ABOUT THIS BOOK

Welcome to Havenwood Falls, a small town in the majestic mountains of Colorado, where nobody is what you think, where truths pose as lies, and where myths blend with reality. A place where everyone has a story, including the high schoolers. These are only but three...

Written in the Stars by Kallie Ross

The Kasun wolf pack has always been led by a female alpha, and now that Willa Kasun's about to come of age, she'll be taking that role. Except Willa hasn't shifted yet. She has until her next birthday to shift and claim her place as alpha, or she'll lose it forever. But Tarron Wilde, a sarcastic and striking elf, makes her wonder if being alpha is really what she wants. The future of her entire pack relies on Willa's choice—embrace what was written in the stars so long ago or choose to fight for what her heart desires.

Reawakened by Morgan Wylie

Like all young witch hunters in Havenwood Falls, seventeen-year-old Macy Blackstone has been spelled to control her killer instincts. Reawakened too early, though, she's overwhelmed and flees town, only to discover more witch hunters living nearby. They are nothing like her family, and she has one moon cycle to uncover their nefarious plans and return home before the town's wards wipes her memories of her family, her home, and her one true love. And if she can't remember them, she won't be able to save them.

The Fall by Kristen Yard

Seventeen-year-old Serena Alverson has no interest in a social life. She's never had a serious boyfriend and has rarely left the safety of Havenwood Falls. But she has big dreams for her future. When Mother Nature finally comes knocking, she hands Serena not only her womanhood, but also a wicked lifetime curse with the potential to destroy everything and everyone she loves.

HAVENWOOD FALLS HIGH
VOLUME ONE

A HAVENWOOD FALLS HIGH COLLECTION

KALLIE ROSS   MORGAN WYLIE   KRISTEN YARD

HAVENWOOD FALLS HIGH BOOKS

Written in the Stars by Kallie Ross

Reawakened by Morgan Wylie

The Fall by Kristen Yard

Somewhere Within by Amy Hale

Awaken the Soul by Michele G. Miller

Bound by Shadows by Cameo Renae

Fata Morgana by E.J. Fechenda

Forever Emeline by Katie M. John

Reclamation by AnnaLisa Grant

Avenoir by Daniele Lanzarotta

Avenge the Heart by Michele G. Miller

Curse the Night by R.K. Ryals

Blood & Iron by Amy Hale

Shadows & Spells by Cameo Renae

Falling Deep by J.L. Weil

Saving Infiniti by Rose Garcia

Willful by Liz Ferry

Cast in Moonlight by Ali Winters

Promise the Moon by Kallie Ross

Blurred Lines by Daniele Lanzarotta

Ascending Darkness by J.L. Weil

Finding Infiniti by Rose Garcia

Unicorn's Lament by Megan Linski

Paper Bird by Amy Richie

Predestined by Valia Lind

Rediscovered by Morgan Wylie

Ashes of Fate by Apryl Baker

Stay up to date at www.HavenwoodFalls.com

WRITTEN IN THE STARS

BY KALLIE ROSS

Havenwood Falls High

Written in the Stars

KALLIE ROSS

~ A Havenwood Falls Young Adult Novella ~

OTHER BOOKS BY KALLIE ROSS

Descent: A Lost Tribe (Book 1)

Defend: A Lost Tribe (Book 2)

Evelyn: A Cupid Chronicles Novella

Unbreakable: The Cupid Chronicles

Dedicated to my wolf-shifter-loving bestie, Gaby.

CHAPTER 1

*O*n her first day back in the Havenwood Falls High lunchroom, Willa Kasun leaned on the doorframe, watching the human and paranormal students carefully shelve themselves into the right sections, as if it were a grocery store. Vampires hovered around a refrigerated soda machine in the corner that served more than cola. Most humans, unaware of the supernatural community around them, wondered why the bottom left button never worked for them, so they stopped pushing it. Elves basked in the sun at a wall of windows to the left. Shifters huddled with their kind, clustered around tables at the center of the room, where Willa's wolf-shifter pack made the most noise. And humans, well, they actually outnumbered them all.

Humans unknowingly fist-bumped shifter athletes, sipped soda with vamps, and made plans to go to the Burger Bar after school with supes. Living a normal life was the point of living in Havenwood Falls, and Willa looked forward to stepping out of the comfort of her pack and into the melting pot of high school. She wondered where she'd fit in. She wasn't human and she hadn't shifted. She belonged nowhere and everywhere.

Havenwood Falls High was the picture of diversity. Every kind, color, and race walked the halls, but pride, fear, and ignorance had a way of keeping most supernaturals with their own species. While popular teen movies about supernaturals missed the mark about much, they nailed their angsty adolescent attitudes, even with nearly half of the population in Havenwood Falls being supernatural. Their ability to shift or exert super-strength didn't make life any easier, because they hid all the messy magic stuff from the humans who walked the hallways with them.

Willa heard and felt a growl vibrating from her right, and as she glanced up, she caught the dark eyes of a brooding dragon shifter. He set his tray down as another student, an elf, scooted over for him. But, as a shifter, he should have joined the other dragons three rows back.

Willa tilted her head, confused.

The dragon—Bale, if Willa remembered correctly—made himself comfortable with a group of supernaturals who resembled the checkout lane of the grocery more than the aisles—an array of items piled together. Multiple supernatural races had convened, all courteous and reticent, and no one outside their bubble seemed to take notice. Willa certainly hadn't regarded them in years past.

"Hey, Will," Willa's brother, also named Will, short for William, called.

Willa rolled her eyes. "Hey, *li'l* Kase."

Growing up with a sheriff for a dad and no mother had Willa acting like another one of the boys in their small community, so she'd often been called "Will." To keep the confusion to a minimum, though, and because her brother was the mini-me to their father, everyone called Will "li'l Kase." Half of the nickname fell by the wayside when Kase outgrew his dad. Among the pack that lived in the woods, the Kasun twins had a reputation for being mischievous, and the nicknames helped distinguish between the two when their older brothers wanted to blame one of them for something. A few of the elders had referred to them as *the boy version* and *the girl version*.

"It's Willa at school. I don't want you giving your entourage any ideas," Willa warned her brother.

He nodded his consent. "I'll add the *a* if you subtract the *li'l*." He nudged her with his shoulder. "Come sit with me and Ana."

Kase had a way of ordering his twin sister around with a smile. He could make a demand sound like a gentlemanly request, just like their dad, Sheriff Ric Kasun. Willa loved her brothers and her alpha father, but there were days her heart ached for her mother.

"I think I'll pass." Willa straightened the hem of her top so that it met the waistline of her skirt. She hated the skimpy cheerleader getup, but until this year, she'd loved cheering for Kase at football games. If only he hadn't recently hooked up with one of the co-captains, Ana Novak.

As if Willa's junior year hadn't started off badly enough, she had been yanked into the seat next to Ana in history. She didn't have enough empty brain space to listen to another cheer idea or dreamy remark about her brother.

"I think I'm going to try something new this year." To make her choice clear, Willa tucked a piece of black hair behind her ear, making her edgy bob look even more fierce, and shot a smile at her brother. She didn't wait for him to respond, and turned toward the most supernaturally diverse table in the lunchroom.

As she approached, Willa recognized a few of the occupants from her earlier classes. Most of them had grown up in the same small town, and with that came rumors and stereotypes. A witch, Scarlet, noticed Willa first. Scarlet's long red hair swung over her shoulder as she looked back and forth from Willa to the empty seat next to her.

"Is that seat taken?" Willa asked.

Scarlet's lips parted, and one eyebrow pulled up in wonder. "Well, uh—"

A lean, white-haired guy slid between them. "No, it's not taken." He patted the seat and grinned. "Join us. I'm Tarron, and you're in my history class, right?"

Willa had seen the freckle-faced guy earlier, but his boyish grin contradicted his broad shoulders and square jaw. Tarron had sat at the back of the classroom, quiet with his pen to paper, not giving any attention to the reunions taking place after the three-month summer break.

Willa had thought the excitement overrated. She'd seen her pack throughout the summer and run into the other students at the Burger

Bar and Coffee Haven, not to mention Paddlefest. The annual summer rafting event on Mathews River had come with extra tourists and drama this year. The pack dared Willa to swim against the river's current, and while the others used their wolf-strength, she couldn't dog-paddle five feet without revealing the fact that some of her powers were manifesting. She'd promised her dad she'd keep the development between them. That night, after her brother jumped into the water to pull her out, she felt so humiliated she moved out of her childhood home while her wolf pack enjoyed the bonfire.

"Hi," Willa greeted. She maneuvered around Tarron and sat between him and Scarlet, setting her bag in her lap. "And, yes, I think we do have history together, but you two," she pulled an apple out of her messenger bag and pointed it at a blonde girl with alabaster skin and the young dragon shifter who'd growled a few moments ago, "aren't in Ms. Bast's history class?"

Her apple bounced in the air back to the blonde, before she took a bite. The blonde nodded with the hint of a smile.

"You're new, too, aren't you?" Willa asked after swallowing, but then the blonde's mouth turned down as she realized her mistake. Willa sensed something supernatural about the new girl, and her cool stare and the scent of blood when she unscrewed her "water" bottle confirmed the stranger was a vampire. Willa set her apple down, wiped her hand on her skirt, then held it out. "I'm sorry. The sort I tend to hang out with don't pay much attention to manners. I'm Willa Kasun."

The blonde's stony palm slipped into Willa's warm one. "Hi, I'm Elliot. Well, most people call me Elle."

Just as the new girl shook Willa's hand, the table at the center of the lunchroom burst out into laughter. The Kasun pack's antics served them well on the football field and in the forest on a moonlit night, but trash talk and arm wrestling in the cafeteria had led to busted tables and busted lips in the past.

"See what I mean?" Willa joked. "It's probably my twin doing his impression of the biology teacher."

The growling guy leaned in and scanned the area. "So, you're the shifter girl from the Kasun pack who can't, you know—" He snarled and cupped his hands above his ears, mimicking a wolf. Willa thought they must all be supes if he felt confident enough to bring up her sort of being a werewolf, but she played it safe anyway.

"Can't what?" Willa's eyes narrowed, and her blood began to boil. She took the pendant hanging from her necklace between her thumb and finger, and slid it back and forth. A calming, methodical motion she'd perfected since she'd received the gift.

"Bale didn't mean anything by it." Tarron leaned in and nudged Willa's shoulder with his. "Did ya, big guy?"

Bale shook his head, and she caught a half-smile before a curtain of shoulder-length dark hair fell forward. "Nah."

"What Bale meant to ask is, how did you get out of wearing one of those gigantic bows the other cheerleaders are wearing?" Tarron nodded in the direction of Ana and her friend Maria, both giggling at Kase. "Are you sure they're not the twins?"

Everyone chuckled, including Willa. Then she caught her brother looking their way. She quickly moved her attention back to Tarron and bumped him back with her elbow.

"The co-captains were pretty ticked when I chopped off my hair right before cheer camp, but those bows are a hazard when I'm flying or tumbling."

"I like it." Tarron smiled as his gaze slid from the top of her head to her cheer uniform.

Bale looked up. "Flying?"

His question broke her own examination of Tarron. "When they throw me up in the air. Wolves tend to like it on solid ground, but I'm not like the others." Willa picked up her apple and took another bite. "And, for the record, I may not have shifted yet, but that doesn't mean I'm any less a Kasun."

The defense she'd built over the last few years sounded rehearsed, and for good reason. Willa repeated the same words to herself whenever a pack member doubted her. She'd moved out of the pack's community in the forest more than a month ago. It hurt too much to be surrounded by a world she couldn't be a part of. Her dad knew the bullying had become intolerable, and he spent most nights with her. It was the best way to keep the rest of the pack from noticing her developing strength and speed, while he secretly investigated if there was another reason for her not shifting yet. Being away from the skeptics and having most of her family's support kept her anxiety at bay.

"So, Elle, where are you from?" Willa asked, trying to divert the eyes from her.

Bale's eyes widened. "Oh, don't start the list again."

Elle giggled.

"Hey." Scarlet pointed a finger at Bale. "Let the girl speak. I don't want to have to use this."

"You can't, and you wouldn't." Bale ran his hand through his hair, revealing a handsome face with high cheekbones and full lips. "Anyway, you'll just get all sad that you haven't been to any of the places she has."

Elle looked from Bale to Scarlet to Willa. "How about I keep it simple? I'm from a little bit of everywhere. My family came to Havenwood Falls so I could finish high school with my own kind. But I've never had vamp friends before, so I don't know why they think I'd want them now."

"Well, I'm glad you came to sit with us," Tarron said to Elle. "None of us are misfits, except maybe Willa here, but we like it here with each other more than our own." He shrugged and pressed his lips together into a tight smile.

Willa filled her mouth with another chunk of apple, trying to keep her retort to herself. She didn't know if Tarron was flirting or trying to allude to something else. Willa remembered her oldest brother, Conall, telling her that other supernaturals had a way of knowing things they had no business knowing. Maybe Tarron was referring to her moving out of the family's cabin.

But she couldn't be the only one with family issues. She regularly heard humans complaining about curfews and siblings as she maneuvered the halls between classes.

"What's so bad about the elves?" Willa asked Tarron and noticed his jaw tense. "Or the witches?" She turned to Scarlet to avoid Tarron, then looked at Bale. "Or the dragons?"

"What's so bad about the Kasun werewolves?" Tarron pushed back, but didn't sound angry. His mockery wasn't lost on her, though.

"Point taken," she conceded. Something about being different kept her and the others from revealing *how* different they were. No one at the table made eye contact, and Willa realized her social skills needed help. "Can I try this whole first-impression thing again?"

Tarron inched closer to Willa on the bench and nodded for her to proceed, while everyone else at the table gave her silent permission. A cacophony of teenage hormones and competing voices served as background noise until she came up with a question to redirect their conversation.

"So, what did you guys do for fun this summer?" she asked, forcing a smile.

"Hmmm…" Bale rubbed the stubble along his chin. "I hiked up to the falls a few times, slept 76% of each day away, met a girl, and binged on Netflix. Is that basic enough?"

"You met a girl?" Tarron's eyebrows were lost in the fringe of white hair falling across his forehead.

Bale looked across the table at Scarlet, where his eyes lingered a moment too long. Tarron followed his gaze, and Scarlet fiddled with the hem of her skirt.

Willa leaned forward, blocking Tarron's line of vision, and propped her chin on her fists. "What about you, Elle? Did you move here from somewhere exciting, like New York City? I bet summers in the Big Apple are amazing."

As Willa took another bite of her apple, Elle twisted a few strands of her long blond hair between her fingers. "We actually moved here from Alaska. It was as cold and dark as it sounds, not that the cold really bothered me. Moving here and getting a tattoo that allows me to be out in daylight was the highlight of the last decade for me."

Tarron cleared his throat, and all eyes turned to him.

"Don't do it," Bale warned Willa, folding his arms over his chest. "Don't ask him about his summer. Tarron is baiting us."

"Why would he want to—" Willa was cut off when a hand slapped the table. The sound startled her.

Kase.

His bicep flexed as he leaned over the table.

"Hey, guys," Kase gritted, his face straining to maintain a smile. "Will, I need to talk to you."

"Will-*a*," she growled back.

"Willa, a word?"

Willa reached past Tarron and placed her hand over Will's. "Sure thing. How about after practice?" She squeezed, released it, and looked to Tarron. "My new friend here was about to tell us what he's been up to this summer."

Will's frown deepened in frustration.

"Hey, man," Tarron said to Kase. "You're more than welcome to join us."

Willa marveled at the two guys' familiarity with each other. Everyone in Havenwood Falls knew about each other, but it didn't mean they were friends. She wondered if her brother and Tarron had a class together. No. Tarron played football last year.

"No, but maybe I'll run into you on the field," Kase snarled at Tarron.

The elf leaned back in his seat and kicked his feet up. "Not this year. I'll be leading the archery team to State, instead of carrying the football team."

Kase flinched. "Come on, Willa, I never see you anymore. Eat lunch with me." His eyes inspected the table's occupants. "And I don't have the patience or time for whatever charity work you're doing here." It was a line straight from Ana's arsenal, her influence oozing out of him.

"Excuse me?" Scarlet seethed behind Willa, looking between the twins.

Willa stood, not amounting to much compared to her brother's six feet of muscle. "Shut your muzzle, Kase. I'm not sitting with or talking to you, because I'm tired of the crap your friends say behind my back. Every one of them thinks I'm a dud-wolf. For the past two years, I've only sat with the pack at lunch and cheered at football games for you. I'm doing this," she waved at the group, "for me."

Kase opened and closed his mouth without a sound.

"I'll talk to you after practice." Willa sat back down.

Kase blinked. "Fine." He walked back to Ana and let her coddle him with whispers and kisses, testing the strict no-public-display-of-affection policy.

"Well, he's a peach." Scarlet rolled her eyes. "How are you two related?"

Willa shifted in her chair. "He's not always that bad, just protective."

"Don't you have two older brothers, too?" Bale asked. "Deputies or something? That's gotta be rough."

"Yeah, one's a deputy and the other is still a cadet. They used to be more like Kase, constantly checking on me or giving me the third degree, but now they're too busy working," Willa explained.

"There's no way you can really be related to Kase." Tarron shook his head. "I still think those cheerleading bow-heads are the twins," he added with a grin.

And he winked at Willa.

CHAPTER 2

*W*illa, surrounded by blue and silver pom-poms, spotted Tarron across the football field as she took her place at the top of the Wolf Wall Pyramid. She figured Ana chose the cheer stunt because of the name—one more way for her to slight any other supernatural in her midst. Tarron's white hair stood out in the sea of green grass past the blue jerseys as he stretched a bow and arrow in his hands. His muscles pulled taut as he aimed at a bale of hay painted with red circles. Tarron paused, glanced over his shoulder at the stacked cheerleaders, and released. The arrow pierced the small red circle at the center of the target. A human, Ginny, gasped as her eyes widened at the feat. When Tarron turned and saw her, he shrugged and acted just as surprised.

The crack of plastic football helmets smashing together startled Willa, and her twitch had a domino effect.

The pyramid shook. The girl holding Willa wobbled and pulled her leg. With the bend of her knee, the center of the formation crumbled. The co-captain, perched on the third level of their pyramid, tumbled down as well, and her backside thumped the turf. The wall had become a pile of bloomers and bows. Willa untangled herself from the pile of limbs and tried to escape blame by searching for her water bottle.

"Which of you inbreeds took your eyes off the mark?" Ana seethed as she stood. She pressed her hands down her skirt, not that it covered much. "We have a pep rally this Friday, and a game to follow. I will not be humiliated by one of you." Her pointer finger bounced up and down in front of her.

"It was my fault." Willa stepped forward. There weren't allegiances among the girls, and any of them would have outed her. They all pivoted to look back and forth between Ana and Willa.

Ana looked to her big-bowed best friend, Maria, then back at Willa. "Well, don't let it happen again."

The girls from the Kasun wolf pack had known each other all their lives, and everyone was practically family, but Ana had been trying to needle her way into Willa's immediate family for years.

"Of course. I'm sorry," Willa offered and twisted her lips. Apologizing was torture. "I think I need a break."

"I think she needs to head to the weight room," Maria said under her breath. The two girls giggled, and a few of the other girls joined in. Willa forced herself to wear a blank face. Standing so far away, she shouldn't have heard the snide remark. She picked up her messenger bag and cheer duffel, and waited for Ana to dismiss her. With a wave, Willa bailed.

They didn't know Willa could hear from so far away, or see Tarron so clearly across the field.

The pack was aware Willa hadn't shifted yet, and the town had quickly caught on when the kids her age started training, while Willa worked at her family's outdoor supply store. At the age of twelve, her friends in the pack, including Kase, all shifted for the first time and all received a special marking. The enchanted tattoos kept them from being hunted while in the forest, but they were also tied to wards at the high school enforcing a no-magic policy.

Because Willa hadn't shifted, she never went through the marking ceremony. So the wolf traits she'd developed, like heightened hearing, agility, and sense of smell, weren't being blocked on the field. She did wish her sense of smell was less heightened during football practice.

Even though her abilities were a secret between her and her father,

17

the hint of power gave her hope the first few months. But by the end of her sophomore year, Willa had resigned herself to never shifting.

"Willa!" Her brother's voice called from a huddle of players as she walked down one of the racing lanes around the track.

She waved, only able to differentiate Kase by his number, and hoped he would leave her alone. As the starting quarterback, she had a feeling he wouldn't be able to get out of practice.

He'd pestered her every day via text to move back to the family cabin, but she'd been content in the apartment above Backwoods Sport & Ski. The family's store had belonged to them for a century, and while some of the pack members were employees at the town square shop, she still had privacy on the second floor.

Before she moved in, Willa's dad had used the space to hunker down when he was working on a case all night. Her dad still spent four nights out of seven on the couch in the living room, but this way Willa didn't have to wake up every morning and endure the inquisitive stares on her way to school. No one else seemed to care she'd moved, except Kase.

"Hey there, wait up." Tarron's voice called from behind her. "Why are you leaving practice early?"

"I guess my heart isn't in it today," Willa said with a hint of sarcasm.

One corner of Tarron's mouth pulled up. "Today?"

Willa burst out laughing. "I only cheer because of my brother. Otherwise, I would not be able to put up with the bow-twins."

It was Tarron's turn to laugh. "Ana Novak has been a conniving bully since kindergarten. She talked me into giving her my vanilla pudding at least three times that year."

"What did she trade you?" Willa asked.

"That's the thing. It was always something disgusting, like carrot sticks."

Willa frowned. "That's horrible, but I can outdo you. So if I don't shift before my birthday in October, Ana will assume the position of alpha for our pack."

"No pressure." Tarron patted Willa's shoulder with a tight grin. "But, can a girl really be alpha? I thought your dad was in charge."

The comment earned Tarron a swift punch to the arm.

"Ow!" He rubbed his bicep and pouted. "That came out wrong. I like a woman who can take charge."

"Did that come out wrong?"

"Nope." Tarron winked at her again.

"My dad is standing in until I shift. But if I miss the cut off, the responsibility will be passed to Ana, since her dad is beta. My pack always had a female alpha—that is, before my mom died."

"Wait. Beta? Does that mean you're related?" Tarron's face soured. "She's dating your brother, right?"

"Beta means he's second in command." Willa tilts her head. "Our families are old, like ancient, so there's a good chance we're related. I think the Novak bloodline is related to Kasun blood from when our pack lived in Croatia. It's been several generations since our bloodline split, but it's the purest."

"Oh." Tarron shook his head. "It still sounds really bad. Kentucky bad."

The two chuckled as they approached the school's parking lot. A few students hung out in the lot, but fewer eyes watched them than the athletic fields behind the school. Tarron pulled his bow over his shoulder, against his quiver, and then started removing his arm guard. Willa's head tilted, inspecting the metal weapon and shooting gloves.

"What?" Tarron asked.

Willa shrugged. "I just thought your bow would be wooden."

Tarron placed his hands on his slim hips. "You're thinking about Lord of the Rings, aren't you?" He pulled his hand through his messy blond hair. It was long on top and shaved short around the sides. Willa thought she noticed a slight point at the top of Tarron's ears. "Sorry to disappoint, but I'm not glamouring waist-length hair or leather armor under here." Tarron motioned at his chest, covered by a graphic T-shirt sporting a taco with the words "Let's taco bout it."

"No need to be sorry, and if it makes you feel any better, I've never

19

seen the movie. I've only read the books." Willa folded her arms across her chest.

"Impressive."

"Well, I've had a lot more time to myself lately. Living in town has its benefits, including more reading time and less fighting over Netflix." Willa fiddled with the strap of her messenger bag, wanting to ask Tarron if she could hold his bow. The request sounded crazy, and a little dirty in her head, so she filed it away for another time.

"Where do you live in town?" Tarron asked.

Willa turned down the sidewalk that led to the town square. "Off Eighth." She pivoted to walk backwards and smiled. "I'll see you tomorrow."

Stepping down onto the next slab of concrete, Willa didn't take into account the roots of an old oak having shifted the path or a student speeding out of the parking lot. She tripped into the street, the car screeching to a halt, but unable to stop fast enough. Tarron darted to her side. His reaction appeared in slow motion to Willa. She saw panic widen his eyes and fear pull the corners of his mouth into a frown. As he reached for her hand, she glanced at the driver of the car. Zara Shannon, a junior, jerked the steering wheel of her car to the left. Her friend, Viv, sat in the passenger seat and lifted her arms over her face. The front end of the blue vehicle still threatened to bash into Willa, and instinct kicked in. Willa flexed every muscle in her body, bending at the waist and changing the direction of her fall. She found her balance on the curb unnaturally.

Zara's car screeched to a stop and her head peeked out of the driver side window. Tarron shoved two fists into the air and bumped their sides together twice, successfully flipping off the girl like one of the characters from *Friends*.

Zara's mouth gaped open at Tarron as she started to get out. "Are you okay?" Zara asked Willa in an exaggerated British accent.

"I'm fine." She waved the human back into the car. "I promise." She placed her hand over her heart and felt it racing.

"You sure?" Zara asked as Viv opened her door.

"I am, thank you." Willa straightened the straps of her bags over her shoulders. "I'm good."

Willa tried to act distracted, hoping the two girls hadn't noticed her using her wolf abilities. They looked at each other, and Zara patted the top of the car.

"Well, if you're good, then . . ." She buckled back into the sedan, Viv following suit.

"Yeah, I'm good." Willa nodded.

"Okay, see you tomorrow." Her accent drifted off as they drove away.

Tarron turned to Willa and his eyes widened. "How did you—"

Willa ran her fingers along the chain of her necklace. "I can explain."

"We're still on school grounds, and the wards—" Tarron pointed to the Havenwood Falls High signage less than twenty feet away. His eyes narrowed, and he shoved his hands into his pockets. "Go ahead, start explaining."

"I really gotta get home. How about I explain tomorrow? Or, we could forget about it?" Willa scrambled to get out of telling Tarron the truth. She figured she could trust him with town gossip, but keeping the secret about her abilities was a level of trust she hadn't even given her brothers. The most she knew about Tarron was that he liked to flirt and could hit a target without looking.

"How about you explain while I walk you home?" Tarron suggested.

"I don't want to inconvenience you." Willa started walking, annoyed at herself for being so careless. "Thanks, though."

Tarron followed. He met her pace and remained five steps behind her all the way to First Street. Along the way, he started whistling. The tune floated on the August breeze and lulled Willa's footsteps into a steady cadence.

Willa tried to ignore Tarron, watching the cars pass by and the townspeople of Havenwood Falls tidy their yards. One neighborhood on the outskirts of town—Havenwood Heights—had become primarily exclusive to the Old Families, but the streets surrounding the town square were more like a mixed bouquet of wildflowers—supes ingrained in the everyday, normal lives of the townspeople. Tourists who made their way to town couldn't tell that a witch lived down the street from the town drunk, and if she was being honest, Willa wouldn't be able to tell either if it weren't for her wolf instincts.

Willa passed a man mowing his lawn and waved. The burly, bald guy had spent a few nights in the town's holding tank for getting too loud after a few drinks earlier that summer. Willa had brought her dad dinner at the station, and the man had made a pass at her. She'd laughed it off, but her dad threatened to charge him with indecent behavior with a juvenile.

At the end of the block, a street sign reading "2nd Street" towered over Willa. She waited under the metal guidepost for a car to pass, and Tarron stepped up next to her. He happened to be on the opposite side of the metal pole, and Willa remembered elves and faeries having an aversion to iron. He stood almost a head taller than her, and when he looked down in her direction, he smiled. Dark freckles peppered the bridge of his nose and cheeks, each a stark contrast to his pale complexion and hair.

"Can I ask you a personal question?" Tarron asked.

Willa folded her arms over her chest and pursed her lips. "You can, but that doesn't mean I'll answer."

He nodded, "Fair." He rubbed his hand against the back of his neck, hesitating. "So, do you really want to shift and be the next alpha of the Kasun pack?"

Willa's head tilted to the side. No one had ever asked her what she wanted. "If I don't try and implement the training I've received, if I don't give myself over to the wolf, I'll be letting my whole family down."

"It just seems like a lot of pressure in addition to ACTs, driving tests, showing up to cheer for your brother every Friday night, not to mention any potential dating relationships on the horizon."

Willa let a snort escape her, and quickly covered her nose with a hand. "Ever since my twelfth birthday party, I've been living in the shadow of my brother. And, there's not one pack member who'd ask me out. I'm a dud-wolf. You wouldn't want to date me. I mean, you've only met *one* of my brothers."

"Actually, I think I met your oldest brother when I got pulled over for speeding this summer." Tarron grinned and stepped into the street. "He didn't seem that bad. With a little of my elf charm, I got off with a warning."

"No way!" Willa sped up to catch him. "You know one thing I do want?

Tarron paused in the middle of the street and turned to face her. "What?"

Willa had slightly softened toward the elf, but at her core, she felt the need to tread carefully. "To learn archery." She walked past him to finish crossing the street.

"Oh."

"What? Did you think I wanted a social life?" Willa laughed.

"Maybe I could help you with both."

Heat rose into her cheeks as she reached the sidewalk. Willa looked to the quaint blue house on the corner to keep Tarron from noticing. She admired how the white shutters and door made the place look anything but supernatural. Willa waved at a small woman watering plants on the porch, a witch with waist-length red hair. A white streak of hair grew from her temple, making it difficult to guess her age.

The witch waved back.

"You know Ms. Howe?" Tarron asked.

"Not really." Willa shrugged as they passed the white picket fence. "Her herb shop is a few doors down from Backwoods Sport & Ski, and I've watched her sweep the sidewalk in front of her store countless times. How is she related to Scarlet? I noticed her coming and going from the shop a few times."

"She's Scarlet's grandmother." Tarron nodded back at the house. "All the women in her family look alike. From a distance, I can't tell Scarlet's mom and grandmother apart. Her mom, Rose, doesn't have as many wrinkles, or as many talismans hanging from her neck."

Willa looked up at him, confused.

"You know, like the one you're wearing." Tarron nodded toward the necklace. "It's pretty. Did you get it from their shop?"

"I'm not sure who made it into a necklace, but the stone was my mother's." She looked down at the pendant. "Do you know what talismans do?"

Tarron shrugged. "It depends."

$\sim$

Chapter 2.5

MONDAY 8:25 PM
    Willa: Are you home yet?

9:04 PM **The BOY Version:** On my way
    Willa: Don't text and drive

9:49 PM **The BOY Version:** Ok, home
    Willa: Do you remember where dad had my necklace made?
    The BOY Version: Where is this coming from?
    Willa: Never mind, forget it
    The BOY Version: Wait . . .

10:13 PM **The BOY Version:** I just asked Tate
    Willa: Ugh. Why did you have to pull him in?
    The BOY Version: He was playing D&D online, he didn't even blink
    Willa: Fine
    Willa: What did he say?
    The BOY Version: It was mom's ring
    The BOY Version: Sheriff asked the Novaks to change the setting
    Willa: I hate it when Tate calls dad Sheriff

Willa: Maybe I'll change Tate's name in my phone to Sheriff

The BOY Version: Give him a break, it's his way of dealing

The BOY Version: Kinda like you moving out

The BOY Version: Curious . . . Am I still 'the boy version' in your phone?

Willa: . . .

The BOY Version: You need to get over yourself

Willa: Same

The BOY Version: And you need to watch out for that Tarron kid

Willa: Same

The BOY Version: SMH

The BOY Version: Love you

Willa: Same

CHAPTER 3

*W*illa held her topaz stone at the end of her necklace and pulled it from left to right while she waited for the bell to ring. Students scrambled into the classroom, hoping to avoid a tardy notice being emailed home on the second day of school. She made a point to sit at the center of the pattern of desks, in a neutral and new seat.

A brunette girl bounced in, then a tuft of white hair caught Willa's eye. Tarron, wearing a T-shirt with a kitten roaring on his chest, strutted to the empty chair next to her.

"Is that seat taken?" he asked.

"Nope." Willa looked down at her black T-shirt with white bold letters. It read, "The book was better."

Tarron sat with a grin.

"What?" Willa asked with a furrowed brow.

Tarron's grin spread into a wide smile. "Good morning."

The bell sounded, distracting her from the knowing look he gave her, and their new history teacher, Ms. Bast, stood. She began drawing shapes on the whiteboard behind her desk. Her black-and-white-checked capris and fuzzy yellow cardigan would have aged anyone else fifty years, but Ms. Bast pulled it off with the help of a messy bun, black-rimmed glasses, and red ballet flats. Her warm brown skin glowed, even in the unflattering florescent light. The new teacher had to be the youngest person on staff at Havenwood Falls High.

Tarron leaned to the side and whispered, "Wanna come by the archery fields after cheer practice today?"

Before she could answer, a low, familiar growl vibrated in the air around her. Kase had run into the classroom and frozen at the sight of his sister and the elf sitting together. He quickly took the seat in front of Willa.

"Sorry, Ms. Bast," he apologized as he pulled a notebook and pen from his backpack.

"Don't make it a habit, Mr. Kasun." The teacher continued scribbling on the board. She grinned, her pearl-like teeth a stark contrast to her mahogany lipstick and bronze cheeks.

Kase swiveled in his chair and placed his elbow on Willa's desk. "Of course, Ms. Bast. Besides, I wouldn't want to lose my favorite seat in the room again."

His eyes flashed gold at Tarron, and he curled his lip.

"Give it a rest, Kase." Willa folded her arms across her chest and avoided making eye contact by focusing on the board.

Ms. Bast had sketched five different masks and started on a sixth. A few of the patterns appeared African, and one looked like it belonged on an Egyptian mummy. The next drawing only covered the eyes, like it would be worn to a masquerade, then she drew a few helmets. A total of ten masks covered the board when she finished and faced the students.

The class had started speculating about the drawings, and the layered whispers had grown into a rumble.

Ms. Bast cleared her throat. "Through the centuries, mankind has gone to great lengths to hide themselves. Some would argue helmets are for protection. Others might say masks allow for someone to be who they really are without being judged." She paused as her gaze drifted over the class. "Today I will be assigning partners for a project due at the end of the month. The presentation and paper you turn in will be worth half of your grade this six weeks. Every pair of students will be researching one of the masks on the board."

Ms. Bast picked up a stack of worksheets and gave a few to the first person sitting at the front of each row. The papers slowly made their way back to Willa, and she perused the instructions as she passed the stack behind her.

"Remember, deception is ultimately a disguise, and some facades give the illusion of sameness, so I'll be mixing things up to keep everyone honest. Let's start with Elle."

Everyone looked up at the new girl sitting on the front row.

"You'll be working with one of Havenwood Falls' natives, Kase."

Ana, who sat with the rest of the pack, huffed and jutted her chin in the air, and Will's buddy Joseph burst into laughter. Kase cut his eyes at the linebacker, silencing him.

Ms. Bast continued to pair students, surprising the class a few times by mixing supernatural races. Willa especially enjoyed Ana's name being called with Aurelia Petran. It wasn't until she heard Tarron's name that she realized how much she wanted to be paired with him.

She liked him.

The feeling wasn't like anything she'd heard a pack member describe with their mates, but Willa genuinely wanted to get to know Tarron better. She smiled to herself.

"Maria Horvat, you and Tarron will be working together on this helmet." Ms. Bast pointed to an open-sided, flat hat.

Willa's shoulders slumped, and her chest tightened with envy.

"As for this mask, I'd like Bale Grayson and Scarlet Howe to partner up."

Willa looked over to Bale, who was peering at Scarlet. She didn't bother to look over her shoulder. In the corner of her eye, Willa saw Maria's hand waving in the air.

"Yes, Ms. Horvat. Do you have a question?"

"No. But I do have a doctor's note specifying that I cannot be exposed to anxiety-inducing situations, so I would like to be paired with someone else."

"You would?"

Maria nodded.

Willa looked over at Tarron, and he'd pinched the bridge of his nose between two fingers. She set a hand on his shoulder and asked, "Are you okay?"

"Would you be okay if you had Maria as your partner for a project worth half your grade?"

"I guess not." She patted him reassuringly. "I'm sorry."

Ms. Bast looked at the list of students in front of her, then glanced over the sheet of paper toward Maria. One more glimpse at the list, then an inspection of Tarron.

"Ms. Willa Kasun, would you be so kind as to partner with Tarron?" The teacher readied her pen over the paper. "I had planned for you to work with Joseph, but I think he's better suited to Maria's predisposition."

"That is fine with me," Willa answered, working hard to keep her smile to herself. She itched to look over her shoulder at Maria, but looked over at Tarron instead. A giddy expression lit up his face, and the thought of Tarron wanting to be her partner, too, made the classroom suddenly warm. And then she remembered her hand on his arm.

Struggling with what would be more awkward, she decided to pull her hand back, and then Tarron placed his hand over hers. The contact left her skin tingling.

"You'll have the rest of class to discuss your project, but after today I expect the work to be done on your own time. Tomorrow, come to class having read Unit 1, and be ready to tackle the beginning of time through 600 B.C.E."

The class erupted into a roar of voices trying to talk over each other. Students swapped seats and settled in with their partners. As everyone began working, the chaos quieted into a harmony. A few partners sat in silence, including Ana and her moroi partner. The mean girl of the wolves and the mean girl of the vamps had never been so quiet. Other pairs argued, like Maria and Joseph.

Willa inspected the room, focusing her attention on anything but Tarron. Her fingers found her pendant as she finally pulled enough courage together to face him. His eyes were already on her, not staring but observing. He rubbed his chin as if he were trying to figure her out.

"So, where do you want to meet?" Willa asked. "Your house?"

Tarron's eyes widened. "I'm not sure that's such a good idea. How about your place?"

"I don't think you'd get off with a warning if my dad or one of my brothers caught you up in my apartment."

Tarron picked up his pencil and twirled it between his fingers. "Well, if you still want archery lessons after practice, I guess we could discuss the project then. Maybe plan a trip to Broastful Brew later this week?"

Willa wanted to say yes, but she noticed her brother watching them. Will's lip curled, and she didn't know if her brother was mad or disgusted at having a vampire for a partner. The two supernatural species had been natural enemies in the world, but within the city limits, peace among the races reigned.

"So, what's so special about that necklace?" Tarron interrupted her thoughts.

"This was my mother's stone. My dad had it made into a pendant for me."

"It looks old," he said. "Can I take a closer look?"

Tarron lifted a hand to take the stone from her, and their fingers brushed against each other. He leaned in closer, inspecting the golden rock. The color reminded Willa of the shade a shifter's eyes flashed when close to releasing their wolf.

"I can take it off if you want to get a better look," Willa offered.

Tarron smirked. "I like this view."

But, he wasn't looking at the stone anymore. He'd met her eyes.

She snickered.

"Too cheesy?" he asked.

"Just a little." She held up her finger an inch above her thumb. "Do you ever give up? Or are you eager for disappointment? You have to realize that all your flirting won't get you anywhere."

"As long as it gets you to the archery field after school, I'll feel like I've accomplished something."

"Low expect—" Willa started.

"No." Tarron took her hand, and people in the room noticed. A hush fell over the classroom, and Tarron whispered, "Baby steps."

The self-deprecating tactics Willa typically used to avoid a guy's advances weren't working with this elf. He pushed past her walls and landed too close to her heart for comfort.

His warm hand slid off hers, and he went back to spinning his pencil like a baton. The silence between them had been compounded by the curious stillness of their classmates. Seconds dragged into minutes, and Willa resorted to doodling arrows along the side of her notebook.

The bell rang, announcing the end of class, and Tarron stood to leave.

Willa reached up for his hand and met his gaze. "I'll be there."

CHAPTER 4

*S*itting in the bleachers, waiting for the squad to disband, the
football field to clear, and the white-haired boy with the bow
and arrow to wave her over, Willa thought about the best part of her
day. It had been lunch, again. She'd sat with her newly acquired
Scooby gang. Of course, they all argued about who would be cast in
which roles, and since Willa hadn't shifted yet, Bale claimed to be the
best Scooby. When Tarron declared he would make the perfect Shaggy
and Willa exuded Velma, the conversation stuttered. Elle was the first
to break out into laughter, and the others joined in quickly.

An elf and a werewolf being anything more than acquaintances
would be social suicide. Tarron had flirted with Willa, unashamedly,
but there couldn't be anything more than friendship between them.
Hence, Willa's reasoning for casting herself as Scooby. They could end
up the best of friends, but someday Willa would shift. And with the
pack came impenetrable devotion, fierce protection, and a mate.

Willa spaced out trying to remember a Kasun pack member who
mated with someone outside their supernatural race. Conall, her oldest
brother, was the only one who'd mated, but Tate once had a fling with
a witch. It had been the summer before Kase and Willa turned twelve.
They wouldn't have started high school for another year, but she

understood a stigma came with stepping outside your coven, pack, or gene pool.

Willa remembered asking Tate, "Why do you like that witch?"

Tate pinched his nose and shook his head. "It feels good to be liked for me, and not the Kasun name, or the expectation that comes with it. Everyone struggles to fit in, but if someone wants to be with you because you aren't like everyone else, hang on to them." He mussed her hair. "Someday, you'll understand."

Willa now grasped what her brother had told her all those years ago.

"Hey, you coming?" Tarron called from the lined track.

Willa shook her head to clear it.

"Oh." He turned and started walking away.

"Wait, no!" Willa stood and maneuvered down the bleachers awkwardly. "I was in a daze, and I didn't see you wave me over."

"Really?" Tarron smirked. "You must have been thinking about someone pretty dreamy."

Willa ignored the innuendo and began the trek to the archery field. "Are you ready to multitask?"

Tarron jumped in front of her and walked backwards. "I think you'll find it's crucial to focus when wielding a weapon. How about we head over to the Burger Bar after I show you a few things?"

Willa tilted her head, wondering if the invitation was meant to be a date.

Tarron pivoted to walk beside her. "We can do a little recon on the helmet we were assigned and decide how to split up the paper we have to write."

"Yeah, um, that's a good idea," Willa agreed, but only because she could explain it away as a study session if anyone asked.

Tarron's lesson in archery started with a demonstration. Willa watched as the muscles in his arms stretched and tightened. His feet, clad in worn-out black Converse, were planted shoulder-width apart with one in front of the other. He took a deep breath and his chest widened.

Something buzzed at Willa's core, and the corners of her lips lifted. Being attracted to Tarron didn't feel wrong or weird. It felt good.

Releasing his grip with an exhale, Tarron froze in place until the arrow struck its target. He turned to face Willa, and his smile reached his gray-blue eyes. The arrow jutted from the center of the solid red circle.

"Your turn."

Willa's mouth fell open. "Are you sure I'm ready?"

"Nope, but you definitely need to get a feel for the bow while we're out here."

Willa had expected him to tease her or flirt, but on the archery field, Tarron had grown more serious than she'd ever seen him. His brow flattened as he pulled an extra shooting glove from his bag and strapped it to her right hand.

"How did you know I was right-handed?" She asked.

He didn't stop to think about it, but answered, "I'm observant." And he winked.

The playful elf Willa had grown to like hadn't gone anywhere. Tarron focused, and as his fingers gently tugged the glove down to her wrist, his mouth tightened into a straight line. As he concentrated on tightening the band, a few strands of his hair fell in front of his eyes.

Lifting her left hand, Willa tucked the hair behind his ear. She paused when her fingertip grazed the top. His ear came to a point like the petal of a flower and was just as soft.

"Does it weird you out?" Tarron asked softly.

Willa's eyes met his. "Not at all." Her lungs felt empty and full at the same time. She hadn't ever been so close to a guy, except for her brothers.

With a tug on the leather strap, Tarron stepped back.

"I think you're ready." After handing her his bow, he moved out of the way and rubbed the back of his neck. Avoiding eye contact, he said, "Let's take a few minutes and work on your posture. If you decide to get a bow of your own, it will probably be smaller and lighter."

Willa was pretty sure he hadn't meant the comment as a slight, but being the youngest of four and the only girl, she took his words as a challenge. She lifted Tarron's bow and squared her shoulders. It took a little of the strength she normally hid, but she pulled back on the string and pretended to aim at the target.

"Nice, but—" Tarron pressed his fingertips upward, along her elbow.

Surprised at his touch, Willa released the string and her elbow snapped back into Tarron's chest.

"Oh, crap! I'm so sorry!" She set the bow in the grass and quickly lifted her gloved hand to Tarron's chest. She rubbed circles where her elbow had hit him and kept her eyes down.

"It's okay," he assured her softly as he caught her wrist.

Willa's eyes watched as his hand slid to cover hers against his chest. She blinked, and as she looked up to meet his eyes, her feet shuffled closer to his.

A whistle from an onlooker sounded from behind Tarron. Willa pushed up on her tiptoes to glance over his shoulder and watched as Kase, Joseph, and a few of their teammates strutted toward them.

Willa patted Tarron's chest and asked, "Will you let me handle them?"

"Sure, but say the word, and we're out of here." Tarron moved around Willa and picked up his bow.

Willa made her way to the track to meet her brother and keep him as far away from Tarron as possible. "Hey, Kase, you headed home?"

"Yeah." Kase squinted past her to watch as Tarron packed away his glove and arrows. "What are you still doing up here?"

"Oh, just working out some details about the history project." Willa twisted her hands together and felt the leather glove still strapped on her right hand. Carefully sliding her hands behind her, she shoved them into her back pockets. The evasion didn't fool her brother.

"What you mean is, he used the excuse to get you here for a study session, and now he's giving you archery lessons and using his elvish sorcery to get close?" Kase shouted over his sister at Tarron, "Normally, I'd be impressed. But if you try anything with my sister, I'll make sure your life is miserable."

Willa's lips twisted, unsure of what to make of her brother's accusations. "Sorcery?"

"You know," Kase kept on, "his charm."

"Magic isn't allowed on school grounds," Willa defended.

"True," her brother agreed. "But we can't help it if a little seeps out every now and then. Isn't that right, Number 22?"

"22?" Willa asked.

"It's why your boy here quit the football team," Kase pressed.

Tarron had picked up his bag, along with hers, and met them on the track. "I don't know what you're up to, but give it a rest. Your sister and I have to work with each other on the project, and it's none of your business why I'm not playing this year. You're just angry because you'll actually have to throw this year for the team to win."

Kase made a threatening move toward Tarron, and he dropped the bags, ready to defend himself. At the same time, Ana and Maria came around the corner of the building, looking for their ride home.

"Come on, Kase!" Ana whined.

Kase looked from his girlfriend to his sister. "I'm not leaving without her."

He crossed his arms over his chest, looking more like a stubborn toddler than a concerned brother.

"Don't be a bully," Willa warned. Her chest started to grow tight, and a burning sensation warned her that her wolf was close, but still out of reach.

Ana jogged over to them, with Maria not too far behind. She placed her hands on her hips impatiently and huffed. "This is ridiculous. If she wants to stick around with the imp, so be it. We have stuff to do."

She placed a hand on Will's shoulder and tugged. Kase tugged back and ignored Ana.

"I'm not leaving without you." He spoke directly to Willa.

Willa looked from Tarron to her brother, not wanting to give in, but not wanting to make things worse. She reached for her pendant to calm her nerves and moved to stand next to Tarron.

Ana assumed Willa was taking a side. "Thank God!" She rolled her eyes. "I don't have time for this sideshow."

Willa squeezed her pendant and turned to face her pack. "It's a good thing Tarron and I are the main attraction then."

"Those are some big words coming from a girl who can't shift." Ana stepped in front of Kase and curled her lip.

"Do you need me to dumb it down for you?" Willa asked, then looked to her brother, hoping he would take the hint and leave with his girlfriend.

"You—" Ana growled.

"I'm done listening to you," Willa exclaimed. Her chest burned with power as the words left her lips, and the magic cut Ana off.

Maria took hold of Ana and stopped her from taking the confrontation any further. "She still has two months to shift."

"Like that's gonna happen." Ana waved dismissively at Willa and Tarron. "If she was going to shift, she wouldn't be wasting her time making toys with one of Santa's helpers."

Ana's insult provoked a snarl from Willa. Her wolf clawed at her insides trying to get out, but nothing happened outside. Being alpha had always been her destiny, and now she might actually have the chance to choose her own path. The problem was that the innermost part of her felt caged.

Willa had never been so mad before. Ana was so close to taking her pack, her future, and her brother. In the past, she'd struggled with being mad at her mother for dying, and later she blamed the powers that be for taking her away. Willa even hated herself for a time. She'd reconciled with herself by moving away from the pack.

"I may not ever shift," she admitted through gritted teeth, "but at least I won't have to live my life playing fetch for the Court of the Sun and the Moon."

Ana turned her nose up at Willa and hooked her arm through Will's, ignoring the dig. "Let's get out of here."

Unable to tamp down her anger, Willa interrupted, "No." She let go of her necklace and squeezed her hands into fists at her side. "You leave."

The command was palpable. The blood of an alpha ran through her body, and her words carried an unexplainable weight. They all felt Willa's power.

Kase stepped aside, out of Ana's reach, and looked at his buddy, Joseph. "Can you take them home?"

Joseph nodded.

"Come on, baby." Ana pouted. "Don't make me ride in Joe's truck. It's more ostentatious than your sister's necklace." She giggled and cut her eyes at Maria when her friend didn't laugh with her.

They had all attended the twins' twelfth birthday party. Each of them had watched Willa open the velvet box her father handed her, and they listened to the story he told of it belonging to her mother.

"How are you even with her?" Willa asked her brother with tears in her eyes.

He turned to whisper to Ana, and Willa heard something about leaving and talking later. Before she could listen to any more, Tarron placed his hand on her lower back. The distraction was welcome, but when she turned to face him, she knew something was wrong. He bit at his bottom lip and looked down at their feet.

"Why don't you go with your brother? It sounds like you guys need to talk." He peeked up at her from behind a mess of hair and let a corner of his mouth turn up. "I'll take a rain check if you still want to go to the Burger Bar sometime."

"Give me your phone?" she asked.

He handed it over with his screen unlocked. Willa quickly texted herself. "Now you have my number, and I have yours."

By the time Willa finished and turned to face her pack, most of them had vanished behind the school building. Kase remained, waiting for her. He looked defeated, almost sorry.

Tarron started to leave, to give the siblings some time. As he walked by, a low growl rumbled in Kase's chest.

"Kase," Willa warned, mustering the last of her energy. "Stop."

And he did.

Her brother moved to her side and took her bag from her. He'd already strapped his backpack and duffel across his shoulder, so what was another messenger bag?

Walking to the parking lot, Willa thought things had never gotten this complicated between them. The reason she'd left their community in the forest wasn't his fault, not entirely. She just hated how, in the last few years, he'd taken the pack's side.

Ana's side.

◇

Chapter 4.5

Tuesday 4:52 PM

Willa: Want to redeem your raincheck this Friday night?

5:04 PM **Tarron:** Shouldn't we get together b4 then about the project?

Willa: Don't think you're getting out of teaching me archery lessons that easy . . . We can talk then

Tarron: Ok, see you tmw

Wednesday 11:28 AM

Tarron: Is it possible for your bros hate for me to grow daily?

Willa: Yes. It's because you sat next to me in history again.

Willa: Save me a seat at lunch.

6:37 PM **Tarron:** You did a good job today

Willa: Thanks! I'm going to try to convince my dad I need a bow over dinner tonight

Tarron: Good luck . . . leave my name out of it

. . .

9:43 PM **TARRON:** How did dinner go?

Willa: He's thinking about it. Ugh.

Willa: I just showered Wikipedia and found out our helmet is called a Kettle Hat!

Willa: Stupid autocorrect! I spelled scoured wrong!

Tarron: LOL!

THURSDAY 2:24 PM

Willa: I have to cancel today! I'm sorry!

Tarron: You ok?

6:14 PM **WILLA:** Yeah, just had some errands to run after school

Willa: I have a surprise tmrw!

Tarron: Please tell me you're wearing a big bow, no don't, I want it to be a surprise

Willa: LOL! G'night

Willa: I almost forgot . . . Do you want to leave the game tmrw night together and head to Burger Bar?

Tarron: . . .

Willa: We can meet if you're not planning to come to the football game

Tarron: I'll be there . . . Wouldn't miss it

CHAPTER 5

*T*he crowd of blue and silver cheered their way out of the Havenwood Falls High School stadium. The first victory of the season would spill over to the Burger Bar, and Willa looked forward to downing a chocolate milkshake and greasy cheeseburger.

Even though it was the first day of September, the summer heat continued to press on. As the sun set, the cool night air calmed the restless fans. Willa searched the bleachers for Tarron and didn't see him until the last quarter. She looked forward to hanging out somewhere other than school and wondered if they'd have enough in common to carry a conversation through dinner.

"See you at the drive-in?" one of the other cheerleaders asked Willa.

"I'll be there," Willa answered as she bent down to stuff her pom-poms into her duffel. Rummaging around in the depths of her bag, she noticed a hint of body odor emanating from her armpits. "Hey, do you have some deodorant I can borrow?"

"I actually didn't think to bring any with me," Tarron's voice answered. He squatted down beside her and sniffed. "I think you smell okay, but you're the one with superscent." He smiled.

Tarron wore dark jeans, his Converse, and a gray-blue T-shirt that brought out the color of his eyes. Willa couldn't make out what his shirt said, because his hoodie was half zipped. She was relieved he hadn't made things more awkward by showing up in something more formal. The last four days had been uneventful, and the drama-free days had given Willa time to think.

"Are you ready?" Tarron asked.

"Yep." She zipped up her bag and lifted it, but he took it from her before she could place it on her shoulder.

"I've got this."

The path to the parking lot still buzzed with Havenwood Falls Dragons, so Willa took Tarron's hand and pulled him up to the bleachers. She'd been waiting all day to reveal her surprise, but the timing hadn't been right in history or at lunch.

"How about we hang out here until the lot clears out?"

Tarron followed her up to the top row. "Sounds like a plan."

Just as they sat, the stadium lights turned off with a loud clack. The two broke out into laughter, and as Willa's eyes adjusted to the sky above them, it blinked to life.

Scooting a little closer to Willa, Tarron asked, "So, what's the surprise you texted me about?"

She looked up at him with a wide smile and answered, "My dad said yes. He's letting me pick out a bow and arrows from the store."

"That's awesome." He bumped her with his shoulder. "Maybe I can swing by tomorrow and help you pick them out?"

"Oh, well, I have ACT prep in the morning, so it would have to be later."

Tarron grinned.

"What's so funny?" Willa asked defensively. "If I don't want to have to work at the store my whole life, I'll need a good score."

"I'm not making fun, Willa," he assured. "I'll be there too. Actually, I think Bale and Scarlet are enduring the course with us."

"With four Saturdays of ACT prep and Friday night games, how are we going to get this history project ready?"

Tarron's grin spread wider. "I guess we'll have to spend a lot of time together."

Willa liked the prospect of studying with Tarron, and she didn't care if everyone else had something to say about it. People had been talking about her behind her back all her life. When she was little, she'd been called the poor little motherless girl, and during the past four years, she'd been referred to as the dud-werewolf.

"How about we spend some time together at the Burger Bar? I'm starving," Willa said.

She stood and grabbed Tarron's hand to pull him up. As she made her way down the bleachers, she attempted to release him, but he didn't let go.

They walked to the parking lot, now almost empty. Willa noticed a few of the players' cars waiting for their owners to shower and change. Her hand slipped out of Tarron's when she started walking down the sidewalk, toward the drive-in. Students frequented the place located across the street from the school throughout the week and especially on game nights. Positioned along the river, teenagers roamed along the water's edge, hooked up, and swam in the summer.

"Where are you going?" Tarron asked from a few feet behind her.

Willa paused. "Food." She pointed to the vintage neon sign in the distance. "Hungry." Her finger shifted to point at her stomach.

"Car." He pointed to a light blue vintage convertible parked at the back of the lot.

Willa stepped closer, looking for some kind of emblem on the hood. "Is it yours?"

"It is. It's a 1961 Corvette," he explained. Glancing at Willa, he noticed her eyes gloss over. "And that doesn't matter."

Willa shook her head and turned to face him. "It matters if you're a car guy." She glanced at the car, then back at him. "Go ahead, tell me all the stats. We can still be friends."

Tarron chuckled. "I'm really not that into cars. This one happened to belong to my dad, and he gave it to me for my sixteenth birthday."

Willa stopped in front of the car and stuck her hand out to shake his. "Hi, my name is Willa. Have I met you before? You look so familiar."

Taking her hand, he pulled her close instead of shaking it. "There is a lot you don't know about me, but with some time, I think we can remedy that."

Willa wanted to get to know him better, but the more time they spent together, the more she liked him. A year ago, she would have chalked Tarron up to a distraction. She'd been convinced that's all he was a week ago. His breath brushing across her ear called attention to the lack of space between them. Her smile flattened, and she closed her eyes to compose herself.

"Your cheeseburger awaits." Tarron stepped back and opened the car door for her.

Willa blinked and watched as he tossed her bag in the trunk. She slid into the passenger seat and grinned when Tarron made his way to the driver side and jumped over his door with supernatural grace. The engine roared with the turn of his key, and Willa leaned her head back to enjoy the breeze as they crossed the street.

The Burger Bar hummed with teenage hormones and souped-up trucks and cars. Tarron circled the lot twice before someone vacated a parking space. When he pulled in, Willa noticed the cars on either side of them were empty. Most occupants congregated inside or at the front of the drive-in, but some dispersed to a less rowdy location near the river.

"So, what can I order you?" Tarron's finger hovered near the call button.

"A cheeseburger, plain, and a large chocolate shake, please."

He placed her order and added a burger, strawberry shake, and tater tots for himself. Sitting in the car, waiting, Willa wracked her brain for something interesting to say. Subconsciously, she held the pendant of her necklace and pulled it from side to side along the chain.

Tarron unbuckled his seatbelt and shifted to face Willa. "Uh-oh, what's wrong?"

"What do you mean?"

"Well, you have a tendency to do that," he pointed to her neck, "whenever you get nerv—wait, do I make you nervous?"

A knowing grin spread across Tarron's face, and Willa couldn't decide if she wanted to kiss his full lips or run away more. She pushed both notions down and swallowed. Her throat had grown dry, but she needed to tell him the truth.

"Yes," she admitted. "It's just that I've never liked anyone before. All my life I thought I'd shift, become the alpha, and eventually find my mate. In less than two months, all of those plans will shatter if I don't shift. I'm starting to accept my fate, and the choices that come with it."

"And you don't want to make the wrong choice?" Tarron asked.

"No, I mean yes—" Willa covered her face with her hands.

A cute brunette wearing roller skates glided around to Tarron's side of the car with a tray full of food. "Hey, honey, that'll be $24.67."

Handing her two bills, he said, "Thanks, Maggie, keep the change."

She hooked the tray on the driver side window and winked at Tarron before skating away.

Willa pointed her thumb over her shoulder towards the trunk. "I have some money—"

"I've got this."

"But—"

Tarron handed her a large styrofoam cup. "You can pay next time, but only if you're the one doing the asking out."

"Hey! I asked you out this time." She took a long sip of her milkshake and cringed. Strawberry.

Tarron's face stretched into a similar frown after taking a drink from his cup. "Bleh, sorry." He handed over the chocolate milkshake to Willa. "I believe this is yours."

She handed him the strawberry shake and asked, "Do you want me to get you a new straw?"

"Nah, I think I'll be okay."

The two ate while debating which flavor of milkshake was best. The only flavor they could agree they both liked was vanilla. Willa stole a few tater tots, starting another discussion about which foods were appropriate to share. Both conceded to finger foods being acceptable, but anything eaten with a spoon verged on disturbing.

Tarron piled all of their trash onto the tray and set it under the intercom. He started the car and pulled out of the Burger Bar, set on a course to the town square. Willa didn't want the night to end. She enjoyed hanging out with someone who didn't know everything about her. It forced her to think through why she only liked whole strawberries, but not strawberry flavored food. And she had no clue what Tarron had against chocolate, but it made her question whether they could really be friends. The topic had made her laugh so hard her stomach hurt.

"Do you want to walk around the square with me?" Willa placed a hand over her belly. "I'm so full."

"Sure." Tarron got out and circled the car to meet her.

The night breeze had turned almost cold, but Willa had enough wolf in her to keep her warm. She walked toward the gazebo at the corner of the square, and as she came to the steps up onto the platform, Tarron's hand slipped into hers. She looked down, and thought no one in Havenwood Falls would be able to tell which of them was the werewolf or elf by just looking at their entwined fingers.

"Do you know any couples in town who are different supernatural races?" Willa asked.

"I do." He nodded and pulled her under the twinkle lights strung around the pavilion. "Why do you ask?"

There had to be couples in town made up of two races of supernaturals. Being raised in the forest by her pack, she hadn't been around any mixed-race couples. She'd seen a few in town now and then, and she understood some supernaturals didn't care about blending bloodlines. With tension constantly high between the werewolves and vampires, and witches, and hunters, and any other supe with an aversion to authority, Willa guessed wolf shifters were probably the last race another supe would want to date. Not to mention, she'd been groomed since birth to be alpha and hadn't ever considered the possibility.

Willa faced Tarron. She'd asked out of curiosity in general, but she also wanted to get his reaction. "There hasn't been a werewolf in the

Kasun pack who's mated with another supernatural race that I've ever heard of, not to say they haven't dated another supe—"

"You're starting to ramble." He grinned and tucked a strand of hair behind her ear. "What do *you* want, Willa?"

"I think I want to change things, and not just for me," she answered, looking up to meet his gaze. "I want to put together a team of our friends to compete in the Founders Day Games."

Tarron blinked a few times, taken back by her answer. "Do they let teams with mixed supernatural races compete?"

"Sure, but not from the high school." She beamed. "Are you in?"

"Sure." He grinned at her enthusiasm. "Hey, have you ever thought about why there hasn't been a team from the high school before?"

Willa shook her head.

Tarron slid a little closer, his arm grazing hers. "Most kids want to feel normal, you know, fit in. And sticking with your own kind is an easy way to do that. It might be harder, but finding people who like you for more than your bloodline is real friendship."

"Friendship?" Willa tilted her head.

Tarron rubbed his hand along his jaw in thought. "Sure. Friends like Scarlet, and Bale, and Elle are not easy to come by." He grinned.

Willa understood what Tarron meant about wanting to belong. As the future alpha, she grew up wishing for the other pack members to accept her as one of their own. Instead, she felt the pressure of their expectations and the anxiety from not meeting them.

"Maybe, someday, I won't feel so bound by what everyone else expects, and I'll be free to go after what I want." Willa looked down at her feet.

"Someday?"

Willa's head slowly lifted, and her eyes met his. Her lips twisted in determination. "Ask me what else I want."

He tilted his head. "Okay, but I'm warning you, you can't have my car."

Willa tugged on his hand.

"What else do you want?"

"I want to kiss you."

Tarron's smile grew into a grin. He slid a hand around her lower back and pulled her closer. Willa pushed up on her toes and wrapped her arms around his neck. Tarron's lips gently pressed into hers, and she let her eyelids flutter shut.

Willa tasted cinnamon when Tarron kissed along her bottom lip. She didn't think she could be any closer to him, as her fingers traced his hairline along the back of his neck. Before he pulled away, he left a trail of kisses across her cheek, all the way to her ear. When he reached her neck, he whispered, "I wanted to kiss you, too."

His words stirred a growl in her chest, and Tarron chuckled.

"I'd better get home." Willa stated the obvious. She thought spending time with him would make her feel less awkward, but now they'd kissed. He'd been her first kiss.

Tarron held his hand out for her to take. "I'll walk you."

They made their way across the street, and Tarron grabbed Willa's duffel from his trunk. Once in front of Backwoods Sport & Ski, Willa dug around in her bag for her keys. She unlocked the door, and before stepping inside, gave Tarron a kiss on the cheek.

"Thank you for tonight. I'll see you in the morning."

"Good night." He stepped away.

From inside, Willa peeked her head out of the door. When Tarron jumped into the driver seat, she smiled. He had a similar grin stretched across his face.

"Hey! Tarron, I'm curious," she called before he had a chance to start the car. "Which couple do you know—"

"My parents."

The Corvette roared to life, and all Willa could bring herself to do was wave at Tarron as he backed out of his space.

Chapter 5.5

FRIDAY 11:52 PM

Willa: Thanks for tonight!

Tarron: I had fun . . . let's do it again soon

Willa: . . .

Tarron: Are you trying to figure out how to ask me about my parents?

Willa: I'm def curious, but don't want you to feel any pressure . . .

Tarron: My dad is an elf and my mom is a witch

Willa: Did they have to deal with any crap to be together?

Tarron: Not that I know of

Willa: It must be a wolf shifter thing

Tarron: The Kasun pack is known for being pretty tight

Willa: Yeah

Willa: Wanna save me a seat in the morning?

Tarron: Sure thing

SATURDAY 3:37 PM

Tarron: That was brutal

Willa: I knew the ACT would be hard, but the prep was so boring!

Tarron: You mean easy?

Willa: That too

Tarron: What are you doing?

Willa: Reading up on a certain helmet

Willa: Do you want to handle the paper or the presentation?

Tarron: Presentation, but I don't mind helping with the paper too

Tarron: I'll tell you about my idea when you try out your new bow Monday

Willa: Deal

MONDAY 7:44 PM

Willa: I totally thought I'd be better than I was! I'm going to need a lot of practice!

Tarron: What exactly are you referring to?

Willa: Archery, what did you think I meant?

Tarron: Archery, of course

Tarron: Don't worry, you're a quick study!

Willa: Will you help me with something this week?

Tarron: Will it require spending more time together and lots of practice?

Willa: I want to convince our Scooby gang to enter the Founders Day Games as a team

Tarron: . . .

Willa: If we play, I'll spring for Broastful Brews

Tarron: Lead with that

CHAPTER 6

ounders Day was always held on the autumn equinox, and this year that meant the Havenwood Falls High student body would get out of school on Friday. Willa had successfully convinced Tarron, Bale, Scarlet, and Elle to join her team for the games, but she'd have a big coffee order to fill. It wasn't until the day before at lunch that Willa dropped two bombs.

First, the team had to show up at the town square at eight in the morning. It was an hour earlier than what she'd initially thought.

Her announcement was met with groans from Bale, but the girls took it well. Every team needed to be informed of the rules, even though they were the same every year. The games never changed, and the teams from each supernatural race rarely changed. Everyone sought bragging rights for the year, and while it sounded silly for grown men and women to participate in a wheelbarrow race, it was oddly entertaining.

Willa also told the others that her twin, Kase, would be their sixth teammate.

The silence that fell over the table was followed with a snicker from Scarlet. "You're joking."

"No, we need one more player, and he promised to play nice," Willa tried to explain.

Bale folded his arms across his chest. "I hate to be the one to break it to you, but your brother hasn't played nice since we hit double digits."

"Come on, Bale. Let's try to give him a chance," Tarron said.

Willa woke up early Friday morning to the noise of Founders Day committee members setting up. She dressed in black joggers and a T-shirt declaring "coffee first." She walked past the storefronts of the square and stopped at the coffee shop. Scarlet found her balancing two cupholders full of caffeine.

"Are you ready for this?" Scarlet took one of the cardboard trays and set it on a nearby bench while she pulled her long red hair into a bun at the top of her head.

Willa watched as a group of vampires arrived and exited a black SUV. "Yeah, I think so."

Scarlet moved to block her view, with her latte in hand. "Can I ask you something personal?"

Willa nodded.

"Is forming this team about proving something to your pack in regard to Tarron or do you have another agenda?"

The question hit Willa in the chest and left her speechless for a few seconds. She'd told herself the team was about showing her classmates they could all work together. There didn't have to be outsiders or insiders. But an ache near her heart revealed that Scarlet was on to something.

"Can it be about Tarron and me *and* proving a point?" Willa asked.

Scarlet scooted to stand beside Willa, and they watched Tarron pull up in his convertible with Bale. "Just remember, proving you're right about him isn't about them. If you focus on proving them all wrong, you could lose him."

"Why are you and Bale hiding your feelings for each other?" Willa asked.

Scarlet's eyes grew wide. "How did you—"

"I just had a hunch."

Scarlet looked off at the cloudy sky. "It doesn't have anything to do with me hating on shifters, if that's what you're getting at."

"I didn't think so."

"It's just that women in my family have a knack for getting our hearts broken. Bale and I decided it would be better to move on when school started, and that way we could stay friends." Scarlet shoved her hands into her hoodie's pockets. "Do you mind not letting on about knowing anything happened between us?"

Willa mimed zipping her lips shut as the guys approached. Her mood lightened with Tarron around, but she couldn't help thinking about how self-absorbed she'd been, worrying only about her own problems lately. She would make it a priority to be a better friend to Scarlet going forward.

"Where do we check in?" Tarron asked as he approached them. He smiled and winked at Willa.

"I think we have to wait for everyone to get here before we register." Bale turned and searched the square. "There's Kase." He rolled his eyes and caught Willa watching him. Shrugging his shoulders, he moved to stand next to Scarlet and nudged her with his elbow.

"What was that for?" Scarlet asked with a smile.

Bale tucked a strand of hair behind his ear. "Just making sure you're awake."

The two didn't hide their chemistry well. Willa felt a couple vibe coming from them on the first day of school, and it grew stronger daily. Their eye contact always lasted a few seconds too long. Scarlet would pat or shove Bale's arm during conversations. And Bale always sat directly across from Scarlet. Willa wondered if they played footsie under the table without anyone noticing.

Kase met the group on the sidewalk, and Willa could tell he was mentally counting everyone who stood with her.

"We're still waiting on Elle," she said.

Just as she mentioned Elle's name, the blonde, lanky vampire strutted around the corner in jogging shorts, running shoes, and a Salt Life sweatshirt. When she caught sight of them, her face lit up, and then she noticed Kase. Elle's mouth immediately turned down, but her feet didn't falter.

"Finally," Kase murmured.

Willa slapped his chest with the back of her hand. "Be nice."

There was no reason to play into the werewolf versus vampire cliché. Elle had proven to be friendly every day at school, and she was the only one at their table who didn't flinch when Willa announced her brother would be a member.

The group walked across the street to the registration table together. A few curious eyes watched them. Willa specifically noticed her brother, Tate, standing in the gazebo at the corner of the square. His cadet uniform proved his purpose for being up so early, but Willa could see her older brother's disdain for being forced to patrol at the annual event in the frown stretched across his face. He typically looked twenty-five, even though he was born in 1917, but his misery made him appear as old as their oldest brother. Born in 1867, Conall resembled a handsome mid-thirties version of their father.

"Can I help you, dear?" asked Irene Beckett, a doughy, elderly woman with a nest of gray hair piled on top of her head.

"We'd like to sign up for the games." Kase stepped forward and flashed a grin in her direction.

While trying to separate two forms, Mrs. Beckett, the town's gossip, rambled, "We haven't had a group of young people from the high school play in ages." She passed the paper to Kase, and he handed it to Willa. "Plenty of *families*, all trying to prove their place in this town."

"Don't let her fool you. My sister's trying to prove something, too." He rolled his eyes.

Willa slapped him in the chest with the back of her hand, again.

After filling out each participants' name and age, Willa handed their form over, and the group waited for the games to begin. They watched as humans and supernaturals alike prepared for relay races and tug of war. Willa noticed some of the Court members wading through the growing crowd. Anyone familiar with the Court of the

Sun and the Moon knew Founders Day was a way for the supernatural leadership to complete a census each year.

One of the leaders welcomed everyone and prattled through a list of events for the day. The games were always first, then lunch, and the reenactment typically started at dusk. But this year, they were re-opening the newly renovated library before the games.

"The three-legged race will begin in five minutes!" a deep voice shouted a while later, with the help of a bullhorn from the gazebo.

When Willa looked toward the voice, she saw Tate plug his ears with his fingers. A squat man, impeccably dressed in slacks, a light blue dress shirt, and suspenders, stood next to her brother and had propped the horn up in his direction. She giggled, and when he realized she saw him, he made his way toward her. The last thing she needed was two of her brothers mocking her new friends. Tate tended to be more understanding than Kase and Conall, and he had a stubborn streak similar to Willa's, but that didn't mean he'd take her side.

Willa, hoping to avoid introductions, jogged a few yards to meet Tate. "Hey!"

"Hey, yourself. How are you doing?" Tate wrapped his arms around her and picked her up. He was the tallest Kasun in the family, and Willa happened to be the shortest. Instead of stooping down for a hug, he always lifted her up.

"Things are good." She nodded in Tarron's direction when he set her on her feet.

Tate looked from Tarron to Kase to Willa.

"Er—As good as they can be." She grinned.

Tate laughed. "So, is he what inspired this public display?" He nodded to Tarron. "You've never wanted to compete before."

"Anyone is allowed to play." Willa propped a hand on her hip. "I just wanted to hang out with some friends . . ."

"And."

"And, I may be trying to prove a point. Let's be honest, after my birthday, I won't really belong anywhere."

"What are you talking about? You'll always belong with us."

"Saying it isn't the same as what I feel when I'm with the pack." Willa placed a hand on her temple and rubbed small circles. "When Ana's family takes over, I'm not sure I can—or want to—be a pack member. It will destroy Dad if they replace him as sheriff in addition to Ana being named alpha. And you and Conall, what will you do if the Novaks replace you?"

"It's kind of a scary thought for the town, isn't it? It won't bother me as much as the sheriff and Conall, but you shouldn't be worrying about us," Tate reasoned.

"I need to find a place for myself, but Havenwood Falls High has a way of keeping us all in our places."

"You don't have a place, and if you did, it wouldn't be here in this hellhole." Tate's chest rumbled. "You're better than all of this. Don't you remember what Elder Lav said over you at your twelfth birthday?"

Willa rolled her eyes.

"I know you don't think much of the pack, but our ways are a part of who you are. They will continue to be a part of who you become."

"But he's madder than any hatter, Tate. No one puts any stock in anything he says," Willa argued. "And how can you say all of that when you're wasting away working on the force?"

"I'm just waiting for Elder Lav's words to ring true."

"No pressure."

Tate smiled. "If it's written in the stars the way he foretold, everything will work out. The pack won't just endure, but we'll prosper."

"Live long and prosper." Tarron walked up behind Willa and held his hand in the air with his middle and ring fingers separated.

Tate's head tilted to the side.

"Geek speak, sorry." Tarron held his hand out to Willa's brother. "Hi, I'm Tarron, and you must be a Kasun."

Tate shook his hand firmly. "Officer Kasun, when I'm wearing this." He pointed to his badge. "But when I'm off duty, Tate's fine."

Willa, impressed and perturbed at how quickly her brother could turn his Officer Stick-in-the-Mud persona off and on, shoved her brother.

56

Tarron squared his shoulders and spoke more formally. "So, Officer Kasun, what do the stars have to say about Willa?"

Tate looked to Willa for permission, but she just twisted her lips. Living in a town full of supernatural beings with super-hearing was annoying.

Clearing his throat, Tate began to recite the prophecy in a low dramatic tone, impersonating the ancient elder who roamed the Havenwood Falls forest. "In the stars is written the tale of a valiant warrior, a wolf who will lead her pack to harmony. The moon will call, but there will be no reply. In the silence, the alpha's mind will battle her heart, but courage will make her whole and shine, a beacon of hope . . . Er, something like that."

Tarron squinted his eyes and nodded slowly. "Impressive. I didn't know werewolves had prophets."

Willa crossed her arms over her chest. "There are stories about elders centuries ago who had special abilities, like seeing the future and mind reading, but Elder Lav's nickname is Loony Lav, if that gives you any idea of how seriously we took him. I think he predicted one of the pack members would also defy gravity someday."

"Don't let her fool you," Tate said. "There are a lot of us in the pack who are holding onto the hope Lav predicted."

"Three-legged race, starting in one minute!" A loud voice echoed across the town square.

"We'd better get going." Willa hooked her arm through Tarron's and started to pull him toward the games.

"Nice to meet you," Tarron offered, with a look over his shoulder back at Tate.

"You, too." Tate waved. "Good luck!" His eyebrows raised as he nodded at Willa. She knew he meant with her and not the Founders Day games.

Once they met the others, groups began to line up at the start. A bandana tied two team members together, and Willa anticipated they'd do well. There wasn't much strategy in running around a cone fifty feet away. Scarlet and Bale raced first and held their own with the more athletic competitors. Kase and Elle got off to a rocky start, but by the time they reached the cone, they'd fallen into sync. It was up to Willa and Tarron to make up the few yards they were behind, and with a last-ditch effort, the two threw themselves across the finish line in a dive.

"By the skin of their teeth, or more accurately by the tip of a finger, our team from Havenwood Falls High has taken their first win," the day's announcer reported. "Next will be the sack race."

In the excitement, Willa embraced Tarron. Scarlet gave Bale a quick hug, then pulled back. She looked around them to see who might have been watching. Kase turned to Elle and held his fist out for her to bump. She grinned and pushed her first two fingers under his fist.

"You get a snail fist bump, since we were the slowest of the crew." Elle's smile grew into a grin, and she laughed as Will's mouth turned down.

"Let's see who's the slowest in the sack race," he taunted.

The team of teens managed to scrape by with third place in the next race, but as they prepared for the tug of war, they began to fall apart. Willa couldn't put her finger on what was said, or who said it, but they went from encouraging each other to comparing their strengths and weaknesses. After each competition, they felt less like a team and more like six strangers.

By the end of the morning, they'd avoided last place, but landed in second to last. Tarron and Willa joked about the feat, but Kase stomped away, mumbling something about how embarrassed he was to be seen with them. Willa was proud of Tarron and Bale for keeping their mouths shut until her brother was out of hearing range.

"I'm not sure what he's complaining about. We ranked better than his precious football team has this season." Bale shoved his hands in his pockets. "I'm gonna get a burger. Wanna come with, Scarlet?"

His casual nod toward the cart on the street made Willa think he wasn't as worried as Scarlet about being seen together.

"See you guys later." She shrugged her shoulders, and the two walked away.

Elle, left standing with Tarron and Willa, examined the lawn around their feet. "Well, I think I'm going to head home." She pushed at the grass with the toe of her running shoes.

Willa didn't want Elle leaving on such an awkward note. "Are you sure? I think you should stay and hang out a little longer. We could get lunch and eat near the river. Doesn't that sound fun?"

Willa elbowed Tarron.

"Yeah!" Tarron sounded like a used-car salesman. "Stay and have lunch with us. You don't want to miss the reenactment later."

Elle shrugged. "I guess I could stay a little while longer."

The three walked up to the Burger Bar's grill and waited in line for their food. With grub in hand, they made their way down Eleventh Street to Mathews River. The area east of the ski resort had always been a haunt of the teenagers in town. There were picnic tables and park benches scattered along a path that ran parallel to the water.

"Nice job today!" Ana's voice called from the river's edge.

Willa rolled her eyes. "Thanks."

She hoped her minimal response would keep the interaction short. But she had no such luck.

"It's a good thing we all made it to see what a great leader you are." Ana gestured to the pack members with her. "I mean, we can't wait to be besties with vampires and—what are you, exactly?"

Ana had turned to speak directly to Tarron, but it was Elle who responded first. "You don't even know what you have here." She spread her arms wide. "Why would you waste living in this town and only be friends with shifters?"

Tarron and Willa looked at each other, then back at Elle. She was being sincere, and Ana laughed.

A growl grew in Willa's chest, and everyone but Tarron and Elle took a step back. Willa felt her supernatural power pressing against the inside of her skin, eager to be released. She curled her lip and snarled.

"What was that?" Kase asked as he walked up from the river.

Willa wanted to shift, right there, in front of everyone. But it would have been against so many of the Court's rules. Not to mention, she still felt like her magic wasn't enough. Not enough to shift. Not enough to be alpha. Not enough to keep up this charade.

"Nothing," Willa mumbled.

She walked away with Tarron and Elle on either side, wondering if she deserved to have them in her life. She glanced back at her brother and the others, knowing deep down she belonged with them. Kase wrinkled his nose as he watched them leave, and his eyes lingered on Elle. Willa had failed to bring her team to work together, and she felt like giving up. No matter what Loony Lav prophesied, her fate couldn't be written in the stars, because she'd run it into the ground.

~

Chapter 6.5

FRIDAY 4:02 PM

The BOY Version: I noticed you bailed

Willa: So

The BOY Version: Smart to make a clean break

Willa: What are you talking about?

The BOY Version: Noticed your elf and vamp getting cozy at the gazebo

Willa: Don't.

The BOY Version: For real, r u ok?

Willa: Yes

The BOY Version: You can do better

Willa: Same

SATURDAY 10:52 AM

Tarron: You up?

Willa: Yep

Tarron: Can you work on the project today?

Willa: Nope

Tarron: What's up?

Willa: Work
Tarron: I'll come by
Willa: It would be better if you didn't

SUNDAY 1:16 PM
Tarron: Want to grab some coffee?

3:27 PM **WILLA:** Sorry, lost track of time
Willa: Check our Google folder, I got some work done
Tarron: I thought we were going to work on it together
Willa: I was on a roll
Tarron: Will I get to see you today?
Willa: I don't think it's a good idea
Tarron: Why not?
Willa: I had a heart-to-heart with my dad
Tarron: Everything ok?
Willa: There's no way you can understand
Willa: My dad asked me to give the pack another chance
Tarron: What does that even mean?
Willa: I'm torn
Tarron: What do you need from me?
Willa: Please, don't make me type it out
Tarron: . . .
Willa: Space, I just need some space

CHAPTER 7

*M*onday, Willa hated herself for walking past her Scooby gang and sitting with the Kasun pack. She'd promised her dad to give her brother and the others another chance. A chance to allow the bond connecting pack members to strengthen. But she felt her alliance with Tarron and the others fracture after she turned to face the opposite direction.

Tuesday, the ache in her soul to exchange a smile with Scarlet or Elle kept her focused on the speckled linoleum floor. In her classes, she buried her nose in her textbooks. In the hallways, shoulders pressed close, but she sensed herself growing emotionally distant.

Wednesday, she survived the day without saying one word out loud.

Thursday, she slept, ditching school. It wasn't until noon that she remembered her project with Tarron was due the following day. She pulled out her laptop and quickly opened up their shared files. Tarron hadn't opened them.

Willa wouldn't bail on the presentation or paper. He didn't deserve it. She started compiling the research she'd gathered and worked through points for the presentation. After organizing a slideshow, she scribbled out some thoughts on notecards. The notes served as an outline for the paper she typed and printed.

Before she knew it, her dad strode into their apartment. His broad frame, dark hair, and affinity for plaid made him look more like a lumberjack than a sheriff. He pulled off his jacket and hung it in the front closet. It only took four steps to reach her at the other side of the room, and he leaned over and kissed her forehead.

"You're up late. Homework?" he asked.

Pressing a thumb to her phone, she saw that it was after ten. "Yeah, a history presentation on an Archer's Banded Kettle Helm."

"Cool." Her dad plopped on the couch and stretched out, propping his boots on the coffee table. "Did you eat dinner?"

"I lost track of time." She clicked to save the file as she closed the window. "But now that you mention it, I'm starving."

"Pizza?" He guessed.

Willa shook her head.

"Hmm . . . Chinese?"

"Burgers?" Willa countered.

Her dad nodded his approval. "Want to take my truck? I'm beat."

"Sure," she answered with a grin. "The usual?"

"Yeah." He leaned his head back into the cushion and closed his eyes. It wasn't often Sheriff Ric Kasun let himself get caught in a vulnerable position, and in that moment, he seemed more peaceful than when he was armed and patrolling the town borders.

Willa had always thought peace and security went hand in hand, but her dad being relaxed and exposed had brought him the most peace. Being able to let go of the outside world and the expectations that went with it, allowing himself to be comfortable.

"Dad, can I ask you something?"

"Sure, but if it's about helmets or archers, I'm not sure I'll be much help," he said with a smirk.

Willa moved to plop down beside him. "You want to keep me safe," she said, feeling so small next to him.

"Yes, it's my job as your father, as your acting alpha, and as the town's sheriff. Why?" He peeked through one eyelid.

Willa shifted uncomfortably. "What if I don't become alpha, and the Novaks replace you?"

"Ana Novak becoming alpha may seem like the end of the world, but we'll survive. The Kasuns have made it through much worse. Plus, Ana is young. Her father and the Court won't allow her to make major decisions on her own for years," he explained.

"But what if they replace you as sheriff, too?"

Ric closed his eyes for a moment, processing the notion. "Honestly, I hadn't thought about it. The Court appointed me as sheriff, and I'm not sure the Novaks could make that kind of call."

"Well, I've been taking your advice. Hanging out with Kase and the others more." She winced. "And, I know it was meant to help me fit in and protect me, but—"

"But you're miserable?"

"Yeah." She frowned. "I've been managing to keep myself together, but the tighter I try to hold on, the more out of control I feel. And, I don't want to let you down."

"Come here." He shifted to his side and wrapped his arms around his baby girl. "There's miserable, and then there's miserable. You have to ask yourself which is worse—the way the pack makes you feel when you're with them or the way they treat you when you're hanging out with your new friends. Once you decide which miserable you can live with, you'll know how to move forward."

"Would you be mad if I chose an elf, witch, vampire, and dragon shifter over the pack?" she asked.

Her dad laid his head against hers. "I'm not sure that's what you're doing. Your mom would say you're adding to your pack, and while there is a Novak or two that don't deserve it, I believe you'd risk your life for any of ours."

"No pressure." She pushed against his chest teasingly, but not so hard that he'd loosen his embrace. It felt like home to be in her daddy's arms. Not because he held her captive, but because he was beginning to let go.

"How about I make you a PB&J? Then we don't have to leave, and we can try to catch a late-night lip sync battle."

"Sounds perfect," she agreed with a smile.

In bed by midnight, Willa lay under a mound of blankets looking beyond her window at the moon. Its power filled her. It felt like the joy overflowing from the time she spent with her dad. Willa wouldn't go another day without talking to Tarron, Scarlet, Elle, and even Bale. It took some time to find sleep, but when she did, a weight had been lifted, and she felt a peace about her decision.

A morning freeze had frosted every window pane in the apartment, blocking the morning light. Willa woke up with a jolt, immediately worried she would be late. Reaching over to her phone, she tilted it, only to see that she'd woken up twenty-four minutes early. Perfect. She had time to pick up coffee.

Arriving at Havenwood Falls High early, with her Americano and an extra hot cinnamon latte for Tarron, Willa stood on the front steps at the entrance. She hoped to catch Tarron so they could go over their project before class, not to mention so she could apologize.

Tarron had given her space, just like she'd asked. He hadn't stopped by her locker or visited her at work. In that moment, as students rushed into the building before the first bell, Willa wished Tarron stood directly in front of her. But he never arrived.

She wouldn't blame him for bailing.

Willa turned and tossed the two drinks in a nearby trash can. Tugging on her backpack's shoulder straps, she took the steps two at a time and mentally prepared to give the presentation on her own.

Just like the second day of school, Willa stopped short of the back section the pack sat in and took a seat in the middle of the room. When the final bell rang, every desk was occupied except the one next to her. Ms. Bast had worn her hair down, and as she turned her back to the students, her dark curls obstructed Willa's view of the names she started writing on the board.

"Psst!" Someone called from behind Willa.

She looked over her shoulder, and everyone looked busy, pulling their papers out of their backpacks or reading over notes for their presentations. She turned back around and did the same.

"Psst!"

Willa wanted to ignore the noise, but it sounded familiar. She turned one more time, and her brother leaned forward in his desk with his eyebrows raised.

"Are you going to be okay if Tarron doesn't show?" he asked.

Ana's eyes darted up at the elf's name.

"I'll be fine." Willa waved her brother's worry for her away. "It's not like I didn't bail on him all week."

Ana rolled her eyes. "We'll just tell Ms. Bast that Santa's helper wasn't very helpful. She'll totes understand, and hopefully you'll never have to mutt-it-up again."

"What did you just—" Willa pushed up from her desk, but Ms. Bast's knuckles rapped on the white board and forced her back to her seat.

"The order of the presentations is listed, and I expect everyone to show respect for their classmates." Ms. Bast moved to stand in front of Willa's row. "You will all be graded on peer reviews as well as your presentations, so take a worksheet and pass them back."

After divvying up the papers, Ms. Bast walked to the empty desk next to Willa. She sat and called up the first pair. Willa attempted calming herself by perusing the list, but found her name at the bottom. She pulled on the pendant of her necklace, hating the anticipation of having to go last.

Ms. Bast leaned toward Willa and whispered, "Tarron asked if your presentation could be the finale."

The request had to mean he'd show, but how did he get out of having to sit through everyone else's project? Willa wanted to take a nap during Maria and Joseph's list of facts, then Kase and Elle presented. The two did a thorough job describing a steel helmet from the Renaissance shaped like a lion's head. They even had the class laughing when they compared it to other helmets worn in in the same period shaped like animal heads.

A few other students gave entertaining presentations, including Ana and Ivan, as much as Willa hated to admit it. Her favorite had to be Scarlet and Bale's take on modern masks and makeup used for disguises. Willa slowly became aware of the masks she and her friends wore on a daily basis. Camouflaging themselves among their own kind, covering up their fear with fake smiles, and obscuring their curiosity with insults were all ways to fit in, hide, and protect themselves.

Then the room grew silent, waiting for her to take her turn, without Tarron.

She walked up to the front of the room, her eyes darting around like she'd find him somewhere hiding behind a bookshelf or desk. Taking her time, she plugged her thumb drive into the computer on Ms. Bast's desk. A few whispers distracted her, and when she glanced over her shoulder, a glint of metal caught her eye.

Tarron had entered the room in full costume.

A flat, open-sided silver helm pushed down his hair, and a leather breastplate covered his chest. He held a longbow at his side and arrow feathers peeked from behind his shoulder, strapped to his back in a quiver. A sword hung from his belt, and he wore brown pants and boots. There were extra touches to the costume Willa noticed, as they were a part of her research.

Willa tilted her head, curious about where he was going with this stunt. Tarron grinned. He showed up. He hadn't planned on letting her fail. A wave of emotion built up in her chest, making her want to apologize to him in front of the class.

Then Ms. Bast cleared her throat.

"As promised." Tarron bowed toward the teacher.

Ms. Bast nodded with a smile. "Just remember, weapons are not allowed on campus. It doesn't matter if it's a personal collection or plastic props, you have to leave directly after your presentation and get all of that off the school property." She waved up and down at his costume. "Or the principal will be torturing both of us."

"Yes, ma'am."

Willa pulled up the presentation she'd prepared, and with the first slide, introduced herself and her partner. During their lesson on the kettle helmet, she described how the helm and other armor was worn through history while Tarron gave a quick demonstration. Students laughed as Tarron modeled each piece of his armor. He'd brought an apple, and while she hoped to place it on top of Ana's big blue bow, he set it on top of a bookshelf at the back of the room. Gasps filled the room when the fruit was pierced by an arrow.

Everyone had been enraptured by them, well, everyone except Ana. She sat with her arms crossed and frowned through every slide.

To bring the presentation to a close, Willa added, "The kettle helmet was worn mainly by infantry, or foot soldiers. En masse, with matching armor, they all appeared to be identical, but many of the soldiers were ripped from their own lives and forced to fight for causes that weren't their own. I don't know about you, but I'm glad I don't *have* to hide or push someone else's agenda. I have the power to fight my own battles."

When they finished, the class clapped, and Willa retrieved her thumb drive. As she turned to walk back to her desk, Tarron exited the room. She looked from her empty chair to the doorway and decided to go with her gut. She walked out after him.

"Hey!" she called. "Tarron, wait up!"

He turned the corner, and Willa almost stopped when he didn't hear her. But, an urgency inside quickened her pace.

"Please, stop!" she hollered, not caring who heard her. "I'm sorry, please hear me out!"

As she reached the end of the hallway, she turned to follow Tarron and collided with a leather breastplate. She shook her head and looked up at a grinning elf. He had waited.

CHAPTER 8

$\mathcal{O}$n the one hand, everyone got enough sleep the previous night to take on the ACTs. On the other, most of the junior class moped into the high school cafeteria, depressed after losing last night's football game. The team had proved less successful than in seasons past, having only won three of their six games. Morale was low, and four hours with a number two pencil wasn't going to help.

For the last week, Willa, Tarron, Elle, Scarlet, and Bale had spent every evening going through a set of notecards Scarlet put together to study. Everyone else at Havenwood Falls High School had been consumed with football. Kase and his buddies rallied at their lunch table every day leading up to the big game. If they'd won, the blue and silver Dragons would have been a wild card team in the playoffs the next weekend. There hadn't been a season in four years that the team didn't cross over into the basketball season.

Thanks to their loss, this year's homecoming would feel less like a ticker tape parade to celebrate a group of guys who won their version of the Super Bowl, and more like a dance. Willa was torn between ignoring the tradition and asking Tarron if he wanted to go with her. The more time she spent with Tarron, the more she knew not inviting him would be a cop out.

"Good morning," Scarlet greeted. Her wide smile and the bounce in her step as she met Willa wasn't typical Scarlet behavior.

Willa was the first to arrive in the transformed space. The tables had been folded and rolled to the far end of the cafeteria. In their place, over a hundred desks filled the room. The public high school served as the host for today's test. If Willa didn't make a great score, she could take it again when Sun and Moon Academy, the private school, hosted. She wasn't surprised when she didn't recognize a few of the teens trickling into the empty seats.

"Morning," Willa answered. "You seem wide awake. What kind of coffee did you order?"

"I drink tea, and you know that." Scarlet took a seat at a desk and patted the chair next to her. "I need to talk. Girl talk."

Willa's eyebrows pulled up behind her dark bangs. "I'm a girl. But, are you expecting me to talk or listen?"

"Listen."

Willa swiped her thumb and finger across her lips and twisted them like she was locking them shut.

"Bale asked me to homecoming," Scarlet started and stopped. She didn't say anything else.

Willa waited.

More students began to fill empty seats, and Willa looked down at her watch. They had fifteen minutes before the test began, and she knew the rest of their Scooby gang would arrive soon. She needed to speed this girl talk along.

"So, what did you say?" she asked.

Scarlet fidgeted with one of her long red braids. "That's the thing. I stuttered a yes, then said something about how all of us could have dinner and make a night of it. His whole demeanor changed. I think he was asking me out, and I ruined it."

Willa felt bad for Scarlet, but she also felt a twinge of jealousy. "I'm sure we can fix this."

"You think so?" Scarlet's voice was hopeful.

Willa rubbed her chin. "I know so. But I need the truth. Do you want to go with Bale alone or do you want to all go together but as couples?"

"I'm not saying we can't all hang out, but I think I want it to be the two of us," she admitted.

As Tarron entered the cafeteria, with Bale and Elle close behind, Willa leaned over and whispered, "Okay, I can work with that."

"Hey guys!" Scarlet waved the others over.

"Are you two ready for this?" Tarron asked.

Willa noticed Bale take the chair farthest away from Scarlet and avoid eye contact. Elle took the seat on the other side of Scarlet, and Tarron sat in the seat next to Willa. He nudged her for an answer.

"I even sharpened an extra pencil." Willa waved her writing utensils in the air. "What's everyone doing after the test?"

"I don't have anything planned," Tarron answered first, then Bale shrugged.

"Hanging out?" Scarlet asked.

"Yeah." Willa glanced at Elle to make sure she felt included. "How about everyone come over to my place this afternoon for a movie marathon?"

Elle picked at her nails. "Are you sure?"

"Of course," she answered.

"Everyone, take your seats!" Ms. Bast's voice echoed from a table buried by stacks of paper.

Willa understood why Elle might have reservations about coming to her house. Any vampire would want to avoid an encounter with a pack of werewolves in the woods. She would feel the same way about walking into a nest of vamps. Willa probably needed to clarify that she lived above the family's store.

A group of teachers fanned out through the room, checking everyone's pencils. Ms. Bast placed red-rimmed glasses on the tip of her nose and read over the instructions while the tests were passed out, and Willa pushed thoughts of homecoming and dating and dresses to the back of her mind. Willa wasn't sure what her college plans were yet, but she hoped her test score would allow her to keep her options open.

"Break the seal and begin," Ms. Bast directed and scanned the room with her black eyes.

Willa flew through English and reading, and when she finished before her friends, she enjoyed peeking over at Tarron. He had the cutest way of tapping the end of his pencil against the tip of his nose while he read. Science kept Willa second-guessing herself, and the math section made her want to stab herself in the ear.

Just before they began the writing portion, Tarron leaned over and whispered, "Relax, the hardest part is over for you."

"You'll do fine," she assured him.

Ms. Bast cleared her throat to get everyone's attention. "You may start."

Earlier that week, they'd all agreed to meet in the school parking lot to discuss how they did. One by one, they each turned in their tests and walked out into the brisk fall afternoon. Bale had been the first one out of the cafeteria, and Scarlet walked out last.

"How do you think you did?" Willa asked her.

Scarlet pulled gloves out of her jacket pocket and fitted them over her hands. "Terrible. I completely froze on the writing and didn't finish."

"I bet you did great." Elle consoled her. "I didn't finish the science."

Scarlet zipped up her jacket and started to walk over to her vintage VW Golf. "Let's talk about it at Willa's. I'm freezing!"

"Okay, girls in Scarlet's car, and boys can meet us there," Willa suggested.

Bale and Tarron nodded their approval and jumped into the Corvette. Willa offered the front seat in Scarlet's car to Elle and slid into the backseat of the witch's silver hatchback. Once inside, and clear of being heard by the guys, Willa explained to Elle that she lived in the town square over the store and not in the forest with the rest of the Kasun pack.

Elle pressed her lips together, trying to restrain herself.

"Go ahead." Willa kneed the back of the passenger seat. "Say whatever is on your mind before you explode."

Elle hadn't been around other supernaturals before her family moved to town, so she observed everything. It seemed to be her way of getting to know all of them without sticking her foot in her mouth. The first week they met, she'd asked Tarron if Puck from *A Midsummer Night's Dream* was real, and if his family knew Shakespeare.

"The Kasun pack, your family, lives east of Havenwood Heights, in the forest . . ."

"Yes," Willa confirmed, "in cabins. It's a small community, but it allows them to shift without having to worry about being seen."

Relief flashed across her face as she pressed her lips together and nodded. "Okay. I mean, good. It's just that, I didn't know if, er, I wanted to make sure I wouldn't wake up to—"

"A wolf encounter?" Willa asked.

Pink blotches spread up Elle's neck to her cheeks. "Sure, um, yes."

Scarlet pulled out of the parking lot, onto Main Street. "Now that we've settled the Kasun sleeping arrangements, can we please address how I'm going to clear things up with Bale? He's been avoiding me all morning."

"I noticed that, too. What happened?" Elle asked, eager to change the topic.

"I fumbled up my words, and now he'll never go to homecoming with me," Scarlet wailed. She leaned forward, and as they slowed to a four-way stop, she banged her head against the steering wheel.

"You could not have fumbled any worse than my brother at last night's game," Willa joked, but neither of the girls laughed.

Elle suddenly lit up with excitement. "You need to do one of those prom-posal things!"

"But it's homecoming," Scarlet argued.

Willa stuck her head between their two seats. "I agree with Elle. You need to let Bale know he's not just a friend like the rest of us."

"Pot calling the kettle black much?" Scarlet teased, and this time Elle giggled, but Willa wasn't in the mood.

She still liked Tarron—really liked him. She felt like she should try to accept that he only wanted to be friends. Willa didn't blame him. If Scarlet and Bale went to next week's dance as a couple, maybe she and

Tarron could still go as friends with Elle. The problem was the theme required everyone to dress up as famous couples.

Willa leaned back in her seat and sank down a bit before responding. "Fine. I like him, but I messed it up when I asked for space. I'm a chicken for not bringing it up. But I bet he doesn't want anything more than friendship, and if that's all I can get, I'll take it. Anyways, we need to focus on fixing your problem."

Elle turned to face Willa. "What if you ask him?"

"I bet he'd say yes!" Scarlet encouraged.

"I don't know." Willa shook her head. "I'd rather not mess things up with him any more than I already have. Plus, if I don't ask him, the three of us can go together."

"Oh, well, I won't be here." Elle turned back around, avoiding eye contact.

"What?" Scarlet's mouth hung open.

"Yeah, my family has to go out of town for a few days. We'll be back by Sunday night, but my mom has already called the school office and gotten my Friday absence excused."

Scarlet pulled into the town square and parked in front of Backwoods Sport & Ski, next to Tarron's car. The guys weren't waiting for them, so Willa examined the sidewalk. Shoppers walked in and out of the stores and restaurants, but she noticed a few of them pointing to the center of the square.

Willa opened her door and stepped out. As she turned to see which quirky town event she forgot about, she watched as a crowd of people surrounded the gazebo. The people moved around the fountain at the center of the quad and pushed up on their toes for a better look.

"What do you guys think is going on over there?" Willa asked.

Scarlet and Elle made eye contact over the top of the car, and Willa picked up on a knowing exchange between them.

"Let's go see." Elle hooked her arm with Willa and pulled her across the street.

Scarlet followed and caught up to Willa's other side and whispered, "Don't be mad at me."

Willa's brow furrowed. The closer they came to the gazebo, the less she could see. Sparkling twinkle lights draped from the ceiling covering the platform, and thumping dance music drifted over the growing crowd.

"Excuse me," Elle said. The young couple in front of them turned and scooted over.

Scarlet tapped on a young girl's shoulder. "Pardon us."

As she slid to the side and let them by, Willa's brother Tate came into view. He didn't have his cadet uniform on, but wore the store's standard work uniform—jeans and a Backwoods Sport & Ski long-sleeved T-shirt. He was supposed to be covering for her while she took her ACTs.

"Tate? What are you—"

Tate pivoted to let her by, and she noticed two things immediately. First, Tate hadn't smiled that widely in a long time. Second, Tarron stood in the middle of the gazebo. Large silver stars hung around his head, and he held one in his hands.

"Go on," Scarlet said.

With a nudge, Willa took the first few steps. She realized the stars, fluttering in the afternoon breeze, were signs with words written on them.

She started to make out her name written on a star, then her eyes darted to read them all.

Willa & Tarron
Written
in the
Stars

Willa covered her mouth with her hands. She finally met Tarron's eyes, and he lifted the star he held to cover his face.

Will you be my date to homecoming?

"Yes!"

～

Chapter 8.5

. . .

SUNDAY 11:43 AM

The BOY Version: Tate told me that you're going to homecoming

Willa: And

The BOY Version: Are you sure about him?

Willa: More sure than I am of you

The BOY Version: Ouch!

Willa: Be honest, you're more worried I'll make you look bad

The BOY Version: I really am just looking out for you

Willa: He makes me happy

The BOY Version: Then I'll try harder to get on board

Willa: You do that

The BOY Version: Same

Willa: But does she really make you happy?

The BOY Version: . . .

SUNDAY 3:22 PM

Scarlet: BTW, Bale and I straightened everything out

Willa: When?

Scarlet: He walked me home when we left your place

Willa: Since the theme requires a costume this year, who are you guys coming as?

Scarlet: He joked about dressing up as Astrid & Stormfly

Willa: How to train your dragon? Bwahaha!

Scarlet: Yeah, I think he just wants to see if I'll dress up like a Viking

Willa: Good luck with that!

SUNDAY 7:56 PM

Willa: What have you been up to today?

Tarron: Bale wants to show up to homecoming shifted

Willa: I heard

Tarron: Who do you want to dress up as?

Willa: Shakespeare is too obvious

Tarron: Probably

Tarron: And you won't get me in tights

Willa: I just got a mental image

Tarron: Sorry

Willa: LOL

Tarron: How about Gatsby & Daisy?

Willa: Meh

Willa: I'd almost rather go as us…but with a happily ever after

Tarron: I'm down for that

Willa: And if anyone asks we can say we're Winston and Julia from 1984

Tarron: I'll have to look that one up

Willa: Really?

Tarron: . . .

Willa: How can I call you my boyfriend if you haven't read Orwell?

Tarron: Boyfriend?

Willa: . . .

Tarron: I like the way that sounds

Willa: Then you better start reading

CHAPTER 9

*W*illa walked home after school on Friday, with Tarron close at her side. He'd offered her a ride, but she enjoyed the colder temperatures. She told him it was silly to walk her home, then walk back to the school to retrieve his car, but he insisted.

The week had been less hectic with football season over and the ACTs taken. Willa spent the afternoons with Tarron and their friends. She'd memorized all their favorite drinks at Coffee Haven and favorite pizza toppings at Napoli's. She didn't think things could get any better. Then, Tarron kissed her goodbye and promised to pick her up by 6:30.

Scarlet had planned to get ready at Willa's apartment and would be arriving soon. While Willa waited, she pulled out her dress and shoes, laying them out on her bed. The sweetheart neckline and shorter length would normally be worn in the summer, but Willa had a vintage motorcycle jacket she'd wear over it and studded high tops.

At the sound of knocking, Willa ran to the door and invited her friend inside. One of Scarlet's arms had a hanging bag draped across it, and the other held a tote stuffed with her heels and styling products. Willa grabbed her dress and waved Scarlet inside.

"This is going to be fun." Scarlet bounced inside.

"Yeah." Willa set the garment bag on her bed next to her dress. "I hate that Elle couldn't make it. Do you know what her weekend out of town was all about?"

"No idea." She hung her tote on a hook on the back of Willa's bedroom door. "I wouldn't blame her if she made the whole thing up to get out of going without a date. Not that she would do that!"

"I'm going to text her, and make sure she knows we miss her."

"Good idea." Scarlet unzipped the bag her dress hung in, and what she pulled out surprised Willa.

"No. Way." Willa giggled. The red flowy wrap dress draped to the floor, dramatic but also simple, almost identical to the one worn in *The Princess Bride*. The movie was one of Willa's favorites, and immediately Willa knew who Scarlet and Bale would be impersonating.

Scarlet wrapped her arm around the fabric, pressing it against her stomach. "You don't think it's lame?"

"No! It's brilliant! And, I can't imagine Bale in anything but a black outfit. Which one of you thought of it?"

Scarlet rolled her eyes. "I did, but only after he suggested characters from Game of Thrones. Come on, let's get changed. I want to see that on you." Scarlet pointed to Willa's dress on the bed.

"As you wish," Willa said with a laugh.

The two girls changed and helped each other with their hair and make-up. Neither one of them went overboard, but their costumes didn't call for heavy eye liner or thickly layered red lipstick. Scarlet pulled a few locks of hair back loosely, but left the rest down and wavy. Willa tucked a clip with sparkling amethysts in her hair. The light purple added to the concept she and Tarron had come up with for their costumes.

A buzz pulled Willa away from the mirror, and her phone screen lit up with a message from Tarron. He planned to pick her up in fifteen minutes. They wouldn't all be going to the dance together, because Scarlet wanted to make sure Bale understood they were on a date. The dragon's bruised ego needed a boost, and Willa didn't mind the idea of some extra time alone with Tarron.

He hadn't held her hand or tried to kiss her since before she'd asked for space, and she was hoping they could fix that tonight. Willa swiped to check the time on her phone.

The front door of the apartment opened and closed, making Willa's heart stop. Had Tarron arrived early?

"Willa?" Her dad called from the living room. "Is it safe for me to enter?"

Willa looked over at Scarlet, who shrugged and turned back to smooth out her dress with flat hands against her hips.

"Yeah, we're decent."

"We?" he asked and stepped into her bedroom. He took in the clothes strewn on the floor and bags opened on the bed, then he noticed Scarlet standing in front of the mirror. "Miss Howe, right?"

"Yes, sir. Scarlet. It's nice to meet you." She stepped forward and stuck her hand out for him to shake.

He smiled and replied, "It's nice to meet you, too. Princess Buttercup?"

"Yes, sir."

He grinned and waved her formality away. "Please, call me Ric."

"The theme is Written in the Stars this year, so we're all dressed as famous couples," Willa explained.

"Ahh." He inspected his daughter's black cocktail dress with a cosmic print wrapped around her waist and glinting stars intricately placed on the bodice. "Then who are you going as?"

"I'm going as the stars, but you'll have to wait to see Tarron's costume."

Ric's head tilted, confused.

"At first he wanted to go as an astronaut, but I convinced him the suit would be too difficult to work around in the bathroom."

Ric chuckled. "I'm sure he just wants to impress you. I love that you're wearing your mother's stone." He leaned forward and kissed her cheek.

Willa placed her fingers over her necklace. "Thank you." She pushed up on her toes and gave her father a kiss on the cheek. "You know, I figured everyone would be showing up as—"

"Romeo and Juliet?" Her dad interrupted. "Your brother fell into that trap."

Scarlet let out a laugh from the bathroom, and Willa and her dad joined in.

Their laughing abruptly ceased at the sound of three raps on the door.

Scarlet jumped. "I bet that's Bale." She moved into the bedroom and started throwing all her things into her bag.

"Don't worry about your stuff." Willa put a hand on her arm to stop her. "You can come by later and grab it."

Ric had already started for the door.

"You'll want to be ready to leave before my dad interrogates Bale."

Scarlet gave herself one more once-over in the mirror and walked into the living room. Willa stepped into the doorway, and she couldn't believe how perfect Bale's costume looked. From the black mask to the sword to the boots, Bale had captured Westley in his Dread Pirate Roberts outfit. The only difference was the dark hair that escaped his mask.

Whatever her dad was asking him, Bale froze at the sight of Scarlet. "You look amazing."

"Thank you." Scarlet blushed.

"Sheriff Kasun, we have a stop to make before we head to the dance. Did you have anything else you wanted to add?" Bale asked, his smile faltering.

Willa understood the feeling. Her dad was intimidating. But he was also a great dad, and she figured he knew that Scarlet didn't have a father figure to instill fear in her dates.

"Just make sure she has a wonderful time." Ric narrowed his eyes at Bale.

Bale nodded. "Of course." He reached out a hand toward Scarlet, and she took it.

As they exited, Scarlet glanced over her shoulder and mouthed thank you to Willa's dad. She waved at Willa and said, "We'll see you and Tarron at the dance."

"Or now," Tarron's voice echoed down the hall. "Hey guys, you both look great."

Tarron passed Scarlet and Bale and stopped in the doorway. His mouth fell open at the sight of Willa. Ric stepped into view, and he quickly pulled himself together and shoved his hands in the pockets of his black suit pants. Underneath his jacket, Willa made out the image on his T-shirt. She hoped everyone would get the reference they were trying to make. Her dad would be the test run.

"Would you like to come in?" Ric asked.

"Thank you." Tarron stepped into the living room and slid his jacket off his shoulders. The black T-shirt he wore had an image of the moon printed on the front. His white suspenders were a surprise to Willa, but she liked them.

"So, what are your plans with Willa this evening?" Ric asked.

One of Tarron's eyebrows lifted. "I was hoping to keep it a surprise—"

Ric's chest rumbled, and Willa giggled. "Dad, give it a rest. Did you ask Kase what his plans with Ana were?"

"No, but—"

Willa laid a hand on her father's arm. "Would you feel better if I gave you Tarron's cell number? That way the surprise isn't ruined, but you can trace his phone."

"I wouldn't—well, unless it got really late." Ric corrected himself with a grin.

"I'll text it to you."

Ric's jaw flexed. "What time do you think you'll be home?"

Willa looked up to Tarron.

"The dance is over at eleven, but I'd like to keep her out until midnight." He hadn't asked a question, but raised his eyebrows like he needed permission. "If that's okay with you, sir?"

"Midnight." Ric held his hand out to shake on it.

"Thank you."

Ric tightened his grip. "Don't thank me yet. You lose the right to take her out again if you're late. Or if you harm one hair on her head —or her heart."

"Okay, Dad, you can let him go now," Willa assured.

Ric let Tarron go, and the elf shook out his fingers.

"See you later, sweetheart." Ric waved goodbye as they left. As Willa reached for her key, he said, "Don't worry about that. I'll be up."

Willa giggled as she grabbed her vintage leather jacket instead. "Goodnight, Dad."

She and Tarron made their way down the stairs and out the building's back door. The last thing she wanted to do was parade through the store all dressed up. At least wearing studded black high tops, she didn't have to worry about tripping and wobbling on heels all night.

"So, your dad is funny." Tarron smiled as he held the passenger side door open for her.

Willa slipped into the Corvette. "That's one way to put it. He actually mentioned his concealed handgun last year when Joseph Greg asked me out." Her face soured at the thought.

"What? You didn't want him to be the moon to your stars?" Tarron asked, referencing their costumes, as he revved the engine.

"Don't you remember that freshmaen hazing you guys went through on the football team? I've seen Joseph's full moon."

The two laughed, and Willa watched as Tarron focused on a few turns and some oncoming traffic. She really liked being with him. He didn't like her because she could be the next alpha or dislike her because she couldn't shift. He hadn't been scared away by her brothers, and he gave her space when she needed it.

"What's wrong with you?" she blurted.

Tarron glanced at her, but quickly moved his eyes back to the road. "Ummm . . . where to begin? I always miss the hamper when I try to toss my dirty clothes in it, and I rarely pick them up off the floor. My mom says I spend too much time playing video games. My dad is always pestering me about work—"

"Tarron, really, is that all you've got?"

The car slowed down, and Willa looked out her window. Tarron had driven them as far on Main Street as they could go, to Danzan Park. They pulled over on the other side of Bels Creek. As he shut the car off, the headlights faded, and Willa could only see a few feet past the hood. She didn't have the ability to see in the dark like her werewolf family. Even Kase only had it when in his wolf form.

"What are we doing out here?" Willa asked.

"Surprise, remember?" Tarron jumped out of the car and reached for a basket and blanket in the trunk.

Tarron spread the blanket along the bank of the creek and opened the basket. He pulled a lantern out first and lit up a small area around them. The peaceful sound of water running toward Mathews River and the thousands of stars beaming above them made the setting perfect.

"Are you going to be cold? I have another blanket—"

"I'm good." She moved to peek in the basket. "What else is in there?"

"Food."

"What kind of food?"

Tarron paused above the basket and looked at the blanket. "Can we sit first? I want to tell you something, but I'm not sure I want to hand you something you can throw at me first."

"Okay . . ." Willa tilted her head. "Is it serious?"

"Kind of. It might be something you'd categorize as wrong with me." He sat on the blanket, his legs remaining straight in front of him, and patted the space next to him.

"I'm all ears." She smiled reassuringly and placed her hand next to his so that they brushed against each other.

"I quit the football team because I have the ability to convince or manipulate other people to do what I want. The power didn't fully develop until our sophomore year, and my mom thinks that my witch side amplifies my elfin abilities when my emotions are heightened."

"That's crazy, but why would that be something wrong? I mean, you recognized it and dropped out of football. If anything, you should think I'm a horrible person for not telling anyone about my abilities."

Tarron shook his head. "I don't think you understand, Willa. When we first met, I was so worried I'd say or do something that would cause you to like me more than you would have if I didn't have this power. I have to be so careful, especially with humans."

"I can't remember ever feeling like you influenced me. I mean, you may have used your mystical power to get me to try that disgusting strawberry shake at the Burger Bar." She nudged him with her elbow.

Tarron sat up and crossed his legs in front of him. "I never want to influence you to do anything you don't want to do. When you told me you needed space, I realized my abilities didn't work on you. At least not as strongly as they had with others. I just need to tell you before things get serious—I mean—"

Willa's mouth spread into a wide smile. He planned for things to get serious. Instead of being scared or nervous, she welcomed the stir of emotions in her stomach. She leaned forward slightly and took in his features. His white hair, messy as always, made him appear wild and mischievous. His light eyes and freckles gave him a boyish charm, but his full lips and jawline made her want to lean in closer and kiss him.

"Are you doing it right now?" she asked.

He whispered, "Doing what?"

"Making me want to kiss you?"

"I'd have to say it out loud." He grinned. "Plus, I told you, it doesn't work on you."

She leaned forward and brushed her lips softly over his, testing his response. Tarron's eyes searched hers.

"Are you sure?" she teased and kissed him again.

CHAPTER 10

arron and Willa entered the high school gym looking like they could be a centerpiece on one of the tables. Black paper and giant silver stars hung from the ceiling. Lights twinkled along the walls. A stage had been set up under one of the basketball hoops and a space cleared in front of it for dancing. The area was surrounded by tables covered in black tablecloths and glitter.

The tables and refreshments were swarming with students, but the dance floor remained empty. The music lilted through the air, not exactly romantic or energizing. Willa had been dreading dancing with Tarron. She looked down at his black boots and hoped he had plenty of polish at home, because she had a feeling she'd be scuffing them up.

"Do you want something to drink?" Tarron asked.

Willa glanced around the room in search of Scarlet. "Sure." She pointed to a red dress at a table toward the back of the gym. "I'll head over to meet Scarlet and Bale."

"Any food?" he asked before walking away.

Willa pushed up on her toes to kiss him on the cheek. "Thank you, but I don't think I can eat another bite. Maybe later, if we dance off some of the burgers."

Tarron had made an effort to recreate their first date, without actually going to the drive-in. After eating, they went for a walk and lost track of time. It had been easy to leave the town on the other side of the creek.

"Hey, you two," Willa greeted Bale and Scarlet. They'd both sat down at a table, with their chairs so close their shoulders touched. Willa grinned at their affection. "Where did you take Scarlet for dinner?"

"Oh, well—"

"He cooked for me!" Scarlet's face lit up. She wrapped her arm around his and squeezed. "It was the best steak I've ever eaten."

"You cook?" Willa's eyes widened in wonder.

"I grill. There's a big difference," he corrected, then rubbed his hand over his mouth and mumbled, "And, my mom shmunted-a-mean-squirrel."

Willa's nose wrinkled up in question.

"His mom wanted to meet Scarlet," Tarron clarified as he sat down next to her. He set a plastic cup filled with blue liquid in front of her. "I had to meet her, too, before I could take Bale out." He laughed.

"Shut up, man. She's protective." He leaned forward. "And you don't want to make a dragon shifter angry, especially a mother."

"I bet my dad could give her a run for her money," Willa said.

"Nah, your dad's intimidating, but imagine him shifting to the size of a school bus and breathing fire because you're out past curfew."

Willa looked to Tarron and Scarlet, who both shrugged. She'd actually like to see Bale's mom shift. Some nights, she looked up to the sky to try to find one of the dragons flying overhead. A few of them worked with her father and patrolled the skies, but she'd only seen the shadow of one gliding above at night.

A group of students barged into the gym in a commotion, and Willa immediately recognized Ana's whiny voice. "This is not music. It's elevator crap. Someone tell that DJ we aren't paying him to be put to sleep."

Scarlet giggled and whispered to the rest of them, "I wish someone would put her to sleep."

They all laughed, but Ana and Scarlet both had a point. The music needed to change, and someone needed to put Ana in her place. Willa could at least do something about one of their problems.

"I'll be right back." She stood up and walked over to the stage. Marching up the steps near the DJ's booth, Willa slid behind a set of speakers in search of the person in charge.

A woman in ripped jeans and a crop top was stooped over on her cell phone. She had her phone against one ear and a finger in the other. Willa patted her arm to get her attention, and she jumped. The woman yelled something into the phone and hung up. She cocked an ear upward and frowned.

"What the—"

"Can I make a request?" Willa asked.

"Sure! Anything would be better than this." She moved to open her laptop, cords protruding from one side. "I asked your principal to click the Havenwood Falls High homecoming playlist, but it sounds like he chose the list at the top of my screen, Assisted Living Bingo Night. What do you wanna hear?"

"How about some Sylvan Esso or The Wombats?"

"Done and done," the DJ's hot pink lips exaggerated. "Have fun, honey!" she yelled over the song's beginning.

The fresh tempo called to the students lingering around the outer edges of the dance floor. As Willa made her way off the stage, she saw Tarron, Bale, and Scarlet move to meet her. Taking her hand, Tarron winked at her and pulled her behind him to the middle of the crowd.

By the fourth song, Willa was thankful she'd worn her high tops. A small pile of heels had amassed at the foot of the stage. The beat of the music bounced off the walls of the gym and vibrated through Willa's chest. As the music slowed, a few loners cleared the area, but most of the couples gravitated together.

Tarron relaxed his arms around Willa's waist and leaned close to her ear. "Are you having fun?"

She smiled. "I never thought I'd have this much fun at a school dance. I feel so cliché."

"It's because we're here together." He squeezed Willa gently.

"Awww," Ana cooed. She wore a long gown, revealing a generous amount of cleavage, and her hair had been braided and piled on top of her head. She'd pulled away from Kase, and her face contorted. "You two are sickeningly sweet."

"Ana, not here," Kase warned. "Someone spiked the punch, and she's had three cups so far." He turned and tried to explain away her horrible behavior.

"Whoa!" Ana put her hands up in mock surrender. "You have about as much control over me as she does."

"Please, Ana, let's get you some fresh air," Kase coaxed. He settled a hand on the small of her back and attempted to gently pull her away.

The downbeat of the music boomed faster, and some of the seniors ran through the crowd causing a ruckus with a machete prop. Distracted, Willa glanced at the stage where Serena stood, Logan at her side.

A surge of heat burned Willa's chest, and she caught a glimpse of her pendant glowing under her chin. The wave of magic emanating from her seemed to have a similar effect on several supernaturals in the room. She saw Scarlet place a hand over one of her bracelets, and a guy shake his ring-clad hand in the air.

Suddenly, the chain at Willa's neck pulled, yanking her head forward. Clattering sounds echoed in the gym, along with a few ouches and gasps. Her pendant hovered an inch over her chest, and with a jerk, the chain snapped. Willa yelped as her mother's stone skittered out of sight.

Ana, eyes wide in astonishment, hurtled out of Kase's reach and tried to stop herself by flailing her arms in front of her. She fell on her face when Willa stepped out of the way.

"The necklace!" Ana frantically searched between heels and loafers and boots. Her teeth gritted together in a sneer at Willa.

Scarlet and Bale moved protectively to stand next to Willa.

Ana pushed herself up and looked Willa up and down. "It won't matter. Everything is set in motion, and that hideous thing can't save you now."

"Ana!" Kase took a step away from her, toward his sister. "What is wrong with you?"

"Wrong with me?" Ana got to her feet and pointed at Willa. "If there's anything wrong with anyone, it's her. She can't shift, she moved out of her house, she cut all her hair off just to avoid wearing a bow, and she's dating that—"

A growl stirred in Willa's, Kase's, and Bale's chests. Tarron took Willa's hand in his. "It's okay," he whispered.

Scarlet lifted her hands out to her sides and chanted something under her breath. Her eyes widened with surprise and amazement as the students around them panicked, charging in every direction, unsure of where to go. Inside whatever refuge Scarlet provided, the chaos was muffled.

"Yeah, it's okay, Willa," Ana snarled.

Kase stepped up to Ana and reached for her hand. "Leave her alone. Let's just get out of here."

"You are such a wuss!" Ana yelled up to the paper stars. "Our pack needs a real alpha, not some elf-loving, witch-bestie with a pet dragon." She laughed at her insult, but everyone around them took a step back.

Willa bared her teeth.

Ana laughed deliriously. "Like you can do anything about it! Your magic has been suppressed for so long, I'd be surprised if you ever shift."

"Suppressed?" Tarron asked.

Willa seethed at Ana, her inner wolf unable to focus on words. The supernatural powers she'd kept secret for so long wouldn't be a secret much longer. She balled up her hands into fists, her nails digging into her palms, to tamp down her desire to grab Ana's shoulders and toss her out of their lives.

"Your father should never have assumed the role of alpha," Ana began to ramble. "The next woman in line should have taken over— my mother. Instead, the Kasun pack has weakened, and it'll be up to me to strengthen every member. I'll start with your family." She pointed from Willa to her brother.

Some of the crowd around them had begun to disperse, and Ana's attention wavered. "I'm bored." She turned and walked toward the exit.

Scarlet's arms fell to her sides, and Willa could feel the bubble of magic she'd concealed them in pop.

"Thank you," Willa said.

"Are you okay?" Tarron interrupted. He took her hand in his and she flinched. Willa was bleeding.

Unable to slow her heart rate, Willa knew she had to stop Ana once and for all. She looked Tarron in the eyes and said, "I'll be right back."

Her body broke into a full run after Ana. As she ran, Willa watched Ana heading for the parking lot. The air above her pressed down on her shoulders. She peered up into the sky and found the moon. Only a sliver lit the path ahead of her.

Using the pressure built up in her chest, Willa barked, "Stop!"

And Ana froze in place.

"I'm tired of you." Willa's posture slumped, as she panted for breath.

"Well, that's mutual," Ana slurred. "My family has always deserved to be in control. I have proven myself worthy to be alpha, while you've run away and mated with a garden gnome."

"Your drunken insults won't make you alpha. Walk home and sober up, and leave me and my brother alone from now on," Willa ordered, following her across the football field.

"Oh, I will. And my family will find another way to put you down. I'm surprised that stupid necklace suppressed your magic as long as it did." Ana's eyes darted past Willa, where her friends and their pack gathered. "I was only planning to string your brother along until your birthday at the end of the month. Once I'm officially alpha, I won't need him or your talisman anymore."

Willa's hand flew to her mouth in shock. She'd always known Ana was cold, but her admission had Willa's blood boiling again. "I get doing what you did to me, but how could you even think of using Kase the way you have? You know our birthday is more than a celebration for us."

"Oh, here we go again! Let's sing praises to the perfect alpha and mother who died giving birth to you two. Get over it already!" Ana waved her arms up and down wildly. "She's dead! And there's nothing you can do about it."

Willa swallowed the harsh truth, but the sorrow didn't mix well with her disgust at Ana. Only half of what Ana said was true. It was how she got away with making people feel small. Ana blended the truth with hurtful, debilitating lies.

Willa's mom had been gone a long time, but Willa *could* do something. She didn't have to sit by and let Ana and her family take over. It might not happen right away, but eventually they could manipulate the Court to replace her dad and brothers. They could twist the Kasun reputation until they had to leave town. Fighting her habit of walking away, Willa stepped toward Ana, allowing her supernatural abilities to reach their potential. She felt her shoulder muscles ripple, and she heard Ana's heart begin to race.

"What do you think you can do to me?" Ana asked and took a step back. She broke eye contact and inspected the area around them. They'd moved beyond the athletic fields, and the crowd had followed. "I will be the next alpha, and I plan to make your life a living hell."

"You already do." Willa didn't want to live another day having to answer to Ana, and she knew the only way to remain in control of her fate, as well as protect her pack, would be to take control herself. To shift.

Unsure how to channel the moon's power or the magic inside her, Willa opened up to the wolf calling. She expected the same hindrances she'd felt in the past, but something had changed. The barrier her necklace had created was gone. She supernaturally flexed her strength and hearing, and she felt stronger than ever. Her magic reached up to meet the moonlight, and it shimmered like the stars above her.

Willa heard someone move behind her, and in the same moment Ana rushed them. In her peripheral vision, Willa noticed Tarron's white hair. Her protective instincts took over, and she leapt between them.

Willa's muscles tensed, and her bones cracked. The cool air

around her did nothing to soothe the sharp pain erupting at every joint. As her body healed, it broke again, until the rhinestones on her dress flew in the air and the fabric ripped from her body. Her teeth and fingernails grew to points, pushing through gums and skin. Canine teeth brushed against her lips as she snapped protectively, and Willa knew she could rip Ana apart if she wanted. Dark glossy hair covered her body. She'd never felt stronger or more aware. By the time she landed, a black wolf stood guard in front of Tarron.

A growl erupted from Willa, and Ana, still in her human form, bowed her head in submission. Tarron was the first to move, and he hesitantly placed his hand on Willa's neck. She responded by rubbing her head against his hip. Something in the air around her vibrated, and Tarron gasped. As Willa turned her head, a gray and white wolf advanced.

Ana, in her wolf form, stood a few inches shorter, but she'd had more experience controlling her animal nature. Her snarling teeth bit at Willa's neck, but Willa shuffled back and swiped her sharp claw at Ana's face. Ana yelped and retreated, cowering on her belly a few feet away.

Willa looked back to check on Tarron. The pack watched intently. She let a growl rumble in her chest as she stepped toward Ana. The bark that followed caused Ana to flinch, but she quickly bared her teeth in dissent. Willa prowled closer, and Ana thrust herself under her belly, desperately pawing at anything to gain an advantage. Reacting to the pain, Willa snapped at Ana's neck and flipped her over. The gray and white wolf whimpered in submission.

Tarron rushed to Willa, checking her fur for blood. As he stood, he gritted out, "Ana, I think you should be going."

She left without a word.

Willa walked on all fours to where her dress had landed. She nudged it with her snout in Tarron's direction. She was surprised at the control and understanding she had in her wolf form. Growing up in the pack, she'd heard stories about werewolves who had lost their connection to their human form. She had a good feeling shifting wouldn't be too difficult, just painful and embarrassing. Her dress was ruined.

"Give me a minute," Tarron said before running back into the gym. He waved the crowd back into the dance with him.

Willa watched Ana mope away while she waited. She knew their feud was far from over, but Ana had lost any chance of becoming alpha when Willa released her wolf.

Her ears perked up when she heard the door open. Tarron raced out with a pair of blue running shorts, probably from the locker room, and a black t-shirt with a moon graphic. She cocked her head to the side, wondering if he had another shirt on under his suit jacket. Then, he started to take it off.

Nope. No shirt.

He raised his jacket like a curtain and waved it around. "You can shift behind this and put these on."

Willa knew this was crazy. She'd finally let her wolf out, at homecoming, and now her boyfriend was going to lend her his T-shirt so she could shift back. Her brothers had needed her help with their transitions before, so she was prepared for the change. Willa just hoped Tarron could handle the sounds of her bones breaking and skin tearing without glancing to check on her. She walked over to the brick wall and waited for Tarron to meet her. He lifted the jacket, and Willa yelped at him.

"Fine, I'll close my eyes." He grinned.

Willa thought of her human reflection and stretched her legs in an effort to stand. The shift followed, and the sound of ripping muscles and popping joints made Tarron's face cringe. The change hurt, and Willa struggled to get the T-shirt over her head at first. She slipped the shorts on, then fell into Tarron's jacket and arms.

He didn't pull away.

Someone cleared their throat behind them. Willa pushed up on her toes to look over Tarron's shoulder and saw Scarlet, Bale, and her brother. Scarlet frowned as if repulsed, and Willa knew they'd at least heard her shift. The others had firsthand experience with the process.

"Dad's gonna flip!" Kase exclaimed.

Willa looked down at the watch strapped to Tarron's wrist. It was only a few minutes past ten. "Only if I'm late for curfew." She grinned up at Tarron.

"What do you want to do now?" he asked.

"I want to kiss you."

Tarron leaned down and wrapped his arms around her waist. He nestled his lips against her neck and pressed a trail of kisses up to her lips. Willa's hands slid up his bare chest to his shoulders. She tilted her head back and took his bottom lip between hers. Deepening the kiss, she savored the flavor of cinnamon he left behind.

She pulled back to look at him. "Ask me what else I want?"

"What else do you want?"

"To dance." She winked at him.

EPILOGUE

Friday afternoon, in the school cafeteria, Willa joined Tarron, Bale, and Scarlet at their designated table. Much of the student body buzzed with gossip about the latest *it* couple getting together and the hardest biology test they'd taken. Willa caught a blue bow in her peripheral vision and turned to find Maria sitting with a group of cheerleaders, all donning uniforms for that night's basketball game. Willa smiled as she reached to tug the hem of her top down and remembered she was wearing a comfy tee.

"Do you miss it?" Tarron asked. He noticed the smallest things when it came to her.

Willa rolled her eyes. "Only the bow, but I have a much bigger bow I plan to wear after school."

"I get why you quit the squad, but you're going to miss flying," Bale interjected.

Scarlet nudged him with her shoulder. "You mean you won't give her a lift, Drogon?"

"Sounds fun!" Willa clapped.

Bale scoffed. "You're no dragonrider. You're an alpha. Plus, I don't give rides to just anyone."

Willa smiled to herself as she retrieved her apple and a protein bar. Things were good. She'd chosen to fight for Tarron, but she'd never imagined it would take giving in to her wolf. What she thought were two worlds warring within her turned out to be one world she was ripping apart by trying to live up to everyone else's expectations.

With her shift came other changes. Her pack learned of the Novaks' betrayal and that Willa could have shifted with the others her age if it hadn't been for the talisman they'd imbued with dark magic. Her openness about her relationship with Tarron had even offered some of the other pack members permission to pursue friendships outside of the pack.

"Hey," Tarron began. "What is your brain up to in there?" He tucked a few strands of hair behind her ear.

She cased the cafeteria one more time before answering, "Just looking for Kase and Elle."

"They'll be here," Scarlet said. "It's not like they can get into any trouble. Everyone is watching them. It's kind of creepy."

"Kase said he's not jumping into anything too fast, so I'm afraid *everyone* is going to be disappointed," Willa informed the group. She'd moved back into the cabin with her dad and Kase, while her brother Tate moved out. Tate explained that her choices helped him to make his own.

Tarron wrapped his arm around her shoulders. "Let's talk about something fun. Like your birthday." He waggled his eyebrows up and down.

"Since it's on a Tuesday, it's not like we can throw a crazy party," Willa said, hoping the others would take the hint that she'd like to keep it low key.

"How about we get coffee, then try our hand at some trick or treating?" Scarlet asked with a wink. Thankfully, her newest bestie had asked what she wanted to do a few days ago.

"That would be hilarious." Bale leaned forward and whispered, "Too bad your costume from homecoming was shredded into ribbons."

Tarron chuckled, and Willa swiftly jabbed him with her elbow. He rubbed his abs, feigning discomfort. "We could get coffee, and maybe just hang at one of our houses."

"That sounds perfect," Willa agreed, as she nestled into Tarron's side.

TUESDAY 5:16 PM
Willa: Is everyone still good for coffee @ 6?
Tarron: Yep
Elle: I'll be a few minutes late
Willa: Are you with the boy version?
The BOY Version: I heard that
Scarlet: I'm already here studying
Bale: Me too
Willa: B, are you studying a book or Scarlet?
Bale: :p
The BOY Version: We'll be there soon
Willa: Great! I may be a few minutes late
Bale: Where's T?
Tarron: studying ;)
Scarlet: Curious, why are we meeting?
Willa: Ha. Ha. Just want to get the Scooby gang together
Tarron: You know, now that Willa's shifted we'll have to recast. Maybe we should let her be Scooby since it's her birthday?
Bale: Not a chance

ABOUT THE AUTHOR

Writing unique adventures with heart.

Kallie Ross has a passion for writing that has become an adventure in itself. She desires to create unique young adult fiction that incorporates legend, conjecture, fantasy, and conviction.

In addition to loving her life as a writer, Kallie adores being a wife, mother, friend, and teacher. She began her creative journey with books, a blog, a podcast, and lots of caffeine. Ross never imagined her own adventure would be filled with so many wonderful people or words!

KallieRoss.com
Kallie Ross Facebook Page
@KallieRoss Twitter
@KallieRoss Instagram

ACKNOWLEDGMENTS

I want to give a shout out to the amazing Kristie Cook. Her confidence in me as a writer and her dedication to making me better is real friendship! I'm so thankful to have her in my life, and I feel honored to write characters who live in Havenwood Falls. Other friends like Morgan Wylie, Gaby Robbins, and Megan Kennedy inspired me to have fun writing Willa's story, and their support is always a blessing.

Thank you readers! Your enthusiasm for fiction keeps me writing, and your passion for fantasy and the supernatural inspires me.

REAWAKENED

BY MORGAN WYLIE

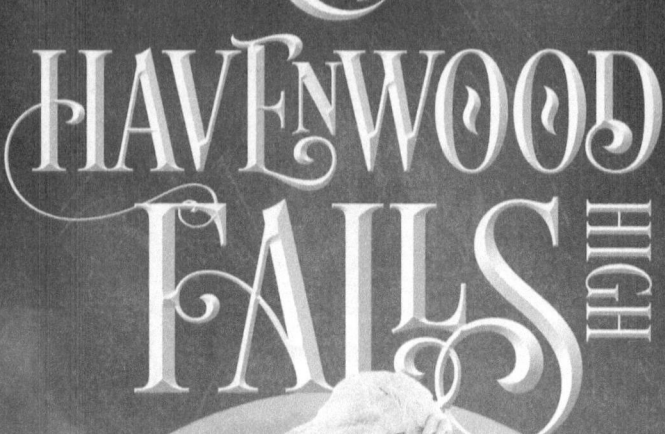

HAVENWOOD FALLS HIGH

Reawakened

USA TODAY BESTSELLING AUTHOR

MORGAN WYLIE

~ A Havenwood Falls Young Adult Novella ~

OTHER BOOKS BY MORGAN WYLIE

∿

YA FANTASY

Silent Orchids (Book 1)

Veiled Shadows (Book 2)

Daegan (Novella 2.5)

Fractured Darkness (Book 3)

Fading Light (Book 4) (Fall 2017)

The Sol-lumieth (Book 5) (Winter 2017)

The Rise of the Paladin (An Alandria Short Story Prequel) (Free with Newsletter subscription)

∿

YA PARANORMAL/SUPERNATURAL

HAILEY: The Necromancer (A Shadow Realm Novella 1) (previously released as Supernatural Chronicles: The Necromancers Novella #7)

JAX: The Doppelgänger (A Shadow Realm Novella 2)

WILLOW (A Shadow Realm Novella 3) (Coming soon!)

SOLANGE (A Shadow Realm Novella 4) (Coming soon!)

∿

NA/ADULT PARANORMAL ROMANCE

RYLEN (The Tangled Web Book 1)

MATHER (The Tangled Web Book 2)

JET (A Tangled Web Novella) (Exclusive in the Creatures Box Set)

～

COLLECTIONS

Supernatural Chronicles: New Orleans Collection

(The Necromancers: Novella #7)

This story is dedicated to YOU, the reader. I hope you have as much fun in Havenwood Falls as I have had!

I can't wait for you to meet the Blackstone family!

CHAPTER 1

*M*ost seventeen-year-olds about to enter their senior year of high school enjoyed every last bit of their summer break. Some even went on vacations. Not me—Macy Blackstone, witch hunter. All I wanted to do was forget the title and be normal at least for a day, but apparently that day was not today.

Nearing the end of August in Havenwood Falls, Colorado, the weather had already began to change—not that it ever stayed any particular temperature for long. Up in the mountains especially, fall came earlier than in the lower elevations. The nights grew chilly earlier, and mornings like this one reminded me what I loved about fall.

Cozy in my oversized, chunky cable-knit wrap sweater, I snuggled into the corner of a large outdoor sectional sofa in front of a giant rock fireplace. Stretching out my legging-clad legs, complete with warm Uggs on my feet, I sighed with contentment. I watched the town come to life below me while I slowly sipped from the steaming mug of coffee in my hand. Rays from the sunrise streaked down to touch the edge of our deck, stretching as far as the fire pit and the uncovered section of deck. The reverse would happen just the same again at sunset. Tipping my head up, I closed my eyes, absorbing warmth from the sun's kiss as it crept up my face, inching as far as the roof above would allow it.

"Beautiful, isn't it?" My mom's voice floated from the doorway separating the kitchen from the outside living area.

"It is," I answered, looking back at her. My mom, Lilith Blackstone, was a beautiful woman, appearing in her mid-forties—though she was actually a bit older. For a human, she looked forty-five, but as a hunter, she was still relatively young at seventy-eight years old. Most of the women in my family were hunters—witch hunters to be exact, though we didn't actively hunt witches. My mom was descended from the founding Blackstone family, a strong lineage of witch hunters. She also held a seat on the Court of the Sun and the Moon as the representative and matriarch for our entire family.

"Are you seeing Gallad today?" she asked, moving toward the railing, carrying her own steaming mug.

"I'm supposed to meet him at the vineyard pretty soon, actually." I checked the time on my phone.

Her eyes were on me, watching me, the weight of her assessing stare boring into me. Turning to face her, I couldn't place her expression. Was she upset? She seemed more questioning than anything else.

"Is something wrong, Mom?"

"How are you feeling?" she returned, avoiding my question.

"Um, fine thanks, but don't think I am that easily diverted. What's up?"

Coming over to me, she placed her hand on the back of my neck, now free from my silky blonde locks since I piled them on top of my head in a messy bun that morning. "How is your injury?"

"It's much better since the witches gave us that healing salve to put on it." Reflexively, I touched the back of my neck as well after she pulled away. "There's some scabbing where the stupid tree limb tore my flesh off, but otherwise I think it's good. See?" I pulled the neck of my sweater down, and tugged my T-shirt back for her to see it.

In a reckless attempt to be normal, I had climbed a tree and tried to jump to an adjacent tree like some damn spider-monkey wannabe. The new tree didn't want to be my friend and wouldn't let me grab hold of it until I had slid down part way, taking my flesh off as I went.

"Your hunter marking looks to be untouched. However, your protection tattoo got a bit roughed up. Did you have Saundra Beaumont look at it like I asked?"

Saundra Beaumont sat on the high council of the Luna Coven, making her one of the most powerful witches in town.

Since I was born, my parents and the Court knew what I would become based on a stupid skin discoloration on the back of my neck in the shape of a cluster of small stars. All hunters were born with it, like a birthmark—or a beacon of doom.

"Yes, Mom. She said it looked fine, and I shouldn't have any issues with the wards within my tattoo. Addie looked at it, too. She said she'd need to touch up a few of the lines but would wait until the skin was fully healed. They both agreed the tattoo held enough magic that it shouldn't be an issue to wait until it was time for the permanent one."

In Havenwood Falls, all the supernatural residents received a tattoo infused with magic. The markings were there for not only our protection, but also for the town's. They protected each individual race, but also helped temper and conceal magic from our human residents, who made up about half of our population. Visitors also had to register with the Court of the Sun and Moon to receive a temporary tattoo for the duration of their stay.

As I grew older, into double digits, the Luna Coven placed a magical, invisible-to-the-eye marking in the shape of a crescent moon with a dragon right below my birthmark. The tattoo was a temporary marking intended to suppress any hunter tendencies until I turned eighteen. According to our traditions as witch hunters, at the age of eighteen we go through a ceremony, committing ourselves to abide by the rules and laws of Havenwood Falls. Hunters can choose for themselves then if they are going to go out on their own, never to return to Havenwood Falls, or become a suppressed member of the Blackstone family and town at large. Good options, right? Normal human high schoolers didn't have to deal with that kind of crap. Choice made and ritual completed, we then receive the permanent tattoo of an adult, thus becoming an official citizen of Havenwood Falls.

"Speaking of which, Macy, I need to speak with you about your upcoming birthday and marking ceremony." A slight edge laced Mom's words, anticipating my reply.

I sighed. This was an old conversation. My eighteenth birthday was coming up the beginning of October.

"Mom, we've talked about this. I still have some time. Can we not talk about it yet? School is starting soon and I want to enjoy the last of summer. Since I can't go anywhere interesting, I want to try to be as normal as possible while I still can." Even I could hear the bitterness and whiny petulance in my tone.

"Macy," she practically growled enough to rival one of the Kasun wolves. The Kasuns were not only the largest werewolf pack in Havenwood Falls, but their alpha, Ric Kasun, was also the town sheriff. "You have put this off for too long. The ceremony will happen, and you need to be prepared. There are things you should know and things to prepare for."

Jumping up from my no-longer-quiet space, I faced her. Then she did something I was not expecting. Moving to the side, she revealed another woman standing behind her in the kitchen, watching the interaction with a frown. Looking from the new arrival back to my mother, I scowled.

"You brought Grandma into this?" Fury pulsed through my veins. I loved my grandmother, and I was normally a reasonable—okay, *somewhat* reasonable—person, but she went behind my back like I needed some kind of intervention.

Eva Blackstone, aka Grandma, was regularly brought in when my mom didn't get her way—at least it looked that way to us kids, my two brothers and myself.

"Now, Macy, be rational. There are many details to attend to and your orientation to complete," Grandma chided from the kitchen, beckoning me inside. Tall, slender, and confident, my grandmother held an air of regality and pride. Her hair had been a fierce blond bob since I could remember, mirroring the same edge in her personality.

"This is my last year of high school, and I'll spend most of it as an official Blackstone hunter. I just want to spend the rest of my summer as an irresponsible teenager. Is that too much to ask?" I huffed and folded my arms across my chest.

"Yes, it is," Grandma said flatly. "You have a responsibility to this family and this town. It is time you owned up to it."

I put my mug in the sink and took several slow drags of air, cooling my growing temper.

"Macy, nothing changes once you are marked. It's all in your head," Grandma added.

I shot a glance toward my mom still standing in the doorway. Her gaze was off in the distance, watching the rising sun or something else farther away, locked in the recesses of her mind. Distracted, she finally felt my stare and looked back to me. I frowned.

"I don't know about that, Grandma," I whispered. My mom definitely had times when she was off, but lately, it had been more obvious. She was hiding something, but I didn't know what.

"Oh that's ridiculous, child. You have until the end of summer and then you will take your place in this town as a Blackstone hunter or . . ."

I spun my head in her direction, mouth open wide. "There's an 'or' in your sentence?"

"Macy, you know the rules of Havenwood Falls. If a witch hunter will not choose to be permanently marked, they cannot remain a resident here," my mother interjected. "And because of the memory wards around the borders, whoever chooses not to stay and follow the laws will forget everything about Havenwood Falls, including their family."

"I know the laws, but I don't need my family threatening me with them either." My heart suddenly felt heavy and sad. I knew they didn't mean to hurt me, but still they did. I grabbed my messenger bag off the counter and moved swiftly through the large, rustic yet modern kitchen-dining-great room toward the front door.

"Where are you going, young lady?" Grandma's voice echoed through the room.

"I'm meeting Gallad at the vineyard, then I have to go into the square to pick up my check at Broastful Brews." I sighed, then schooled my voice to an acceptable tone. "I'm sorry, I just need some space. I'll be back later."

"Let her go, Mom. I'll talk to her again later." My mom's voice reached me before I opened the front door.

CHAPTER 2

I took the shortcut from my house in Havenwood Heights over to Stone Falls Winery without having to head down to the main road. My brothers and I had cut through the fields and forest since we were little, thus wearing down our own path from our main house to our home away from home at the vineyard.

My family had several businesses, including the one I headed to now. Stone Falls Winery had been in my family for generations—since the first hunter, Marie Blackstone, had set up camp. More recently, we added Soothing Sips, a wine-tasting bar in town square, and NamaStays Inn at the Vineyard—a quaint B&B boasting six cabins with picturesque mountain views set amidst the vineyard. My family added them about ten years ago, when we started to see more tourists and visitors to the town.

My father, Reginald "Reggie" Benton Blackstone—the men who married into our family took the Blackstone name—was human and ran the daily operations of the vineyard. Even the extended family was heavily involved with each endeavor, always had been. Grandma's cousin, Great Aunt Letti—Letitia Blackstone, former family matriarch—even oversaw the Yoga in the Vines classes, and she was practically 116 years old! Okay, so she looked like she was in her seventies, but still. Long life ran in the Blackstone family.

Everything about Stone Falls Winery was designed to bring soothing relaxation to your senses, and calm was a necessity for the hunters of my family. The drives and instincts of the witch hunters were strong even with the Luna's magic suppressing the bulk of it. At just the right height, the winery sat above the town providing a view of all of town square. When night blanketed the valley, the town lights and sounds mesmerized even the grumpiest of guests. But when a large moon crested over the tips of the craggy peaks, the sight stopped me in my tracks; I could stare for hours like nothing else mattered. I had memories from when I was small of reaching up, thinking I could touch the tip of the moon because it appeared so close.

Several buildings, modern yet mixed with rustic architecture—similar to our home—were laid out with designed precision. Each was positioned to ensnare the majestic views of snow-capped, jagged mountains.

I maneuvered my way quickly through those buildings, hoping to not get caught by Aunt Letti, lest I be roped into some odd job I was not assigned today. Plus, I already had plans.

"You really shouldn't text and walk at the same time. You're liable to miss something right in front of you." Gallad's voice arrested me. I smiled. Leaning against the back wall of NamaStay's lobby, with one booted foot propped up behind him and sheltered in the shade from the roof line, Gallad was the image of a bad boy in his black leather jacket covering a rock band T-shirt accompanied by gray-washed jeans.

"You really shouldn't wait in the shadows for people. Someone might think you were stalking them." I tried to shake off the small fright with sarcastic wit, but my accelerated heart rate said otherwise. When I looked into his eyes, however, my nerves calmed. His love and concern packaged with his cute signature lopsided grin took my breath away.

"You're right." He pushed off from the wall and moved in close. His cologne wrapped around me, the intoxicating aroma pulling me in close. I loved the way he smelled of pine and spices—it made me feel cozy and safe every time. "I'm sorry. I bet I can make it up to you." His grin turned from innocent to devilish in a matter of seconds as he leaned in to steal a kiss. In that moment, I felt our connection—I was home.

Gallad Augustine, grandson to another Luna Coven High Council member, was a witch prodigy. Remarkably handsome with his windswept dark hair, fair skin, and bright green eyes, he was truly an all-around good guy—though he wore the exterior of a bad boy at times—and he was my boyfriend. Yes, it was unheard of for a witch hunter to date a witch, but stranger things had happened in Havenwood Falls.

I couldn't help but cover my heart with my hand. The beats sped up when he was near—they always did. Those girlish butterflies took flight in my stomach no matter how much I tried to suppress them.

"You definitely have a way of making it up to me," I mumbled in a swoony state. If anyone had told me I would be the type to swoon, I would have laughed in their face. But Gallad could make me swoon pretty much without trying. Grabbing my hand, he laced his fingers in mine and pulled me alongside him as we strolled through the vines of grapes.

"Have you seen any of the Perseids meteor shower? I saw several shooting across the sky last night. It was amazing, Gallad." I couldn't help the awe I heard in my own voice, but they were truly a sight to see.

Gallad's face turned down to me with a smile so big it reached his eyes. "I did. The meteors looked like shooting stars." He looked up as if he could see them already, but the sky still had plenty of color. "I thought of you the whole time, wishing I was lying on the ground somewhere with you, watching the meteors together."

I blushed. The rush of heat ran up my neck and into my face. Squeezing his hand in mine, I changed the subject. "How was your morning?"

He shrugged casually. "Pretty uneventful. You?"

Frowning, I didn't want to talk about my morning. *Way to start a conversation you didn't want to participate in, Macy*, I scolded myself. Too late—he caught my frown.

"What's wrong, Mace?"

"My mom tried to push the marking ceremony on me again." I sighed. "This time she brought my grandmother in on it. That didn't go over too well."

Running my fingers through the tendrils of hair that slipped down from my messy bun, I felt guilty for bringing the topic up. "I'm sorry. I didn't want to drag you into it."

"What are boyfriends for if not to be there when needed?" His cute smile melted my heart and soothed my guilt.

"Thank you," I said sheepishly.

"Hey, how is your back where you were almost skinned alive by a revenge-hungry tree?"

I laughed out loud. "That tree *was* out for revenge, wasn't it?" Shifting my shoulder blades as if testing out my injury for his benefit, I smiled. "It's almost healed."

Gallad kept quiet as we continued walking, but I felt him glance my way several times. I could practically feel the wheels turning in his head.

"Come out with it already, before you burst."

He blew out a gush of air and raked the fingers of his free hand through the hair sliding down into his eyes. "I know you don't need me to add to it, but you know how important your permanent tattoo is. I'm sure Cousin Addie would do it as soon as your skin fully heals."

"She would, and she offered." Slowly, I brought air in through my nose as I calmed my inner nerves. The idea of being permanently chained left me raw, no matter how much I loved my town. I mean, I knew I'd be able to leave town someday. Since I was little, I always wanted to step outside the boundaries of Havenwood Falls—even just for one day, to see what else was out there, how other people lived, what it might be like to live in a normal town. Just once. I wanted to travel!

Mom and Dad left often for short business meetings and quick getaways, but they had never taken me or my younger brother, Brice. They always returned within the necessary twenty-eight-day moon cycle. In fact, they had never risked more than two weeks. As a human, my older brother Brock got to go with them a couple times, and even had tried attending college outside of town, but he didn't have much desire, it seemed, to travel. I would do anything to leave for college, but apparently it wasn't in my cards—or so I'd been told—because I was marked as a hunter. Literally. Alas, I would have to wait a little while longer. Until then, I would do what I could to pretend I was a normal seventeen-year-old, headed into her senior year at Havenwood Falls High.

"I'm just not ready yet."

"I won't push you, Mace. But I have plans for us, you and me, and don't want anything to get in the way of them." Gallad turned a smile on me that rivaled a rogue pirate.

My heart thumped up into my throat. All salivary glands stopped working at once, drying out my mouth. And those damn butterflies took flight so fast, they almost knocked me off my feet. Words. I couldn't find words.

Gallad laughed at me. He actually laughed. "It's all right, Macy. Seems I caught you off guard." Turning toward me, he grabbed my other hand and tugged me close, so close I could feel his chest rise and fall with each breath.

"Ha! Just a bit," I forced out shakily.

Gallad let go of one of my hands. He brought his up and tucked a stray hair behind my ear. His fingers skimmed lightly over my face, sending shockwaves of excitement through my body and launching those same butterflies into a frenzy. Just when I thought he was going to kiss me, his forehead rested against mine. His voice lowered, and he said, "I love you, Macy. And I think about the future with you. There's no question in my mind we were meant to be together."

"You're my other half, Gallad. My soul mate," I whispered in return. For some reason, I couldn't say the "L" word just yet, though I felt it about to bubble over the rim of my heart.

We stayed forehead to forehead, standing in a row of grape vines for more than a couple minutes. At least until we heard some of the workers headed into that section of the vines. Gallad pulled back just enough to get a better angle, then came in for a gentle, teasing kiss;

long enough for me to feel cherished but short enough to make me want him more.

Hand in hand, we walked out of the vines and headed for the road to take us into town.

"You headed to work?" I asked him.

"Yep. Where you off to next?"

"I don't work today, but I need to grab my paycheck, and I'll meet Ruby in the square for lunch."

Once we walked out from the main entrance of Stone Falls Winery, we hit Blackstone Road. Just sayin'—it's pretty cool to have a road named after your family. Casually, we chatted as we walked together, slowing down as we approached the intersection at Eighth.

"I'll call you later. Have fun with Ruby," he said as he left me with a peck on the cheek.

"Bye, Gallad."

I watched him walk away toward the Sun and Moon Academy. During the summer, Gallad worked in the private school's *Histories for Supernaturals* program, a course for those who wanted to learn more about their heritage—humans not included. The Luna Coven had made available most of the information they had collected on all the races for the program. Gallad hoped to one day be positioned high up within his own family, the Augustines, and on the Luna Coven's council. In order to do so, it was required he learn the histories of all the supernaturals in town. He gave off the vibes of a bad boy, but deep down he was actually quite the bookworm. The Luna Coven basically ran the town—you didn't want to cross them or the rules of Havenwood Falls—but they also protected us from the outside world and from each other.

Gallad turned back and blew me a kiss. Why something so simple could make me blush even from a distance, I would never know, but it warmed my heart. I waved back and headed down Eighth Street toward the town square—the heart of Havenwood Falls.

CHAPTER 3

*R*uby Jean Milton—my best friend—stood waiting for me at the corner of Eighth and Stuart Streets, outside the entrance to Broastful Brew, where I worked as a part-time barista. Her strawberry-blond hair blew into her face as she wrestled it into a ponytail high on her head. I laughed. She hadn't spotted me yet. Ruby, who wasn't human, either, but came from a family of lynx shifters, looked up just as I passed in front of the firehouse. Her warm brown eyes lit up with her smile.

"Ruby!" I waved, crossing the street toward her.

"Hi, Macy! You're late. I bet you just couldn't tear yourself away from Gallad's kisses." Her hands crossed over her heart, and she sighed dramatically.

She could always make me laugh. "Not quite."

"Don't spoil my visions of the two of you, Macy Marie Blackstone. I don't have my own love life right now, so I live vicariously through yours."

"All right, so maybe there was some kissing and hand holding then." I winked at her. Ruby came at me with arms wide open. I let her embrace me, not that I had a choice in the matter. Ruby was a hugger; always had been, ever since we met in kindergarten. She was also the most loyal person I knew—and that said a lot, since I was born in Havenwood Falls and I knew everyone . . . mostly.

"I knew it!" Ruby declared with a fist of victory and a giggle as she pulled away from me.

"I just need a minute to run in and grab my check, then we can go get lunch and more coffee over at Coffee Haven."

"Why don't we just stay here?" Ruby frowned. "I mean, isn't it strange that you go in to one coffee shop to get paid to then spend said money over at a different coffee shop?"

"Well, yeah it sounds strange when you say it that way." I laughed. "I don't want to feel like I'm at work. Plus Broastful Brew is usually filled with the older residents or the morning meeting clientele. I want to feel the energy over at Coffee Haven."

"Then that's what we're going to do." Ruby nodded her head decidedly. "Go get your check. Hurry, though. I'm hungry and I can't wait to see what Willow made today!"

Willow Fairchild was the owner of Coffee Haven and, being one of the fae, a strong empath.

I ducked into Broastful Brew and breathed a lungful of freshly brewed coffee. A low din of chatter filled the atmosphere, but it felt more like a library than a coffee shop. I waved to some of the regulars, but headed toward the employee area. Mabel, the owner of the shop, manned the register. She smiled at me and said hello as soon as she finished with her customer.

"Morning, Mabel, I'm just grabbing my check."

"Morning to you, too, Macy. It's in the usual place on the desk in the office, dear. Would you like a coffee to go?"

"No, thank you, I had one at home this morning already."

As quick as I could, I retrieved my check and snuck back out while Mabel visited with a customer. Otherwise I'd be leaving with another coffee.

On our way to Coffee Haven, we passed Backwoods Sport & Ski and Howe's Herbal Shoppe, owned by Ruby Howe but now run by her daughter, Rose.

"Hello, Ms. Howe." I waved to the older woman as she swept her walkway, muttering under breath. She barely raised her head to look at us, let alone wave back. Ruby and I exchanged a smile—the old woman added her own flavor to the morning.

We found a table outside at Coffee Haven, then placed our order. Coffee Haven was quite the popular place even at lunchtime; the interior was abuzz with voices and activity. For some reason, the white noise satisfied something internally with me, but it was such a nice day, so we stayed outside.

Sighing, I slumped and took my seat. Ruby took hers across from me. I shifted in my seat, pulled at the neck of my sweater, and ultimately took the thing off; it was warm now that the sun was high in the blue August sky.

"Does it hurt?" Ruby asked, watching me intently.

"No, it itches. I think it's irritated or something. I either need more salve or to get it checked again." Not realizing I did it, I reached over my shoulder and attempted to scratch where the itching was most intense.

Ruby's frown intensified. "I'd get it checked."

Her head shot up and looked at something behind me. "Gallad's mom approaching," she whispered under her hand suddenly in front of her mouth.

Whipping my head around, I spotted her myself.

"Covert, Macy." Ruby's sarcasm complemented her eye roll.

"Subtlety is not one of my qualities, you should know that."

"Good afternoon, ladies," Mrs. Augustine greeted as she approached our table.

"Hello, Mrs. Augustine," we said in unison, and sounded like schoolgirl robots.

"How are you?" I added quickly after.

"Fine, dear, but please, I've told you, call me Ronya," Gallad's mom corrected. Ronya's bright smile was so much like her son's; it was like an explosion of joy and good looks all at once. Gliding in, wearing leggings and a flowing chiffon tunic, she turned her joyous expression, accompanied by her long and curly dark hair, toward me. "Good to see you, Macy. You, too, Ruby, dear."

"You, too, Ronya," I replied with not as much gusto as I would have normally, but something felt . . . off. Again? What was going on? Absently, I scratched my bare arms. The itch persisted, and I wanted nothing more than to scratch my skin off. I sat on my hands before my nails drew blood.

Ronya's sharp and intense eyes evaluated me. "Macy? Are you feeling all right?"

"Yes, I'm fine. The scrape on my back is itching its way to a complete healing."

Ronya's gaze traveled to my neck and shoulder then back to my eyes as a new frown formed. "Maybe you should get it checked again. Injuries have a tendency to get worse if left untreated."

An unexpected sensation suddenly rose in me—like something inside me clawed to get out, something agitated . . . something dark.

"Thank you. I had Ms. Beaumont look at it already. You know how scabs itch when they heal." My laugh sounded hollow even to me. "I'll get her to look at it again."

"See that you do, dear." Ronya's pointed stare pinned me in my seat and made me feel small. Fear uncharacteristically reared its ugly face in her eyes. "A darkness stirs inside you. I can see it, and I fear for you—and my son." She spoke quietly so no one next to us would hear, then turned and walked away.

Rage boiled in my chest. Like I would ever hurt Gallad! He was my other half. My soul recognized him like no other.

"Whoa! She did not just say that!" Ruby gasped. Her hand found mine on the table and gave it a squeeze. "Mace, you okay? Don't worry about her. She must be having an off day."

"Or I am." Unexpectedly, I was afraid for the first time that I really didn't know what would happen to me if I wasn't protected by my Havenwood Falls tattoo. "What if the magic in my marking didn't hold up from the injury?"

Would I really not be able to control the hunter within me? Was that what this was all about?

"Don't be so dramatic. I'm sure you're fine," Ruby encouraged, but her tone lacked the usual confidence. Ruby leaned forward and whispered, "Saundra Beaumont, the head of the Luna Coven herself, checked it. If she says the magic is intact, then it is."

Slowly, the blood drained away from my face until it became lead in my feet. "What if she was wrong?"

"Nope, I don't buy it." Ruby looked around at nearby tables at Coffee Haven. Many of the lunchtime crowd had moved on or gone back to work. Only a few stragglers like ourselves enjoyed the last rays of the season. "You look like you've seen a ghost."

"Hmm?" Shifting my back against the chair, itching what I couldn't reach with my hand, I finally noticed Ruby staring at me. Concern and alarm briefly flashed across her eyes before it flitted away. "Don't look at me like that, Ruby Jean Milton. I'll be fine, you'll see. They'll all see."

Ruby laughed. She could have been hurt or put off by me, but instead she pushed back. "There you are. Come on back to the now."

"You're right. Sorry."

"Before I get going, remember tomorrow is the eclipse?" Her eyes lit up with excitement.

"You know we don't get a total eclipse here, right?" I hated to burst her bubble but I didn't think it was going to be as spectacular as she imagined it would be.

"Of course I do. I've learned all about it. I got us glasses, too!"

I didn't like the sound of silly party glasses. Wrinkling up my nose I asked her, "What for?"

"To protect our eyes, silly."

"Of course." Rolling my eyes, I flopped back in my chair. "Tell me again why this is a memorable moment?"

Ruby sighed, but of course I knew she wanted to tell me more about it. "So this is special for several reasons. This particular solar eclipse happened like thirty-eight years ago but it also falls on a new moon. But not only that—"

"Interesting," I slipped in.

"No, listen, Mace! This *is* interesting." Leaning forward, she slapped my thigh, gaining my attention. "This new moon is a Black Moon, ushering in a total solar eclipse. This is a rare combination of events that especially witches love because of the heightened power unleashed."

Sitting forward, I absorbed all she said. "That actually is interesting. I feel like I've heard some of it before." I pinched the bridge of my nose, racking my brain. "Oh! I remember Gallad told me the witches planned a ritual to strengthen the magical protection wards around the schools after the Parade of the Perseids tomorrow night. Apparently, the darkness from the new moon would be the best time for it."

"That makes sense. It's also during the meteor showers—there should be increased supernatural energy streaking above us—not a bad plan." Ruby nodded her approval. She didn't have a single magic bone in her body, but she loved to know all the things going on she could—a bit of a busybody if you asked me, but that was one of the things I loved about her. One of the other things I loved about her was her ability to quickly shift subject matters.

"Speaking of the parade, are you coming by after work tomorrow to see the finished product?" Her face stretched tight in nervous anticipation.

I laughed out loud, startling a nearby coffee drinker. "You look like a lizard."

"I'm worried our float won't be good enough," she admitted.

"I saw what those wolves were working on, and the Kasuns' float looks pretty good, but I think ours is up there, too—it maybe even has a chance at winning." Folding my arms across my chest, I held tight so as not to scratch. "I'm not sure the Luna Coven will be able to pull it off this year. Pretty sure the trophy will have a new mantel to sit on," I rambled. I rarely ever rambled unless I was nervous or trying to keep my mind off something else, which apparently I was doing.

Ruby huffed. "Oh gods, you're like a prepubescent shifter before their first full moon. Can you not hold still? It's like you're reacting to the pull of the moon or something."

I inhaled sharply. "Well, that's ridiculous. I'm not a shifter." If I kept furrowing my brow, I was going to get a headache. "Why would I be reacting to the moon? I never have had a reaction before. Oh, maybe I *am* a shifter!"

So maybe I was being a little dramatic, but my skin crawled, begging me to scratch it.

"All right. You're losing it. That's my cue to leave."

"Take me or leave me! You'll feel bad when I shift, and you aren't there to guide me through it." Shrugging my shoulders, I gave her a wink.

"I'll keep ya! Where you headed now?"

"I'm supposed to stop in at Soothing Sips. Brock's there and will drive me home since he's coming for dinner." My older brother Brock had moved into his own gorgeous cabin-esque townhouse in Havenstone.

"Bye."

Hugging Ruby, I squeezed extra tight, and she returned the love. Her information about the new moon and the eclipse triggered a thought in my mind—or gut—that I wanted to follow up on tonight with my computer.

CHAPTER 4

*S*oothing Sips, my family's wine-tasting bar on the east side of the square, served as a front to the more nefarious side to the Blackstone's endeavors for Havenwood Falls.

I headed north through the center of town square toward the fountain. Beautiful and sparkling at the interior, the fountain was gifted by Mayor Barbie Stuart's ancestors when the town was founded. Town square was a popular hangout, especially when the weather was nice. Several people simply loitered, basking in the sun, while others used the opportunity to exercise around the square. Spotting Viv Freeman and her best friend Zara Shannon jogging, I waved to them. Both waved back excitedly. They were also seniors at school, and I hoped we would be in classes together this year again.

I was about to cross the street to Soothing Sips when tendrils of unease crawled down my spine, and I broke out in a cold sweat. A toxicity rose in my stomach, bile forcing its way up my throat. Running—faster than normally possible for me—to the closest garbage bin, I expelled all the wonderful lunch I had just eaten.

"Oh no," I moaned. I gripped the garbage can as dizziness threatened to steal the ground out from under my feet. Swaying, I held on tight.

"Macy?" My brother's voice broke through the haze fogging my brain. He jogged toward me, concern written all over his face.

"Macy? Are you all right? I called you like five times. Are you sick?" Brock put his hands on my shoulders and attempted to calm me.

"I . . . I'm not sure what happened. I think I ate something bad, maybe?" Shaking my head, I tried to loosen the fog wrapped around my brain. Something felt wrong, but I had no idea what.

Brock's dark eyes narrowed as he studied my face, and his equally dark brows pinched in a frown. But he didn't say anything. For that I was grateful, but I knew it was only a momentary respite. Of course, Mom and Dad would hear about it for sure, especially since he was taking me home.

"I think I just need a minute, Brock. Could we sit in Soothing Sips for a bit, get some water, and see if I can shake whatever that was?"

"Sure thing. I need to clean up before closing anyway. Come on, little sister," Brock said gently. Placing his arm around my shoulders, he guided me back with him.

Frowning, I couldn't understand what was wrong with me. Did I have food poisoning or was I reacting to something else? But if so, what?

My hands shook. I couldn't stop the tremors. Hiding them in my pockets so Brock wouldn't see, I let him guide me into the small storefront we used in town right next door to Sanguine Elixirs. We partnered with the liquor store to sell our wine and specialty drinks, including an exclusive line for the supernatural population. Because my family was in the business of wine, I knew a lot more than most and have tasted more than I should have, as I was still underage. It was tradition in my family to train us up with all the knowledge for taking over the business when we were older. Luckily for us—at least those who were hunters—we lived longer than the average human.

However, most of the men in my family were not hunters, even some of the women ended up simply human, and sadly, we lost them long before those who were hunters. I have no idea why it worked that way, it just had . . . until now. My younger brother Brice was the first male hunter in centuries, and we didn't yet know what that meant, if anything.

Many people didn't realize Soothing Sips was actually a front for an underground—literally—weapons-making operation for the entire town, if needed. Now don't get me wrong, we hadn't needed weapons for quite some time, but they were there and ready for when the Luna Coven decided we needed to defend Havenwood Falls. For example, back a few years, during the Vampire Massacre of 2005—our weapons saved the town from a drug-crazed bloodsucker. For generations, my family had been making specialized weapons, going back to when the first hunters began hunting witches in the 1800s, and since then, they kept up the practice and skills to train generation after generation of Blackstones. Managing the town's weapons stores was one of our many responsibilities.

It may seem ironic hunters would be in charge of making weapons in a town basically run by witches, but it was done with full knowledge and supervision of the Luna Coven. Plus, the wonderful markings we wore from youth subdued our hunting drive. So there was that—at least I thought so.

Another responsibility we hunters bore was to inform the covens if any of the witches practiced black magic. I still wasn't sure how we did that. I was told I would learn all I needed to know during the orientation before my marking ceremony and initiation into adulthood. I was beginning to think I needed to have that talk with my mom.

I looked up to find Brock carefully watching me.

"Are you sure you're all right, Sprite?" he asked, using my nickname from when I was little. He was the only one who still used it.

"Who are you calling Sprite?" I countered with attitude. "I'm not as small as I used to be, in case you hadn't noticed."

He laughed and gestured to the top of my head and where it hit him mid-chest. I rolled my eyes. "Sure, point out the obvious."

"Well, there's not much else to point out." Brock's teasing took a back seat to a more serious expression and tone. "What happened outside, Sprite?"

"I don't know for sure. My arms felt like they were going numb. Then I felt so sick to my stomach. I couldn't stop the maelstrom of evil that needed to forcefully be ejected from my system. And that's where you found me."

His face contorted into an expression of sheer repulsion—probably remembering the image of the state he found me in. "Sounds like food poisoning to me."

I moved the neck of my shirt and pulled it open for him to see. "My back has been itching like crazy today. I think it's just healing, but could you be a big brother and, you know, scratch it?" I growled with frustration, moving my shoulders back and forth.

Brock laughed, but did as he should and looked at the scabbed area first. "Looks agitated and angry. Do you have more salve from the witches?" But then he scratched, and the relief felt so good, I practically purred.

"At home. Addie Beaumont said it wouldn't heal it super fast. That I would have to have some human patience with that part of it, but it should still cut the healing time in half, if not more," I explained.

"Probably going to leave a scar. Sorry."

"No biggie. Not the first time I've been scarred. I'm a tough hunter, remember?" I smiled and winked exaggeratedly at him.

"Yeah, a tough hunter who thinks she's a spider monkey but is really just a klutz," Brock said with a laugh.

"Ha ha, very funny." I frowned. "I'm not usually klutzy. And don't you have work to finish up here so we can go home for dinner?" Reminding him of his duties usually did the trick. Brock was the responsible sibling.

He went to work cleaning up, while I stared into space, thinking about the mixture of hunters and humans in our family. "Brock? Can I ask you a personal question?" I hesitated because I didn't like to bring it up, and we didn't talk about it very often, but I worried about him sometimes.

"Yeah, Sprite?" he consented without looking up from where he wiped down the counter and put glasses in the dishwasher.

"Do you ever wish you were a hunter? I mean, does it bother you that you aren't one?"

Brock stilled, then wiped the rest of the counter before he looked up at me with those deep, dark eyes of his.

"Do I wish I was a hunter? No. At times, it's hard for Mom to control the power of the hunter side—she thinks no one sees her suffer, but I do. I hope all the time it doesn't affect you and Brice in the same way." He breathed deeply, then let it out. "Does it bother me I'm not a hunter? Every day." Brock placed the dirty rag in the sink. "I'm different. I stand out like Dad does. Sometimes I doubt my place in the family," he replied honestly. His response was so genuine, I paused, almost forgetting to speak.

"Brock . . . I had no idea you felt that way. I wondered, but you've never said anything that straight up about it before."

"No one's ever asked. Well, Dad has, but I figure he had to."

"I'm sorry, Brock. I'll be more sensitive." I reached toward him for a hug. He pulled me in tight and kissed the top of my head.

"Don't change, Sprite. I don't want to be treated any differently than your brother. Just wanted to be honest with you. Now it's your turn."

Uh-oh, not sure I liked where this was going.

"Are you experiencing hunter symptoms early?"

I thought for a minute. "I don't think so, but Mom hasn't given me the entire 411 on what I need to know—though lord knows she keeps telling me I have to get ready for my ceremony. I'm just not ready yet."

He watched me longer than necessary, but I knew he didn't have any "extra" gifts to see with beyond his human eyes. However, he did have brotherly intuition. "All right, but you need to talk to Mom. Deal?"

"Deal," I replied, thinking of what Gallad's mom had said to me earlier. Why was everyone so worried about me? There hadn't been a witch hunter attack in Havenwood Falls as far as I was aware. I didn't feel any need to assault anyone, and my boyfriend was a witch!

"I'm finished. Let's go home." Brock pulled me out through the back of Soothing Sips, which had another door leading down to a secret display room in the cellar below where we stood. He locked all the doors, and we went out the back to his shiny black 1968 Pontiac Firebird. He had a magical silencer put on the muffler so he didn't break sound ordinances inside the town, but it still roared to life when he turned the ignition, and I loved it.

CHAPTER 5

The town wasn't so big I couldn't walk from one end to the other—and I've enjoyed that walk from time to time—but when we drove, it felt like it took only seconds to get from the center of town to our house. Once exiting the square, we headed straight up Eighth Street, crossed Blackstone Road, and began the climb at slow intervals. We arrived at the big metal security gate bearing the words Havenwood Heights. With the click of a control button, Brock opened the gate, and we rolled slowly through it. Havenwood Heights —or the Heights, as I liked to call it—was the old money part of town. The secluded and exclusive lap of luxury, it was filled mostly with the Old Families, the ones who had descended over time or the ones who literally had been here since 1854, when Havenwood Falls was settled.

The sun had made its retreat behind the mountains to the west, but the lingering colors painted the sky, dusting the tops of the aspen and evergreens bordering each property for privacy—not to mention they were just everywhere in Havenwood Falls. Antique lampposts lined the streets, awaiting the chance to shine bright once darkness had fully fallen.

Over the years, parts of our home had begun to descend into old age. In the last decade, the family had our home updated, mixing old log-cabin style with more modern amenities and architecture, giving it the magical Colorado Mountains touch.

Brock sighed. "I do miss this view. It's not quite the same down in Havenstone."

"You could always move back in," I teased. "I'm sure the parentals would love that . . . and so would we young'uns." I smirked at him and jumped out of the car.

"Being on my own has its own magic, too, don't get me wrong. I'm just saying nothing beats this view."

Our home's entry greeted you with gray stone tiles, warm wood beams, and large pieces of art Brock had painted. It guided you to the heart of our house where we spent most our time—the large great room including the kitchen, dining, and living areas. One of the best features was the wall-to-wall windows, broken up only by thick beams of dark-stained wood. My favorite piece of the room, other than the windows, was the floor-to-ceiling rock fireplace with a wide glass front, topped with a hefty chunk of wood for a mantel.

Brock smiled, admiring the original handiwork of one of our relatives, untouched by the more recent remodel. Other aspects of the home, including the underground weapons area that mirrored the one under Soothing Sips, also remained untouched.

"Where is everyone?" Brock asked. "And I hate to disappoint you, but I don't smell anything cooking in the kitchen."

Frowning, I realized he was right. I didn't hear anyone. "Where are they? Tonight's taco night, right?"

A car door shut, and the clacking of heels swiftly arrived at the front door before it swung open, revealing my mom. Confident and powerful, she carried in a large square box, giving off a most delicious aroma.

Upon her arrival, a warmth hummed under the skin at my neck. My hand found its way to the scabbed section but jerked back—it was hot to the touch. My stomach suddenly unsettled again, I lost my appetite.

"I have pizza from Napoli's!" Mom headed straight to the dark gray, granite kitchen bar.

"Mom? Don't we have family dinner tonight? What's going on?" I stood by Brock, both of us just watching, at a loss to what was happening.

She finally looked up at me and cocked her head. "Didn't your father call you?"

We both shook our heads.

"Oh. Well, too late now. I had a meeting come up, and your father ended up having a late meeting at the vineyard." She paused thoughtfully. "Brock, I'm sorry. He was supposed to tell you, so you could make other plans. There's more than enough. Brice should be home soon."

"Sure, Mom, I'll stay for pizza." Brock patted his stomach. He walked over and wrapped his arm around our mom's shoulders. She paused for a moment and relaxed into his embrace.

"You and your father have a way of bringing me a calm when I feel it least." She patted his cheek as he let her go. Then her eyes found mine and narrowed. "Something happened today. What's wrong?"

No, my mom was not psychic—at least not that I knew of—so either she had some mom voodoo going on or Ronya had called her.

"It was nothing, I think my injury is irritated, and I might have food poisoning. I got sick in the square today, and I still feel a bit queasy." I didn't mention the warmth at my neck, growing even hotter the closer she came. She watched me with those mom eyes, but turned her head as soon as the front door opened again.

"Mom? I'm back!" shouted my fifteen-year-old brother, Brice, while he propped his skateboard by the front door.

"In the kitchen," I yelled back at him and took note that the tingling in my neck increased. Brice was adorable in a nerdy kind of way—a cross between a stylish skater and a computer geek with his shy tendencies and thick-framed glasses. And he was the only male hunter we knew of, which made him kind of rare.

"I'll be late," Mom said, grabbing her purse in a hurry. "Macy, we need to talk about your upcoming birthday and ceremony. No more delays. We'll make time the day after the parade." I nodded. The chat was inevitable and maybe even necessary now more than ever. "Brice, in bed by eleven. Macy, you still have to register for your classes or you may not get the ones you want. The information is on the counter." She gave me a stern look, underscoring the seriousness of her message.

"Fine. I'll do it tonight." Resigned, I grabbed the Havenwood Falls High stationary with a blue and silver dragon on it that read "Registration Information" as the subject line.

"Good night, Blackstone children." Mom left, her heels clacking on the tile once more on her way out the door.

As soon as she was gone, the strange feelings at the base of my neck receded drastically. I sighed with relief. A low buzz remained, but it was easily ignored. If it didn't go away on its own, I would have to bring it up.

After we devoured all the pizza, Brock left, and Brice went to play video games in his room. I was left with the damn paper staring at me, taunting me to pick classes for the coming school year—my senior year. After not receiving a reply to the text I sent Ruby, I went ahead and began registering before I picked up the house phone and called her. Cell coverage was spotty in Havenwood Falls, whether from being up in the mountains or too much magical energy interfering or a combination of the two.

"Stupid cell coverage. I tried to send you the same text like ten times. So sorry, but you'll get flooded with texts next time you get reception." Ruby's irritated but friendly voice floated across the line.

"No worries, I know it sucks. Did you register for classes?"

"Yep. My mom already registered for me." Her voice grated with true irritation now. "How's that for over-parenting? I don't know if I can change any of them, but we can go over it if you want."

I laughed. There wasn't much else to do. "Damn. Okay, tell me what classes you have, and I'll see if they are ones I need to graduate."

"Okay, so looks like I've got history with you and Serena and Viv for fourth period with Ms. Bast so far. She's new. I wonder what kind of teacher she'll be," Ruby added.

"I know! I heard she's from Egypt. That should be interesting. Oh, and I'm so excited to ski for PE again!"

"Oh shoot! I'm sorry, I gotta run, Macy. You'll be at the eclipse shindig I planned after the big float reveal tomorrow, right?" Ruby interrupted.

"Yeah, I'll come straight from work so I'll be a little late," I said absently, looking over my work schedule. "You said the float was finished, right? So I don't have to do much else for it?"

She laughed. "Your family is the sponsor of the prize this year *and* the founders of the parade. Do they know you hate the floats?"

"I don't hate the floats—at least not totally—just building them. I have no problem watching them float by me, though, while I sit on a bench with an ice-cold latte or a bag of popcorn."

"Count me in! That sounds divine. Although, I admit I like the idea of riding on one. Okay, gotta go!"

I hung up, shaking my head. Ruby, Gallad, a few other kids from school, and I had joined together to form a team. I was really only on it because my parents told me I had to represent, but I didn't see them out there building a dumb float. We'd been building our monstrosity of a float in one of the old grape-press rooms on the vineyard property —that was my main contribution.

Just as I settled in my room for the night with my latest book, my phone buzzed on the nightstand beside my bed. It buzzed again and again and again. I reached over to it and saw the multitude of texts from Ruby finally come through. I couldn't help but laugh because they were quite intense and irritated. I could hear her practically shouting at her phone through the texts. Then the final text came through, but it wasn't from Ruby. It was from Gallad. Even though it was a stupid text, my heart practically beat through its cage.

G: Hey Macy, just thinking of you. How are you?
  Me: Hi! Good. Reading. You?
  G: Wishing I was with you *kissy winky face emoji* (lol)
  Me: awww <3
  Me: Will I see you at the eclipse party tomorrow?
  G: I'll be there! I bet you'll be cute in those protective glasses ;)
  Me: lol. See you then! Good night, Gallad.

G: G'night Macy. You know you're my world right?!

Me: *blushing emoji* And you are mine. See you tomorrow.

LAYING BACK ON MY BED, I shifted from one side to the other while I looked up information about the eclipse and the new moon tomorrow. Apparently, it could be seen in the late morning over Colorado. I got off work just as it started, so at least I wouldn't miss it.

"Grrr! This itching is driving me crazy!" I jumped up and put more salve on my back where the healing scabs were, but couldn't reach it all. I was so not waking up my little brother to put it on. Maybe I *should* have it looked at again. Feeling responsible about my decision, I prepared for bed and turned out the lights. Dreams of darkness surrounded me with images of witches surging through it—weaving spells around me, hunting me, provoking me, angering the hunter within me until I lashed out. Free . . .

Reawakened at last.

CHAPTER 6

$\mathcal{M}$y morning at Broastful Brew had flown by, but I couldn't help how distracted I was after my night's dreams. I couldn't shake the intensity of the magic that had assaulted me through them. It felt dark, leaving me with a sick feeling in my stomach similar to what I felt yesterday before I hurled in the square. I knew last night was simply a case of bad dreams, but man, they shook me. I woke up drenched in my own sweat, trembling with the exertion of running from the witches, which was backwards since I would be the one chasing them, if I'm the hunter, right? Not that I would. I had no issues with the witches—at least, the ones from Havenwood Falls.

Walking up Thirteenth Street, I headed toward the vineyard. Small decorative evergreens, accompanied by large barrel planters filled to overflowing with colorful flowers, bordered the parking lot. A slight breeze tickled the aspen leaves, delighting the senses with soft pleasing sounds.

As I dodged through the winery, the large building used to create the float came into view. A group of teenagers had gathered off to the side, where I could see Ruby handing out protection glasses for the eclipse. She threw one to new guy Rylan Gilles and tossed several to Will "Kase" Kasun, who handed them out to his usual wolf pack posse. Viv Freeman, Zara Shannon, Aurelia Petran, and several others were there too. So many faces—Ruby had gone all out gathering friends old and new from both schools.

Suddenly, a wave of agitation hit me, causing me to stumble. I sucked in a great breath. Tingling shot up my arms and straight into my heart. I had to stop and clutch my chest. Breathing hard, I couldn't help but wonder if I was having a heart attack.

"Macy, dear, are you all right?" I vaguely heard Aunt Letti's voice penetrate through the fog engulfing me. Strangely, as she approached, I felt a different feeling start at the base of my neck, though this one was more of a familiar warming sensation compared to what I felt the previous night. What was happening?

"I . . . I'm not sure. Can teenagers . . . have . . . heart attacks?" I huffed out, trying to regain my breath.

"Well, I don't know about that, dear. Come sit down and catch your breath while we figure this out." She tugged me by my arm over to a bench in front of the NamaStays Inn main cabin, next to a hand-lettered chalkboard sign advertising "Yoga in the Vines" with the times of the next classes. Aunt Letti was in charge of the bed and breakfast and oversaw the yoga classes. "Sit and enjoy the beauty of the vines and the fresh mountain air. You do have my flair for the dramatic, I fear."

Aunt Letti to those who knew her well—Letitia Blackstone to those who didn't—was my grandmother Eva's cousin, but they couldn't have been more different. Average in most ways, round in the middle —Letti didn't participate in the yoga—with wavy, reddish-blond hair that hung to the middle of her back, Aunt Letti really was the life and spirit around the B&B. Where Grandma was classy and pretentious, Letitia was casual and unassuming, yet they were quite close. I supposed when you outlived most of your family members, you embraced those who remained even more, differences and all.

Aunt Letti kept her gaze trained outward at the new crop of grapes soaking up the sun. We boasted high-altitude crops, though sometimes we used a bit of magic to ensure a harvest during the coldest parts of the growing season. Patting my back in a soothing fashion, she helped me calm down. She casually glanced at me from time to time, but seemed to know watching me would make matters worse. After a few moments, I was able to inhale normally again. I sucked in a deep rush of air and slowly let it out.

"Thanks, Aunt Letti. I think I'm better now. Must have been a panic attack or something," I rambled out something ridiculous.

Her eyes narrowed slightly, taking all of me in, but she smiled and nodded. "Don't kid a kidder, dear. I bet the power of the eclipse was overlooked when the injury to your marking was evaluated." Her gaze, full of wisdom and keen observation, pierced directly into my eyes. "You should go home, Macy. Talk to your mother."

"I'll be okay, Aunt Letti. I can't miss the eclipse!" I jumped up.

"The eclipse has begun, and your reaction will only intensify as the moon advances."

I gave her a quick hug, noting the warmth at my neck surged at the closer proximity. "Be careful, Macy, with yourself and your friends," Letti warned before I dashed away.

Instead of heading into the gathered group of eclipse watchers, I jogged to the building to check out our finished float for tonight's parade. As I moved away from Aunt Letti, the warmth behind my neck receded, but the tingling in my arms remained. In fact, it grew stronger. Shaking my hands, I attempted to rid myself of the feeling, to no avail. The warmth at my neck, I realized, happened only around my family members—except not at Soothing Sips with Brock— meaning only hunters. As for the tingling, I still wasn't sure.

The smells of aging wine hit my senses, and I breathed deeply. It was in my family, in my blood. The smells of the wood oak barrels soothed something deep in me, which was one of the reasons we originally entered the wine business—to calm and soothe the inner hunter.

"There you are!" Ruby yelled, coming in behind me. "I've been waiting for you. You have to see the finished product!" She grabbed my arm and pulled me along behind her. "Ta-da!" Ruby announced with arms flung wide, before a monstrosity of a float transformed into a beautiful spectacle.

"Wow! It looks great!" I admired the float. "Being the new moon tonight, will anyone see it, with how dark it will be?" I asked, eyeing the star decorations.

"Oh, Macy, that's the best part!" Ruby clapped her hands. "The stars all have LED lights behind them, see . . ." She plucked one off the cloud-like bottom of the float and turned it over so I could see the tiny lights. Then she turned her beaming smile toward me.

"I love it. That will look great at night!" I couldn't help but be a little excited about what they had done.

"I can't believe the parade is tonight! I'm so excited to see it lit up!"

"It should be magical," I agreed. "Speaking of magic, when does the eclipse peak, Ruby?"

"Oh! Anytime now," she said excitedly and pulled me outside. Ruby raced around, handing out glasses to anyone she'd missed, before she came back and placed some in my hands, too.

I laughed at Ruby's exuberance.

The rest of the group gathered out by the fire pit while I hung back by the barn. Catching my eye, Gallad smiled and waved as he moved closer to me. My arms tingled more intensely than ever. Clenching my fists, I did my best not to react, but failed. Gallad's eyes narrowed on me. He grabbed my hand with his. I flinched. I didn't mean to, but he took me by surprise. The area between his eyes puckered as he frowned. "You all right, Mace?"

"Little tired from work this morning, I guess. It was busy." I gently pulled my hand away from his touch, from the sizzle where my skin burned against his. I could see the hurt in his eyes, but also something else.

"My mom said she felt something yesterday when she ran into you," he whispered.

"She told me."

"She was worried about you." He placed his hand on my shoulder, but everywhere he touched me, agitation surged underneath my skin. I needed space.

"I think she was more worried about you, actually," I mumbled.

"I'm worried about you." His words were soft and sincere. Gallad's brows pinched momentarily, but he let whatever he wanted to say slide for the time being, making the conversation seem as natural as possible.

Needing to change the subject, I put the glasses on and looked up to the sky. As the moon moved, daylight faded slowly, like it would as it neared evening. The protective glasses kept me from seeing anything other than the round black orb moving in front of the sun. As suddenly as the agitation had hit me earlier, now a surge of energy shot through my arms. My hands flexed and fisted against the pain.

"Gallad, I'm sorry, but I need to go home." I hesitated, but took my glasses off to see his face. His expression gripped my heart. You'd think he lost his puppy. "Don't worry, I'll be fine, you'll see." I forced a smile, a feeble attempt to convince him and possibly even myself.

"No, Macy, talk to me. What's going on?" Leaning his head close to mine, he tipped my chin up with his free hand and stared deep into my eyes.

Breathing slowly through the pain, I held myself perfectly still, all sensations bottled up and contained for the moment. I couldn't let my guard down even for a second.

As if reading my thoughts, Gallad spoke to my heart. "I would never fear you, Macy Marie Blackstone. I trust you. I know you. Do not for a second pull away from me. I see the fear in your eyes. It's looking for a place to control you. Don't let it."

He always had a way with words. They reached into my soul and anchored themselves there, knitting together with the fibers of my being. I let out a slow breath. "I didn't want to admit what might be happening, but I might be losing control of my hunter. Somehow the magic on my tattoo isn't holding. I don't want to lose you, Gallad. I was afraid they'd keep me away from you," I admitted quietly.

"Ooh! Look! The moon is almost all the way in front of the sun!" Ruby's happy voice floated to me from one side. I put the glasses on and looked up to see the eclipse. The sight was amazing, but my attention tore away as something sharp stabbed me from the inside out. I gasped and hunched over. My breaths shortened. I felt on the verge of a breakdown.

"Gallad!" I started to call to him, but my vision swam and the tingles in my arm ratcheted up to becoming nearly unbearable. I crossed my arms, trying to contain the raw shooting pains. Breathing in and out through my nose seemed to calm me and give me a focus to channel the pain, but it started to move through my entire body.

"Macy?" Gallad asked, suddenly way too close. With his hands on my back, he whispered soothing words in a language I didn't know.

Intense pain not only shot through my arms, but my entire body hurt as a power of some kind rushed through me with great force. I fought for a breath. I reached out, then quickly pulled my hand to my chest. Gallad was too close.

"Get away . . . Gallad, go," I managed to say between gritted teeth and short breaths.

"I'm not leaving you."

"Witches . . . away," I panted the only warning I could manage. I could hear a commotion beyond me, but all was fuzzy in my head except for a blasted high-pitched ringing sound. The only thing I could focus on was not acting on my overwhelming urge to hurt Gallad. I refused. I couldn't hurt him; I loved him.

"You're reacting to him, as a witch, aren't you?" Ruby spoke with a hushed tone, coming up next to me, too. More people drew closer as the edge of consciousness faded from my tenuous grasp.

"I . . . can't . . . stop . . ." Curling in on myself, I crouched to the ground, covering my head protectively with my arms. A keening, wailing sort of sound pierced my hearing, but I quickly realized it came from me.

"Macy, look at me." Gallad's soft dulcet tone attempted to draw me back to him, out from the dark hole I crawled into. But as soon as he added magic to his words, all hell broke loose.

I lunged at him like some kind of possessed wildcat and knocked him down to his back.

"Macy!" he shouted at me, but his voice sounded fuzzy and distant.

I didn't have a weapon, so I used fingernails and fists. The sounds of his grunts and hisses told me I landed some hits. His arms protected his face, but otherwise he didn't do much to stop me.

"Macy, stop!" Ruby cried, pulling at my shoulders. "You have to stop!"

"Macy, I love you." Gallad's pained words shot straight to my heart, thinning the haze over my mind and body. Suddenly I could see what I had done.

"Gallad." I could scarcely whisper his name; disbelief, guilt, and horror laced that one word. "What have I done?"

I scrambled off him and away as fast as I could. Panic surged through my being. I couldn't breathe.

I looked up to find the eyes of all my friends trained on me. Disorientation set in. I reached out for the wall and barely found it before I would have fallen over.

Gallad jumped up off the ground, barely even injured. He held his hands out for me. "Macy, let me help you to the inn."

His eyes were not full of hate, but love. How could he even look at me, let alone like he loved me?

"No!" I shouted at him and scooted as far away as I could without falling away from the wall. His head reared back in shock. "I'm sorry, Gallad."

I couldn't explain. I shook my head, and tears slipped from the corners of my eyes. Breathing labored, I felt the world closing in on me, suffocating me from the inside out. I had to leave, to get out of there. Steadying myself, I ran.

"Macy!" Gallad and Ruby both yelled after me.

I sprinted through the vineyard, cutting across the fields at the base of Mt. Alexa toward the backside of Havenwood Heights. I needed to run, to shake off the remnants of what I felt. I needed to feel the freedom of nothing but the breeze through my hair and hear the splashing of the falls in the distance.

I wasn't prepared for this. I was becoming the hunter I wasn't ready to be, and for the first time, I was afraid.

CHAPTER 7

*A*t the back of my house, I closed my eyes and let the magical energy of the falls seep into me. I could always hear the falls pretty clearly from my house. After a few moments, I felt strong enough to head inside. With no one home, I slid into the mud room and ran through the house to my bedroom.

Leaning over, I panted to recover from my winded state. My heart pounded so hard, it felt like it was going to explode through my chest. The squishy gray and pink tufted comforter was practically calling my name to come back to bed and snuggle under the thick blankets, to go back to sleep and start this day over again. *If only*. Sighing, I walked toward my desk in front of large windows with a view of Havenwood Falls below me.

"Oh, Marie, I've let you down. I've let my family down. And I let myself and my boyfriend down." My heart broke as I said the words out loud to the woman in the picture frame on my desk. Taken at the turn of the century, it showed my grandmother Eva, great-grandmother Rhea, Aunt Letti, her mother Janella, and Rhea and Janella's mother Marie Marcella Blackstone—my great-great-grandmother and founding member of the Blackstone family in Havenwood Falls—right before she died. I often talked to her. I wasn't sure why, but something about the knowing twinkle in her eye and the slight grin of her lips made me comfortable, like she understood me or what I was going through.

I stepped out onto the balcony, and the instant I did, I felt it— something different than what I had felt earlier with Gallad. A toxic and nefarious feeling overwhelmed me and made me want to vomit. I held my breath and fled back into the safety of my room, shutting the door and the dark feeling out behind me.

"What the hell was that?" I gasped as I fell back on my sturdy bed with thick log beams at the foot and the head. Nope, lying there wasn't going to cut it. I jumped up and ran into my attached bathroom to empty whatever I may have had in my stomach into the toilet.

"Oh, that is not good," I moaned, slurping water from the sink to rinse my mouth out. *Bleh*. The feeling reminded me of the dark feeling from my dream. *Black magic*. The thought flitted through my mind. Black magic was illegal here in Havenwood Falls. Who would dare to practice it and why?

"Macy Marie Blackstone! Are you here?" My mom's voice shouted angrily, shocking me out of my discovery that someone might be using black magic. Other voices joined with hers and wafted up to me from downstairs in the main entry foyer. I froze.

"Oh shit," I whispered, looking around frantically as if there was anything in the bathroom that could help me. "I'm in trouble."

Basic instincts took over. I scurried through my room, grabbed my empty backpack off the floor, threw in some clothes, ran back into the bathroom for my toothbrush, then back out to my desk. I scribbled something quickly on a notepad, a note to my family.

Mom and Dad,

Something happened. I attacked Gallad. Gallad! I didn't mean to, but I'm not ready for what it may mean. I need some time to myself. I'll be back when I can think clearly. I'm sorry. I love you.

Macy

P.S. I think I felt black magic, but I'm not sure.

· · ·

THE VOICES DOWNSTAIRS seemed to be growing impatient. I listened as my mom offered tea and cookies. Their feet shuffled from the entry into the main part of the house. Stealthily, I snuck out of my room to my parents' room, but stopped at the door. Several feet away from their door was the family library. I quickly moved in that direction and peeked my head inside. When no one stirred, I ran in, grabbed a specific book off the shelf closest to the mantel, and shoved it in my bag. Back at Mom and Dad's door, I slipped inside.

"I thought I heard something. I'm sure I felt her upstairs. Please make yourselves comfortable and excuse me. I'll go and get her." Lilith's voice echoed from the kitchen.

Quickly, I moved through their large master bedroom to a door leading to a much larger back balcony with a staircase down to the ground level. I couldn't even explain why I was leaving, except I couldn't face what I had done yet. I hated being a hunter right then. All I wanted was to be normal for even one day, to see beyond the mountains, to not feel like everyone was watching me, waiting for me to screw up or attack a witch—and now I had! One or two days of freedom from the awful humming in my body so I could think was all I needed.

Decision made, I jumped down half the flight of stairs and took off at a dead sprint. The exhilaration took hold of me, and the rush of the fresh air and the knowledge of my forthcoming freedom caused a giddiness to bubble out of me. I ran as quietly as I could all the way down to Blackstone Road, which would curve along the outskirts of town, leading down to the main exit, Country Road 13 aka Burdorf Pass. Once I started to slow down so as not to be too conspicuous, but then I would feel it—the tingling up my arms, into my chest. My mom never talked about having these types of feelings as a hunter. It must have been because of the injury to my tattoo, or maybe some kind of punishment. Or maybe I was simply broken. Instead of Brock being the one who didn't fit into the family, it was me all along. Somehow I always knew it would be me.

I ran again, not wanting to feel, not wanting to hurt, not wanting to be afraid.

At the edge of town I stopped, attempting to catch my breath. I had never been beyond this point, and my nerves flared up.

"Is this a mistake? What will I do once I get down the mountain?" I asked myself. "I'll figure it out, that's what. I'm resourceful and smart. I can do this. Besides, it's only a couple days. No worries."

I felt fearless already. I sucked in a huge gulp of courage and took the first step. When lightning didn't strike, I took another step. There was quite a distance still before reaching the actual boundaries of the wards around the town, but my mark kept a tighter control on me than most.

I took one last look back at my little town, my home. It was time for me to stretch my wings a bit.

As I took the final step over the immediate boundary—the road into town—Havenwood Falls was literally behind me. I thought I heard my name being called, but it was only in my head. Now, as my own determination grew stronger, the tangible fear lessened with each step I took. The next thing I knew, I was running down the gradual decline of the mountain road. I ran. And I ran.

Slowing to a walk after some time passed, I rested a few moments and paused to admire the nature surrounding me, from the forest trees on either side of the paved road to the ferns and ground-covering plants to the smallest flowers poking through the rough forest floor. It amazed me how they survived with even the smallest glimpses of sunshine. The sun would go down soon, and underneath the tree canopy it would grow darker earlier. Even though it was summer, in the mountains the evenings cooled very quickly. I untied my heavy sweatshirt from around my waist and put it on. Wishing I had grabbed a bottle of water from the shopping center before I left town, I decided to slow my walk to conserve energy. I didn't actually have time to look at a map, so I didn't know exactly how far it was to the bottom, especially on foot.

A rumble came from behind me, and I froze. What kind of animal made a rumbling noise? I racked my brain, until finally the large bus used to bring tourists and guests up and down the mountain with a big sign for Havenwood Falls moved around the corner I had rounded seconds before. It slowed when the driver saw me and pulled over as much as he could on the narrow road and still leave room beside him —for who I didn't know. It wasn't like traffic was abundant on this road.

The driver, whom I didn't recognize, climbed out of the bus and gave me a friendly wave. He eyed me suspiciously, but shrugged it off. "Hello, miss, would you be needing a ride down the mountain? It's a long ways yet, and I've got room for ya."

I thought about it for all of two seconds, and the idea of saving my feet persuaded me. "That would be really nice, thank you."

"Well, come on then. I've got a schedule to keep." He winked at me, then got back in the bus. I hurried behind him.

"Thank you," I said as I passed him.

Heavily cushioned seats sat two to each side of the center aisle. I took the first empty row, which thankfully happened to be a few from the front. I wouldn't mind chatting with the driver on any other occasion but I didn't feel like explaining why I was obviously underage and leaving in a hurry. The bus was far from full, but a few other people filled some seats. Thankfully, all the strange sensations circulating through my body had found peace and quiet. Perhaps so could I.

I STRETCHED and yawned after stepping out of the bus once we had stopped. I couldn't imagine having to walk the entire way down the mountain. And thankfully, I picked the best time of year to take an out-of-town adventure so we didn't have to deal with extreme weather conditions. According to the bus driver, I was in Durango. The several hours' drive seemed like forever, and evening had fully fallen. Back home, they were about to start the Parade of the Perseids. Looking up, I hoped to see some of the meteors falling, but there was too much light down here in this part of town. Sadness fell upon me when I thought of not saying goodbye to Ruby and the others. I couldn't even think about what I did to Gallad.

I needed to find somewhere to spend the night. The bus driver had pointed in the direction of restaurants and accommodations for those of us who chose to stay in Durango. A motel would be my first stop, then food.

Finding a quaint little inn proved to be easier than I had thought. At first, the clerk didn't want to rent me a room as I appeared underage. She was a sweet, plump older woman who seemed like one to fuss over everyone. However, after I pointed out it was safer for me that she give me the room and knew where I was than for me to be wandering the streets, her last resolve broke. I paid with the cash I borrowed from my parents' emergency fund hidden in the book I'd grabbed from the library.

I settled into my room and decided it was too late to go get food in an unfamiliar town, so I raided the vending machine for snacks. The inn had a continental breakfast, and in the morning, I'd stock up before I hit the town. But tonight I would allow the sadness and guilt of what I'd done drown me into sleep.

CHAPTER 8

aking up far from home, I felt as if a weight had been lifted from me. It was like coming up for much-needed air or emerging after a long sleep from a cocoon. Stretching my arms, none of the tingling or sensations of dark power flowed within me. As I thought of Havenwood Falls and my parents, I felt a pinch of guilt in my chest. If I had hurt Gallad, I wouldn't be able to live with myself.

After breakfast, I gathered what food I could and stored it in my room, then hit the street. At first, exploring the small town of Durango was exciting and everything was new. I started to check my cell phone, but stopped myself. I was sure Mom or Dad—or Gallad or Ruby, for that matter—had left messages. I turned it off when I left Havenwood Falls so they couldn't talk me out of leaving. This was something I had to do; I knew it deep down. Sighing, I glanced at the phone still held in my palm and put it back in my pocket. They could wait a little while longer.

Friendly people caught my eye and smiled as I passed by their storefronts and fruit stands near the corner. Families walked hand in hand. A street performer mimicking a silver tin man stood at one corner, and a young man played a guitar at the opposite corner. Many signs and shops promoted the local museum and railroad paraphernalia. As the day went by, I had become familiar with the lay of the land, at least in my little section of Durango.

Sitting at a little café with an outdoor seating area, pondering my next move and what I would do tomorrow, I noticed a girl a little older than me standing across the street. As soon as I caught her eye, her lip curved up sardonically like she was waiting for me to notice her, then she turned and went the opposite direction down the crowded sidewalk.

"Wonder what her issue is?" I said out loud to myself, barely noting the warm sensation crawling down my neck.

Having eaten my dinner, it was fun to simply sit and watch people. After a little while, I couldn't keep the guilt at what I had done to my parents away any longer. Of course, I could have handled all that had been going on with me better. But at the time, with all the new feelings I had been experiencing, I couldn't think straight. I was in for some big trouble when I went home. I stared at my phone like it would bite me, and perhaps it would with all the messages about to flood through it when I powered it on. Well, no time like the present to rip off the Band-Aid. I turned it on. After a second, it buzzed with text after text, then voicemail after voicemail—mostly from my family, and even one from Brice, which surprised me. I listened to his first.

"Macy, Mom shut herself in the library today, muttering how it was all her fault. I don't know what all is happening, but come home now. Your momentary show of rebellion or whatever this is needs to end. And we're worried about you . . . okay, even I'm worried about you. It isn't like you to just leave." Brice hung up.

"Sprite, what the hell? You have no idea what it's like out there on your own. I'm worried about you. Mom's going nuts in her not-speaking-hiding-in-her-room way. Dad's got a search party getting ready to come look for you. Hurry back before the ward's effects start to mess with your—" Brock's message was cut-off as the call dropped. I'm pretty sure he was going to say mind. We were taught early on that without special permissions and arrangements from the Luna Coven, if you were outside the town's boundaries for more than a moon's cycle, roughly twenty-eight days, then you would lose your memories of the town and its location. I wouldn't be able to get home if I wanted to. Well, I'd only been gone one day so far, so I was pretty sure I didn't need to worry yet.

The next message was from Ruby. She yelled at me to get my butt back to Havenwood Falls, adding that Gallad was fine and didn't blame me. Even though it made me laugh, it hurt my heart to hear her voice, so I skipped on to the next message from Dad. He also yelled at me to call home and tell them where I was so he could come get me. I could hear the fear and worry in his voice. I hated that I put that there. My resolve started to fail. *I should go home.* I had proven I could leave town on my own.

The message I had been skipping, the one that meant so much to me, sat waiting to be heard. Gallad. I'm sure my disappearance hurt him deeply. I was a coward. I attacked him, then couldn't even face him. Instead, I ran. Suddenly I couldn't stomach hearing his voice, the guilt weighing heavily upon my heart. My food sat like a stone in the pit of my gut.

I paid my bill and headed down the road. I wanted to walk a bit more before turning to head back to my room for the night. It dawned on me my mom had not left me a message. Did she think since everyone else did, she didn't need to? Shouldn't hers have been the first one on there? I mean, I knew she raised me to be fully independent and capable even at a younger age, but still . . .

My mother loved me. I knew she did. But at times, she seemed more caught up with her seat on the Court, the vineyard, and her own frailties from being a hunter that perhaps she thought her job as my parent was finished. Or maybe she was mad at me for not letting her tell me all I should have already known by now.

Sighing, I saw a flash of long blond hair fly around the corner up ahead of me. The same feeling of warmth spread down the back of my neck like it did before.

"I thought these feelings would be gone once I was away from Havenwood Falls," I mumbled to myself. I must have been wrong when I associated that feeling with proximity to a hunter. As far as I knew, there were no other witch hunters around here.

"Did you say Havenwood Falls, my dear?" a kind, curious voice emerged from an elderly woman as she stepped out of a soaps and lotions storefront. The mix of fragrances wafted out with her. I froze. Outsiders weren't supposed to know about Havenwood Falls.

"I think you may have misheard me," I started to reply.

"I know someone who lives there . . . at least she did. I doubt she lives there anymore," the woman prattled on.

"No, I'm sorry, I don't know," I replied. My head began to hurt, I was so confused. Rubbing the back of my neck, I recognized the same warmth, though not as strong. I saw the flash of blond hair that had disappeared around the corner only moments ago step into a different shop across the street. "Excuse me, ma'am, but I have to go."

"Oh, of course, dear. Don't mind the ramblings of an old woman." Then she did something odd. Reaching out to gently grip my arm, she added with a straight and serious tone, "Don't ignore the feelings. Let them reawaken within you."

Without further explanation, she simply turned and left. For a moment I debated whether to follow her to ask exactly what she meant or to go after the blonde who had been watching me. The blonde won.

It could have been any random blonde woman, but something about this one triggered a reaction in me, and my gut told me to follow her. Only, when I crossed the street and ducked into the store I watched her walk into, she was nowhere in sight.

"Well, that didn't work out, did it, Macy?" I scolded myself. With hands on my hips, I decide to call it a night and headed back to my comfortable little room at the inn.

The next few days went by in a similar manner. I didn't know why I stayed longer than I had planned to, except I kept seeing the girl with the long blond hair right before she elusively slipped past me and out of my sight—almost as if she was taunting me. But I had no reason to believe she would be spying on me, let alone playing some game of cat and mouse with me.

After another failed attempt to sneak up on my mystery girl, I took a break and grabbed a coffee at the little café I had now deemed as my place to hang out. Staring at my phone once more, I chewed my lip and contemplated calling someone from home, perhaps even Gallad. But the longer I was away, the harder it seemed to simply check in and let them know I was all right. *Ugh.* That shouldn't be the case with family and friends, but I felt foolish for my responses and for leaving the way I had. Once I let the messages come through, I turned on airplane mode; it was too overwhelming, and I wasn't ready to be located.

I pulled up a selfie Gallad and I had taken on a day we worked on our float for the parade. We had made goofy faces, but it still made my heart thump erratically to see his gorgeous face so close to mine. Tears sprang to the corners of my eyes and threatened to spill over. The indicating warmth seeped into my back just before I looked up.

"Hello, dearie. From Havenwood Falls, right?" The elderly woman from the other day sat down at a table next to me. "Such a coincidence to meet you again."

She was probably in her early seventies—not that I was any good with guessing ages when most of the people I knew from home were often quite a bit older than they seemed. I smiled, but something niggled in the back of my mind. I didn't believe in coincidences, though she seemed harmless enough to chat with from another table.

"Lovely day today, isn't it?" I asked, making small talk, nodding up at the bright blue skies of the warm August afternoon. The weather had been cooling down quickly at night, but the afternoons remained pleasant.

"Indeed. Are you staying near here, dearie?" she asked innocently enough, but my alerts went on full volume.

"Perhaps. You?" I rebutted in my not-so-subtle teenage way of not entirely caring if it came out rude or not. Fortunately, she simply laughed at my response.

"Touché. I was merely trying to make conversation, I apologize. But yes, I do live near here. This is my favorite part of town. It can be lonely for an older woman these days, and I like to get out where I can watch the people." She pointed at me where I was seated facing the street. "It doesn't look like you are doing much different."

"Touché." I repeated her word and shrugged. She seemed harmless enough, but unless the warmth crawling up and down my spine when I talked to her before and again now—as well as when I was near my family—was also a coincidence, then I had an unknown hunter chatting with me.

"I'm Macy. What's your name?" I decided to go on the offensive and find out as much as I could.

"Nice to meet you, Macy. My name is Grace Blackstone."

She simply waited for me to acknowledge what she had said, but I couldn't. I was frozen internally. Externally, I schooled my features and willed them not to give anything away. How could there be a Blackstone—and a hunter to boot—only hours away, living in Durango? Could this woman be my family? I gulped, possibly loudly. I needed more information.

"How long have you lived here in Durango, Mrs. Blackstone?"

"Not long, actually, maybe a few months. I moved here with my family."

She set me up, I was sure of it. Curiosity may very well have killed the cat, but I was smart—I'd ask a few more questions. It would be responsible of me to gather information to bring to the coven and my family back home.

"Family?" I asked, prodding her to continue. "Is it a big family?"

"Oh, there are quite a few of us Blackstones. Right now I'm out with my niece. I'd like you to meet her, if you don't mind. She's not far."

"Of course, invite her to join us," I offered.

A sneaking suspicion shot through my mind as soon as she mentioned having a niece. *Yep, sure enough*. The back of a blond ponytail rounded the entrance to the café.

"Nala, come meet my new friend. The game is not necessary," Grace supplied as she waved the girl over to her table. I'm not sure "friend" was a word I would have used quite so early in our meeting, but we'd see.

Nala was older, probably in her early twenties, and taller than I had been able to surmise from across the street. Her long blond hair, tied up and pulled away from her face, allowed her striking features to draw all eyes to her. Watching me were large almond-shaped, blue eyes framed with thick, long eyelashes I was instantly jealous of. Flawless skin matched with high cheekbones and defined features added to the badass, Norse goddess vibe she sported. I wanted to be her, and at the same time, I wanted to tell her to relax unless she was late for the movie set.

"Nala, this is Macy. Macy, this is my niece, Nala." Grace gestured with her hand for Nala to sit. Nala nodded but stared at me as if she waited for me to speak first. Fine.

"Nala, I've heard your name somewhere before . . . Oh! I know, it was the name of the lioness from an old Disney movie. Is that who you were named after, for your intense prowess and stalking abilities . . . to hunt?" I asked with a bit too much snark for someone I had newly met, but something about her rubbed me the wrong way. How hard was it to say "nice to meet you"?

An awkward moment passed where Nala stared me down. Then the side of her lip quirked, and a muscle twitched in her jaw. Was she laughing at me?

"I remember hearing something about that movie." She sat down gracefully in the chair across from her aunt, from which she could watch me. In what might have been the only way she could relax, she crossed her legs and folded her arms. "So you're a Blackstone, too?"

My mouth fell open.

"You are, aren't you? There's really no point denying it." She turned to Grace. "Or dancing around it, Aunt Grace. We know. She knows—at least if she's any kind of a hunter, she knows."

"I guess we're not pulling any punches here, are we?" Was this good? Was it bad? I was in unfamiliar territory here.

"No reason to." She picked at a nail she focused on too closely. Apparently reading my discomfort, she added with an exasperated sigh, "Listen, Macy, we just wanted to see who you were and if you posed any threat to us. As long you don't, we can be friends."

"I could pose a threat." Not sure why I got a sudden case of defensiveness. I didn't need enemies right now. *I should back away and run home.* "If I wanted to, I mean. Not that I do," I quickly backpedaled.

Nala laughed, and Grace simply looked at me with an entertained twinkle in her eyes, both obviously humoring me.

"Why do you want to be friends with me?" I asked, suddenly quite suspicious.

"My dear, we're family. Why wouldn't we want to be friends with you?" Grace asked.

Okay, that made sense. Then a thought struck me that I apparently asked out loud. "Why did I not know I had other family out here?"

Nala looked out at the street, then back at me.

"Maybe they didn't know?" she supplied weakly, then shrugged. "Or maybe they didn't think you were ready to know?"

"Well, whatever the reason, we can remedy it now, can't we?" Grace took a sip of her iced tea. She smiled, then looked to me.

"Perhaps. I will be heading home soon, but could we meet for lunch tomorrow?" I asked, needing a little space to think and perhaps even call my parents to tell them I found lost family members.

"That sounds lovely, dear." Grace stood up and grabbed her handbag. Nala also rose from the table.

"Same place?" Nala asked.

"It's a date!" I exclaimed with a little more jubilance than I meant to. Quickly, I felt a pang in my chest with the name Gallad written all over it. I missed him. Apparently it showed in my face.

"Call your young man, Macy. You never know when the next time you might get to speak with him will be. Don't regret it," Grace encouraged, as if from the depths of some place in her heart.

"How did you . . ."

"Know about your boyfriend? I saw you longingly look at a photo when I came over," she explained.

I nodded and waved my phone at them as I left the café, heading to my room for the night.

Maybe I could bring them home with me to Havenwood Falls. Wouldn't that be the surprise of the season!

CHAPTER 9

*A*lmost a week had passed, and I couldn't believe how fast the time had gone by. Guilt swamped my emotions, flooding me with visions of my family, of Ruby, and of Gallad. I missed them all, and I couldn't believe what I had put them through. Everyone had suffered enough, not that I intended for anyone to suffer. My only intention had ever been for me to escape the plague caused by the simplest act of stupidity and a tree.

Walking to the café, I decided to tell my family I was coming home on the next bus out of Durango. My money had almost run out, and I wouldn't have enough to pay for another night at the inn. Perhaps my dad would even come get me. I checked out of my room and filled my backpack with food from the inn's breakfast.

After turning my phone on, I went through the countless text messages once again from Ruby and other friends, these asking if I would be back in time for the first day of school. I looked at the calendar on my phone and realized school was scheduled to start the next day.

"Oh no! I can't miss the first day of school," I muttered out loud. Just as I had said it, my phone chimed—voicemail from my mother. My heart quickened. She had yet to call me. I wanted to hear her voice as desperately as I wanted to slam my phone down and ignore her call altogether. Sighing, I gave in and held the phone up to my ear.

"Macy," her voice began, and with it, a sliver of pain stabbed into my heart. Tears rose in my eyes, but I quickly squelched them back. I paused to lean against a brick building while listening. Mom's voice broke, and for the first time in my life, I heard fear and guilt laced in her shaky words and hesitation. My mom, Lilith Blackstone, matriarch of the Blackstone hunters, was never afraid—or at least never showed it. "Macy, I feel an urgency to tell you . . . I should have told you sooner . . . I put it off, I thought I had more time before your hunter began to reawaken. I didn't prepare you for what you would feel. We didn't understand how the energy from the eclipse would interfere with your healing tattoo. This is my fault. I'm sorry, child. Please come home. I understand, more than I hope you ever know, I understand the drive to run. It's overwhelming, scary, and even painful. Oh, Macy, be careful out there. You needed time. I understand that, too. I tried to get everyone to give you time. Your father has been searching for you, but I know you'll come back when you want to be here." She paused for an uncomfortably long moment, but I could hear her heavy breathing. "Please listen, Macy. Run when you have feelings that make you intensely, toxically sick. That is a witch's black magic. I can tell you more when you get home, but the lesser feelings, usually where your hunter marking is located, tell you when other hunters are nearby . . . And Macy, there may be other hunters nearby." Her volume grew and her pace quickened as if she was suddenly in a hurry. "Other Blackstones have been sighted in the area. They are dangerous. If you run into any of them, stay away from them, Macy. I love you, child. Please call home."

I stood silently stunned. My mother rarely said she loved us. She must have been afraid for me. She seemed afraid of the other Blackstones. But the ones I met seemed nice enough. Well, Grace did. Nala I could see being dangerous, but she hadn't tried anything so far.

Choked up, I didn't think I could speak yet. I texted a family thread to Mom, Dad, Brock, and even Brice. I told them I got their messages and would be home tonight on the next bus out of Durango.

I said I was sorry and told them I loved them. Then I texted the same to Ruby, but Gallad I called. I needed to hear his strong, soothing voice right then. He picked up on the first ring.

"Macy? Is that really you?" He sounded panicked and relieved all at the same time.

"Hi. It's me. Gallad . . ." I paused.

"Mace, are you okay? Where are you? I'll come and get you right now!"

"Calm down, G." I laughed. It was so good to hear his voice. "I miss you."

"I miss you, too. Seriously, can I come get you?" The hurt in his voice broke my heart—hurt I had put there.

"Gallad, I . . . I'm . . ."

"No, you don't need to explain."

"What the hell are you talking about? Of course, I do! I attacked you—the other half of my heart. You tried to help me, but I was a coward and ran away. I didn't understand the feelings overwhelming me, and I couldn't think straight. Gallad, I'm sorry. I . . . I love you." There. I said it. I had never said it to him before now, even though he had said it to me countless times. But I didn't want to be like my mom in the same regard and wait until it was almost too late. Although, that was exactly what I had done. I didn't want to be closed off with my heart—not with Gallad, not ever.

Silence permeated the other end of the line. I was too late. I had ruined my chance with him, and now I didn't know what I would do without him.

"Come home, Macy . . . please." His voice cracked. If I closed my eyes, I could almost reach out and touch him, his voice was so close. His brown shaggy hair, the cocky air about him he would call confidence, the way he held my hands or held me close . . . it all called me back to him, but nothing more than his striking green eyes that held my gaze and instilled the promise of his love.

"I'll be on the next bus out of Durango. I told my parents. I'm coming home," I told him quietly. "Gallad, I am sorry. I hope you can forgive me in time."

"Just come home, Mace." He ended the call, and I stood there solemnly, catching my breath and guarding my emotions before I met my newest family members for lunch to tell them goodbye—at least until I could come back with my parents and introduce them all together. I had enjoyed meeting up with them this week and getting to know them a little.

With a new plan and renewed excitement about seeing my family and Gallad, I held my head high and headed toward the café to meet Grace and Nala. I tipped my head up briefly to feel the warmth of the sun on my face. Today, a light breeze ruffled the ends of my hair and brought a feeling of fresh perspective to my soul. I was going home, and now that I had decided, I couldn't wait to get there. Nothing terrible had happened, and my little getaway proved I could do it on my own in the future.

Spotting Grace and Nala already seated in the outdoor section, I waved when they caught my eye. Both smiled and waved me over to them.

"Good afternoon, Macy." Grace welcomed me. All I got from Nala was a nod and a brief smile. At least she didn't frown at me.

"Hello," I said as I sat at their table. "Did you order already?"

"No, we waited for you, dear."

Taking the menu she held out for me, I looked over it quickly and decided.

"Are you ready already?" Grace asked, with a light chuckle.

"I'm pretty simple. I know what I like. They have a wonderful tomato basil soup and grilled three-cheese and bacon sandwich here. I want to savor it one last time." I sighed gleefully at the mere thought of it as my mouth began to water.

"Oh, I want that now," Nala chimed in unexpectedly. When I raised an eyebrow at her, she shrugged.

"What? It sounds good."

The waitress came by to take our order, then quickly dashed off to her next table of new arrivals.

"Did you say last time, dear?" Grace asked, bringing my attention back to her right as something strange flitted swiftly behind her eyes.

Cocking my head, I didn't hide the fact that I caught it. "Um, yes. Tomorrow is the first day of my senior year, and I need to get back home. My little getaway has come to an end."

"It has been so lovely getting to know you. I do hope we can see you again," Grace said with a spark of sadness in her eyes.

"Let's just eat and enjoy our last day then," Nala urged, strangely focused on Grace.

"Of course, of course." Grace patted my arm on the table next to her. "Did you have a chance to call your young man, Macy?"

I blushed. "I did."

"Good. Good." She winked at me.

"You had mentioned knowing someone from Havenwood Falls. Who was it? I'm not supposed to talk about it, but I figure since you already know about it, it couldn't hurt." I looked up at her expectantly.

"Yes, it was long ago, but one doesn't forget the connections of family easily. It helped she had come to meet me outside of Havenwood Falls. I suspect there were consequences of some sort, as I didn't hear from her again after that time."

Intrigued, I leaned forward. "Who was it?"

"She may not even still be alive, but she was a cousin of sorts. Letitia Blackstone is her name." Her words exploded in my mind like a dropped bomb. She waited, watching my reaction.

"Well, I can tell you she is still alive. She's my grandmother's cousin. I see her almost every day. I can tell her I met you, and perhaps in the future I can even bring you to Havenwood Falls or bring her here to meet you!"

A spark lit in Grace's eyes; the news seemed almost shocking to her. Quickly she used her napkin to school her features, but it was too late. I saw the longing in her eyes, but for some reason she felt it should not be there or be seen. Seen by me? Or possibly by Nala? I let it go for the moment, but I would try to ask her about it before I left her. Nala eyed Grace curiously as well, but she didn't ask for an explanation either. A strange, awkward silence descended on the table. But then the server brought our meals, and for several minutes, no one said anything while we dug into our food.

"When do you leave?" Nala asked. "And oh wow, this is good. I'm going to have to come back for this again."

"Right?" I beamed, amazed I got her to act somewhat normal for even a mere second. *Score one for me!* "I'll be leaving right after we have lunch. It's a bit of a journey, and I want time to settle back in before school tomorrow."

"Macy, would you be a dear and ask the server to refill my iced tea?" Grace asked, holding out her glass to me. The server would have been back to check on us momentarily, but I didn't want to be rude to my elder, so I took the glass up to the counter to be refilled.

When I returned to the table, there was a sudden tension between Grace and Nala that hadn't been there before I left.

"Everything all right here?" I asked, eyeing them both.

"Of course, dear, thank you for the refill." She took a deep pull from her drink and smiled.

The next half-hour flew by with Grace asking me random questions about myself and about my boyfriend—though I was selective about what information I gave her. Knowing she was from our family of hunters, I wasn't sure of her views on dating a witch. Nala chimed in occasionally, but mostly she stared out at the street.

"We wish you didn't have to go, Macy," Grace finished. "I've enjoyed our time out here, getting to relax at this wonderful café."

"It has been lovely. I hope to see you both again in the future," I replied, even including Nala. Uncharacteristically, she gave me a big wink.

"Oh you will, you can count on that," Nala countered, watching me intently.

"Ok . . . well, I should be going soon." I started to stand up, but my knees felt wobbly, like they couldn't hold my weight. "Whoa, maybe I need just a minute." My head started to spin, and I clutched it tight.

"Are you all right, dear?" Grace's voice came through the fog permeating my brain.

"I . . . I don't know. I don't feel so good." The fog spread thickly in my brain, and fuzziness crept in front of my vision. Was I fainting?

That fight-or-flight drive surged in my chest, but my limbs felt like lead. Was I even moving them? I couldn't see. But I could still hear.

"You'll be fine, dear. I'll keep an eye on you," Grace's voice whispered in my ear.

"Let her go, Grace. Dante wants to meet her." Nala's words stuck with me as I tried to process what she was saying. Who was Dante? Why did that name sound familiar?

"Whaz happen . . ." Was that my voice slurring? "I can't fweel ma tung . . ." Seriously, what was wrong with me?

Suddenly, the ground was torn out from under my feet, and the air moved on my face. Was I being carried?

"Get her in the car, boys," another woman's voice echoed in my head. Boys? What boys? Panic bubbled up in my chest, but all I could manage was a groan. What was happening to me? The next thing I knew, I was slipping into darkness. I fought it as long as I could, but the darkness won. As I went under, the last thought I had was of Gallad. I saw his face in my mind, his eyes twinkling when he said he loved me. I felt his tender but firm lips over mine as he kissed me and heard his masculine and confident voice as he said my name. I wanted to go home.

CHAPTER 10

*V*oices penetrated through my brain like rays of light breaking through dense fog with sporadic effectiveness. Sometimes words were recognizable, and other times only indistinguishable sounds hit my brain as I tried to comprehend what I heard. I didn't know if it was days or minutes that passed before I heard a familiar voice cut through the haze.

"Macy, it's time to wake up."

"Mom? Is that you?" I croaked, my voice scratchy and thick. I wasn't even sure what I said was decipherable as words. My cracked lips smacked as I moved my tongue around in my mouth, trying to get it to work properly. Had I been eating cotton? *Yuck.*

"No, dear. Have some water." A glass was put up to my mouth, and I began to slurp down my liquid savior. "Slowly now. You don't want to choke." The voice soothed me as she spoke.

"Am I blind?" Panic started to erupt. I absently patted the space around me.

She chuckled. *Seriously?* I was concerned about being blind the rest of my life, I had no idea where I was or what was happening, and someone *laughed* at me? I growled in response.

"Your vision will slowly return. Don't worry, dear."

"I know you . . ."

"Yes, it's Grace, child." I felt her warm breath closer to my ears as she whispered the next part. "I'm sorry it had to happen this way." She sounded sad.

I needed a minute to breathe, to calm my overactive heart. I couldn't do anything blind. I needed to get my body back under my control. I pushed air in through my nose and out through my mouth. I let the act of breathing help me to gain command of myself. I remembered Grandma Eva instructing me when I was younger. She taught me ways to master not only myself when I felt powerless but also when I felt the drive of the hunter pushing to the forefront. I just wished I had remembered those lessons before I fled Havenwood Falls. Then I wouldn't be in this mess. Suddenly, the memory of my mom's voicemail warning me about other hunters rushed back to me. She was right. I didn't even know entirely why, but something here was very wrong.

The fog lifted from my brain, and the darkness receded from the edges of my sight. Slowly but surely, my vision returned. I just couldn't tell if Grace was on my side or planning to hurt me.

The prison they held me in came into view. I lay on a twin-sized bed in a pink room. The room had a closet full of girl clothes, a desk with books stacked on top of it, an overflowing hamper near the door, and posters of eighties bands and movies. On a chair right next to me sat Grace, her eyes full of concern as she watched me come out of the sleep-induced fog I was battling.

"Grace? Why have you done this?" My voice cracked. Fear crept in. What did she mean the way it had to happen? "Where's my phone?" I patted my pockets but felt nothing.

"We have it, and you will get it back. But until you've heard us out, it's being held in a safe place."

I practically roared, I was so upset. I had been kidnapped by an elderly woman and her ninja Nala posse. How lame was that?

"I need to go home. My parents will come looking for me if I'm not home tonight."

"Sweet child, you have been asleep for a week."

"WHAT?" That was a bomb I didn't know how to recover from. I sat up with a rush, quickly regretting it as I did. "Did you say a week?"

"Slowly, or you will make yourself sick." Grace reached over to pat my arm, but I pulled it back, not wanting her comfort. She had betrayed my trust.

"You said we were family. How could you do this to me?" Anger seethed. I fought my emotions for control. Placing my head on my knee, I tried to regain my balance. The more I allowed my body to recover, the more I felt the warmth bloom behind my neck. The sensation was much stronger than before with Grace—which meant more hunters were present.

Her sigh sounded remorseful, but I didn't care or believe it now. It was too late for remorse.

"I missed the beginning of school." Yes, I pointed out the obvious, but I was still muddled a bit in my head.

"I'm sorry, dear," she whispered. Her head hung low, and she seemed truly sorry. Still no grace for Grace.

"Tell me why," I demanded. Slowly, I raised my head, and I turned my glare on her. I hoped she felt the sting of betrayal in my gaze.

"Because I asked her to." A male voice flowed into the room a second before the body it belonged to followed. A tall, handsome man strode confidently into the room. He appeared in his early sixties, with graying hairs at the sides of his otherwise black-haired head, and was clothed in a gray business suit with even darker gray dress shoes. He had kind of an old Hollywood style about him, but with cold eyes— Hollywood with an edge. His eyes shot to Grace, disapproval striking within them, and I found myself rearing up internally, wanting to protect her even though she betrayed me. What was up with that? *No, she should be on her own*, I thought . . . but maybe she already was.

His steel-blue gaze swung to meet mine. Something dark and malevolent hit me in the chest. I had never encountered anyone with such an intense gaze that it physically assaulted me. Chills erupted up my spine.

"Who are you?" I asked with a bravado I had to pull out of my backside. His lip twitched as if he knew exactly where I pulled it from.

"My name is Dante Blackstone. And I believe you are a member of my family, Macy," he replied. The way he said "my family" did not escape my still slightly fog-addled brain, as if he was the ruler and not just a member of it. It irked me he knew my name. I guessed Grace and Nala were some kind of spies who reported back to this guy.

"Why am I here?" I swung my legs over the edge of the bed, needing to be grounded on the actual ground in case I needed to get up quickly—though I wasn't sure I was physically able to yet.

"Stand down, Macy. I am not planning on hurting you." The side of his mouth quirked up, as if it was funny I thought I had any chance to run or fight at all. "You are here because I have been searching for the rest of my family for a very long time. I wanted the chance to get to know you and for you to get to know us."

"I'd like to go home, please." I hated the whimper I heard in my own voice—like some weakling. I was a hunter, the same as these people, although possibly quite different from them as well.

"Of course. You are not a prisoner here. But you have cousins and relatives who would like to meet you before you do. Would that be all right?" He stood with his hands clasped behind his back.

His way was totally manipulative, but it also worked. Of course I wanted to meet family members. Why wouldn't I?

"It would. It still doesn't explain why I was asleep for a week." The anger surged up once more. *A whole week!* Anything could have happened during that time, and I wouldn't have had a clue. The very thought made me want to throw up, but taking stock of myself, I didn't feel violated in anyway. In fact, I oddly felt stronger the more time went by.

"You have a strength about you, Macy. However, I can tell you have not yet allowed your hunter side to come to the forefront. It has somehow been dampened . . . magically." He said his last word with a tone of disgust accompanied by an ugly sneer. He didn't seem finished, so I remained quiet, though everything in me wanted to lash out with a smart remark. "You see, all those in *my* family are given the freedom to be who they were created to be, to engage in every facet of their being, to awaken the hunter from birth." Those sharp eyes shot directly into my soul. His voice grew in strength as the shadow of something rose up behind his eyes. "Your hunter needs to be reawakened."

"Compelling. Is this where I jump and ask to follow you and remain here with *your* family?" Who did this guy think he was? Slowly, I stood from the bed. I felt Grace move back to allow me space, then inch her way toward the only exit in the room. I didn't blame her. "You took me away from *my* family just so you could see what kind of hunter I could be? Who gave you that right? You have *kidnapped* me! My hunter is just fine, thank you very much. I want to go home. Now."

"We are above the law, Macy. Your hunter called out to us. We deserve our freedom, as do you. They need their freedom."

Oh gag. He talked as if we and our "hunters" were separate beings in the same body. I mean, I've talked about my hunter side, but I'm pretty sure I've never heard my hunter talk to me. Dante paced slowly in a tight circle, as the room hindered his need for space.

"As supernaturals in this world of humans, we have been given the upper hand, the abilities to govern and police our own. It is our responsibility. There are those who have taken liberties to exist outside the *natural* law. Those who conjure and collect the magical elements with a spoken word to do as they will and to harm others. It is our job to govern them. It is unnatural!"

Witches. He was talking about witches, and I did not like the turn this conversation was taking. My skin crawled with a very bad feeling.

"And how do you govern them?" I asked hesitantly, pretty sure I knew where he was going.

Turning to me, his eyes lit up as if excited I was interested in learning his ways. "Excellent question. It is about restoring balance. We remove the unnatural abominations, thus creating a more natural state."

"But don't you think as supernaturals, we are not 'natural' ourselves?" Oops. As soon as I said it, I realized my mistake.

His gaze shot toward me once more. A muscle twitched in his jaw, and another at the corner of one eye gave away his impending anger, but he calmed it quicker than my parents would have. Perhaps he wasn't used to anyone questioning him, or perhaps I hit a nerve.

"We are created to restore the balance. You should know that by your age. Your parents have let your education of our race slide. I can remedy that. Outside of human schooling, those in my family grow up knowing exactly who they are, what they can do, and their position in this world." Holding his hands behind his back once more, he straightened his shoulders—though I had no idea how they could be any straighter—and his facial expression became one of a semi-hospitable host. "I would like to extend the same opportunity to you, Macy. It might take some work at first, but I'm willing to do it."

Gee, don't I feel special. I wanted to roll my eyes so badly, but I refrained and chose my words carefully. "Thank you for the offer, Mr. Blackstone." He smiled and gave a curt and approving nod. Yeah, I could be a suck-up when I needed to be. "But I'm going to have to decline. I can see your family is very important to you, so you'll understand I need to get back to mine. They'll be worried sick and looking for me."

"No need to worry there. We have scouts out looking for them. They will be proud when they see how I have helped you engage your hunter side." Like a peacock, he puffed out his chest as he straightened a lapel.

"I don't think so. They are the ones who agreed to have my hunter tendencies suppressed until I'm eighteen and can choose for myself." Wow. To hear myself speak, I might sound a bit resentful about the fact.

Dante stopped moving and held completely still. Supernaturally still. "They suppress their young, not allowing them to engage with their hunters?"

His voice held a deadly calm, like when the air became electrically charged right before a storm of epic proportions.

"I thought you understood," I said cautiously.

"I thought perhaps you were an anomaly, unable to fully engage," he began matter-of-factly.

"You mean, you thought there was something wrong with me?" I didn't know why that bothered me more than anything else at the moment—maybe because I felt there was truth in it, deep down inside.

"It happens from time to time. All it takes is some kind of trigger to truly engage the hunter, to realign what might be off internally." He shrugged, an unusual action for someone dressed the way he was and carrying himself the way he did. Like a boomerang, he brought the conversation back around. "You were suppressed magically. That leads me to believe you live cohesively with those who do the suppressing? With the magic users?"

"Yes."

Through gritted teeth, he responded. "How can this be? They have gone against their very nature to live in the same community as the witches! I knew long ago my sister decided to fight her hunting urges. She didn't understand the true need for balance, the true cause of our mission. She was misguided and ran from it like a coward . . . But to live with witches . . . to commune with them . . ." He didn't finish his rant. I was done.

"Yep, in fact, my boyfriend is a witch." Why, oh why, couldn't I keep my mouth shut?

"They let you . . ."

"They don't *let* me. I chose him!" I shouted. Gallad was the best thing that ever happened to me, and I wasn't about to let some deranged stranger claiming to be my family belittle that. Okay, so it may have been stupid timing, but whatever.

Dante held his chin high. He breathed in through his nose, held it for a count of three, and then slowly released it again. He appeared to be enacting some kind of control over himself. For that I was grateful, but I was not sorry, and I wouldn't take it back.

"Come, let me introduce you to the rest of your family." Instantly, Dante had flipped a mental switch. This guy was crazy, I was pretty sure of it. But following him would lead me out of this room, and from there I could discover where I was and what I had to work with. Then I would make my move.

174

CHAPTER 11

*A*fter following the most stoic man ever, with the assistance of my elderly captor, down a long hallway adorned with several doors not unlike an apartment building or hotel, we finally arrived at a large room at one end. Through double doors was a wide-open room with no interior walls, a ballroom at its basest function. This room, however, was full of couches, a large screen television with smaller screens on either side connected to game consoles, an extra-large table with a lot of chairs, and overflowing bookshelves lining one wall. Occupying several seats within the room were roughly ten people. Most appeared younger than fifty, but a few older ones sat at the big table and played cards. When Dante stepped in, the room quieted, and all eyes turned toward him without him even saying anything. The way his presence affected everyone gave me the creeps. Their eyes looked to him first, then fell on me. Mixed expressions surveyed me, but mostly they seemed curious and open.

"Everyone, this is Macy Blackstone. Introduce yourselves and make her feel at home. I have business to attend to and will be back for dinner." He turned to Grace. "Keep an eye on things, Grace."

She nodded and reached out for his arm, but then retracted it. Her face remained in control, but her eyes held sadness. Dante turned on his heel and stopped at me. "Macy, I do hope you enjoy your time getting to know the rest of your family. If you would still like to leave, the morning would be the earliest opportunity, as this evening will be too late to travel. If you wait until the morning, I will escort you home myself."

Seeing my flinch, he quickly amended his words. "Or I would be happy to have Nala or one of the others drive you, if that makes you more comfortable."

I nodded. "I'll think about it."

I had no intention of thinking about it. I would find a way out of here, but I needed to find my phone so I could call Dad to come get me, or at the very least, let him know I was alive. Maybe I could strong-arm—or sweet-talk—Grace into getting it back. She seemed to have reservations about the way they brought me here. I could use that. Dante strode out of the room with great intention. I felt a collective sigh throughout the room, a releasing of the tension as they returned to what they had been doing.

"Macy, come meet some of the others," Grace said, pulling me along by my arm over to the main table where three ladies watched me, not yet picking up their card game again. "Ladies, this is Macy. We're not sure yet how we are related, but she says Letitia is still alive and kicking."

Introductions were made at the table, but honestly, they seemed more interested in knowing about Aunt Letti than anything about me at all. Fine by me; I didn't want to get attached. They had all been very sweet, when I had been expecting animosity—animosity would have been easier. Then I wouldn't think of them like people—or like family I would turn my back on.

Grace then took me over to the couch area where there appeared to be three different video games going on simultaneously. I was dizzy trying to figure out which screen to watch. Brice was a gamer; I played with him sometimes, but never really got into it.

"Macy, this is Sunny, Charlie, and Rachel on the couches." Grace pointed at three different girls about my age. "Girls, introduce yourselves."

"Hey, I'm Sunny." The girl with short blond hair and bright blue eyes and a smattering of freckles on her nose waved with a small smile. She was obviously the youngest.

"I'm Charlie," the girl next to Sunny on the big couch said. Her shoulder-length brown hair with soft waves framed her pale skin, green eyes, and sharp features. She and the other girl, who must have been Rachel, most likely were a bit older than me. She smiled, and her welcoming aura made me relax and think we could be friends. Thinking of friends brought Ruby to the forefront of my mind. I missed her. I hope I got to see her and the others again.

"Hi Sunny, Charlie, and Rachel." I waved, then put my hands in my front pockets, unsure what to do next. I didn't want to be here, making nice with new people, no matter how much I could see familial resemblances in each of them. Rachel lounged in a reclining game chair in front of one of the small screens. She paused her game to look up at me, nodded, and shot me a brief gratuitous smile before returning to her game, which was obviously more important. I didn't blame her. Who was I to her? A random stray brought in off the street. Well, I was not looking to be fed or coddled.

Two boys over on the small couch played their own games.

"Hey, I'm Luke, and this is my brother Jeremiah. We're twins," the one with longer brown hair sweeping across his eyes announced. His twin, Jeremiah, gave me a wave. His hair was cut shorter all around, but other than that, they were practically identical.

"They call us the hunting Houdinis because we're great at disappearing when necessary," Jeremiah chimed in with a chuckle. They couldn't be more than twelve or thirteen. Brice would probably like them. Thinking of Brice . . .

"You both are hunters?" I asked, attempting to hide the surprise in my tone. According to the eyes that all swiveled my way, I failed.

"Of course! Do you see a ghost right now? Because you're kinda pale," Luke said.

"No, but there are no male hunters in my family . . . well, until my younger brother that is." I clamped my mouth shut. I shouldn't have said anything.

"Seriously?" Jeremiah guffawed.

I nodded. Oh well, too late now. Maybe I could find out something about it.

"We have lots in our family," Sunny, the youngest of the girls, supplied. Two other boys, one younger and one closer to my age, were on the floor in bean bags that looked well used. They hadn't been introduced yet, but were quite focused on their game, or at least appeared to be. "Are all your males human then?" Sunny continued.

"Yes, except Aunt Letti—I still have a question on that by the way —she married a dragon shifter awhile back." I heard snorts of disgust from the table behind me, where Grace had sat herself down. I turned with an eyebrow raised in question. "Care to comment?" I dared.

"Letitia stayed with us quite some time ago. She thought she wanted to stay, then she met her dragon and eloped with him. She said he was from a town called Havenwood Falls, where she was originally from as well, and she returned with him to become the family matriarch there. We never heard from her again," said a woman appearing to be in her early sixties, with Easter egg purple hair piled up on top of her head and a glint of hurt in her eyes.

"Granted, we were not living so close at the time. We didn't know how to get ahold of her," Grace supplied with a sad shrug.

"She was a lot of fun back in those days," a different woman commented with a big smile—I thought her name was Gladys.

"That sounds like Aunt Letti," I said with a smile before I realized I had.

"So are you all hunters?" I asked, looking around the room at each of them.

"Most of us are," Rachel chimed in, "but we have human members who have married into the family and offspring that are either human or half hunter."

"Really? Some of you are half hunter?" I was surprised to hear that and realized I rambled. "That's pretty cool, I mean it makes sense, but we don't have any. Offspring from a hunter and a human where I am from produce either a full human or a full hunter—one or the other.

And in my family the girls are mostly hunters and the males are human."

"Except for your brother," Charlie put in.

I nodded. "Except for Brice. So how can you be half hunter?"

"A half-hunter half-human mix basically dilutes the full hunter experience. They can sense the same things we do, but only at half the strength," the older boy on the floor explained without taking his eyes off his screen.

That made sense.

Rachel turned to me, a suspicious expression on her face. "So you can't tell which of us are hunters or not?"

"I should be able to, right?" I asked, uncertain.

"Oh yes, definitely," Sunny blurted, nodding her head. She was like a cute little ray of sunshine on caffeine. Brice would be so annoyed.

"I'm learning, just a little slowly, I guess. Back home, my mom doesn't inform us of everything until our eighteenth birthday—though I see that needs to change." Now that I said it out loud and looked at those around me, it seemed a silly thing. I should have known more about being a hunter. I should've known what to expect when I began to experience symptoms.

"No. Way," Luke and Jeremiah said at the same time, in stereo, really making a girl feel confident.

"You mean, they don't let you be a hunter, or fulfill your responsibilities as one until you are eighteen?" Charlie asked, her jaw practically hitting the seat of the couch.

I had already learned my lesson. I wasn't about to tell them that not only did we live near witches and agree to suppress our hunting nature to be a part of their community, but that I also had a witch boyfriend. Wow, the shit would really hit the fan in this room if I did.

"I guess when you put it that way, it doesn't sound quite right," I admitted, trying to think of something to change the subject.

"What do you do where you live then?" Sunny chirped.

"I guess the same as any teenager. I have a job, I work at a coffee shop. I hang out with friends, I go to school—hey, speaking of, why aren't any of you at school?"

"Oh, we homeschool," Charlie answered.

"We move around a lot," the older boy, still intent on playing his game, answered flatly.

"Do you have a boyfriend?" Sunny asked with stars in her eyes. She couldn't be more than twelve maybe.

I hesitated, feeling the blush suddenly rush up my neck.

"Ooh you do! I knew it!" Sunny practically bounced in her seat. "Is he a human?"

"Uh . . . no, not exactly," I hedged. I took a step backward, looking to Grace. Dizziness suddenly swam in my head. I reached up to try to keep my head from rolling to the floor.

"Hey, are you okay?" someone asked.

"I'm not sure. I feel funny. Grace? Did you give me something else?"

"No, dear." She sounded worried.

As quickly as it hit me, it was gone. Widening my eyes, I looked around the room. Nothing had changed, but I felt something in my head I couldn't explain. Rolling my shoulders and neck, I shook it off. "I'm not sure what that was, but it's gone now."

"Is he a dragon, like the one your aunt married?" Sunny asked.

"What?"

"Your boyfriend, is he a dragon or another shifter? Or maybe a vampire?" My potential answer had her on the edge of her seat, more intriguing than the games being played on the screens in front of her.

"He's a witch, isn't he, dear?" Grace totally outed me, and I didn't know why.

"WHAT?" roared too many people's voices to differentiate. I had to hold my hands over my ears.

"What kind of Blackstone are you?" Rachel's vehemence shot at me.

"The kind who lives above the archaic prejudices you seem to be stuck on," I shot back. I would not be put down because of who I chose to hang out with. I edged myself back toward the wall slowly, not wanting to appear like I was backing down, but needing to move around. A window came into my view. I needed to see where I was.

"Careful, you're in our house, Macy," Charlie warned.

"Yes, and not by my choice. Is kidnapping something you're all okay with? Because I'm pretty sure the law wherever we are is not."

I heard a couple stifled laughs.

"We're outside the law, Macy. You should be thankful that we found you in time and brought you here where you can learn your hunter side safely before somebody got hurt," Rachel informed me.

"What are you talking about, before somebody got hurt? In time for what?" I asked, totally confused and yet feeling the stirrings of something inside me that felt dangerous and desperate to be freed.

"If your hunter surfaces and you don't know how to control it, something terrible could happen. If you got out of control, you might even hurt an innocent passerby without meaning to. An unchecked hunter is dangerous, Macy," Charlie added, sliding a look over to Rachel, then back to me.

I thought of Gallad. I shouldn't have at that moment, but I couldn't help it. I was out of control, and I did hurt an innocent.

"She's right," Rachel jumped in. "And just think if you did happen to come across a witch while your hunter tendencies flared to life and you weren't ready for it or the witch. You could get hurt. Witches are powerful and dangerous, especially when threatened by a rabid hunter intent on killing them."

My heart started jumping in my chest. I would never hurt someone intentionally, let alone kill them just because they were a witch. Glancing out the window, I noticed a street, then a park down below, maybe three stories. Not too far, but I'd still probably break something, or a lot of things, if I jumped. But maybe I could figure out how to get outside.

The room closed in around me, and shortness of breath assaulted my lungs. I could feel my eyes frantically searching for anything to use to my advantage.

"Macy, are you all right, dear?" Grace asked from somewhere near me, her voice echoing like in a cave. "You don't look so well."

"I think you should lie down," Charlie suggested.

"Is she going to throw up?" Sunny's little voice asked with slight disgust.

"Eww, no, get her out of here," one of the boys yelled.

"Yes! Air, I need air," I begged. Holding one hand against the wall so I didn't fall over and the other against my chest, I grabbed at my neck collar, hoping to alleviate the tightness in my chest. "Grace, where is my phone?"

"I . . . I'm sorry dear, I don't know. Dante took it into his office."

With my limited ability to discern the situation around me, I noticed Charlie glare at Grace for even telling me that much.

"Come with us." Rachel stood up and gripped my upper arm with her warm hand. "Charlie, help me. We'll take her out to the courtyard for some air."

"Thank you, thank you," I panted, practically clawing at Rachel's shirt. Charlie came up and took my other arm, supporting it as they led me out of the room. Instead of going back to my room the way we had come, we descended a stairwell I hadn't seen on my way in. Two flights down, the landing opened up into an unassuming entry complete with a solid wood door—the gateway to fresh air.

Rachel punched a code into a keypad to the left of the door so fast there was no way I could have seen which numbers she put in. Charlie reached forward and opened the door as soon as the green light next to the keypad indicated it was unlocked.

"This is a short visit outside. We can stay out longer tomorrow, but why don't you catch your breath and sit for a minute. I'm sure it's a lot to take in." Charlie almost sounded caring or even understanding. But I didn't trust her tone, no matter what her words suggested.

"Thank you." I gulped the fresh air as we stepped out into it. Closing my eyes, I took a moment to slow my heart and my breathing. Rachel tugged my arm.

"There are benches in the courtyard out here." She pointed to a little area to our right. It was small, but still managed to include a lovely garden area and a pleasant seating area with a table, chairs, and an umbrella. Along the bottom of the high fence were several benches put end to end to create a long one. Hearing the soothing sounds of water, I jerked my head back to see a fountain at the end of the area.

"It's really nice," I whispered genuinely.

"It is. We enjoy it most evenings. We even have a fire pit at the other end," Charlie said as she pointed to it.

Rachel and Charlie seemed to relax a bit as they led me to the seating area. They kept me close, and their eyes never left me.

"Doing better?"

I nodded slowly. "I think so. My breathing has slowed down a bit, but I'm still dizzy."

As I answered, the fence opened from the outside, and a mail carrier walked in with a package. The girls said hello, and Rachel jumped up to receive the package. While she signed the slip, the postman handed Charlie the rest of the mail. Out of the corner of my eye, I spied that the gate had not latched. Now was my chance.

I stood up and swooned dramatically, my hand draped across my forehead. I gasped as I started to fall forward. All eyes turned to me in surprised confusion, but mail dropped all over the ground as they leaned forward to assist me. In the moment of their shock, I bolted for the gate, flinging it wide and slamming it behind me. I didn't know where I was or where I was going. I simply ran.

Yes! It worked. I knew I should have gotten an A in drama last year.

After a half hour of running faster than I knew I could, making sure no one was following me, I stopped in a busy area by the side of a street. I had nothing. No phone. No backpack. No ID. No money. Nothing. This sucked. But I was free.

Spying myself in a nearby shop window, I was shocked to see my eyes were bright and fevered. Perhaps I wasn't faking what I was feeling as much as I thought I was. My breathing was still shallow, but more normal than it had been. Shaking off the edges of dizziness that legitimately plagued me, I looked for anything that could help me.

"Excuse me," I asked a nice-looking elderly woman, though cautiously, since the last elderly woman burned me.

"Yes, can I help you?"

"Could you tell me what the name of this town is?"

She looked at me funny, probably wondering if I was a runaway. "You are in the outskirts of Durango. Do you need help?"

So not that far from where I was before then. Good. My parents knew I was in Durango. Maybe they were looking for me!

"You don't look so good, child. Can I call someone for you?"

Could she? "Do you have a phone I could use?"

The woman retrieved her phone from her bag and handed it to me after unlocking the screen. I opened the phone app and started to dial then hesitated. "I . . . I can't remember the number . . ." I frowned and shut my eyes tight. "Why can't I remember the number?" I whispered harshly to myself.

"Take your time, dear, it will come to you."

Inhaling a deep breath, I simply dialed something without thinking about it. Thankfully it rang, though I had no idea who I just called.

"Hello?" a man's voice answered.

"Daddy?"

"Macy? Baby, are you okay? Where are you?" His voice was rushed and panicked.

"I'm okay, I think. I'm outside Durango, but not sure where. Dante Blackstone and crew took me to their home. Can you come get me? Tell Mom. She'll know what to do about them."

"Where have you been? No, we can talk later. I want to get on the road. Macy, find somewhere safe. I'm on my way. It will be late when I get there. Do you see a restaurant or something near you we can make a meeting place?"

Looking around, I saw several shops, a bakery, a restaurant, and a few taverns. "There's a small park across from a restaurant called Jimmy's that's open late. I'll find a place to wait there, then meet you at the restaurant."

"Be safe, baby. We'll be there as soon as we can."

"Maybe Uncle Tranner could get you here faster," I suggested of Aunt Letti's dragon husband.

"I'll see what I can do."

"I love you, Daddy."

"I love you, too."

I handed the woman back her phone and thanked her before I ran across the street to the small park to look for a place to hide. The sun was already going down, and hopefully I could use that to my advantage.

CHAPTER 12

*H*ours later, the full darkness of night had fallen upon the outskirts of Durango. I was still sitting in a tree I found that allowed me to pull my legs up and hide. I felt like such an imposter cowering in a tree. It wasn't in my nature. I was supposed to be a hunter. And I was getting hungry. I hadn't seen or felt any sign of hunters nearby, or anyone at all, for that matter, in quite some time. I ventured down to see if I could find food without having to resort to stealing or begging.

Hopping down from my safe haven above ground, I scouted my route through the forest at the edge of the park. I could make out the street I had been on earlier. People still milled about, but most were patrons of the taverns, which could be their own kind of trouble. The chilled air had a bite this late at night as the weather descended into fall. I jumped around to get my blood flowing. Sneaking through the copse of trees like a spy, I watched where I stepped and stuck to the shadows. Once a break in the dense canopy opened, I looked up to find the moon at its peak fullness. Unexpectedly, my arms tingled, and the sensation traveled up to my shoulders.

Uh-oh. I hadn't felt that since I was in Havenwood Falls, but I knew it meant I was near a witch. I thought I was alone out here. More carefully, I headed toward the people. If I was near more people, perhaps I had a better chance of blending in. Almost to the edge of the park, I felt the warmth at the back of my neck too late before I saw the shadow of someone up ahead. A hunter. Not knowing who it was, I kept my guard up. Of course they had felt me, because everyone was better at being a hunter than I was. Did I take my chance with them? Or head the opposite way and try to avoid the witch? I recalled what Charlie and Rachel had said earlier: when the hunter surfaced for the first real time on their own, they could lose control.

Taking my chance with the witch, I turned and hightailed it as fast as I could go away from the hunter. I had no idea where the park ended or if it even did. Outlines of mountains in the distance were visible in the moonlight. Distinguishing if there was a river or thicker, denser trees was almost impossible from my location. Someone watched me; I felt eyes all around me, closing in on me. Similar to the feelings I experienced earlier at the house, the nausea and dizziness came over me, but so much more intense.

My vision blurred. I heard things on either side of me that didn't sound natural, but I couldn't be sure. My stomach rolled. A new sensation, one of epically toxic proportions, punched me in the gut. *Black magic.* I doubled over, thankful I had eaten nothing to bring back up. The buzzing in my ears brought with it a fogginess that swarmed my eyesight. I was about to faint as the toxic sludge forced its way through my veins.

I stumbled forward, urging myself to move.

I ran blind, as fast as I could. I ran faster than I should have been able to. My ears burned with sensitivity at every sound of the forest all at once. And my sight, instead of going completely black, sharpened and went into some kind of night-vision mode. If I didn't know better, I'd say I was turning into a shifter like Ruby or our friend Willa Kasun's family back home at Havenwood Falls, but I did know better. My hunter side was surfacing in full force, and I had no idea what to do about it. One thing I did know for certain—I needed to stay away from the witch.

Feeling a sharp poke in my butt, I swatted my hand and came back with a small needle-like thing with a fluffy top. Someone hit me with a tranq dart! I kept running.

The next thing I knew, the ground jumped up to smack me in the face. Voices screamed my name, and then I blacked out.

~

"MACY! Macy! Oh my god, you have to wake up!" A panicked female voice shouted at me as hands shook my body.

Groaning, I tried to open my eyes, but they felt so heavy. "What happened?"

"You killed a witch," her voice said with a bit of pride.

That did it. I jolted my head up and forced my eyes to open. Looking around, I was on the ground not anywhere near where I thought I had been. In front of me was a body of a young man about my age, his neck at an odd angle. I leaned over and threw up, or at least tried to, but I had nothing. Tears ran down my cheeks. I studied my hands. They felt foreign to me, capable of such a deed. I sobbed uncontrollably—the vision of the corpse forever burned in my mind.

"Macy, get a grip!" Rachel crouched down next to me. When she had my attention she continued. "We had just found you when you ran from us, then you went crazy like an uncontrollable animal, screaming. We followed you, then we sensed the witch. But we got here just after you took him down. You were so fast! Then you passed out," she explained.

"I . . . I don't understand . . . how could this have happened? What do I do?" Panic tore through my chest. My dad was on his way. Oh no! My dad was on his way, he couldn't see this, couldn't know his baby girl killed someone. The other Blackstones had been right. My hunter was out of control. Something was wrong with me.

"Macy. It's time to come back to the house with us before the authorities find the mess you made." Dante spoke unfeelingly from the side as he looked on. "Let us train you, prepare you for next time."

I was numb. "I deserve to be taken to the authorities. Let them come to me," I said quietly.

"Don't be silly. It's just a witch," Charlie said from somewhere beyond me.

"Shut up, Charlie," another voice hissed. Nala. I recognized her voice, but hadn't seen her since I had been with the Blackstones. "Give her a minute. She'll come around."

"Macy, we cannot allow you to be caught by the authorities. It puts us all in jeopardy. We will correct the problem. You will be trained and won't lose control again. This one here," Dante pointed to the body, "was dabbling in black magic. Did you notice a toxic feeling as you got closer to him?"

I nodded. I would never forget that sensation. I remembered feeling it back in Havenwood Falls before I left, too. The Luna Coven would want to know about that for sure. The thoughts of home pierced my heart. I couldn't go back, even if I wanted to or if I tried to. They wouldn't let me now that I had done the unthinkable. Gallad would never look at me again. I had nothing and nowhere to go.

Dante held his hand down to me expectantly. "Will you come back with us?"

Hesitating, I found no other option. I nodded.

Dante whispered behind me to someone, telling them to clean up the mess. We headed back to the Blackstone compound.

"If you let us, we could be your new family."

Numbly I followed along with Nala and Rachel on either side of me to what would be my new home.

BACK AT THE COMPLEX, I received my own room. It turned out I had been using Sunny's room before, as she was the only one willing to give it up for me. This one was plainer than plain, with nothing more than a twin bed complete with a beige comforter, a plain white dresser, and a small wood desk. No window. It didn't matter. I didn't deserve to be comforted by the light of day. I showered, then curled up on the bed and cried myself to sleep.

I woke to a hissing sound. With no idea or concern for how long I had slept, I covered my head with my pillow, went back to sleep, and dreamed of Gallad.

In the dream, he called to me, his voice a soothing balm. He spoke to me as if I could respond to him, but I remembered what I had done and tried to shut him out. Gallad was relentless and persistent—telling me how much he missed me, and I needed to come home. He talked about random things, as though filling the time. He told me my dad was searching for me. Could I tell him where I was? But I couldn't speak. Hearing his voice was more than I deserved. It wasn't real anyway, but I could allow myself this indulgence for a moment.

"Tell me about school, Gallad." I finally tried to talk to him. Since it wasn't real, what could it hurt?

"What do you want to know, Macy?"

"Everything. I miss you so much, it hurts." I cried some more but kept it to myself.

He proceeded to tell me exactly what I had asked for—everything. Gallad went on to share with me about all his classes, his teachers, the other students at Havenwood Falls High School. It was our senior year, and I was missing it. Gallad was on the football team, but his heart wasn't in it this year, he said. People kept asking about me and when I was coming home. *Home.* I didn't have the heart to tell him it could no longer be my home.

"Macy, I have to go now. The sun is coming up. I'll try to contact you again. The full moon assisted me this time, but I don't know when the next time will be," he explained, though I thought I had a pretty good imagination for concocting such a story for him. "Don't forget me, Macy. I will always love you."

His voice faded out of my mind. "Oh Gallad, you wouldn't if you knew what I had done," I whispered to myself as I woke up fully to the sound of knocking at my door.

"Time to get up, Macy. Training starts in one hour!" Sunny chirped too cheerfully for any time of day, let alone after just waking up.

That's exactly how my days began for the next week. Training.

Breakfast. Schooling. Training. Free time. Dinner. More Training. Bed. I was exhausted.

Training consisted of working out intensely with weights, aerobics, and yoga. I was also educated about how the hunter gene worked, the different sensations I felt, what they meant, how to control them so they didn't overpower me, and how to use them to my advantage. I worked harder and studied more than I ever did at home. Every evening ended with yoga training. I didn't remember doing it before now, but my body already knew the moves, and I loved it. Something tugged at the back of my mind, perhaps a memory, but I couldn't place it. After an intense day of training, we gathered around the fire pit out in the courtyard and roasted marshmallows.

Every day that went by, the ache in my chest for somewhere called home grew less and less. I knew I had a mom and a dad and even siblings, but some days it took longer to pull up my memories of them or the sounds of their voices in my head. The layout of the town I came from, and even its name, sometimes eluded me like a lost memory trying to resurface, poking its head out occasionally for air to survive one more day, then be forced back under the water of forgetfulness.

"Macy," Dante called me into his office one day. "You have been excelling at your training. How are you fitting in here?" he asked.

"I'm beginning to feel like this is home. I know Charlie doesn't really like me, but I'm used to her and can hold my own."

"Do you miss home? I was thinking it was time to return this to you." He pulled out a desk drawer and handed me a cell phone. I rubbed my forehead where a slight headache had been forming.

"This is mine?"

He looked at me strangely. "Do you not remember?"

"It feels familiar in my hand, and I'm having flashes of memories, but they're not strong." I rubbed my head again. "I can't remember some things. I feel like the memory is there, but it takes me longer to grasp than it should."

"Why don't you go through your phone and see if it brings back any memories. Maybe call your mom or dad. I was thinking it was time to arrange a meeting with them so you could visit. Would you like that?" He watched me carefully for my answer. But I wasn't sure how I felt. Part of me wanted to jump up and down and say yes! But part of me wanted to hide from it, from the thing I had done, the shame I still felt.

"I think so. Could I take some time with this to see what I remember?" I asked, feeling odd I was even asking at all. My chest felt tight with emotion, but I wasn't sure why.

"Of course. You know where I am if you need to talk." Dante stood up from his seat and waited while I exited his office. I paused outside his door, hearing him talk. I thought at first he was still talking to me, but I paused before responding. My sensitive hunter hearing came in handy sometimes.

"She's starting to forget. We can't let her forget how to get home. If you see it get worse, let me know. We'll have to move up our timeline." He hung up what must have been the office phone.

I quickly dashed down the hall, using my new stealthy skills they had instilled in me. What had he been talking about—a timeline? What for? Lost in thought, I almost ran straight into Nala at the end of the hall.

"Oh! Sorry, Nala, I was lost in thought," I rambled when I was thrown off.

She cocked her head, watching me. "You all right, Macy? You seem off."

Off? Yeah I'd say so. "I just have a headache. Do you have anything I could take for it?"

"Grace does. I would find her. Maybe get some sleep too."

"I haven't been sleeping well. I know I'm having dreams but I either can't remember them in the morning or they're of people and places I can't put my finger on."

"Get some sleep then."

Yeah, thanks, Captain Obvious.

"Thanks," I said politely as she moved passed me. I turned around and went to find Grace. Her room was on the second level, and I made my way straight there. I didn't have to wait long after knocking on the door.

"Macy, lovely to see you, dear." Grace moved aside and welcomed me into a room twice the size as mine.

"Thank you, Grace. I have the mother of all headaches beginning and Nala said you might have something to take the pain away?" I asked, pinching the bridge of my nose after she offered me a seat.

"I do indeed. Just a moment." Grace walked into a bathroom and came back holding a bottle.

"You have a bathroom in your room?" I was so jealous.

She laughed. "I do." Grace handed me a couple of the small pills and a glass of water. I swallowed them quickly.

"Thank you." I downed the rest of the water. "Grace, I never asked you . . . well, maybe I shouldn't. I mean, I'm wondering how you are related here, especially to Dante. You're a hunter, right?"

She nodded. "Yes, dear. Well, technically, I'm half hunter, half human. As such, we age more closely to a human but get a few extra years in there. I am Dante's granddaughter at eighty-five years old."

"Well you look pretty good for eighty-five. I had you around mid-seventies." I smiled at her. "I hope I didn't make you uncomfortable asking."

"Of course not, child." She patted my arm and sat down in the chair next to me. "I see you have your phone back."

Looking to the device in my hand, I held it out. "I do, though I don't remember it very well. I get glimpses of memories and just when I think I have a solid grasp on them, they fade from my mind. It's infuriating. Dante thought maybe if I looked through it, I would remember more. He said maybe I should try and call my parents . . . Their names are slipping past me, though. Ugh. Why can't I remember? I feel like I should remember more." I flung my head down on my arm on the table in a most dramatic fashion.

"The important things will come to you, dear. Though I remember when Letitia started forgetting things, she found writing them down was helpful for a time."

"But why am I forgetting? I can't even remember that!"

"Seems there was something she said about wards and protecting the town from outsiders, though she didn't tell me too much. Said I talked too much, but I don't know what she could ever mean." Winking at me, she raised her own glass of water and took a sip.

I opened my phone like I knew how to do it and powered it on. Immediately it started buzzing, and text message after text message popped up, accompanied with voicemail notifications. The very sight was overwhelming. Dozens of messages of concern, love, and worry were left by names that rang a bell but not clearly enough to give me a visual impression. Obviously, the ones titled "Daddy" and "Mom" had to be my parents. But the ones from Gallad stirred something strong in my chest—a mix of emotions from pain and guilt to joy and excitement. It was fuzzy, but something about his name brought an image of green eyes that pierced my soul. Thinking of pictures, I opened the photo app and scrolled through the images of me with other people, some who looked like me. Visions of places and names of people and voices flooded through my head, but almost as quickly, they funneled back out.

"AH! I almost had the memories strong enough to latch on to them!" I mimicked grasping at them with my hand into a fist. My head started hurting again. It was more than a headache this time. It was almost like a pinprick behind my eyes.

"Maybe I should just call somebody and see what they say, do you think?" I asked Grace as she watched me carefully with concern and almost sadness. "Don't be sad, Grace. Maybe I'm not meant to remember." I sighed. But deep down I really wanted to remember. The pictures of those people looked like they had a ton of fun. A girl with strawberry-blond hair posed with me in some kind of rock T-shirts, making funny faces. There were more of me and a very handsome guy with the same green eyes I had just envisioned. Others might have been family, but I couldn't place them.

"Yes, Macy, I think that might be a good idea," Grace confirmed.

"Grace? What's the date?" I asked, not even sure why I did.

"It's September twentieth. Oh, and it's also the new moon tonight, ushering in the autumn equinox tomorrow."

"Well, aren't you full of information?" I laughed, but something about what she said nagged at the back of my mind. Probably something else I forgot about. I went to the voicemail app on my phone and listened to the first message.

"Macy, it's Mom. I don't know where you are, and I hope you're okay. I believe in you, so I know you're okay, you have to be. There's a lot we need to talk about. I'm sorry I didn't prepare you the way I should have. None of this would have happened otherwise. Please come home, baby. We miss you. Gallad's going out of his mind, showing up every day, asking about you. Today is September seventeenth. I just want to remind you in case you are already starting to forget things . . . after twenty-eight days, September twenty-first, you will forget all about Havenwood Falls. It's a safety precaution, but right now I'm ready to overthrow the Luna Coven to keep you remembering. I wish I could. You will forget about your family. Me, I'm Lilith, and I'm your mother, Daddy is Reggie, your brothers are Brock and Brice, and your best friend is Ruby Jean. And you'll forget how to get home. Please know, we will never stop searching for you and believing you will find your way home. I love you."

That was the end of the call. Slowly, tears found their way from my eyes down my cheeks and onto my lap. Her voice brought up an image of her face. She had outlined everything I basically needed to know right now.

"I have to call her back!" I fumbled with the buttons on the phone as my eyes kept blurring from the tears. Grace handed me a tissue without saying anything, and for that, I was appreciative.

Finding her number, I hit the button, but nothing happened. I wiped my eyes, sure I had hit the wrong one, and tried again. Nothing.

"What is wrong with this thing? It's not working!" I looked up at Grace. She, too, had a tear in the corner of her eyes.

"I'm so sorry, Macy, I don't know."

Desperately, I tried again and again, until right after my last attempt when there was a sizzling sound, the phone vibrated, and then the screen went black.

"What just happened? No, no, no, where did everything go?"

Frantically I tried to power it on, but nothing happened. It was dead. "It fried." I stared numbly at the phone.

"This won't do." Grace tsked to herself. "I must tell Dante."

"You do that," I mumbled. "I'm going to my room."

"Macy?"

"Huh?"

"Write down all you can remember immediately. Describe pictures, sounds, names, everything. Before you lose it all again, but this time for good," she warned softly.

I nodded and left her room. I had lost my family once again.

CHAPTER 13

*A*fter a somewhat awkward dinner with everyone at the long table in the dining room, I heard some of the girls talk about starting up the fire pit, and some were going to play cards. I couldn't shake what I had heard on my voicemail, and I was doing everything I could to hold onto the images and descriptions I had seen, to the point of ignoring the others.

"Macy? Macy!" I heard my name shouted repetitively.

"Oh, what?" I looked around for the source of the shouting.

"I said—after several tries, I might add—are you all right?" Rachel asked.

I had a sudden case of déjà vu from not too long ago, when I couldn't come to terms with my hunter side and tried to run away. A few memories from even before that, before I came to Durango, started to resurface, but they felt fuzzy.

"Sorry, I have a headache." To prove my point, I rubbed at my forehead.

Nala sat quietly off to the side like she often did and watched me closely.

"We forgot to grab the new bag of marshmallows, Rachel," Sunny whined as she looked through the basket of supplies they brought out.

I stood up. "I'll get them. I want to get more aspirin from Grace."

"Thanks, Macy!" Sunny beamed and did a little skip around the pit and into the courtyard.

Before I got to the door, I felt eyes on me. Looking around then finally up, I spotted Dante watching me from his office window on the third floor of the five-story building. Unabashedly, his eyes followed me until I couldn't see him any longer, but when I turned back around before entering, I caught Nala giving him a curt nod. What that could be about?

After I retrieved the entire bottle from Grace, I made my way up to my room to grab a sweatshirt. Nights were too cold for long sleeves alone. I made the decision to try to enjoy tonight with the girls. The boys had opted to go to a movie in town with some of the adults that had come back from a recent hunting trip out of state. So there were more people milling about inside than normal. Practicing my stealth mode, I crept lightly down to the end of the hall where Dante's office was. Whispers had reached my sensitive ears, and I was simply a snooping teenager. Something was going on, I could feel it. I just didn't know what.

Getting as close as I possibly dared, I held completely still and even slowed my breathing.

"Dante, she's not doing well. Something needs to happen to force the issue, otherwise she'll forget everything for good." Nala. I thought I left her outside. Guess that was what the nod was for.

"Tonight is the new moon and the cusp of the equinox. Perhaps the energies could intercede and assist us." Dante's voice seemed thoughtful.

"What do you mean?" asked one of the adults I hadn't talked to much—I thought his name was Bob. He was Charlie's father.

"She hasn't gone out on a hunt yet since she's been trained. Let's set one up for tomorrow, a celebration to thrive in the autumn equinox and the turning of the seasons. Witches will be out in force. We'll call it an initiation," Dante expounded with satisfaction.

"I'm unsure where you're going with this, sir?" Nala asked. "I don't think she's ready for a hunt yet."

I fist pumped for Nala. I didn't think she would be the one to stand up for me.

"You misunderstand, Nala. The hunt won't be real," he began.

Wait, what?

"It will be the catalyst that sends her over the edge. Because you're right, she's not ready. I need her to try to find her way home. I need her to lead me to Havenwood Falls—there will be a treasure trove of not only witches but the rest of *my* family." He slammed his hand on something, creating a loud noise. "My sister Marie took them from me, hid them from me, and now I have the one chance we've been searching for to lead us straight to them."

Insert maniacal laugh accompanied with creepy music here, please. What the hell? They've been using me?

"They will either join me in my quest to bring all witches to justice to pay for their crimes, or they too will pay for theirs."

"Oh no," I whispered. I quickly made it back to my room. My heart beat heavily in my chest, my breathing quickened. Not knowing what to do, I paced in the tiny space of my room.

"I can't believe they used me! I can't believe I didn't see it!" I whispered, in case someone walked past and heard me.

"Sit on the bed, Macy. Calm down," I told myself. I breathed slowly—in through my nose, out through my mouth.

"Macy? Macy?" another voice called to me. I went to the door, but no one was there. I didn't have a window, and even then, I was three floors up.

"Macy, can you hear me?" The voice was urgent and the most intoxicating masculine voice I had heard. It called to something deep inside me. Looking around, I couldn't find the source.

"Hello?" I whispered back.

"Thank the goddess you can hear me!"

"Where are you? I can't find you."

His enticing chuckle rang through my head all the way down to my toes, affecting me in ways I hadn't remembered feeling before. But maybe I had.

"I'm in your head, so to speak."

Cocking my head, I was totally confused. I moved my jaw around, popping my ears, and shook my head.

"Still there?"

"Yes. Unless you learned how to block my spell, you can't get rid of me." His voice sounded sad now.

"Who are you?"

Silence flooded my head, the strangest feeling.

"You don't remember me?"

"I'm not sure. Your voice is familiar. Do you have green eyes? I'm envisioning green eyes."

"I do. It's okay, there's not time to explain it all right now. The wards are really strong. I should know, my family helped create them."

"Are you from Havenwood Falls? That name keeps coming up."

"I am. Just know that I'm a friend—well, more than a friend—and I care about you."

"Okay . . . Are you the guy that was in pictures with me on my phone?"

"I hope so, otherwise we have another set of issues." He chuckled again. I really liked the sound of it. "Yes, I am. My name is Gallad Augustine. I'm your boyfriend. At least, I was when you left us."

By the hurt I could hear in his voice, he must have really cared about me, maybe even . . .

"Do you love me, Gallad?"

"With all my heart and soul," he breathed out with so much emotion, it gripped my heart and squeezed tight.

"Things are going down where I am, and I'm not sure what to do about it. You contacted me for a reason. So what can you tell me?"

He told me all about Havenwood Falls and where I lived and my family and friends as quickly as he could. He had given me enough information that lined up with some of the pictures I had seen for me to trust the stranger in my head.

His relief was almost palpable through our mind connection, though I had no idea how he was doing it. He had said "spell." Did that mean . . .

"Gallad, are you a witch? Is that how you're speaking to me?"

He hesitated. "Yes. It's a spell I have been trying to get through to you with, but I think the added energies from the equinox helped strengthen it."

"Then you and your family are in trouble." I proceeded to tell him what I had heard from Dante and the others. Gallad took everything in stride and didn't freak out like I had. I told him everything I could remember, even the part where I took the life of another witch . . . that I would never forget.

"Gallad, I have to get out of here. I know they are setting me up, but I can't go through with an actual witch hunt to play along and not give away that I know their plans."

"Here's the plan. It will work with your current situation." He told me what he, along with my parents and something he called the Luna Coven had come up with.

"Founders Day . . . is that the day with all the outdoor games, like the three-legged race and tug-o-war?"

He paused. "Are you remembering it?"

"I'm not sure, but maybe. I also saw some pics in my phone that had you, me, the girl you called Ruby—please don't tell her I didn't remember her—and some other kids in front of a gazebo with a banner that said 'Founders Day' on it."

"That's the one. So it begins in the morning, then after dark is when the covens gather at the falls to strengthen the wards around the town. You should be able to feel the power, or energy, from quite a distance. Let energy and the images I'm putting in your head guide you."

I laughed quietly. "Sorry. It makes me sound like I'm a computer you just plugged your thumb drive into."

He laughed, too. Talking to him had completely calmed me down, centered me, and brought me a peace I forgot I had until now, when I was with him. He reminded me I didn't need to be a hunter who lived like a traveling nomad and killed witches. There was another way.

"Macy, be careful. It could be dangerous, and it will be dark."

"I will. And Gallad?"

"Hmm?"

"I can't wait to remember you."

LATER IN THE EVENING, the adults had finally come outside to join us by the fire. It was late, and night had fallen like a black blanket. Several of us huddled under blankets to keep our backsides warm away from the fire.

"I have an announcement," Dante said from where he leaned against the brick façade of the building, not sitting by the fire with the rest of us. "Tomorrow ushers in the autumn equinox and the turning of the seasons. We are going to celebrate together by going on a hunt."

A few cheers erupted and shouts of "yeah," "about time," and "we'll get those witches" fed the darkness. Dante turned an eye on Charlie and some of the boys who had joined us as well.

"Voices lowered please, Charlie and Luke. We have neighbors with ears," Dante growled. A few others, whom I had only recently met as they had been out of town hunting, joined the group for the announcement.

"Am I to go on this hunt, too? Do you think I'm ready?" I asked, nervously. No lie there.

Dante searched my face in the dark, then nodded. "I believe you are. It is time."

I nodded back, unsure what my response should be. It would raise suspicion if I showed any excitement.

THE NEXT DAY passed way too slowly with the anticipation of what was to come that evening. Like all other days, we trained and even did some schoolwork, then we waited it out by playing a huge round of video game racing. I had never played so many video games before—at least I didn't think I had—but it helped time go by. Evening finally arrived and with it, a full case of butterflies for what I was about to do.

On our way out, all the hunters and I said goodbye to the humans that stayed behind. As I passed Grace, I felt a mix of sadness to leave her, but also hurt at her betrayal to me the entire time. I don't know why I hoped for an ally in her, maybe because she knew Letitia Blackstone, who I think was my aunt, from what Grace had said. She reached out and grabbed my elbow.

"Be careful out there, Macy. Always follow your heart. It will lead you home," she said quietly.

I cocked my head and frowned at her. Did she know my plan? Did she mean to come back here if I got separated from the group? Simply patting my arm, she whispered, "You'd better get going."

"Right. Goodbye, Grace," I replied and turned to follow the others outside into the night.

I was so glad I geared up with warm clothes. The other girls had pitched in to give me clothes to wear, and Dante surprisingly had one of the adults shop for me. I layered on as many clothes as I could. I had no idea how long I might be out in the cold night.

"Come on, Macy, keep up!" Rachel hollered at me from the front of the group. "It's your first hunt. Are you excited?" she said with exaggeration to pump me up, failing miserably.

"Um, I'm not sure about excited. Nervous, definitely nervous." Better to be honest, I thought.

After a lengthy time of walking, we entered a denser part of the forest nearby. Dante had instructed that there was a coven of witches he had heard about across the river, in the next community north of ours. My nerves rose with each step I took. My heart fluttered in my chest. I felt like everyone was watching me, waiting to see if I would go through with it. Of course, they weren't all watching me; it was my own paranoia about who knew the insiders' secret. Finally approaching the river, I could hear it rushing by from quite a distance away. We slowed, looking for the bridge to lead us across to the coven. The tingling in my arms started growing stronger and stronger the closer we came. They weren't lying. There really was at least one witch across the river. And judging by how strong the tingling was, I'd say there were definitely more. Due to the training I had received, the sensations in my arms no longer bothered me. No longer were they uncontrollable.

Thinking about it, I either had to go through with the hunt and watch these people who called themselves my family wipe out an entire coven of witches in one night, or I had to create a diversion and leave immediately. I knew what I had to do. I'd always known deep down—there was never really a choice.

"I . . . I can't do this," I announced. Everyone turned to face me. I was met with expressions of satisfaction from those who hadn't expected me to go through with the hunt and anger and hurt from those who had.

"You what?" Rachel shouted with anger.

"I'm sorry. I'm not meant to stay with you."

With that, I took off at a dead sprint. I knew they would follow me. However, I didn't expect the loud expletives shot my way. But I kept on running. I could feel the hunter in me emerging as I ran faster and faster. Unfortunately, many of them were gaining on me, running almost as fast.

I followed the river for a time, knowing it led north. I could hardly remember anything, but I knew I had to go north until I started climbing the mountain. The darkness surrounded me, but my night vision kicked in to guide my path. The terrain was rough but I maneuvered it better and more smoothly than I had anticipated. I knew the others would have the same advantages—I only hoped my determination would outweigh theirs. After a few minutes, I didn't hear as many of them as I had before. Perhaps some of them turned back.

The path grew steeper and steeper the more the ground climbed toward the mountains. I saw a reflection of the light from the sliver of moon where the river curved around a boulder and headed toward the east, away from me. The sight brought back a flash of an image I had seen recently, but couldn't remember why. The night approached midnight of the autumn equinox, and I felt something stir inside me. I didn't know what, but it felt peaceful, so I let it lead me. Almost instantly, the pictures I had seen before, when that guy had spoken into my head, came rushing back into memory—what was his name? He said he cared about me. Gallad! That was his name. He told me to follow the pull—the pull to what? I couldn't remember, but I trusted him, I knew that much. Other landmark sights started popping into my head, so I turned toward them or swerved around them, but follow them I did.

I didn't know how many hours had gone by, or where I was, but I was exhausted. I didn't hear anyone behind me, but that didn't mean they weren't there. Dante had said they wanted to follow me somewhere—I couldn't remember where, but it was where I was trying to go, where what's-his-name was leading me . . . Ugh! Gallad! Why couldn't I keep him in my head?

The farther I went, the more defeated I felt. I couldn't remember most of the time where I was headed. I only followed a gut feeling and the pull of my heart toward somewhere north. I hoped something or someone waited for me when I got there, because I was the one being hunted now. The Blackstones were the epitome of stealth, but I still felt that faint warmth behind my neck, indicating a hunter was near.

Unable to take one more step, I stopped to rest for a minute. My breathing was labored, and my heart was about to explode through my rib cage. If I stopped for long, though, I wouldn't want to keep going. I never thought I might die from exhaustion until now, but it was highly plausible. Voices sounded in the distance, though I couldn't discern how far away or who they were.

"Macy? Can you hear me?" the voice in my head spoke to me again.

"Where are you?" I panted, catching my breath.

"You're close, Macy. I can feel the connection between us stronger than before."

"I don't remember where I'm going. I keep trying to remember you, but right now you're my conscience. I know I trust you, but the memory of you keeps slipping through my fingers!" Tears fell down my face, air stuck in my throat as I hiccupped, and I crouched down, lowering my head in defeat.

"I believe in you, Macy. You have always been strong. Know that I love you, trust that. We're waiting for you."

"Where do I go?"

"Look up into the sky. Can you see the light coming off the horizon in the east, where the sun begins to rise?"

I looked but didn't quite see it from where I was near the ground. I stood to see better. The sky was beginning to lighten to my right, though just barely. He must be higher up than I was still.

"Yeah, I think so."

"Head that way. Your real family is waiting for you."

My real family. I wish I could remember them.

I turned around to smack right into Sunny. Cute little Sunny snuck up on me, and I had no idea how.

"Sunny! You frightened me. You shouldn't be out here so late. Are you alone?" I cautiously looked around her, but didn't see anyone. I couldn't believe they would let her out this far on her own. Yes, we might have been hunters, but we were trained specifically for witches —there were still a lot of other dangers in the forest, especially at night.

"I followed you." She shrugged like it was no big deal. "I'm better at following than the others."

"What happens now?" I tried to determine what her purpose was in following me.

"I . . . I just wanted you to know I heard the older girls talking about how they set you up when you first came to live with us," she started, uncharacteristically shy.

I didn't have time for this. She was stalling so the others could catch up, I was sure. She piqued my curiosity, though. "What do you mean?"

"You didn't kill that witch."

"Yes, I did. I woke up and found him."

"You don't remember. They shot you with a tranq dart and staged the entire thing so you would come and stay with us. Charlie is the one who killed him." Sunny looked mad and yet also unsure. I almost felt bad for her. If I could take her with me I would, but then I'd be a kidnapper like they had been to me. When she was older, she could choose.

"Sunny, when you're older, if you ever want to join my family, I will find you." I watched her reaction, but her expression changed. She looked much older than she had seconds ago.

"Thanks, Macy, but why would I want to do that? I'm having fun for now." She turned to leave.

"That's it? You're leaving? You're not telling the others where I am?"

"Nope. You should be able to leave if you want. But I thought you should know the truth. Bye, Macy." Taking off at a run, she didn't even look back.

"Goodbye, Sunny."

That was my cue to head toward the rising sun.

CHAPTER 14

*O*oices assaulted me from overhead. I was so focused on putting one step in front of the other, I almost didn't realize someone called my name. I was beyond exhausted, but had to keep going.

"Macy! Macy!" A woman yelled to me.

I looked up, almost blinded by the sun, but there on a large rock jutting out over my head was a woman. She was older than me, but looked like me with blond hair and the same sharp blue eyes. Running down to meet me was a man who was old enough to be my father with kind eyes the same shape as mine. He, too, called me by name. Could they be . . . could they be my parents?

"Macy! You're really here!"

"Are you all right? Get her some water, somebody!"

"Where are the others? Are they following you?"

All the voices blurred together. I stopped and sagged to the ground, falling to my knees. I had nothing left. The woman ran down to join the man.

"Did I find you? Are you my parents?" I mumbled, my mouth dry from dehydration and exertion.

"She doesn't remember, Reggie. She's still beyond the wards." The woman sank in front of me, pulling me to her chest. Sobs wracked her body. "I'm your mother, Macy. And I'm so sorry. I knew you could do it."

The man next to her embraced us both, also crying. "I'm your daddy, Macy. We were so worried, missed you so much, didn't know how to find you . . ." All his words came out in a rushed jumble.

I didn't know how much time went by. They slowly administered water to me in small doses so I wouldn't be sick and gave me food, too. Slowly I recovered enough to stand up. They helped me and wouldn't let go of me until I was strong enough on my own.

"Let's go home," the woman who called herself my mom said.

"Yes, let's." A man's voice preceded him as he stepped out from behind a large rock formation. I froze. Dante.

"Oh no," I whispered. "They did follow me. I'm sorry."

"It's part of the plan," my daddy whispered into my ear. "Just wait."

"Dante, I see you haven't changed," my mother addressed him, standing tall, every bit the hunter as the rest of those coming up behind Dante. She appeared strong and fierce. I'm sure I knew she could be, but I still couldn't remember.

"Indeed, I have not." He inclined his head like he was being properly introduced. "It's nice to see you, Lilith. I enjoyed getting to know your protégé." He waited for a response, but when she gave him none, he continued, "You look very much like my sister Marie when she was young. Where is she? I should like to say hello." He sneered in the subtlest way, his intention quite clear in his eyes.

"She died back in 2000. I'm sorry to be the one to inform you," Lilith replied flatly. "But somehow I think the sadness of it will be lost on you."

Something flashed across his eyes, disappointment to not get to face her or that he didn't get to kill her? Or perhaps genuine sadness for the loss of his sister?

"Odd she would die still quite young. Might you know why, matriarch of your family?" He taunted her.

"I do, in fact. Because we have chosen not to hunt witches and kill them for sport, our life spans are shortened without the excess energy in our bodies."

I didn't know that.

"Very good. Did you also know that I have many male hunters in my family? I heard you might have one in yours? I'm sure you know how you get one of those, too?" Dante smirked, not waiting for her answer. My mom stood proud, unmovable. The only thing she gave away was the slightest twitch in the corner of her eye, but unless you looked, no one would have seen it. I would have to ask her about that. Based on her expression, my mom had no intention of replying to his comment.

"Now, if you'll continue, we would love to be introduced to your quaint little town. Havenwood Falls is it?"

"Dante, you will never see Havenwood Falls. We won't let you." My dad stepped up to the plate. Though he was a human, he apparently was a badass one.

Dante laughed in his face, but my dad stood strong. "Oh and I suppose you are going to stop me. You and what army?"

He gestured to the hunters standing behind him, lined up and awaiting instructions. Many of them glared at me, but some refused to look at me, including Nala. I thought I could find a friend in her, but I guess not. The only one remotely curious or pleased to see me was little Sunny. I couldn't even believe she was still with them. I gave her a curious look, but she held her finger up in front of her mouth, telling me to keep our secret.

"This army," Lilith said without removing her gaze from Dante. As she said it, other hunters from our family stepped from behind trees and rocks where they had apparently been hiding and waiting, wielding a variety of menacing weapons. Then the biggest surprise was the witches, who stepped out in droves. My arms tingled so badly, I had to grip them to keep them from shaking. How were my mom and the other hunters so still, so unaffected by their presence?

Dante grimaced and released a growl unlike any I had a heard a man make. The other hunters shifted on their feet, prepared for a fight. Instead they got a huge surprise when the witches started a spell in unison. Holding out their hands, they blew a red sparkly dust. With the aid of the wind, the dust carried straight into the faces of all the hunters standing with Dante. I scrambled back closer to my parents, not wanting to get hit with whatever that dust was.

Dante and the others batted at their faces as they turned and headed the opposite direction, down the mountain. My mouth gaped in awe.

"What just happened? They were going to fight, and now they're leaving?" I asked, baffled.

"The witches came up with the plan with the help of your boyfriend, Gallad. It is a forgetting spell that will misdirect them temporarily and cause them to forget what they were searching for. However, it's only temporary. Once the wards are reinforced, they will be redirected anytime they come close again," she explained, helping me up to my feet again.

"Thank you," I said, but then turned to face everyone there. "Thank you, all of you." I sobbed out a hiccup and wiped the tears from my eyes again. It was all over. I was safe.

"Can we go home now? I'd like to try to remember it," I asked sheepishly.

"You'll remember everything just fine, sweetheart," my dad said, reaching for my hand, and I let him take it.

"How can you be so sure?"

"Because the wards are created to protect the town, but once you're back in it, and with the help of the Luna Coven, you should regain all your memories," Mom supplied.

"It could be a slow adjustment, though, so don't get discouraged if it's not instantaneous," my dad added.

"Then let's go home."

"Not until I get to see her," a young male shouted from behind a crowd of witches as he pushed through. Tall, athletic, with floppy brown hair and sharp green eyes I would remember even in my darkest moments—he had to be Gallad. I couldn't remember my connection with him, other than I had one. My arms tingled even more as he came closer. I had to fist my hands at my sides to keep them from shaking again. *Breathe in through my nose and out through my mouth.* I didn't want to hurt him.

"You helped me get home," I stated, not taking my eyes off him as he strode slowly forward. I felt stalked as he did so. The witch pursued the hunter.

"I did. I couldn't go on without you," he whispered roughly, but my ears heard it clear as a bell.

"I felt you here," I placed my hand on my heart, then on my head, "and here, guiding me."

"I knew you could make it." He believed in me from the start.

"Can you forgive me for leaving?" I felt small like a child, but I had to ask, had to know.

"Always," came his reply.

I couldn't stand the distance anymore. I ran toward him and threw myself at him, knocking him onto the ground. Hearing the gasps and shouts from those around us, I pulled back but Gallad wouldn't let go. He gripped me tight and held me to him.

"Stop, Macy. Don't hurt him," hunters shouted at me.

"Get out of the way, boy," the witches yelled.

I looked up in utter shock. "You all thought I was attacking him? Give me a little credit. I learned to control my hunting side—kind of," I said, looking down at my shaking hands, but Gallad covered them in his at his chest. Looking into those eyes, I asked him, "Did you think I was attacking you?"

"Of course not. I might not mind if you did, though." He winked at me. I couldn't believe he actually said it. Though he was still a stranger to me, I had to remember that we had a history and maybe talked like that all the time. I giggled, embarrassed others were watching.

"I didn't kill that witch. They set me up," I confessed to him, since I had told him the entire story.

"I didn't believe it for one minute," he stated, and I saw the truth in his eyes. "My Macy could never do that, even in the worst situation."

My Macy, he had said. It warmed my heart, and I melted into him. "I can't wait to remember you."

"So you've said." Gallad laughed, then kissed me on the lips in front of everyone, including my parents.

My dad cleared his throat. "Okay, show's over. Let's get her home."

EPILOGUE

*T*he week after I returned home was supposed to be for me to rest and regain my memories. Some came back all in a rush when I crossed the border of Havenwood Falls, but others still came slowly or as events and people were brought up. It was maddening how slow it was at times. My parents had given me the week to get ready to start school once October came. Plus, I had agreed my mom could put me through orientation, a sort of Hunters 101, on my eighteenth birthday, October thirteenth.

Gallad and Ruby had come to the house every day, or I met them in town at Broastful Brew or Coffee Haven, depending on the day. I was told I could start up work again part-time at Broastful Brew this fall when I felt ready.

Gallad had shared how he told my parents everything I had told him once he was able to communicate with me. My mom interjected that Aunt Letti had shared with them details of the hunters and her stay with them. My grandmother had been instrumental in retrieving Letitia with her husband a long time ago, and had been introduced to Dante then. My mom had met him later, but I still didn't know the story there yet. She hadn't realized they had been so close to our home. Mom blamed herself, saying she should have known. But after my ordeal, she set a watch schedule for the hunters to be on the lookout for Dante's possible return and even posted someone in the town of Durango on and off to keep tabs on them.

My mom had apologized profusely that she had not prepared me sooner. She thought she still had time, so she let me keep pushing her away. She was upset she hadn't forced the issue, though that rarely worked out well. My mom was not one to apologize, so it was a big deal.

I told Mom and Dad outside of Brice's hearing that Dante did in fact have other male hunters, and I wanted to know why we didn't have any other than Brice. He was going to ask, and I didn't want him to be blindsided like I had been.

"I will tell you, Macy, I promise, but it's not for right now. I will explain it to you and Brice as he gets a little older," was all Mom had to say, though her eyes glossed over with the pain of a time she would have rather forgotten. I guess I had to take it one step at a time with my mom.

The first full day I was awake—I slept the first real day—members from the Court of the Sun and the Moon accompanied by the Luna Coven came to see me. They wanted a full report, which I gave, leaving nothing out. They had asked if I was prepared to receive my Havenwood Falls tattoo, to choose to be a full-fledged citizen of the town, even though I wasn't quite eighteen as my family's custom dictated. It was close enough. They explained how it would work.

Some might say I was trading my freedom to be less than I was created to be and marked by a town in secrecy. All I had to do was envision Gallad's bright green eyes and I knew my future was with him and this town. It was the easiest choice I'd ever made, and in that peace, I felt the freedom I desired.

The day before I would go back to school, Gallad surprised me. I was helping out at the vineyard, soaking in the afternoon sun, and relishing the smells of grapes and smoke from the fire pit as we burned debris in preparation for winter. The aspens had turned colors, and fall was in full swing. It was everything that I loved about living in the mountains. He brought our friends with him to the vineyard and had pre-arranged with my parents a bonfire party to celebrate my official return. As the evening fell and the stars became visible, I realized I could never see the stars and night sky anywhere in the world like I could in my own backyard. It was amazing.

"Macy?" Gallad called from the other side of the fire towering above my head.

"Where are you?" I hollered back, giggling.

"On the other side!"

When I rounded the large fire, passing various friends, I found Gallad standing in a circle of things I loved. Grapes, a stack of books, small glow-in-the-dark stars, one of my pink coffee travel mugs with steam escaping the lid, a bowl of kettle corn, a pile of scattered notes of welcome from my friends, a bottle of my favorite wine from my family's vineyard, and a few things I had given Gallad over the last couple years. I was so stunned, I didn't know what to do.

"What . . . ?" I barely got out, as suddenly my throat was choked up.

"Macy, these are all the things you love . . ."

"With you at the center of them," Ruby shouted playfully behind me, and everyone giggled or agreed around us.

"Yes, I'm hoping I continue to be at the center of them." He gave Ruby a wink, then turned back to me. "Macy, will you go to homecoming with me? The theme this year is *Written in the Stars,* and I want you to know I would travel through time and space to get to you, always."

"Yes! Of course I will go with you!"

I ran to him inside the circle and kissed him full on the mouth. It was going to be an epic time to remember.

I KNEW Dante and the other hunters would eventually seek out a way to discover Havenwood Falls again, but for now I, and the town, were safe. We'd be ready for them. The Blackstone family of Havenwood Falls would protect their own; we had the weapons to prove it. When I saw the witches and hunters carrying the weapons together in the forest I was amazed, but finding out they were our own creation that we made secretly to protect the town, I was even more in awe at my family.

I once thought I had been denied my heritage by suppressing the darker side of it. Truthfully, once I received my new permanent tattoo, the one I chose to be marked with, I realized I was free to be me without the extra fight. I still had all my other hunter tendencies—I would never be denied those—but I could control them and use them to protect the town I loved. I had truly been reawakened, and I never wanted to forget again.

ABOUT THE AUTHOR

Morgan Wylie is an award-winning and *USA Today* Bestselling author with several genres published from YA fantasy to adult paranormal romance, as well as other stories in between! Morgan published her first novel, *Silent Orchids,* one year after moving across the country with her family on a journey of new discovery. After an amazing three years in Nashville, Tennessee, and the release of two more books, Morgan and her family found their way back to the Northwest, where they now reside. Still working every day with great optimism, Morgan continues to embrace all things: "Mama," wife, teacher, and mediator to the many voices and muses constantly chattering in her head, where it gets pretty loud!

You can find her and news on her books at the following:
MorganWylie.net
Morgan Wylie Books on Facebook
@MWylieBooks on Twitter and Instagram

ACKNOWLEDGMENTS

First, I'd like to thank Kristie Cook for her amazing imagination and her generous heart to include others in her vision of Havenwood Falls. It's an honor to work with her and the other wonderful authors that are quickly filling up Havenwood Falls! I've loved working with her; her attention to detail, organization, and patience has strengthened me as a writer.

Next, a big thank you to my family—my husband and my daughter—as they were so supportive and patient with me while working on this project. I wouldn't be who I am today without them. And to my first readers on this project: my mom and my #LoveWriteCreate crew, Gaby Robbins and Kallie Ross. Thank you.

And last, but definitely not least, I'd like to thank YOU, the reader. Thank you for your support and for hanging out in Havenwood Falls with me!

THE FALL

BY KRISTEN YARD

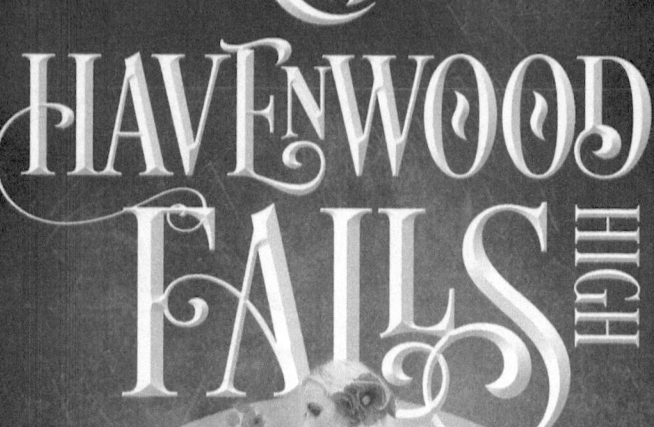

HAVENWOOD FALLS HIGH

The Fall

KRISTEN YARD

~ A Havenwood Falls Young Adult Novella ~

For Alexa
My love for you is water.
Undying, life-giving,
in this world and beyond—always.

If you are falling...dive.
~ Joseph Campbell

CHAPTER 1

*L*ight glimmers through the ceiling of a cavern. Moonlight morphs the water into a sea of diamonds, bobbing gently against rock walls. Water roars in the distance. I sit up, assessing the situation.

Where am I?

How did I wind up in a cave, when I swear I just laid my head down for a quick couch nap? Glancing down at my bare feet, I note the dirt on them. *Where are my shoes?*

I steady myself and then rise to my feet, looking for an exit, but there isn't one. My heart ricochets off my rib cage as I run my hands along the wall, edging my toes over the tiny strip of stone separating me from the water.

"Help!" I call, sifting through memories of the day, trying to piece together what could have led to this.

School, then a Coffee Haven stop with my best friend, Nikki Morris, and her new boyfriend, Max Cooper, then home, and couch.

So how am I here? And what is this place?

My mind flashes to the lagoon behind the tiny distributary waterfall that runs from Havenwood Falls into my own backyard, but the lagoon looks nothing like this. There is definitely an exit to that cavern.

My hands go clammy. Max was the one who grabbed our coffees from the barista and brought them to the table. Logan Andrews, my and Nikki's other best friend, is convinced that Max brought not only designer clothes, but also designer drugs with him when he moved here from New York City.

He drugged us. That's it. Oh my God. Nikki.

Whatever fear I have for my own well-being takes a back seat to the throat-tightening terror of picturing my bestie tied up in a trunk—or worse.

"NIKKI!" My voice breaks into a sob. Then I clamp my hands over my mouth, realizing that Max might still be in the vicinity. *What if I got away and am now luring him back to finish me off? No. I have to find a way out and call for help.*

Losing my footing, I slide down onto my knees, my arms flailing out to catch me before I fall into the lagoon.

I fight to catch my breath and then notice a sound that picks up over the surrounding cacophony of rushing water.

Whispers. Layers of them, building upon one another.

I freeze, trying to focus in, past the rushing falls, so that I can understand what they are saying. All the while, my mind begs me to run, but I cannot move.

The whispers finally come together into one voice.

"Serenaaaaaa."

It comes directly from the water in front of me. With a gulp, I take a breath and then lean forward, until I am directly over the brackish pool.

The inky clouds clear. An emerald light shines from below the surface, revealing a woman in the depths. Her blond hair cascades around her in waves, concealing her face.

I lean in closer, and the current finally moves enough of her flaxen strands that I can make out her features. A porcelain face with a pointy chin, long eyelashes, a slightly turned-up nose, and full, pink lips. The birthmark on her left cheek sends my heart stuttering, but when her eyes snap open, revealing piercing blue irises, I scream.

Because the girl in the water is me.

Her eyes glow. She shoots up, water droplets glittering around her. She smirks and then pulls me in, as I scream and kick, trying to break free.

~

"SERENA? SERENA!" Aunt Odette yells, as I attempt punching my way to freedom. "Hey! Million Dollar Baby! It's just me, your adorable aunt, trying to wake you up to give you cake and presents. Can you please refrain from killing me?"

I blink a couple of times. The warm glow of the fireplace and the log walls of my family's cabin releases the knot in my stomach.

"You feeling okay, honey?" Aunt Odette's face eclipses my view of the room. Her sky-blue eyes narrow in concern, and she places a hand on my forehead.

"Yeah . . . just a wicked nightmare."

"You want to talk about it?" she asks, rubbing my shoulder.

I shudder. "No, I'm good."

Slowly, I sit up and stretch, shaking the dream off. "So, what's this you said about cake? And did you make it yourself?" I ask, eyeing her, because I love my aunt, but she cannot cook to save her life.

She grins. "Yes, I did. But no worries. I've been practicing! Oh, Serena." She sighs in disapproval.

"What?" I yawn.

"Your feet are filthy. Next time, can you please clean them off before you put them on the furniture?"

The knot returns to my stomach, and I lean over to examine them. My eyes frantically search through the pile of shoes by the door, and I try to remember what I had worn to school. Sandals would explain dirt, but it's too cool for sandals. *It was a dream. How would this even be possible?*

"Okay, okay, I'm sorry for channeling Grandma. That even weirded *me* out," she says, misunderstanding my reaction.

I let out a nervous laugh, and she pulls me to my feet, smoothing my hair.

"And about that cake, oh, ye of little faith. You never know, it could actually be the best of your life." She winks and leads me into the chilly October night.

We walk through our yard, nestled beside Mount Alexa and surrounded by the woods on all sides. Our roaring mini waterfall is a curtain to the lagoon I explored as a little girl, sitting behind our cabin. The thought of it brings me back to the cavern in my nightmare, speeding up my heart, as my mind continues to try making sense of what just happened.

The memory of glowing eyes in the water quickens my pace toward our family's business, the Fallview Grill & Tavern, which is on our property, but higher up the mountain.

"Why are we going here instead of just eating in the house?" I ask.

"Man, are you writing a novel or something? Why all the questions? Maybe I just didn't want to burn the house down. You know, since you think I suck at all things culinary."

"But your heart is in the right place," I offer.

She snorts and then gestures toward the entrance of our restaurant. "Hey, can you open the door? I messed my back up earlier."

"How?" I ask in concern, holding the door open for her to pass.

"SURPRISE!" a group of people shout. I fall back against the door, laughing as my aunt winks.

"Gotcha!" she singsongs, leading me over to the small gathering of our family and friends.

The rustic lodge vibe of the tavern is at odds with the very feminine lavender and silver streamers, balloons, and number-18 decorations strewn about.

Nikki and Logan come up to me first. In the time since we left school this afternoon, Nikki's long wavy brown hair has been hacked into a shoulder-length bob. I gasp as I take it in, flashing Logan a confused look. He barely nods in what I take as quiet agreement that he's as shocked as I am by Nikki's new do.

"Oh!"

"Ya like?" she asks.

I gape at Nikki, because her hair has been one of her most prized physical traits as far back as I can remember.

Her face falls. "You don't like. Clearly."

"*I* don't like," my little sister Laurel pipes up.

Nikki narrows her eyes. "Nobody asked you, Felicia."

"Laurel!" Lena, my other little sister and Laurel's twin, scolds her, as I glare at Laurel. She shrugs. Her white-blond hair shines under the lights as she plops down on the couch and starts texting someone. My phone beeps. I pull it out of my pocket and then turn toward Laurel after reading the text.

"You couldn't just say 'happy birthday' instead of texting it?"

She shrugs again, and Lena comes up and gives me a quick hug.

"Happy birthday, sis."

"Thanks, Bug,"

When I glance up, my best friend still looks aggravated.

"Nikki, I think your hair is adorable. You just caught everyone by surprise," I protest, wrapping my arms around her.

"Happy birthday, babe," she says, kissing my cheek.

Honestly, Nikki's new look does frame her pixie-like features, high cheekbones, and doe eyes to perfection. It's just that she has been undergoing some pretty weird and major personality changes over the past few months, which have left Logan and me worrying. The brooding dark-haired guy in expensive clothing trailing her is one of Logan's biggest concerns when it comes to Nikki's strange, new behavior.

"Hey, Max," I say, still uneasy from his appearance in my dream. Misplaced or not.

"Happy natal day," Max says.

I blink and then smile, but Logan rolls his eyes.

"Hey," I say to Logan when he wraps his broad arms around me, pulling me in for one of his famous, all-encompassing hugs. His familiar woodsy scent nestles around me.

"Happy birthday, Rena. Sorry. My, uh, dad couldn't make it," he says to Aunt Odette, who waves it off.

"One Andrews is plenty, and you're my favorite of the lot," she teases, knowing as well as I do how much it hurts Logan that his dad is such a workaholic. Mr. Andrews owns a contracting firm that builds cabins for anyone, from the professional mountain man to the tourist who just wants to build a summer home. He has allowed work to become his new wife in the wake of Logan's mom's death a few years back.

"Thanks for coming," I say, extricating myself from the awkwardly long hug.

Logan grins and slowly releases his hold. His gray eyes sparkle down on me, and he runs a hand through his sandy-blond hair.

Nikki's parents, Aunt Brynna and Uncle Christian, emerge from the kitchen with Simon Turner, the only person on the Alverson property who can cook worth a damn and the chef of the business.

Aunt Odette went to high school with Nikki's mom and dad. She and Aunt Brynna grew up together and have been best friends as far back as they can remember. Hence the whole "aunt" and "uncle" thing.

I catch a whiff of the dish that Simon carries, and my stomach rumbles.

"I even surprised myself with this one. Vegan ratatouille, for our little humanitarian artist." He grins.

"She's not so little anymore, Simon," Aunt Brynna teases.

Aunt Odette sighs, and Aunt Brynna squeezes her lightly around the shoulder.

"Just think, they're us, basically yesterday," Aunt Odette says, staring at me and Nikki.

Nikki snorts. "Yeah, if yesterday was 1972."

Aunt Brynna raises an eyebrow. "Actually, we were 90s kids, brat." We laugh, but I can't tell if Aunt Brynna was just teasing Nikki, or if she meant to be nastier with that word choice.

Aunt Odette eyes the two of us with a smile. "It's weird, looking at them, isn't it?" she says to Aunt Brynna. "Like looking at old pictures of ourselves." She flashes a wistful smile.

"Pfft, they're the knock-off us," Aunt Brynna says. They both dissolve into peals of laughter.

Simon hands them fresh glasses of white wine. "Well, at least they are entertaining," he says to Uncle Christian, nodding toward my two aunts.

Uncle Christian chuckles and then walks up to me.

"Happy birthday, Serena," he says, giving me a hug that Aunt Brynna and Aunt Odette both pile on top of.

"Simon, help!" I squeak.

From his place by the bar, Simon calls the adults over, pouring Uncle Christian a beer, and already refilling Aunt Brynna's and Aunt Odette's glasses of wine that they somehow managed to suck down.

"Man, do you think we will be total lushes like that in our forties?" Nikki says, a little too loudly. "I mean, what else is there to do in the mountains?"

"Nikkola!" Aunt Brynna scolds, glaring over her shoulder. In all fairness, the only time Aunt Odette drinks is when Aunt Brynna comes over. But Aunt Brynna has earned her wino title.

"Not in our forties yet," Aunt Odette calls over her shoulder, before turning back to whatever she and Simon are discussing.

"Hey, beer wench!" Nikki calls to Simon. "I made Serena a birthday playlist. Hook my phone up to the sound system?"

"Depends what's on it." Simon folds his arms across his chest, an unlikely indie-snob-banter-bond existing between them.

"LCD Soundsystem, Belle and Sebastian, Mitski, The Rapture . . ."

"Yes, yes, yes, no."

"Simon . . ." I pout.

"Fine." He accepts Nikki's phone and syncs her music to the speakers.

She grins. "You're a gentleman and a scholar. So . . . what do you want to do first, Serena? Open your presents! I can't wait to give you ours. I almost ruined it eleventy times today alone!"

"Yes!" I grin back.

"Nikkola, that's after dinner," Aunt Brynna calls back.

"Her sense of hearing is annoyingly far-reaching," Nikki mutters.

"Oh, what does it matter, Brynna? If Serena wants to open presents, let her," Uncle Christian says.

"Yeah, the food has to cool a little anyway," Simon offers.

"Okay, ours first!" Nikki claps her hands together. I can feel her mother's eyes on her and glance in her direction.

Sure enough, Aunt Brynna glares daggers. *What the heck?* Nikki isn't even doing anything. Thankfully, Nikki doesn't seem to notice. It's not the first time that her overbearing mom has come down on her hard while drinking.

Nikki hands me a lavender gift bag. I look at my present pile and smile because everything is lavender.

"Man, you guys have my number, huh?" I joke.

The adults laugh, and my friends and Lena grin at me. Laurel is consumed by whatever is on her phone.

Nikki shoves the gift bag in my face. I reach in, and crushed velvet melts into my hands as I pull out a hunter-green vintage Fendi hobo bag, without one drop of leather on it. Charcoal beads stipple the front and back.

"Oh, Nik! How in the world?" There's no way she makes enough to buy this purse, waiting tables here for Aunt Odette and Simon part time.

Max grins, and I have my answer.

"Callie helped locate it. Wasn't easy, since Fendi is known for leather," Nikki says.

Inner conflict wrinkles my nose, because I refuse to own anything that means an animal died for me to have it.

"Callie and I even made sure that the freaking velvet and the satin lining came from vegan sources. Let me tell you how fun that was. I swear, not one creature died in the making of this bag." Nikki reassures me.

"Except for a hippie's bell bottoms," Simon cracks.

"Nikki, this is too much!" I gasp, twirling it around in my hand, and then standing to admire it on my arm.

"My best friend only turns eighteen once. Plus, Callie was really cool about it. She said it's the one piece that has entered her shop that she knows with one-hundred-percent certainty you won't . . . 'defile'? I believe that was the word she chose."

Aw, Callie. I make a mental note to not hack any vintage finds from her consignment shop for at least a few weeks.

"She even let me make payments. Max offered to pay for the whole thing, but that's not how I roll." Nikki winks.

"I love it." I breathe out, still admiring it. All the planning Nikki clearly put into the gift chokes me up.

"Open the inside pocket!" she says.

"But—" I object, because there had better not be anything else.

Four xx tickets slip into my hands.

I glance up, and Uncle Christian and Aunt Brynna raise their glasses, acknowledging their contribution to my amazing gift.

"The xx?" I shriek. "NO WAY!"

They have sold out the past couple of times Nikki and I have tried to see them in Red Rocks.

"Happy birthday, kiddo!" Uncle Christian calls.

"Happy birthday to all of us!" Nikki grins, pulling me up to dance around in circles with her, Max, and the tickets. Logan steps to the side, but still smiles, holding a hand out to spin Nikki.

I set the tickets and purse down so I can hug her and awkwardly hug Max, all the while feeling guilty for my weird dream involving him. Then I head over to Uncle Christian and Aunt Brynna and hug them, too.

"You do have more presents over there." Aunt Odette winks, taking a sip from her glass.

"I'll go put the food back in the oven, because I'm guessing it's cooler than we want." Simon heads toward the table to check on it.

"Sorry!" I call after him, but he waves me off, laidback as ever.

When I head back over to my present pile, I unwrap a beautiful crystal bracelet from Logan, with matching earrings.

"Oh, wow—this is gorgeous. Thank you!" I say. He wraps me in another of those hugs that are starting to feel less friendly and more like something else, so I clear my throat and step back.

Simon's gifts are quite predictable. Two new PlayStation games, because I am the only one who plays with him.

"Are these for me or you?" I ask, holding them up, and he laughs.

"Open mine next," Laurel demands. And since it's weird for her to openly participate in anything these days, I go along with it.

Nikki hands me a lavender box. I open the lid and then narrow my eyes when I pull out the vintage Ramones shirt that *I* bought from Callie's Consignments and spent close to five hours hacking the back of so that I could weave glass beads into it. Of course, I had to hide this from Callie, because she considers my vintage clothing hacks to basically be sacrilege.

I stand up, letting the box fall from my lap, the shirt in my hands.

"Are you *kidding* me? My Ramones shirt!"

I have been searching for it since August. I wanted to wear it on the first day of school and had accused Laurel of stealing it. I even got in trouble, because I had gone after her, and Aunt Odette didn't find the shirt in her room.

Nikki snorts and then covers her mouth, forcing a straight face.

"What?" Laurel demands. "I wanted to give you something I knew you would love."

"Hey, twisted little ray of sunshine," Aunt Odette says to Laurel from the bar. "You and I are talking later."

"Here, open mine?" Lena asks, handing me a large gift bag. "It's actually from Laurel, too."

"Is not," Laurel grumbles.

I pat Lena's hand, because she is forever the peacemaker of the house. I open the bag and find the three-hundred-count Prismacolor pencil set I have been drooling over, along with a portable easel and three sketchpads, all with different types of paper.

"Lena!" I say in shock.

"Check out the easel." Simon points the bottleneck in his hand toward it. "She spent hours at my place painting it for you, so you wouldn't see it."

I pull the easel from the bag. The cherry wood has been covered in cherry blossom branches, with petals falling.

"Oh, Bug. This is amazing." I set it down and pull my youngest sister in so I can give her a squeeze, her face beet-red.

Lena mumbles, "Just wanted to give you something you can hang on to."

"It's perfect," I say.

"Yeah, just like *she* is," Laurel mutters.

Lena's eyes glisten, and she looks away.

"Aaaaaaaaand later is now. Kitchen," Aunt Odette says.

"Big surprise," Laurel snaps, stomping through the dining area to follow our aunt.

Simon sighs. I hug Lena and whisper encouragement that I know falls on deaf ears.

Before hormones, Laurel was one of my favorite people to spend time with. Now, not so much.

One present sits in the once-full pile. A lavender envelope with Aunt Odette's handwriting. She is still in the kitchen, her voice raising as she tries to talk sense into my sister, so I place it in the back pocket of my jeans.

Logan touches my shoulder. "Hey, can I talk to you for a second?"

My throat tightens, because I'm not ready to talk about what I think he wants to discuss. I nod anyway.

Logan leads the way to the patio door. Nikki waggles her eyebrows at us as we walk by. I narrow my eyes at her.

Logan holds the door open for me. The globe lights that Simon strung on the wooden railings and the metal awning cast a hazy glow over the mist coming off Havenwood Falls.

I walk to the railing and glance down at the waterfall that the patio overlooks. I have often wondered if this was the best location for a bar patio.

The roar of the water sends a chill through my spine, reminding me of my dream, and I shiver violently.

"You cold?" Logan asks, shrugging out of his red flannel shirt before I can answer.

I nod, and he helps me slip my arms into it.

"Thanks, but now aren't you cold?" I ask, gesturing toward his black T-shirt.

"The way Coach had us running laps after bombing out last week, I think I'll be toasty all winter," he jokes, referring to their big loss, which wiped out all chances of a homecoming game.

"So, uh, thanks for my gift," I say, glancing down at the charcoal crystals that glitter on my wrist. I realize that it's the exact same shade as the beads on my purse, which is still on my arm, because I am in love.

He smiles. "Nikki and I coordinated."

"I'm so lucky. I really do have the best best-friends a girl could ask for."

He winces a little, and I clear my throat. It feels like ever since we became seniors, Logan and I have fallen out of sync.

"Speaking of Nikki . . ." Logan says. "That's why I asked you out here."

"Oh?" I try to cover the relief in my voice, but I am almost positive I fail.

He hesitates for a moment. "Yeah, I still think Max is giving her drugs of some sort."

"I don't know, Logan. Max seems really nice."

"Why is everyone so blind? Nikki is clearly exhibiting classic signs of drug use, ever since dating him. Drastic change in appearance, ditching school, and she's mean all the time," he says.

"I just feel like if it were the case, I would *know*."

"Oh, are you 'psychic' like she is, too?" He rolls his eyes. As kids, Nikki always teased us that she was a witch. In middle school, that switched to botched fortune telling.

"I won't argue some of those points. Something is definitely going on, but I just don't get that vibe from Max like you do."

"Is it because he bought you an expensive purse?" Logan snaps.

"Um, wow. No," I answer in the same frosty tone.

He sighs and scrubs his hair with both hands. "I'm sorry. That was stupid."

"Yeah, it was." I bump his shoulder with mine. "But I know you meant well. You care about her. I get it."

"Well, talk to her or something, please?" He asks. "Nik and I are in such a weird place ever since that douchenozzle came to town. She doesn't really talk to me or hang out anymore, like it bothers him or something."

"And you're so welcoming and friendly to Max. It's mind-boggling, really!" I tease.

He mutters something under his breath.

"I'll tell you what. I'll work on talking to Nikki, but can you please work on being open to Max? You could be wrong about him. Plus, it will make her happy if we can all be friends."

"The hell does she care what I think?" He mumbles.

I cock my head to the side and flash him a *duh* look. "You know you've always been a sort of big brother figure to her. When she picks on you, it's because she feels like you don't approve of her anymore. She's hurt, so she lashes out at you."

"She has changed so much. I don't even know if I would be friends with this Nikki if we had just met," he grumbles.

"Well, that's not the case. She's always been there for us, Logan. A few years ago, did she leave you hanging when you needed her most?"

Logan looks away. I know bringing up his mom's death was a low blow, but he's so stubborn that I have to get through to him any way I can.

He sighs, and I know I have won. "Why do you girls have to be so damn complicated?"

I snort. "Yeah, *we* are the complicated ones. Reasons why I have basically always been single."

He mumbles something else.

"What?" I ask.

"Nothing. Look, we should head back in." He gestures toward the table that Simon and the other adults are busy filling with food.

"Wait." I grab Logan's wrist as he turns away.

He slowly turns to face me, his eyes sad.

"No matter what happens this year, the three of us stick together.

241

Right? If it's drugs, we deal with it and help her. If it's her psychotic mother, which is more likely the case, we deal with it and help her."

Logan glares at me. "And if it's the douche canoe from New York, *I* will deal with it."

"Logan," I sigh.

He grins, dimples appearing. "I said I would try to get along with him, but I didn't agree to starting tonight."

Logan winks and then takes my hand and leads me inside.

CHAPTER 2

e all sit back in our chairs, stuffed with vegan ratatouille, French bread, various salads, and multiple French side dishes that Simon slaved over in preparation for my birthday dinner.

"Seriously, the best meal I have had in weeks," Logan says.

"Ha!" I shoot up in triumph, digging for my phone.

"What are you doing?" Logan asks.

"Wait." I set my voice recorder and then lean over the table so I am directly in front of him. "Please repeat what you said about a vegan dinner being amazing."

He snorts and bats my hand away. "Dork."

"Nerd," I fire back.

"Good God, get a room already," Laurel whines.

"Laurel!" Aunt Odette snaps, her cheeks rosy from the wine. "Apologize."

"So sorry." She rolls her eyes and then walks out of the tavern, toward the house.

"Laurel!" Aunt Odette calls after her.

"Let her go, Odette," Simon coaxes. "She needs to cool down."

Aunt Odette sighs. "I just don't understand what I am doing wrong with her."

Aunt Brynna leans against her, wrapping a bangle-clad arm around Aunt Odette's shoulders. "Nothing. It's not you. It's the age." She gestures toward Nikki when she says it.

Nikki's fork clatters onto her plate. "That's right, Brynna. Deflect that blame right back on the growing teen instead of the lies and pressure being placed on her by the parents."

"Nikki! That's enough," Uncle Christian thunders. I stop mid-chew. Uncle Christian never yells, but he probably spoke up because both of my aunts are still trying to remove their jaws from the table.

Nikki picks her fork back up and continues picking at the remaining food on her plate, like nothing happened.

"Apologize, right now," Uncle Christian continues.

"Aunt O, that wasn't meant for you, entirely, sorry. Brynna . . . nope," Nikki says, popping the p and then taking a bite of a roll while smirking at her mother.

Uncle Christian slides his chair back to stand, but Aunt Brynna shakes her head, never removing her eyes from her daughter.

"Christian, it's fine. Leave it. Nikkola, we will discuss this at home."

"Once the rosé is on ice, I'm sure," Nikki fires back.

An awkward silence settles over the room. Logan and I meet eyes, and he shakes his head, as if to say, "See?"

I try to catch Nikki's attention, but she won't look at me.

"Hey, I want to see this fabulous cake of yours, Odette." Simon's voice takes on a strained pitch, probably trying to distract everyone.

A smile brightens her face. "Ooh! Yes!"

Aunt Odette leaps from the table, also overly eager to move on from the weirdness, it seems. She returns with a four-tiered chocolate cake that looks like it could be from a wedding magazine.

"Aunt Odette!" My jaw hits the table. "How?"

"I've been practicing on slow days," she says, sticking candles in the cake.

Once they are lit, Simon dims the lights, and everyone sings. I smile through teary eyes, thinking of my mama's missing face, in addition to Laurel's.

I look up, and everyone stares at me.

Aunt Odette drapes her arms around me. "You should probably decide on a wish and blow them out before we eat wax, sweetheart."

"I know, it's just . . . I wish Mama had been well enough to be here," I whisper.

Aunt Odette sighs. "Honey, Margot is here in spirit, along with your father and others we have lost. I firmly believe that. But I do wish they were all here in person, too." She squeezes me.

I close my eyes to make the one wish I have always wanted—for my family to be complete again. For Mama to find a way to climb out of the mental prison she has been locked away in since Daddy died.

My candles flicker out, and everyone claps.

"Okay, drumroll!" Simon commands.

Aunt Odette shakes her head at him but grins as she slices into my beautiful cake.

And then it implodes.

Sticky goo runs all over the lavender lace table cloth, an erupting volcano of cake.

"Oh, crap!" Aunt Odette cries.

Aunt Brynna jumps up and runs into the kitchen to retrieve towels so we can help Aunt Odette mop it up.

"I cooked that sucker for hours!" Aunt Odette wails. "Serena, I am so sorry."

Everyone looks at me, wide-eyed, gauging my reaction.

Laughter rips through my body—painfully, given how full I am. A snort or two later, everyone joins in, tears running down some of their faces.

"I will never be able to cook," Aunt Odette hoots between gasps of air.

"Well, that's why you have me." Simon's eyes crinkle with amusement as he walks out of the kitchen. He'd managed to slip away unnoticed while we were all in hysterics.

In his arms is a less impressive, but hopefully cooked, two-layer cake with cream frosting and lavender pearl candies around the edges.

"I really wanted to support you, Odette. But, I also know you, so I ordered this from Health Nut weeks ago." Simon explains, referring to the health food store in town, owned by Stella Daryn, the mom of one of my classmates, Ellisyn.

"My hero." Aunt Odette winks at him, and my eyebrows raise. Has she finally figured out how perfect he is for her?

"Yeah, a regular knight in shining armor," Simon teases. He and Aunt Odette laugh so hard over that one that she snorts.

"I don't get how it's that funny," I say, one corner of my mouth poking up in reaction to them.

Aunt Odette waves me away, like it's an inside joke or something.

"Vegan carrot cake with cream cheese frosting, made from cashews. A little bird told me it's your favorite." Simon places it in front of me.

"Uh . . . I think I'll take my chances with Odette's cake." Logan winces at the smaller cake and Uncle Christian chuckles.

Simon opens a second package of candles.

"No, don't sing again, please." I blush, not wanting all the attention.

He nods, cutting and serving the cake instead.

I shift in my seat, and something digs into my back. "Ow!"

I glance behind me and pull Aunt Odette's gift from my back pocket.

"Oh, yay! Open!" she demands.

I take a couple of bites of the delicious cake first, trying to rein in my response to how good it is, not wanting to hurt my aunt's feelings. Then I tear the envelope open.

A card with a woman carrying a sleeping little girl, the girl's head on the woman's shoulder, is on the front. The woman faces the ocean, as the sun beats down.

The inside is blank, save for a scrawled note that says:

YOU WILL ALWAYS BE *our baby.*
   Even if you're too big to carry.

Happy 18th!
Love,
Aunt Odette and Mama

TWO ROUND-TRIP AIRLINE tickets to Paris fall out.

"Aunt Odette!" I gasp.

She grins. "I know you have been saving, but I wanted to do this for you."

I jump up from the table and crush her in a bear hug. My plans for a gap year, before finding a university somewhere overseas, and then studying art, haven't always been met with such enthusiasm from her. She squeezes me, and I settle back into my chair, looking at the tickets. I note the departure and arrival dates and have the reason for her excitement right in front of me.

"This is a two-week trip?" I ask.

Her smile falls into a straight line. "Yes, so you can sightsee with Nikki and explore, and then come back to start at a community school closer to home."

"But, I'm not coming back. Remember?" My mouth dries. "I have been saving for this for years. I am taking a year off and traveling. Then I will figure out what art school I want to attend, once I know for sure which country I want to stay in."

"Serena, I'm sorry, but that cannot happen," my aunt says.

"Brynna isn't allowing my Seattle plans, either," Nikki says shortly.

Aunt Brynna's eyes flash at Nikki.

Nikki continues, "Too bad for them that we are adults at eighteen, huh?"

"Nikkola, not another word," Aunt Brynna warns through clenched teeth.

Nikki glares at her.

My hands shake as I place the tickets on the table. Nikki is right. I am an adult now, well, in theory at least. As soon as I graduate, I am free to do what I want. I stand.

"Aunt Odette, thank you for this party, but no thank you for the gift. If they are nonrefundable tickets, I will pay you back from my savings."

Everyone quiets down, and I look around the room. "Thank you, everyone. For coming, and for the gifts. It was wonderful . . ."

I run from the tavern to the house before my tears of frustration fall.

~

SOMEONE KNOCKS on my bedroom door.

"May I please come in?" Aunt Odette asks.

I grunt in response, brushing my hair as I stand in front of my dresser mirror.

Aunt Odette comes up behind me and wraps her arms around my waist.

"I know you are mad about college, but can you please just trust that I am trying to look out for you? What if you don't get in anywhere in Europe? College is super competitive as it is, but internationally? Plus, what if this whole gap year idea of yours messes up your chances?"

My nostrils flare, and she hugs me tighter.

"That came out wrong. You are more talented than anyone else I know, and I believe that you can and will do amazing things. But I am also being realistic. We don't know what is going on with your mother's condition. I don't want to burden you with it, but would you want to be far if we needed you home, quickly? Why not take some basic college courses online, or locally, to start?"

"No," I whisper.

"Look, my gift still stands. Two full weeks abroad with Nikki, after graduation. God help me and my nerves. Brynna, Christian, and I will cover the entire thing, but you *will* return home two weeks later. You just . . .you have to." Her voice cracks.

I whirl on her in defiance. "Why? Will I turn into a pumpkin? Or will you just disown me if you lose control over my life?"

She takes a deep breath. "Let's make a deal. I will explain more to you before you leave. Can you just trust that I will tell you everything that you need to know, as you need to know it?"

"Cryptic much?"

"Serena . . ." she pleads.

I sigh. "Okay, fine. But secrets don't make friends."

Her shoulders sag. Guilt tugs at the loose strands of my anger, unraveling it some.

"Friends also do not bake cakes for friends if they are terrible at it." I attempt a light tone.

She snorts, and then laughs out loud. "God, it was awful. The sad thing is I really tried."

I lean over and kiss her cheek. "You know I don't care about that. And I do appreciate the thought behind it."

I glance at our reflection in my dresser mirror. Passersby in town often mistake us for sisters, and it's no surprise. I favor her features more than my own mama's.

She sighs and plays with my hair. "I cannot believe you're eighteen. I feel like only yesterday you were this pink little bundle of yumminess."

"Wasn't I cross-eyed?" I ask, wrinkling my nose.

"You outgrew it, and you were still the prettiest baby. So, now for the heavy. I have another present for you."

She turns me around and leads us over to sit on the edge of my bed.

"Aw, Aunt Odette, really—it's not necessary."

"Hush."

"It's not food, is it?" I wince, and she laughs.

"I am trying for a moment here between us!" she says, pulling a tiny box, wrapped in lavender paper with a tiny silver bow, from the pocket of her oversized cardigan.

"The last Alverson to wear this necklace that I am about to give you was your aunt Karina."

She deposits the box into my hands. I sit on the edge of my bed and slip a finger under the seam, sliding it through the tape. The paper falls right off, revealing a sapphire blue velvet box.

I glance up at her, and she waves me on to continue, her iPhone at the ready to snap pictures, blinding me with the flash as I pout my way through.

"Is that really necessary?"

"It's a momentous occasion. One day, you will be glad that I took all these pictures."

The box creaks open and reveals a delicate, but upon inspection strong, silver chain. The silver claw setting weaves into an intricate design, cradling a clear crystal with bubbles within it that move around as I rotate the charm in my hand.

"Here, let me help you," she offers, opening the clasp and draping it over my neck.

I hold the crystal of the necklace in my fingers, pulling the silver chain up from my neck. It looks like a geode—rather ugly, save for the bubbles inside the crystal that glitter and sparkle, catching the light.

Feeling Aunt Odette's eyes on me, I glance up. She stares at me expectantly, and I clear my throat.

"Oh! It's really . . . unique." I offer.

She smiles at it in quiet adoration before saying, "I know it's not the most beautiful thing to look at. Some of the more important things in life are the plainest. Every Alverson woman has worn this necklace. Your great-great-great-great-aunt Josie wore it when she traveled to Havenwood Falls by covered wagon with her sisters and her father, your great-great . . ."

"I get it," I interject with a grin.

"Grandfather, Jedidiah," she finally finishes. "Your aunt Karina was the last Alverson woman to wear it before she . . ."

Aunt Odette doesn't like to talk about her baby sister, who died as a teenager, aside from Aunt Karina's birthday each August, when we picnic on her grave, in her memory.

"Aunt Odette!" Laurel calls from downstairs. From her tone, she is clearly over the mood she was in at dinner. "Beulah and Esmerelda ripped the trash apart again! They must have been here earlier."

Aunt Odette groans. "Damn bears. I need a shotgun and a shovel."

"Don't you dare!" I jump to my feet in protection of the black bears, whose curiosity far outweighs their fear of people. From the time she was a cub, Beulah, as we named her, has been a constant presence on our land. Much to my aunt's chagrin, Beulah showed up with a cub in tow this spring. They are basically the closest thing to pets that my sisters and I have.

"Don't worry. Since it's dark, I'm sure she's long gone and safe for the moment."

"You mean, safe forever." I try.

Aunt Odette stands, gathering the crumpled wrapping paper from my bed. "No one is safe for that long 'round these parts." Her voice is light but something strange flickers in her eyes.

She pivots at the door. "Hey—are you feeling okay? I know you said that you had a bad dream, but you looked flushed when you woke up. Do you feel sick—or different?"

She eyes me strangely, her view dashing down to the necklace momentarily before meeting my eyes once more.

I sigh. "I haven't gotten my, *you know*, if that's your down-low way of asking," I mutter, referring to the fact that I am now an eighteen-year-old who *still* doesn't have her period.

She clears her throat. "Well, don't worry, honey. The doctors aren't concerned, so we shouldn't be either. I am sorry to bring it up. I only asked because I have strange dreams and nightmares sometimes before I get mine. So, I thought maybe . . ."

"Ugh." I cover my ears. "Don't really want to know."

She winks and then blows me a kiss, before disappearing into the hallway. Her voice echoes, carrying on about bear stew, bearskin boots, and other things that make my little vegan heart shrivel up and die.

My eyes travel down my dresser, to the picture of me, Mama, and Daddy, taken the day I was born. My throat tightens, and the urge to see her spurs my feet toward the hallway leading to the third-floor home of our own Miss Havisham.

Mama's thin, white-washed planked door stands open, probably to let some air in. It gets hot on the third floor, but Mama doesn't

251

tolerate the central air, so we mostly leave it off up there to keep her content.

The same song that she has listened to nonstop on Daddy's old record player, since the day he died, echoes eerily down the stairs, filling the hallway. A breeze wisps through the open window at the foot of Mama's stairs, the curtain a phantom in a somber dance to the music.

"Mama?" My voice bounces off the log walls, and my bare feet pad against the wide-planked wooden floating stairs.

No answer, other than the steady creaking that I know to be her rocking chair. This is normal, so I sigh and keep going, lowering my head at the stair landing to account for the pendant light fixture. It was added to the hardwood ceiling molding during one of the many updates each generation of Alversons has made to keep our cabin going over the past couple of centuries.

With a deep breath, I steel myself against Mama's ripe stench, growing with each step I take into her room. She used to allow us to bathe her once or twice a week, but now her aquaphobia has worsened to the point that it's almost impossible to make her go near water, except for little fluke instances when she doesn't fight it. The air flowing in through the open window in her bedroom jettisons off the cross breeze from the stairwell, making it slightly more bearable.

"Mama?" I ask again, with less resolve this time. I don't know what I expect her to say or do. I've long ago given up on getting a response.

I vaguely remember the start of it all, when Daddy died the summer before I began kindergarten. Mama slowly slipped into fits where nobody could reach her. She would just sit in this room and stare at their wedding picture, like she's doing right now. But it would come and go. Catatonic, they called it. Aunt Odette gave up the small room attached to the tavern, where Simon now lives, and moved into the main house to help her. But Mama still slid deeper into her darkness, until she never left the room again, unassisted.

"So, it's my birthday. Eighteen! I'm finally old enough to vote, buy a pack of cigarettes, and buy a gun without parental consent." I sink down onto the edge of her bed and snort. "I mean, we both know I will only be doing one of those things."

My smile fades. Nothing. The familiar urgency to connect with this woman who brought me into the world swirls up.

"Mama—I . . . I wish you had been at dinner. Aunt Odette tried to bake me a cake, and it was totally raw in the middle. Good thing Simon predicted that one and ordered a backup."

I glance down and trace my fingers over the strange crystal on my neck. "And then Aunt Odette gave me this necklace . . . she said it was Aunt Karina's and is an heirloom or something. I feel bad, because I think it's sort of ugly, but it seems like it means a lot to her for me to wear it."

The silence of the room catches my attention, so I trail off and look up at Mama. No longer rocking, she sits in her chair, still as stone. Slowly, she glances up and over at me, as if shaking off a dream.

"Mama?" I ask, voice breaking, my hope a pathetic zombie.

Maybe this is it.

"Mama? Please come back to us," I plead, moving toward her, grabbing her hand, but she wrenches it away from me and jabs her pointer finger at . . . my necklace?

"What is it? Do you want this? I'm sorry! You can have it." I move to unclasp the necklace, and it all happens so fast.

Mama stands, one hand clawing at my necklace as I gasp and back away. Then she grabs a framed picture of her, Aunt Karina, and Aunt Odette as teenagers from the table, and flings it at me. I gasp and jump out of the way as it crashes into the framed wedding picture on the wall behind me, spider-webbing Daddy's handsome face.

"Oh, God, no. Mama, I'm so sorry!"

She falls to the floor, sobbing, her eyes on me in accusation.

Footsteps pound the stairs behind me, and Aunt Odette lifts Mama into her chair, as Mama kicks and punches, crying and screaming.

"Here, let me help." I move toward them.

Mama shrieks.

"No! Serena, give her some room," Aunt Odette pleads.

Mama lurches toward the window, almost bumping her head on the angled ceiling, but Aunt Odette deflects the blow onto her own arm instead. Forever protecting her big sister.

"For heaven's sake!" Aunt Odette cries out, shaking her arm and wincing as the twins run into the room. "Serena, please, love, just go. It will be okay."

"What the hell did you *do*?" Laurel rushes to Aunt Odette's aid.

"I didn't—I don't know . . . I showed her my necklace, and she freaked out."

Something dark passes over Aunt Odette's face, and then she waves Laurel off and leans into Mama, whispering in her ear.

Mama's body goes slack. She stops punching Aunt Odette, collapsing into her arms in muted tears.

Laurel glares at me.

Lena yanks me from the room, dragging me back down the third-floor stairs. Once we are in the hall, Mama's screams reverberating through us, Lena threads her thin fingers through mine.

"S'not your fault," she mumbles.

"No, it is. She was fine until I went in."

"Who's to say she wouldn't have had the episode regardless? Maybe it's that new medication Aunt Odette has been talking about that the doctor gave Mama last time."

I smile sadly at my little sister and tuck a stray blond wisp behind her ear. "I love you for this, but it's not your job to make me feel better, or to take care of me. That's my job with *you*."

She frowns. "I like to think it's equal. That the three of us look out for each other."

I smile. "You're a wise little Bug, but I'm fine."

"Serena, you're shaking . . ." she continues, reaching out for my hand, but I step back.

"Really, I'm fine," I say in a firmer tone. "I just want to go think."

I slip down the stairs and out the front door before Lena can say anything else. To the far left, behind our makeshift garage that was added centuries after the cabin was built, I can still see remnants of Beulah and Esmerelda's buffet.

Aunt Odette must've called it quits for the night, which is a blessing. I don't feel like any more talks or inquisitions.

I crave the roaring quiet and peace that only one place can provide. My heart gallops when I kick my shoes off and dip my toes into the small body of water that couldn't decide between forming as a small lake or a large pond.

I feel stupid that a dream has me dipping a toe in trepidation, but it was so real.

Not even thinking, I step in, clothes and all, wading up to my shoulders in the warm water. Aunt Odette says that it is secretly fed by a hot spring, and it's like a lukewarm hot tub without the maintenance. The heat is inviting against the chilly air. With a deep breath I go under, my mind wrestling with the image of me pulling myself in, from my dream—probably nothing more than a weird Freudism about senior year and finding myself or whatever.

Something sears against my chest, and I gasp. Forgetting I am underwater, I suck in a lungful and propel myself to the surface.

Spluttering and hacking, I struggle to clear my airway, and then I open my eyes. The scent of burning flesh registers in the background as the water takes on that weird green backlight from below, like in my dream.

I claw at the necklace, and when I move it from my chest, there is a burn mark in its wake. I open my mouth to scream, but nothing comes out other than a squeak, as the crystal lights up in my hand.

Brilliant colors of the rainbow color my flesh, strobing onto the still water.

As quickly as it began, it stops. I glance up and see shadows against the mouth of the lagoon that peeks out in between strips of the waterfall. That's when I find my voice and yelp, attempting to swim backwards out of the water.

When my feet hit the shore, I glance up at my cabin. Mama's window calls to me. I don't know why. Just like conversations with Mama, it's usually dark and empty. But something white flickers there. I blink and look closer.

Mama stands in the window, staring directly at me, but that's impossible. Even when she had her episode earlier, she couldn't stand alone. Yet, there she is, eyes wide, mouth wide and gaping in a silent scream. A chill threads itself along my spine. I blink, and Mama's gone. I glance away and look back again, clearing my view, just to be sure.

Still nothing. Just a vacuous black hole.

CHAPTER 3

$\mathcal{I}$n the comforting light of day, the strange happenings of last night feel like nothing more than a crazy dream. The events and questions tug at me, demanding answers. Yet I know that after our spat about going away to school last night, the last thing to help my case will be Aunt Odette thinking I am delusional.

I make my way down the stairs and look over the banister, searching for the twins. They are both on the couch, predictable as ever —Lena buried in a textbook, while Laurel cracks her gum, FaceTiming her friend, Alicia.

"What could you two possibly have to talk about at this hour?" I ask in exasperation. "You're going to see her at school in like five minutes."

Laurel rolls her eyes at me and turns over on her side on the couch, hiding behind a curtain of white-blond. She lowers her voice to a grumble and then they both shriek with laughter.

I nudge Lena. "You know you're my favorite, right?"

She flashes a sly smile as I slip into the kitchen and swipe a travel mug from the cupboard, filling it with black coffee. I grab an apple from the bowl on the table and then scoop the keys to the Jeep up with my other hand.

KALLIE ROSS

Aunt Odette looks up from emptying the dishwasher and smiles at me. "Hey, were you night-swimming?"

"Uhh . . ."

"Why?" Her eyes pierce me, and it feels like anything I say here is critical.

"I just needed air, after Mama," I answer.

Her eyes flit down. Score one for me.

"How is she?" I ask.

"Better, but I am going to run it by her doctor today."

I bite my lip, guilt washing over me again.

"The only thing you need to be flashing those guilty puppy-dog eyes over is sneaking out on a school night and then dripping all over the floor. Don't do it again."

"Sorry," I mumble.

She comes up to me and cups my face. "I have to be strict sometimes, but please know I am here if you want to talk." She gives me that same expectant look that she did last night.

As much as I want to ask her more about the necklace, my gut tells me that if I let on that I could potentially be crazy, I will have to kiss Europe goodbye, permanently.

"Serena," she says with a look on her face as if she might be repeating herself to get my attention.

"What? Sorry."

"You okay?"

"Yeah," I lie.

"Okay. Don't forget to hand your excuse in to the office so you can come home early to set up for Harvest," Aunt Odette says, handing me three sheets of paper. One each for Lena, Laurel, and me.

"Wait, *what?*"

Aunt Odette blinks. "The Carnival at the Falls. I need you girls home early to help with setup."

"No, you said, 'Harvest,'" I argue.

She hesitates for a minute and then sighs. "Honey, I am exhausted. I haven't had coffee yet. It's fall. Harvest is pretty much always the theme." She suddenly becomes busy, organizing papers on the table, and no longer meeting my eyes.

Are we both keeping secrets now?

I stare her down for a minute longer and then call over my shoulder, "Lena. Laurel. In the Jeep now, or you're walking."

A growl comes from the living room, and then Laurel stomps out.

"What's your problem now?" I ask, holding the door open for my sisters, with Aunt Odette trailing us.

Lena moves to the side to let her darker half pass. Aunt Odette tries to kiss Laurel's cheek, but Laurel ducks out of the way, as Lena steps in to accept it.

"Turner freaking asked Emily to homecoming," Laurel finally answers.

"You guys have been up for like twenty minutes. How is there already so much drama?"

Laurel mutters something darkly incoherent in response.

Aunt Odette mouths to me, "Have fun," and then pulls the screen door closed after us. I watch her figure recede up the mountain, toward the tavern to begin prepping for the afternoon shift and the busy night that the Carnival crowd will ensure.

I open the driver side door of the Jeep and sink into the seat, weary from a restless night without much sleep.

Laurel clicks away in the backseat, snorting and growling like a girl possessed with each *ping ping ping* of a text.

I glance at Lena in the passenger seat. "Thank you for beating her to shotgun," I say as I back up onto the dirt road that meets our driveway, rewarding myself with a sip of coffee.

"Alicia needs a ride," Laurel chirps when I turn onto the road opposite from the direction of her friend's house.

I groan because I just want to get to school and away from my sisters, so I can tell Nikki about everything that happened after she left my party and find out what the hell is going on between her and Aunt Brynna. I was tempted to call her last night or this morning, but it's not like that is info you can dump on someone over the phone.

"Laurel, we're gonna be late," Lena objects.

"Not with the way lead foot over here drives," Laurel says.

She's not wrong. Sheriff Kasun and Havenwood's finest are the bane of my driving existence. Yet, I still mutter under my breath, pull a U-turn, and drive five minutes out of the way to scoop up a giggling redhead. Her curls flounce like a cartoon character as she skips her way into the backseat.

"O. M. Geeeee! Emily totally just got grounded so Turner is up for grabs for homecoming!" Alicia announces.

Laurel squeals, and they do their weird little handshake-hair-flip.

"We should totally hit Aurelia up after school to go shopping!" Alicia says.

Lena buries herself deeper in her book and her seat. Last year, *she* was the twin Aurelia spent nearly every waking moment with, before moving on to hanging out with Laurel and her friends. I know it isn't fair, but witnessing Laurel leaving our sister out like that has left my patience waning.

I reach over and pat Lena's knee and then glance over my shoulder and mimic Laurel and her friend. "OMG! Maybe Turner will ask me! I'll find the pinkest, most glittery dress in existence, and count how many times he uses the word 'like' in a sentence the whole night."

Meeting their unimpressed glares, I turn around to back out of Alicia's driveway and onto the dirt road to retrace my steps toward Nikki's house.

"Seriously. Loser status, you freak," Laurel snaps.

"So, ReeRee . . ." Alicia tries out her newest nickname for me.

I mouth, "no," over my shoulder at her.

"How's that hottie, Logan?" Alicia asks, applying bubblegum-pink lipstick, using her cell phone as a mirror.

I choke on my coffee as she and Laurel cackle, shooting off more *ping ping pings*, and snorting in between.

For whatever reason, I find myself on the defensive. "He's too old for you. Wait—are you two seriously texting each other right now?"

They *ping* back and forth in response with the occasional "I know, right?" and "So lame."

I pull from the dirt road onto the pavement of Fifth Street, heading to Nikki's house on Seventh.

"Ugh. Why do we have to pick *her* up?" Alicia groans.

"It's my vehicle you're riding in, so, yeah. My friend."

"Actually, it's Aunt Odette's Jeep," Laurel interjects, always super happy to point that one out.

"Shut it," I mutter, pulling up to the gray clapboard Cape Cod with red shutters and wooden stars. Folk art punctuates the side of the house and the yard. Nikki's mom has a serious craft show obsession and will drive for miles just to find a new piece. We used to let her drag us along, just so we could get out of town for a day when we were younger.

Nikki slips out her screened front door, strutting her stuff in a very black, very mini skirt with fishnets and combat boots. One of the torn tee halters I made for her peeks through a jean jacket. I blink against a flashback of years past and all the pink she used to wear. Some of Logan's concerns are becoming impossible to ignore.

Nikki pulls her shades off and pops them into her cocoa hair, delicate nose wrinkling as she sees the shock of red.

"I'll get in the back," Lena says quickly.

Overhearing her, Nikki leans into her open window and winks. "No way, baby cakes. I'm always up for a backseat party."

My head hits my backrest, and I sigh.

Nikki and Alicia's feud is very real and undying, dating back to that one time Nikki babysat Alicia years ago. The little brat framed Nikki for stealing the mad money stash in her parents' safe, when really, Alicia took it herself to buy a billion Barbies and Pixy Stix. Even though Alicia's parents eventually discovered the truth and apologized, the damage was already done. Nikki was blacklisted from her short-lived babysitting career.

"Nancy," Alicia hisses, sliding away from Nikki, in a nod to the deranged goth girl from *The Craft*.

Nikki narrows her eyes and growls. "Weasley. Move your twig-butt over and pull the twig out while you're at it."

I back out of Nikki's driveway while she plugs her phone into the auxiliary jack, Soundgarden blaring as we pull into the Havenwood Falls High parking lot. I slow down, because nobody particularly pays attention or parks in any semblance of order. Kids sit on hoods of cars and hang out of windows, yelling at each other instead of making their way into the building.

"Let us out here?" Laurel asks, waving to Aurelia and their group of friends, leaning against the railing of the school's entrance.

I pull over so they can hop out, glancing at Lena, who remains buried in her book, clearly not wanting to join them.

"Leen?" Laurel asks.

I shake my head at her, and she sighs and then shuts the door behind Alicia after she hops out.

"Have a good day! Learn stuff!" Nikki calls after Laurel and her friend, Satan. Lena remains in her seat, paler than the paper in the book she reads.

"You okay, Bug?" I ask.

Lena nods unconvincingly.

"What is it?"

"Laurel's mad that I'm not going to homecoming," she mumbles. "But I don't see how it even matters. She has Alicia, and . . ."

"Aurelia?" I offer gently.

Lena looks down and blinks, whispering, "I don't know what I even did. I tried to be nice to Aurelia. I feel like something is so broken in me. I just cannot people."

Nikki pops her head between the front seats and nestles her cheek against Lena's in an awkward hug. "Oh, I can talk to Laurel for you. Aurelia, too." An odious grin consumes her face.

"Nik, no. Look, Lena, I know this probably doesn't help, but I can tell you that friends come and go and drift around at your age."

"You have had the same two best friends since kindergarten," Lena says with a glum sigh.

"Serena, Logan, and I are freaks of nature. Our friendship literally doesn't make sense. Worst case, I could always be your homecoming date." Nikki waggles her eyebrows. "Come on, we'll be the talk of the town. Irene will love it."

Irene Beckett is the town busybody, and that would probably give her gossip material for at least a full morning.

"You have Max." Lena sniffs, wiping the creases of her eyes before tears fully fall.

"Pfft. Boy can't dance to save his life. I would choose you first, any day," Nikki says.

"Bug, you know you are always welcome to come hang out with us," I echo. Lena smiles, but shakes her head. "Thanks, but no thanks."

"At least think about it?" I ask as we step out of the Jeep and grab our bags.

She shrugs and then heads off toward school. I sigh and lean back against the Jeep.

"Dude, I am seriously never having children," Nikki muses, so darkly that my gut tells me there might be more to her sentiment than my little sister drama.

"Tell me about it. I quite literally probably will not," I say, my health issues always in the back of my mind.

Nikki gives me a hug. "You don't know that. You and Logan will probably have a little army of mountain men."

I giggle.

"He will have his own football team," Nikki continues.

"Oh, stop. You know it's not like that between the two of us."

"But does *he*?" Nikki asks.

My cheeks burn, and the heat reminds me of what happened last night. The memory brings back the urgency to share it all with my best friend.

"Nikki, I really need to talk to you."

The five-minute warning bell blares across campus, so we head toward the building.

"So, let's leave," she says.

I stop in my tracks. "Uh . . . no. You have Ms. Bast first." She is a fun teacher, but one who will notice if you skip. "What the heck is going on with you, anyway? You never skipped school before and suddenly you just don't care?"

"Oh, you're overreacting," Nikki says as we walk up the stairs into the three-story brick building.

"Nik, you've missed three days this term alone. You cut your hair, like a lot. Your clothes, while interesting, are totally different . . ."

"What are you, my mom?" She snaps.

"Speaking of your mom, what the hell is going on with you two?"

"I'm quite sure I do not know what you're talking about." Nikki pulls the visor down and removes the sunglasses from her hair. Leaning into the mirror, she straightens some flyaways.

"Bullshit. What happened last night?"

She slams the visor back into place. "For the love of cheese, back off, Brynna Number Two."

I flinch, and Nikki sighs. "Look, I know you care, but I am seriously fine. I have spent my whole life doing what everyone wants and expects of me. This is senior year. Time to break free. Let's not take it so seriously, 'kay?"

I try to object, but she covers my mouth with her hand.

"I will release you if you promise we will only discuss *your* problems," Nikki says.

I nod and quickly tell her about my dream (minus the part about thinking Max abducted us) and the necklace as she opens her locker and takes out the books and folders needed for her morning classes.

"You guys are so cool with all your Old Family heirlooms and stories, unlike my boring family. And that dream is full of symbolism regarding all the stuff we are going through right now in senior year. Being in over our heads, loss of control, impending freedom."

"But, the necklace . . ." I insist.

Nikki picks the crystal up and examines it. "Could be more attractive," she ascertains.

"Nikki." I sigh.

"How many hours of sleep have you had this week?" she asks, worry knitting her brow.

"The same amount of time you've actually spent in class," I fire back.

She cocks her head to the side. "Maybe it's a combination of exhaustion and undercooked food?" She teases about my aunt's cake gone wrong.

"No!" I argue. "I know what I saw and felt. You just think I am crazy. I can't believe this."

"Serena!" she calls after me, but I storm away in the other direction toward my locker.

"We will talk about this tonight," she calls after me.

I let the late bell answer for me.

"WELL, I think that just about does it." Simon wipes the sweat from his brow with his forearm. "Thanks for your help, Serena."

"Since you're feeling so thankful, how about sharing the theme of my birthday booth with me?" I ask, nodding toward the red velvet curtained booth—a tradition that dates back as far back as I can remember.

Simon shakes his head. "Every year you try, and every year I say no. What makes this year any different?"

"I'm an adult now?" I offer.

"That means you can wait." He grins as he saunters off to my aunt's side.

"Girls, go get changed. We've got the rest of this," Aunt Odette calls out to my sisters and me. Aunt Odette looks wiped, with dark circles under her eyes. She always seems to be unwell around the carnival—fall allergies or something. Maybe it's the additional hours she invests to pull it off.

My sisters and I file into the house. When I return into the darkening night, I've traded paint-splattered overalls for a pair of jeans, a T-shirt, and my faux-leather jacket.

Nikki, Logan, and Max sit on the steps of my front porch, watching as the final rides are put together.

"Happy Birthday Part Two . . . and I am sorry. You're right, I should have listened." Nikki stands to hug me.

I stiffen at first and then ease into her, unable to remain mad at her for too long.

"You have to admit, it sounded crazy, but I am pretty sure I've approached you with crazier. I promise to keep an open mind. We will figure this out," she says.

"Thanks." I smile back, not feeling as alone and scared with her by my side.

"What was that all about?" Logan asks.

Nikki grins at me and says, "Serena wants to date me." And then she skips the two of us over to the unveiling of my booth.

Logan sighs as we both giggle. Worry still tugs at every corner of my mind, along with the need for answers, but it feels good to laugh and live in the moment.

Simon and Logan both pull aside the curtains on my "Paint Night" themed booth, complete with mini art kits for my friends as souvenirs.

We settle in to paint the Eiffel tower. I lose myself in the colors and textures until Logan elbows me.

"I know I'm not an artist, but since when was the Eiffel tower surrounded by waterfalls?"

I focus in on my painting, and my throat tightens.

Twin waterfalls box my tower in place.

Simon walks by, and I flag him down.

"Hey, where's Aunt Odette?" I ask.

"Oh, she's . . . around." He answers a little too quickly. "Why don't you hang out with your friends for now?"

He heads off to help someone before I can argue, and Nikki peers at my painting.

"Whoa, that's . . . something." She quiets, and I glance over at her. She checks her watch and then pastes a big smile on her face, leaping off her stool.

"Come on! Let's go explore before my shift at the kissing booth."

"Your what?" Max asks.

She pats his arm. "Anything for charity, baby."

"Come on, man," Logan says, clapping his shoulder. "Let's try to sneak into the Soothing Sips wine booth . . . That's your kinda thing, right?"

Max smiles, and they head off together, Logan's sudden effort distracting me.

"Well, that was unexpected," I joke. Nikki grins and hooks her arm through mine.

Weaving our way through the brightly lit cacophony of sounds and rides, we wave at people from school. The scents of fried dough and pumpkin spice lattes assault me, but the thought of food turns my stomach.

"Where are we going?" I ask.

"To get answers," she says.

Nikki pulls me to a dark purple velvet tent with a shimmering sign that proclaims, "Madame Tousseau."

"Oh, no," I mumble.

"What?" Nikki asks.

"You know I don't believe in this crap."

She glares at me.

"Okay, I'll rephrase that. *Your* terrible fortune telling is the only of its kind that I believe in."

"Hey!" She feigns hurt.

A middle-aged woman with fiery red hair and bright green eyes comes to the opening of the tent.

I blush, hoping she didn't hear my outburst, but from the way she smiles at me, I can tell she did.

I open my mouth to apologize, but the woman holds up a manicured hand.

"Eeeets quite alright," the woman says. "Zee soul needs to grow more. "Pleeeze, come seet." She gestures toward the flap of her tent.

"Oh, no. We were just looking," I say and turn to make my exit, nudging Nikki to keep moving.

Claws dig into my shoulder. I turn back and see the woman's sparkling red stiletto nails clinging to me, her face inches from mine. "You must be very careful, child. You are surrounded by eveeeel, and weeeell soon make a choice."

My heart thrums as Madame Tousseau fingers my necklace, dropping it immediately, as though it burns her, too.

"You are much more than you realize just yet." She pats my cheek. "Choose right, giyuuurl. Much eeeees at stake."

She disappears, leaving us outside of her tent, my heart pounding.

"Wow," Nikki whispers.

I stand, unmoving, staring at her tent.

"Are you okay?" she asks. "Freaking psychics. They leave you with more questions than answers."

"But, she went right for the necklace. Nik, that has to mean something," I say in a hushed tone.

"Serena," Nikki laughs. "She basically recited a fortune cookie. You're a teenager, so 'young' with choices to make. The whole world is surrounded by evil, so that was ridiculously generic."

"But, she held the necklace like something is wrong with it," I protest.

"I'm sorry, but that is the ugliest rock I have ever laid eyes on. I feel like they zone in on noticeable accessories like that."

My lips twitch. *Maybe she's right.* When it's broken down like that, the whole thing sounds fake. Normally, I wouldn't have given it a second thought.

"Come on, let's geeeet you some vegan fried dough—if that's even a thing. Eeet's the least I can do, giyuuurl." Nikki mimics.

"I—" The necklace heats up against my skin, and I gasp. My heart slams into my ribcage.

"What now?" Nikki asks.

"I just need to go find Aunt Odette. I'll be back." I lose myself in the crowd, barely nodding at everyone who waves to me and dodging people who yell birthday wishes my way. I need to find her and finally confront her about this damn necklace.

I know that woman felt something, too.

I blow past the wine booth just in time to see Deputy Kasun stroll up behind Logan and Max as they change their master plan.

Logan calls out to me, but I don't stop, storming down each path. I pass the rides, just barely waving at Lena on the Ferris wheel.

Aunt Odette is nowhere to be found.

With a sigh of annoyance, I head to the waterside to plop down in defeat. That's when I hear a laugh that I had almost forgotten.

Mama?

I scramble to my feet and follow the sound, toward our backyard. There she is, treading water close to our little waterfall, in a white gown that matches the white gown Aunt Odette wears, beside her.

I hide behind my favorite weeping willow tree, peering out as men join them in the water. Mama flirts and laughs with . . . *Dr. Nance? From the hospital!* He set my arm when I broke it in second grade.

Dr. Nance swims out to her, along with the other men. The moonlight hits both her and my aunt in just the right way so that their skin shimmers—they look like goddesses afloat in the water.

Mama accepts Dr. Nance into her arms, lovingly stroking his cheek before planting her lips on his. Aunt Odette follows suit with one of the others.

"Mama?" I cry out, my voice carrying.

Why would she lie to us? All these years of guilt over her being sick and me living my life. Yet here she is, just fine. Doing awful things with these men who aren't my father.

I glance over to my right. A figure rustles the bushes. I narrow my eyes to get a better look at a man with something metallic glinting by his side. I lean in and connect eyes with his sea-glass green ones for a moment, and the breath freezes in my lungs.

Before I can focus in on more details, he backs away, slipping into a camouflage of greenery. Aunt Odette appears in front of me. Her dress clings to her soaked body.

"What the hell is going on?" I demand. "What happened to Mama? Who are those men, and what is wrong with you?"

Aunt Odette's eyes glow. She murmurs in a weird language, and my mind swirls into blackness.

CHAPTER 4

*T*he final bell rings. I cringe. The headache I woke with after a late night at the Carnival still hits hard. Tylenol hasn't even taken the edge off. At least the weird brain fog has somewhat disappeared. I'd better not be getting sick. Homecoming is tomorrow.

Mr. Milner frowns. He's just getting revved up on his speech about what the founding fathers would think of the current administration. There's nothing he hates more than being interrupted. Groans from classmates turn into cheers since we have all been saved from it.

"Don't forget, your first project is due Monday. Extra points will be awarded to anyone who goes with a historical, non-fiction theme for their homecoming costume tomorrow. But, as you kids say nowadays, 'pictures, or it didn't happen'!" He chortles to himself as he fills his briefcase.

The groans return. Chairs scrape the floor, and we shuffle out the door into the neutral halls that only help to encourage the unshakeable wave of sleepiness that eighth period AP Government imparted.

I trip over a shin and bounce into the locker belonging to the sometimes pleasant, but mostly scary, Ellisyn Daryn. I wonder for probably the millionth time how the hell her mom, Stella, spawned Ellisyn, when Stella is such a calm, health-food-store-owning hippy.

Ellisyn's flint eyes bore through me, proving my point. She snaps,

"I know walking while talking must be such a challenge for you, but maybe try a little harder?"

"Uh, sorry," I squeak, hating myself for doing it.

"Don't you have a kitten to sacrifice or something?" Nikki shrills in my defense, appearing at my side.

Ellisyn's eyes narrow. "Watch it, Nikkola," she hisses. A dangerous smirk dances across her red lips. Strawberry-blond hair swings against the shoulders of her teal cashmere sweater.

Nikki's eyes flash.

Memories of the two girls joking in the halls mere months ago flash through my mind. Nikki always fit right into the fringe of the popular girls, even though she was just a teensy bit edgier than them.

I grab Nikki and pull her over to my own locker. "What happened between you two, again?" I ask, trying to fish for an answer that I was never given.

"What do you mean?" Nikki asks, playing with her hair.

"You guys were never best friends or anything, but you and Ellisyn were never this mean to each other. What happened?"

She shrugs. "I decided I was sick of hanging around that basic wi —basic bitch."

"Nik . . ."

"We don't have time for a friendtervention. I just grew up and realized there's more to life than matching my nail polish with my outfit and joining every school committee."

"Well, how about one committee or club?"

"I still belong to art club."

"It's just . . . I know there's stuff you aren't telling me, and it hurts."

She refuses to meet my eyes once more and says, "If something were wrong, you would be the first to know."

"Promise?" I ask.

She smiles, but it doesn't reach her eyes. "Promise," she repeats, hooking her pinky through mine.

"What's going on?" Logan asks, his face tightening into his serious look, taking in the tail end of our conversation. Max trails him like a confused, well-dressed puppy.

"Nothing, just girl stuff," I say.

"Speaking of which," Nikki says, "Bye, Felicias. We're going shopping."

"Oh." Logan looks a little disappointed and then glances at me. "Did you still want to meet at Burger Bar later?"

Oops! That one totally slipped my mind, along with a good chunk of whatever happened last night. I bite my lip, pondering. "Yeah, sure. After we are done," I say a little too quickly, distracted by trying to figure out why I feel like there's a hole in my memories.

Nikki pouts. "But we can't give you a set time, because there's no limit on how long it will take to find the perfect shoes."

Logan stares at her. "It's Callie's."

"And?"

"It's two floors. One shoe section. Not thinking it will take all night."

"Can we text you guys when we're done?" I ask.

Nikki sashays over to Max, whose skin-tight jeans and leather jacket are the polar opposite of Logan's daily uniform of flannel and denim.

Max is too busy digging in a black leather pouch at his hip to notice. He glances down from underneath a cocked fedora to briefly smile as Nikki presses her lips to his cheek.

"Sure, I guess," Logan says, his eyes widening in horror. "What. Is. That?" He points his finger at the pouch along Max's waist.

Max zips it shut, slinging the bag at an angle.

Nikki blinks. "It's a Gucci belt bag. They're all the rage in the city. Right, baby?" She tweaks Max's nose and nuzzles into his cheek, but Max merely clears his throat.

Logan's face turns red with the effort of stifling explosive laughter.

He doubles over, tears coming to his eyes when he manages to gasp out, "Fanny. Pack!" before completely losing it.

Nikki bristles. "No. It's a vintage Gucci belt bag, Mountain Man."

He doesn't even hear her and clanks back against my locker, shutting it, while he hoots with laughter.

"Um. I wasn't done in there yet," I grumble, but Nikki's words pique my attention.

I turn on my heel. "Max, do you understand how the skin is actually removed from an animal to make something like that for you, which could just as easily be made from another material? Did you know that most of the animal is wasted after? So, you're basically walking around with a dead animal on your hip and back. Does that make you feel like a man?"

Logan guffaws. "Well, I think that ship has sailed. Because it's a *fanny pack*."

"Oh, for the love of God," Nikki says. "IT'S A BELT BAG FOR MEN."

Kids walking down the hall stop and stare, laughing as they pass us.

Nikki turns to Max, whose cheeks are just as red as Logan's.

She hugs him, cooing. "Don't listen to PETA and Joe Dirt over here. *You* are cutting edge. *They* are stuck in 2002."

"Max, if you're bored someday, come on over. I have a few documentaries that would fascinate you. Do you know how they make Uggs? It's extremely educational and eye-opening."

Logan bumps into me lightly. "I think he's suffering enough by having to wear that thing."

And then he cracks up again, shaking his head as he walks away from us.

Max glares down at Nikki, mumbling, "I told you it was a little much for . . . *here*."

"Hey, would you rather fit in with future L.L.Beaners of America?" She asks, fitting snuggly into his arm to walk him to his car.

"I'll meet you at the Jeep," she calls over her shoulder to me.

I turn back to my locker, thankful that I will be able to miss out on their little lovefest as I grab the rest of my books.

"Saving the world one leather good at a time, are we, Alverson?" Mr. Weaver, my art teacher, teases from behind.

I jump. He's good at sneaking up on people.

"Well, someone has to speak for the poor animals," I huff.

KALLIE ROSS

He holds his hands up. "Do your thang, girl. Speaking of which, when do you want to meet up to discuss your portfolio?"

On top of the dream, the necklace, Mama, Laurel, Lena, Nikki and Logan's weirdness, and really, the stress of creating something that reflects my abilities and goals after high school ends—I am beyond overwhelmed.

I snap. "Can I please just get through homecoming first?"

I slam my locker shut and whirl around to face my favorite teacher, waiting for him to go all "you will not talk to me like that, young lady" on me.

But, of course, he doesn't.

He just nods. "Cool, let it simmer. I can dig. Just don't let it burn to the bottom of the pan, 'kay?"

I nod.

"Have a good night, Alverson. Go reflect by a stream or something. You know, fresh air—nature."

He gestures past the open school entrance, where misty shades of indigo in the mountains mix with afternoon sun, dotted with aspen and pines. He's right. It's stunning and *should* be cathartic. Even though I am an artist, I sometimes take the beauty of my home for granted.

When I glance back, he's gone, sauntering down the hall, whistling a Grateful Dead riff.

I step out into the crisp fall air, squinting against the sun as I dig in my bag for my vintage Ray-Ban Wayfarers and slip them on.

Nikki's lithe body curves over the hood of my Jeep, leaning against it. Her forehead's full of lines as she furiously taps away at her phone.

"You know what I won't miss about this place?" she asks.

I pause at the driver's side door. "Uh . . . flannel, lack of malls, hiking boots?"

"Well, yeah. You would think they could make some fashionable hiking accessories. I mean, they have cute skiing stuff."

"Well, if your indie music label doesn't pan out, there you go," I say.

She rolls her eyes. "The mountain reception is what I won't miss.

I've been trying to text Max for like five minutes now, and it won't send."

We both get into the Jeep and buckle up before I place the key in the ignition. I glance over at her, my shoulders sagging. "You're kidding, right?"

"What?"

"You just left him. Max is awesome, but—girl time. Remember? We're gonna see him in a couple hours, anyway."

She slides down in her seat. Letting out a sigh, she drawls. "You're right, I'm sorry. He just . . . smells so good, and he's so cute, and his hair is so soft and curls in my hand. Did I say that it's soft?"

"Where the hell did my best friend go?"

"To Seattle, with Max, in her mind," Nikki says.

My gaze remains fixed on her, and I leave my eyebrows pointing toward the sky. "Girl, I love you. And it's because I love you that I am going to cling to the string of your balloon. Remember Aaron?"

She scrunches her nose. "Blah, forest ranger mistake."

"And Bill?"

"That was my jock phase," she says flippantly.

"Cameron?"

"The name alone says it all." She sticks her tongue out in an *I'm gonna puke* face.

"Yeah, but you were gonna 'go to Seattle' with all of them." I air quote with my fingers, looking over my shoulder to make sure that all is clear before backing out. I point the Jeep toward town square and Callie's.

"You're jealous," she snaps, incredulous.

Stopping at the stop sign on the corner of Main and First, I let a couple of kids cross.

I scoff. "Jealous of what? Losing myself in a high school thing and turning into a pod person? No thanks."

I chance a look over at her crestfallen face, and my throat tightens. "Aw, Nik, I'm sorry. I didn't mean it. I'm stressed between school, worrying about *you*, worrying about Lena, and this weird necklace thing. I swear Aunt Odette is hiding something."

She rubs my shoulder, proving why she's my bestie for life. Even after a low blow like that, she is still right there for me, for whatever reason.

"Deep breath. Okay? First off, please don't worry about me. For the bajillionth time, I'm cool."

But even the way she says it indicates otherwise.

"We will just be there for Lena, and kick whoever's ass we need to. It's all we can do. As far as the necklace and your aunt, we will figure that out, too. Okay?"

I take a deep breath and nod, lucky to find an open spot on the street in front of Callie's Consignments. I pull in, beating a red Honda Civic. Nikki sticks her tongue out at the driver in victory.

Usually this street is so packed that the two-hour parking allotment is strictly overseen by a guy named Travis. No one seems to know much about him other than he is rumored to have flunked out of police school. Everyone thinks that's why he takes his job way too seriously. He lurks in alleys, waiting to strike if you are thirty seconds late to your car.

"Oh, shoot!" I cry out, remembering that I am wearing my reclaimed Ramones shirt. I frantically dig around in the back seat until I unearth one of Laurel's cardigans.

"What?" Nikki asks as she watches me slip into the very un-me sweater. "Oh, honey. We need to talk about your current life choices . . ."

"No! This shirt . . . Remember? Callie explicitly threated my life over Frankensteining it, and I sort of swore that I wouldn't. I mean, my fingers were crossed behind my back, but . . ."

"Joey Ramone would totally be down with your improvements," she muses. "But I can see both sides."

"Thanks for the diplomacy," I mutter as I slide out of the Jeep and grab my bag.

Nikki's phone beeps, and she pumps her fist in the air.

Imitating the SpongeBob announcer, she says, "Fifteen meeenutes laaaaterrrr, my text went through."

She furiously taps away at her phone, glancing up in apology.

"Two more minutes, and then I'm yours." Nikki finishes her text and slips her phone into her bag.

I open the door to Callie's, chimes tinkling. The familiar smell is one part countless stories that each article of clothing holds, and two parts musky floral incense. I would recognize the scent anywhere.

"Time to do some damage! Hey, Callie," Nikki chirps to the gorgeous brunette bent over the register, helping a customer decide between two shirts.

"Did you get any new shoes for homecoming?" Nikki asks.

Callie straightens up so she stands tall. Her long, wavy hair brushes her shoulders as she points us toward the far end of the store. The newly-curated homecoming display beckons.

Callie's sparkling bluish-green eyes, a sharp contrast to her dark hair, shrink to slits, letting us know that she's watching.

"We mean the shoes no harm. Plus, Serena is on her best behavior because she loves her Fendi." Nikki winks at her, pointing toward my purse. I try to sneak by, but Callie has hawk eyes. She focuses in on my shirt. I wrap the sweater tightly around myself and then slip between racks of dresses.

"So, what shoes would a serial killer's mother wear to homecoming? Sensible or sexy?" Nikki muses. "I need to get in character."

"We aren't actresses."

"Speak for yourself, girly. There are no small roles in life."

"It's a dance."

"It's the last homecoming of our high school career—and more importantly, senior prank kickoff. Get your head in the game, Alverson. Did you find a good pair of scream queen shoes, yet?"

"Not quite."

"Don't worry, we will find something. Worst case, your dress will cover whatever you wear. This detail will not trip up our diabolical scheme."

"Diabolical scheme" is our play on the homecoming theme of love-struck characters from history and movies.

Logan, Max, and I decided it would just be easier to give into Nikki's whims for one of the last times. In her defense, it's sort of a hilarious plot. The only part that's making me feel a little weird is that she is pairing Logan and I off as Carrie White and Tommy Ross, partners in crime to her Mrs. Voorhees and Max's Jason. Because holding a dance for teens on Friday the 13th is an amazing idea, said no adult, ever.

Nikki holds up a pair of white kitten heels and shrugs.

"Perfect!" I say, because I hate high heels, like the pair Nikki tucks under her arm, even more than I hate algebra.

We head toward the register, passing a pile of garments that Callie is in the process of adding to the racks on the floor. Nikki grabs a light blue vintage Jackie O–style hat.

"This is perfect for our cover story," she says, referring to the fake costumes the four of us are planning to wear for parent pictures, before changing into our prank costumes later at school.

"Tab, please, for mine," I mouth as Callie answers the ringing phone.

While she wraps it all up and rings Nikki out, I thank her for her help with my new purse. Then I venture to the back of her store, taking inventory of my handmade jewelry. I count each of the glass-bead, wire-coiled bracelets, rings, necklaces, and earrings, tracking what needs to be replenished. This is what keeps my clothing tab running strong.

On my way out the door, I wave to Callie, and she offers me a tiny side-smile. Out of everyone who lives in Havenwood Falls, Callie and I possibly have the strangest relationship.

"Burger Bar now?" Nikki asks, fishing for her phone. "I'll text the guys. They will be happy that we finished early."

I glance at my watch, my shoulders relaxing when I realize we haven't been parked in front of Callie's for the full two hours yet. Aunt Odette has threatened my Jeep privileges if I bring home another parking ticket. We aren't supposed to meet the guys for half an hour. I told Logan we would be there by six o'clock. It's closing in on five-thirty, but it's never a bad thing to get there a little early, because it's always packed, no matter the day of the week.

We settle into the Jeep after dumping our bags in the backseat. I back out into traffic and head back toward school, pulling into the Burger Bar parking lot across the street from Havenwood Falls High.

The Burger Bar lot is basically a mirror image of the school lot after classes end, just add women on roller skates and trays of burgers and fries hooked onto the car doors.

"You know, I think this is all that we have here that actually impresses Max. He said that drive-in burger places are hard to find on the outside," Nikki muses.

"Oh, that's not all that impresses him here." I wink at her as I pull into an empty spot, and she blushes.

"We're going in, right?" I ask hopefully, not really wanting my Jeep to reek of burgers.

"We can eat inside if you want." Nikki smiles, knowing me too well.

We step out of the Jeep and weave our way through the crowd. I wave to our friend, Paisley Underwood, but she doesn't look up from her new boyfriend, Cole Silver, and I sigh.

"You shouldn't worry about me," Nikki says. "*She* is the one we both need to worry about."

Paisley has started skipping school and her shifts at Coffee Haven, where she works, since she started dating Cole.

The door swings open and "Love Me Do" by the Beatles croons from the jukebox in the corner. Logan and Max wave to us from the counter, where they're saving us a couple of stools. Ha, and here I thought we were the early ones.

"Hey, kids!" Maggie, co-owner of Burger Bar, waves. She pivots on her skates to deposit ketchup at a table occupied by Kase, Greg, Joe, the other football guys, and some cheerleaders, her chestnut curls flying behind her.

"Hey, Mags! Any new menu items?" I ask.

Maggie pulls a pad of paper and a pen from the pocket of her apron. "Yeah, good luck with your save-the-whales-tofurger-pitch today. Frank's in a mood."

"HELEN!" he barks from behind the grill, as if proving his wife's point.

Helen Rigby, a brunette I have only seen in passing at town events, bumps into the counters and stools, making her way over to the window to see what he wants.

"What did I say about abbreviations? Is this an order of rings or wings? It can't be both, sweetheart . . ."

Her face crumples. Maggie waves to us apologetically and then skates over to help, not even bothering to leave us menus, because we all but live here.

We settle into counter seats, casually observing as Helen rips her apron off and then half skates, half soldier-crawls out the front door.

Frank slams the spatula on the grill. "I'm deducting the cost of any uniform items or skates that aren't returned from your final paycheck!" He yells after Helen, but she is already gone.

"He's gonna give himself a heart attack," Logan says, shifting on his stool so that his knee touches mine.

I slowly move my leg away. "One more reason to serve healthier food here. Maybe he will start eating it."

Nikki groans. "We're all gonna die. Let Frank live his best life, will you, Serena?"

Maggie skates back over and takes our orders, and then Frank comes out with a tray full of plates for the football players' table.

I glance over at them, and Ben Siddons, one of Logan's teammates, makes kissy faces at me until he sees Logan's and Frank's matching glares.

Frank and Maggie were school friends of Mama's and friendly with Daddy when he first came to Havenwood Falls. Even though Frank is gruff when it comes to my dietary choices, he and Maggie have always looked out for my sisters and me when it comes to stuff like this, since neither of my parents are here to do it.

When Frank stops at the counter with our food and places a wilted plate of lettuce and tomatoes in front of me, I wrinkle my nose. "Oh, come on."

"What?" Frank barks.

"What is this?" I ask.

"A salad."

"No, it's old lettuce and a mushy tomato."

He points to the flashing neon sign that screams "Burger Bar."

"Can you read? Does that say 'salad bar?' No. It's Burger Bar. If you want falafel, head to Denver."

"Did you ever stop to think that it would be better karma for you to serve more plant-based choices? Cheaper, too, *and* you could make more money. It's a win-win."

"You know, Frank, some of that stuff is actually good." Logan takes a sip from his soda. *What is he doing?*

The vein in Frank's neck bulges. "Serena's hippy not-meat will never touch my grill!"

"Come on, man. Don't you want to give Stella a run for her money? You do know she started selling baked goods at Health Nut, right?" Logan asks.

Frank scowls.

"What if she steals your pie business?" Max pipes up, after swallowing a big bite of his burger.

"When you're the little guy, you've gotta keep up, or you'll be lost in the dust of your competition," Max says. "I used to see businesses fold like that all the time in the city."

Frank snorts. "Well, this isn't the city, and I am NOT the little guy, Tight Pants. Stella isn't even running a diner. I am."

Logan cringes over-dramatically. "Yeah, man . . . I don't know. I saw some tables and chairs being delivered to her last week. She's really pushing the whole café vibe with her smoothies and healthy takeout."

Frank continues to frown, but I can tell that he's thinking about it.

I grin at Logan, and then he bumps against my knee again, and I stop smiling. I clear my throat, turning my attention back to Frank.

"People are waking up to the reality that agricultural monopolies are in bed with the government. Stella is realizing a new consumer need and capitalizing on it." I say.

"You know what the problem is with your delusional generation?" Frank asks.

"No, but I'm sure you're going to tell us," Nikki answers before taking a sip of her chocolate milkshake.

"Your problem is that you kids are so busy with your 'Netflix and relax' that you've forgotten how to work and think for yourselves."

"Chill," Max says.

Frank's nostrils flare, and he starts to walk over to Max, who looks like he's ready to bolt.

"No, Frank! Max means the saying is 'Netflix and chill.'" Logan rushes to Max's defense. Max stares, wide-eyed, and Nikki smiles at Logan, flashing every tooth in her head. Logan shakes his head and looks away.

I sigh and then stand and walk over to Frank, gently placing a hand on his arm. "Don't you want to come in at the ground level of that cash cow, like Stella?" If nothing else speaks to him, perhaps money will entice him.

"Sure, as long as I can chop that cow up and throw her on my grill," Frank fires back.

I gasp, and Maggie skates up in between us. "Ya know, I don't make enough for this. Frank, in the kitchen. Serena, hon, I can whip up a new salad for you."

Frank says, "We are out of lettuce."

Logan glares at him, then turns to me. "How about we walk over to Health Nut and grab you something?"

"It's fine. Forget it," I say as I sink back onto my stool and try to spear a slimy tomato with my fork.

"It's on the house." Maggie winks at me, and then heads into the kitchen after her husband.

"Since when are you into veganism, Mr. Football Star?" Nikki teases.

Logan turns red. "Shut up, Nik."

"Since you've decided to be into a vegan?" Nikki continues, leaning behind me at an unnatural angle so she can flick his ear.

Logan's football team hoots and hollers, waving him over. *Thank God for the interruption.* They yell something about meeting them down at the river. Part of me hopes Logan will join them, because the elephant between us is taking up way too much room. Logan smiles at them but declines, tossing a fry at Nikki's head to silence her.

It's about seven o'clock when we finally surrender our little corner of the Burger Bar counter and step out into the chilly evening.

"Do you want a ride home, guys?" I ask Nikki and Max, but I've already lost them to Lover's Lane.

Nikki hugs me. "I think we're gonna take a little walk. Can I grab my shoes tomorrow?"

It's officially serious. She's ditching designer for dude.

"Sure, no problem. See ya guys." I hug her back.

They wave and then take off, cutting through the square to go sit in the gazebo, where the twinkle lights glimmer against the setting sun.

"You and Max seemed to get along okay tonight." I say to Logan, once Max and Nikki are safely out of earshot.

"I guess it wasn't horrible. So, what are you up to? Coffee?" he asks with that weird gleam in his eye again.

"Aw, sorry. I can't. I have a stop to make, and then homework."

His eyes are on me, and I can't bring myself to look back at him, because I know I will get sucked in to saying yes, when I have other things on my mind that need to be handled.

"Karina," he says, more than asks.

My throat tightens. "How do you do that?"

"Do what?"

"Know everything. Even the things I don't really want to say."

He smirks. "Because I know you better than *you* know you. Well, enough to know that I need to quit while I'm ahead, because you want to be alone with her. Have a good night, Rena."

His chin grazes the top of my head when he wraps his arms around me. I give him an awkward half-hug in return, then he waves and heads toward his truck.

I stand at the door of the Jeep, watching him leave, and it hits me.

He's right. He knows me entirely too well. Maybe that's the problem.

∾

THE SUN PAINTS the sky shades of orange, coral, and yellow as I pull into the cemetery parking lot.

I step along the stone walkway, lined with flowers and foliage, walking past the tombstones and walls lined with plaques. This is the main cemetery, but since my family is a founding family, our burial grounds are in a different area.

In the darkest corner of the graveyard, behind the moss and ivy that line the stone wall, I reach for a handle. The door creaks open to reveal a dank stone tunnel that smells of mildew. A steady dripping echoes in the distance. As much as I hope it is just my imagination, I swear something scurries by my feet.

I activate the flashlight feature of my cell phone and quicken my pace. Whenever I walk this tunnel, I always picture the "other mother" scenes from *Coraline*. I don't care how old I am, it always makes me want to run to the tunnel's exit.

A similar door to the one I just opened appears in front of me. I open it and let myself back out into the chilly evening. A slight breeze rustles the aspen leaves, feathering them against the sherbet sky. I grab Laurel's sweater, which still lays in my bag, and slip it on, wrapping myself in the thin yarn. I step through the elaborate marble arch of the cemetery reserved for the Old Families.

Cooley Creek babbles in the distance. A few stray birds chirp, here and there, as they make their way home for the night. I crunch over twigs and fallen leaves. The familiar chill rushes through me when I cross in front of the weeping angel statue. She is mossy with the years she has spent perched up there, judging the souls of all who enter her realm.

With a shudder, I break eye contact with the creepy thing and make my way through the unkempt pathway that nature has reclaimed. I step deeper into the cemetery, over a hill, into a more secluded, older portion of the land, where caged graves sporadically break up the horizon line of tombstones.

The first grave at the top of a small hill hollows my heart, as usual.

I trail my fingers over the lone, weathered stone with a crack in it and whisper, "Hey, Henry."

Not that I knew him. I mean, he died in 1902, but the fact that he died at 16, his tombstone a riddle of one name that could've been either his first or last, and the way his plot is isolated . . . it makes me sad. Nobody should be alone in death. I have sort of adopted him and can't set foot in the cemetery without checking in.

The breeze picks up again, whipping my hair in my face. The tinkle of hundreds of colorful glass ball chimes, strung up in the trees, trill. They float in the air, bumper-carring against each other, but somehow not breaking. This is the entrance to my family's plot. Regardless of my grand plans to see the world, I can feel it deep down —one day, this is where I will lie. My bones will return to the same corner of earth where they were born. As much as that thought bothers me, as much as I plot to run from this place once I can, it oddly brings a sense of comfort to know where I will end up.

I pass random stones belonging to older ancestors I have heard mentioned once or twice in passing, tapping the stone of the true patriarch of our family, Jedidiah Alverson.

Three smaller tombstones surround his—the resting places of his daughters: Maude, Esther, and Josie. I pause to examine Josie's headstone, and the crystal of my necklace finds its way into my hand, of its own volition. I had never really paid her grave much attention before, but now that I wear a piece of jewelry that was clearly important to her, I feel as though I should.

I drop the crystal back onto my chest, run my fingers over the cold limestone of Josie's grave marker, and then turn away to the grave I truly came for.

Karina's creamy marble tombstone is not nearly as old as all the rest. I pull out the roundie blanket I have wrapped up in my purse, unfurling it over her grave. I lay down on my side and dig out my sketchpad, a smaller tin of Prismacolor pencils, and a box of drawing charcoal.

Settling into silence, I pick up the dying glint of sunshine on the glass ball chimes in the trees, trying to capture the exact gleam and the gem tone hues on my gray paper, before finally speaking up.

"So, there's something weird about this necklace of yours, Karina," I say.

For whatever reason, it's just easier for me to talk to her like that. Really, at death, she was younger than I am right now, so it just feels weird to call her "aunt."

The tinkling glass in the trees is the only response I am given. I treat it as though she nods her white-blond head, sending me an encouraging smile, so I continue.

"I feel like I am going crazy even saying this, but it burns me. The first night I put it on, as soon as I set foot in water, it all but blew up into a crazy light show. Mama freaked out when she saw me wearing it, too. It was the first time she has responded in so long . . . it has to mean something. But Aunt Odette blew it off like it was nothing."

I trail off and swap out a magenta pencil for white so I can work in some more streaks of light. I reach for the twisted cardboard stump from my charcoal pencil tin so that I can blend it, all the while imagining how this aunt I have never met would respond.

"There's more." I breathe out. "Something is wrong with me—with my body." Content, for now, with the scarlet glass ball, I swap the white pencil out for dahlia purple and start working on its neighbor.

"I still haven't gotten . . . you know." I sigh. "It's so stupid that it's hard for me to say. It's not like I'm in middle school and this is all new. It's not like anyone is here. *You* aren't even technically here." My voice shrinks, and tears dot my lashes.

"I'm sorry. I didn't mean it like that. Of course, you're here. I just wish you were on this side of the soil. I feel like you would be different. Mama—she isn't well enough for me to dump my problems on. She needs me to be strong for her. So does Aunt Odette. Plus, whenever I try to talk to her, she changes the subject."

I put my pencils down and hold my sketchpad out to critique my work. Then I place the pad down and crack my knuckles before stretching.

"All the medical tests came out okay . . . but I feel like she's hiding something from me. We have been fighting about college, too. She knows how badly I want to go away, but the guilt over leaving her, the girls, and Mama keeps me here. I feel like sometimes she uses it to manipulate me. Why doesn't she want me to leave?"

I ball up, my arms around my knees, as I lean in to her grave marker. Cool marble calms my fiery cheeks. I blubber all over my dead aunt's grave, wishing she could actually give me advice.

A rustling in the distance bolts me upright. Eyeliner smears the back of my hand as I try to destroy the evidence of my tears.

"Hello?" I rasp.

Nothing.

Anger flames in my belly, and I yell, "Hey! Creeper! Get your freak on somewhere else!"

There's more rustling, and this time a dark form emerges from the shadows. His sea-glass green eyes lock onto mine, and I forget how to breathe. A hazy memory of a man with the same eyes, with a knife, standing by the waterside, smacks into me. I take off running toward the tunnel.

My heart pounds as footsteps follow.

CHAPTER 5

*W*hen I get to the Jeep, I fumble with the key, hands shaking. I look over my shoulder and all around me. No one. But I don't allow myself to be lulled into a false sense of security as I finally get into the Jeep and lock the doors, taking off down Main Street.

It's only then that I realize I must have kept my notebook and my new purse in my hands all along, because luckily, they are on the seat next to me, unlike my blanket. *Damn, I really loved that one—but there's no way I am going back for it.*

I somehow make it home in one piece, which is a small miracle. The entire ride was spent debating whether or not to go to the sheriff's office and report the strange guy in the woods. And what was up with that weird image of a similar figure by the water on my property with a knife? It was like déjà vu, but I have never seen anyone so creepy before.

"Ow!" A deep voice cries out.

I jump, so lost in my own thoughts that I hadn't realized that I walked into the tavern, instead of the cabin as I intended, smacking the door into someone. I peer around the door and come face to face with a slightly annoyed Simon.

"Oh, sorry. Didn't see you."

His forehead crinkles as he looks at me. "Hey, what's wrong? You're shaking."

I plop down onto a leather armchair next to the roaring fire, my adrenaline rush finally wearing out.

"What were you doing outside in just a sweater?" He asks, standing to his full height. His biceps and chest muscles flex under a white T-shirt that he somehow manages to keep clean, even after hours spent over a hot stove and grill.

Simon runs one of his large hands through his trimly cut, loose light brown curls, his bright blue eyes flashing in concern. "Serena?"

"I was in the cemetery, talking to Karina, and this creepy guy was there. He chased me."

Simon stands straighter. "Did he hurt you? Why were you alone in the woods at night like that? Why didn't you take Logan or Nikki with you?"

I flinch, still confused, feeling like I am stuck between the waking world and a dream.

"I'm calling Sheriff Kasun," he says, reaching for his cell phone.

"No, just . . . maybe it wasn't anything."

"We need to discuss this with your aunt when she gets home. She took the girls to town. I still think that the police need to know someone is lurking in the woods like that."

"Maybe it was just a guy from school. I don't know. I am so tired, and I was already upset, talking to Karina, maybe it was my imagination."

The concern in his face deepens, so I move to change the subject before he pokes around any further. If my aunt is the Narnian White Witch, Simon is the damn trees, or that little dwarf with the whip.

"What were you doing back there, anyway?" I ask, nodding toward the door.

He rolls his eyes and saunters over to the bar, pouring himself a beer and popping on the switch for the hot water kettle. "Patching a wall. Let's just say it was an eventful evening here at the Fallview."

"Really? On a school night?" I joke weakly, desperate to move on.

"Two words," he says. "Drunk Rocas."

"Huh, please continue."

"Tase thought that Xandru was hitting on Addie, only—*plot twist*—he was actually here alone, and she was at home. Besides, everyone knows Xan is back with Kaela. Smart choice on Maddie's part to stay home. Tase drank so much that he thought she was with him, so he and Xan wound up tossing fists, and then chairs, until Tase almost fell off the patio into the damn falls. I managed to save him, but then he thought *I* was trying to hit on Maddie, so he swung at me. I ducked, and he nailed Xan *again*. I finally got hold of both those numbskulls and tried to throw them out, and then Xan kicked a hole in the wall." He mutters something else before taking a swig of his beer.

"I was trying to patch it up for now, until I can actually take care of it properly, so Odette doesn't freak out." He eases down into the leather armchair across from me after handing me my steaming cup of green tea.

I smile my thanks to him. "Bet you never expected this sleepy little town to be so exciting when you came here."

He laughs. "Oh, I had an idea. It's always the quiet ones that tend to have the best story behind them—that goes for people as well as places. Speaking of story, how's the art thing going?"

I cock an eyebrow. "My 'art thing'? That's the technical term you're using, huh?"

He grins. "Hey, we aren't all as cultured as you are—going places." Something in the way he says that saddens me.

"Simon, don't talk like that. You run this entire place most of the time, because Aunt Odette is so busy with Mama. Stop picking on yourself."

The grin returns to his face. "Aw, you care?" He jokes.

"Hell yeah, I care. Because if anyone is going to make fun of you, it'd better be me."

He whips the pillow from his chair at my head, narrowly missing my steaming mug.

Simon goes on about something in the background, but a vision of Aunt Odette and Mama, floating in the water, wearing matching white gowns washes over me. It's the same déjà vu sensation that I had in the cemetery before I was chased.

My heart races, and my chest burns where the necklace rests against it. Simon calls my name in the background, but I am too distracted by the skin on my chest all but sizzling.

I yelp and jump from my chair. Burning tea spills all over my lap. The ceramic mug clatters to the floor, where it's reduced to shards.

Simon jumps to his feet, handing me a towel from a nearby table. "Are you okay?"

I blink, shake my head, and accept the towel, patting my lap dry. It doesn't make any sense! Mama won't even take a bath without prescribed tranquilizers, let alone walk downstairs to get to the waterfall.

"I'm going to call your aunt." Simon grabs his phone again.

"No. Please. I'm fine. It's been a weird night." *More like week . . .*

Simon narrows his eyes, assessing me.

"Please don't call her. I just want my pencils, paper, some tea, and quiet."

I bend down to clean up my mess.

Simon waves me off. "Why don't you let me take care of that? I can make you another cup of tea to go. Styrofoam is Serena-proof."

"Not Styrofoam. It never breaks down." I sigh.

He smiles. "That was a test. I wasn't going to let you out of here if you let that one fly."

I laugh weakly as he replaces my tea in one of the biodegradable cups I convinced Aunt Odette to order.

I take the cup and then reach up to give him a hug. "Thanks, Simon. For, you know. Listening to me."

My voice comes out tiny and tired. I wish I could tell him more. I know he is cool, but no grown-up is that cool, no matter how many video games they own.

"Hey, do me a favor and get to bed. Okay? Tomorrow's a big day," he says, reminding me about homecoming.

"And an even bigger day for you," I tease.

Due to her fallout with Aurelia and some other drama at school,

Lena has decided not to come to the dance after all, even with my friends and me. To soften the blow, Simon offered to take her to do whatever she wants. Lena chose an indie movie festival in Grand Junction, the closest largish town, which is a two-hour drive away.

Simon groans. "Please don't remind me. She just looked so sad. I wanted to fix it, and before I knew it, I was agreeing to subtitles. You should never have to read a movie."

"Don't forget, jeans do not count as dress clothes," I say.

"God, I have to dress up, too? What fresh hell is this? How about jeans without holes?"

I snort.

He walks me to the door. "I mean it. Bed."

I nod and head out into the chilly night, wishing it was warmer so I could draw outside. I follow the path to the house, trying to ignore the way the rushing water tugs at me.

Once in my room, I change into flannel jammies. I settle in at my desk, by the window, drawing the falls until I can no longer keep my eyes open.

CHAPTER 6

"Where's Laurel?" Aunt Odette asks, searching the first floor of the house while Logan, Max, and I sit in the living room with Nikki and her parents, waiting to leave for homecoming.

"She went upstairs," Aunt Brynna says.

"Laurel?" Aunt Odette calls up the stairs.

"Can you please help me? My hair keeps falling out of the clips," Laurel whines from the bathroom, her voice panicked.

"Must be serious if she said please," Logan mutters.

Nikki snorts.

A few minutes later, Aunt Odette and Laurel emerge. Laurel's lacy, one-shoulder peach dress sets off her creamy skin. Her hair pinned into a curly up-do reveals the same delicate neck and shoulders all the Alverson women share. My breath falters. *Where did my baby sister go?*

"Laurel, you look amazing!" I say.

Her cheeks flush as she takes a seat next to the fireplace.

"So where is this guy?" Uncle Christian asks, not sounding too thrilled.

"Turner should be here soon." Laurel's grin sparkles like sunshine dancing on water. I find myself mirroring her because it's one of the first times she has been this happy in a while. Hard as I am on her, and as frustrating as she can be, she's still my sister, and it's good to see her like this.

"Well, before he gets here and I 'embarrass Laurel,' let's talk, kids." Aunt Odette dangles the Jeep keys midair.

Her voice takes on a dangerous turn, and she eyes me, as though I don't drive her Jeep every day. "You drink and drive, and it won't be Sheriff Kasun you'll have to fear. Understood?"

"Don't worry, Aunt O. I refuse to be the dead chick who peaked in high school. I have people and industries to conquer," Nikki says, shooting a pointed stare at Aunt Brynna, who narrows her eyes in response.

What is going on with them?

"Although . . ." Nikki's face softens. "If it's *Deputy* Kasun coming at me with cuffs, let's just say I won't exactly resist arrest. Sorry, not sorry, Max." She winks at her boyfriend, as if it will make up for drooling over one of Sheriff Kasun's hot sons.

Uncle Christian turns an impressive shade of purple.

Aunt Odette eyes us before raising her hands in surrender. "Okay, okay. Just doing the obligatory parenting PSA thing. I really do trust you girls, but that's an easy thing to ruin."

She kisses us both on the cheek and then points two fingers toward her eyes and then to Logan's and Max's.

"I'm watching you, boys." Aunt Odette's voice chills the air.

Max visibly gulps.

Logan huffs. "Oh, for crying out loud, Odette. You know I would run in front of a car for all three of them. Obviously, I won't let Fanny Pack over here touch them, but, I mean, he wears a fanny pack, so I think we're all safe."

"IT'S. A. BELT. BAG." Max and Nikki protest simultaneously.

Nikki takes it one step further and grins at Aunt Odette. "You changed Logan's diapers once or twice, right? Zero threat."

A big smile and a tiny squeak emanate from Nikki as Logan chases her. Max stands there, looking like he might puke.

"Nikkola!" Aunt Brynna chides, rushing after her.

Uncle Christian rolls his green eyes and mouths, *"I'm so sorry."*

A cell phone rings in the background. Laurel digs her phone from her purse and disappears into the kitchen.

Aunt Brynna steps between Nikki and Logan, swatting at Nikki's hair, trying to fix it and separate her and Logan, whom she fixes with a set stare.

Logan clears his throat, adjusts his suit jacket, and then returns to my side on the couch. I pet his arm and smirk as he grumbles to himself.

"Okay, get out before you blow the house down," Aunt Odette jokes.

She commands us to line up in the backyard, with the waterfall in the background of the pictures. Aunt Brynna and Uncle Christian jump in, encouraging it, so we grudgingly give into the parents.

"If even one drop of water gets on my dress . . ." Nikki whines as we line up, backs facing the falls.

"It's water." Uncle Christian deadpans.

"It's *vintage.*" Nikki huffs.

Laurel finally returns, her eyes red-rimmed.

"Hey, what's wrong?" I ask.

"Turner is meeting me at the dance," she says quietly.

"What about pictures?" Aunt Brynna asks. Aunt Odette touches her arm gently to silence her.

Nikki holds her hand out. "Give me your phone. I'll have that floaty turd here in five minutes or less."

"God, NO!" Laurel says, stuffing her phone in her purse and coming to my side.

I wrap my arm around her shoulder and kiss her cheek.

"I'm sorry," I whisper into her ear, knowing she doesn't want a scene.

"Come on, I'm very persuasive." Nikki waggles her eyebrows at Laurel.

Laurel shakes her head. "It's fine, pictures are lame. Just like the dumb dance theme."

She and Turner apparently have opted out of costumes.

I squeeze her again, and she leans in to me for a minute before wriggling free.

"Speaking of costumes," Uncle Christian says to Nikki. "Who are you and Max actually supposed to be? I know Serena and Logan are those two doofuses from Titanic."

"Hey! That's the movie we met during!" Aunt Brynna says.

"Please save us the high-school-English-field-trip-love-at-first-sight story." Nikki begs.

Uncle Christian smiles.

"Actually, Serena and Logan are Romeo and Juliet." Aunt Odette corrects.

"We're Jas—" Max begins.

Nikki's eyes fly open. She tackles her boyfriend into a kiss to shut him up. Max's arms fly out at his sides in surprise.

Uncle Christian is between them within seconds, Max trying to extricate himself, as Nikki grins up at her father.

"Hi, Daddy!" Nikki says.

He eyes her.

"We're Jackie O. and JFK." Nikki points to the tiny vintage hat we found at Callie's yesterday that perfectly matches her baby blue A-line dress. She slips on an oversized pair of black shades.

"Well, now that you have the glasses, it's obvious." Uncle Christian shakes his head at his daughter.

Aunt Odette sighs. "I wish that Lena and Simon were here for this. It just feels off without them."

They left earlier this morning so they would make it to Grand Junction on time for the movie festival.

"Wait, I almost forgot!" Logan jogs over to his truck. When he comes back he has a tiny plastic box in his hands.

My eyes question him, and Nikki and Aunt Odette say "awwww" in the background as he unwraps a delicate corsage. A white Calla lily, my favorite flower, surrounded by red roses.

"Oh, Logan . . . it's beautiful! You didn't have to."

"A little bird told me not to show up without it." He glances at Nikki, who winks.

Logan's eyes don't meet mine as he slides it onto my wrist.

I reach into the box and take out the matching boutonniere.

Logan winces. "I have to?"

I shrug. "Guess so."

He takes a breath and moves closer.

I glance over at Aunt Odette for assistance, because I've never done this before. She skirts over to my side, showing me how to pin it to his jacket.

"Thanks for not stabbing me," Logan teases.

"That comes later," Max cracks under his breath.

Nikki snickers.

I smooth the flowing tulle of my white gown and run my fingers through my blond hair. Aunt Odette braided the sides, forming a crown. She left the rest down, in curls that tumble past my shoulders.

Logan follows my lead, awkwardly smoothing the front of his vintage 1970s polyester suit, looking as uncomfortable as ever. He refused to even set foot in Callie's, so we were lucky to find his suit on eBay.

"The things I do for you," he says softly.

I grin up at him and ruffle his hair. He catches my hand in his on its way down, not relinquishing it as the flashes explode around us.

A cool breeze picks up, goosebumps dot my arms and chest, and hair tickles my face. I move the strands stuck to my glossy lips. A few drops of water stray from the waterfall. Carried on the wind, they land on my shoulder blade. The necklace burns me so intensely that I cry out and jump.

"Hey!" Logan says in alarm, hands hovering over me, ready to take out any imaginary threat.

I take a deep breath, and the burning sensation is gone. It's one of those things that happens so fast and so randomly that you question its actual existence.

"Serena?" Aunt Odette asks.

Oh, you know. This psychotic necklace that you gave me keeps burning me. Or, even better, I am losing my mind. File that under conversations not to have in front of most of the people you know before heading to a dance.

"Uh . . . rock in my shoe," I lie.

Aunt Brynna openly glares at me.

I gulp, blinking, and then she's looking just as concerned as the rest. *Am I seriously going insane?*

"You good?" Logan asks softly.

"Yeah."

He bumps my shoulder conspiratorially. "You know, I'm cool with sitting this out. A man's pants should never be this tight."

"Are you sure, Serena?" Aunt Odette asks, not taking her eyes off me. Everything in me begs to tell her the truth. I promise myself that tonight will be the night that I tell her everything and get some answers. Crazy or not.

"No, I'm fine." My shaky voice grows stronger with each word.

"Okay. Well, have fun. But like we talked about, not *too* much fun."

She relinquishes the keys to me, but I hold them out to Logan.

Nikki twirls at the door to the Jeep and calls out, "No worries, Aunt O. We have other ideas for a fun night."

Nikki waggles her eyebrows. Aunt Brynna and Aunt Odette glance at each other in one of their weird bestie silent communications that Nikki and I have grown to copy over the years.

"Oh, I don't know if I like that," Aunt Odette mutters to Uncle Christian.

"Nikkola!" Aunt Brynna warns.

Nikki giggles and hops into the backseat in response.

She hands me a CD titled "Homecoming."

"Start with track number two. The Knife will get us in party mode. *And* they match our theme!" She dances away to the band's opening drum solo, shaking the backseat.

"What are you talking about, weirdo?" Laurel asks her, and then shakes her head. "Actually, I don't even care." She slips her earbuds in and turns the volume of her music up until it's so loud that I can hear distorted bass from the passenger seat.

Logan backs out, and we take off in the streamered nightmare of a Jeep that looks like a party supply store barfed all over it.

CHAPTER 7

*W*e pull into the crowded lot of Havenwood Falls High as the sky takes on a beautiful shade of watercolor spill.

"I still don't see why Logan and I had to lie about our costumes. It's not like *we* are the ones doing anything crazy," I grumble from the passenger seat, massaging my temples. My head has throbbed ever since the flashes of light from the cameras.

Nikki leans forward so that she can whisper-hiss past Laurel. "Because your aunt and my mom share a brain. I'm telling you, they would've seen your weird little number and known that what I had planned was epically worse."

We both glance over at Laurel to make sure she isn't listening. She is still lost in her own world, head leaning against the window as she listens to her music.

"Is it hard for you to walk?" Logan asks, waving at a couple of guys from the football team while pulling into a spot.

Nikki wrinkles her nose. "Well, these shoes aren't the comfiest. Why? You offering to carry me, Princess?"

"No, not your shoes. It's amazing that you can even stand upright with a head as big as yours," Logan counters.

"Heavy is the head that wears the crown." Nikki winks at him, and one corner of his mouth turns up.

"I love your confidence, girl." I smile.

Nikki was devastated when she didn't win Teen Miss Havenwood Falls. Up until a few months ago, she was involved in every charity cause to help the town, so she really thought she had a chance at winning. Even though she was nominated, she lost, and it crushed her. Back in September, our friend Paisley helped me start an underground campaign to try to drum up votes for Nikki and her new-kid boyfriend, which led to their nominations for homecoming queen and king.

"Now, we all know what to do, right?" Nikki asks. "Meet at my gym locker at nine-thirty on the dot."

"Why can't we just get this over with first thing?" Logan asks.

"Because, *obviously*, we will catch everyone more off guard if we do it later," she answers.

"And it gives her a chance to accept her crown." I wink at Logan.

Nikki's face shines with hope. "If I pull that off, it will be one of the only things my Mom and I might have in common."

Her tone is light, but a hint of sadness lingers behind it.

We file out of the Jeep. Laurel removes her earbuds and waves at Turner, who sits in the backseat of a car with a couple of his guy friends, feet hanging out. I narrow my eyes at him.

"Later, dudes," she says and then skips away.

Strobing light, accented by bass, pours from the opened gym doors, pulsating through me as we fall into step with everyone else walking in. Paisley weaves her way to the entrance, her boyfriend Cole by her side. Both are punked out and clad in black leather from head to toe, Paisley's ringlets teased into a blond mop. I wave and move to catch up with her, but they disappear. Nikki's secret-ish homecoming campaign was the last time Paisley and I really spent much time together. It sucks. Especially since this is our last year all together.

Logan takes my hand, leading me into the gym.

I hold his hand for a minute, and then release it, pretending to search for something in my purse, because I don't know what the heck we are doing. Sometimes I let my mind go there and think that we could be together . . . And then I come back to reality and know that I will be leaving, no matter what Aunt Odette says. The last thing I want to do is hurt him and ruin our friendship.

The gym is decked out in black and silver with stars hanging from the ceiling. Glittering lights adorn the walls, giving the gym a dreamy atmosphere. A stage has been assembled and placed against the wall, under the basketball hoop. Star centerpieces and glittery confetti adorn tables covered with black tablecloths.

Nikki glances around and sighs. "They changed the decorations."

"What?" I asked.

"When I was still on the committee, we had a completely different color scheme. I literally spent hours on it." Her chin trembles.

"When you drop out of the dance committee without notice, your ideas get trashed," Zaltana Purser says from behind us, Julianna Fairchild at her side. Both are members of the dance committee. Paisley and I couldn't sway either girl to vote for Nikki because they were too hurt and annoyed by her sudden attitude shift.

"Oh, yeah, let's just dredge *that* body up again." Nikki sniffles.

"You're right, it's pointless. There's clearly no getting through to this 'new and improved' version of you, Nikki. Please give me your tickets," Zaltana says, holding her hand out for them.

The guys fork them over, and then Zaltana turns on her heel, moving to the other end of the ticket table with Julianna.

"Come on, Nik," I say, leading her past the two girls as I throw disappointed looks at them.

Yes, Nikki has completely changed and quit, but I know there's a reason, even if she isn't sharing it. This can't be her new normal.

"Let's dance," she mumbles to Max. He takes her hand, leading her to the dance floor.

Viv Freeman chats with Zara Shannon, off the side of the dance floor. They both wear pastel gowns, covering them from neck to toe, their hair curled and twisted into up-dos with matching baby's breath woven into the braids. They laugh at Mr. Friske, our lanky principal, dancing with poor Ms. Bast, who is clearly super uncomfortable with her situation.

"Frisk-e's getting frisky." Logan snorts.

"You look gorgeous, ladies!" I curtsy toward the two girls, and Viv grins.

"So, uh, what are you supposed to be, Amish?" Logan asks.

Zara pulls an old-fashioned fan out and waves it open. Each slat has a name written on it, and one name only, "Darcy."

"What the heck?" Logan asks.

"Oh, cool! Is that like a dance card? Ah, the Bennet sisters. Very nice twist on the theme!" I say.

I poke Logan in the ribs. "Seriously? 'Darcy' didn't tip you off? *Pride and Prejudice* is only one of my and Nikki's favorite books."

"You know I don't read," he admits as we all crack up.

"Wait . . . was that the one with the zombies?" he asks. "Because I'm pretty sure I saw the movie."

Viv, Zara, and I groan. I wave goodbye to them and make my way toward the drink table next to the stage, Logan in tow, to say hi to Mr. Weaver.

"Andrews, you clean up good!" Mr. Weaver teases Logan, wearing his trademark cords and a sweater.

"Hey! Didn't you get the memo?" I joke. "Where's your costume?"

Mr. Weaver grins. "You're looking at it."

"Well, who are you supposed to be?" Logan asks.

"Who are any of us supposed to be? Aren't we all a little star-crossed at some point? *That* is who I represent. The herd," he says with a bow before ladling cloudy blue punch into cups for us. I wave mine away as Logan accepts his cup.

"Philosophical and handy at a refreshment table. Who knew?" I tease.

Mr. Weaver gives me a look. "And who are you? Wait, let me guess . . . Romeo and Juliet?" He sighs. "Alverson, I have to admit, I'm a little disappointed."

"Well, Mr. Weaver, as you have taught us over the years, not everything is as it seems."

"Intro" by the XX blares through the speakers. Nikki and I connect eyes from across the gym, and I am happy to see she appears to be over her disappointment.

The music moves us toward the dance floor, where we meet. We kick our shoes off toward the wall, and twirl each other.

We giggle, losing ourselves in the beat, not worried about where the guys went, or what anyone else is doing. All fears and concerns melt away. My heart swells with how much I already miss my best friend, when she hasn't even left my side yet for her adventures in Seattle.

The sobering thought stops me in my tracks. Nikki twirls a couple more times and tries to bump butts before realizing that she's now dancing alone.

The song ends, and she leans into me, still giggling. "What is it?"

"I don't want this to be the end," I mumble.

She smiles and tugs at my hair. "Sweetheart, this is just the beginning for us."

"But, you're gonna leave." A song that I don't recognize picks up, forcing me to yell over it to be heard.

Nikki grabs my hand and slips her arm around my waist, twirling and then dipping me. "Actually, *you* are the one who is really leaving. I am just jumping states, while you're going full-blown expatriate."

"About that . . . maybe I don't want to. Maybe Aunt Odette was right."

She stands up and releases me. "It's so loud in here I almost thought I heard you say you've been living a lie for as long as I have known you."

"Nik . . ." I grumble. She twirls me again, picking up her pace to keep in time with the music.

"It's so much more than that," I continue. "I feel like I am drowning in life, it's all moving so fast. Aunt Odette is acting weird, and this necklace keeps burning me . . ."

She raises an eyebrow. "Still?"

"Let me guess. You think I am certifiable now."

She looks at me with such longing it takes my breath away, because I know that look.

"What aren't you saying?" I demand.

She pulls me to the side of the dance floor, away from everyone.

"Let me see the necklace." She holds out her hand.

"Why?"

She shrugs. "You know I'm psychic. I'll scan it or something."

I snort, and then pent-up nervous energy turns into bubbling laughter.

She mimics my laugh and then rolls her eyes. "Very funny. You seemed to listen to that quack at the carnival the other night."

Oh, well. This is better than nothing, I suppose. I reach around to try to unclasp the necklace to hand to her, but it's stuck.

"Ouch!" I cry out as the metal bites into the skin under my nail.

"Here, let me see," she says, turning me around so she can work the clasp. It doesn't budge for her, either.

"Hmm." She muses, stepping to the front of me again so that she can examine the crystal. She places it in her hands and closes her eyes.

"Nik? What the hell are you doing?"

She finally releases her hands, eyes flying open. For a second, I see a mirror image of the fear I have felt toward it, but then she blinks, and it's gone.

"What just happened?" I demand.

She opens her mouth and then lets out a breath. "I am not psychic. That's what happened. Just between us girls, I talk a strong game, but Aunt O scares the bejesus out of me when she's ticked. Maybe don't mess with the clasp too much, in case it breaks. Since that thing is old as sin, and a family heirloom."

"So we're just giving up?" I say. "And since when do you use the word 'bejesus'? Who says that?"

She pats my wrist. "Serena? Just talk to your aunt. About all of this. Okay?"

"But—"

"And for now, please promise me we can live in this moment. I mean *really* live in it? It's our last dance," she says.

"No, there's still the winter formal and prom," I say, bewildered by the sadness in her eyes.

"Well, I meant the last homecoming," she amends, a little too quickly. "You know I am all for girl power, but right now, we have a couple of guys who are checking us out."

Nikki nudges me toward where Max and Logan stand. Logan mingles with the football team, while Max lingers on the fringe. Logan nods at me and smiles, then turns his attention back to Kase and some other guys from the team.

"I know you think I am beating a dead horse, but I have known you your whole life and you have never been as close to a guy as you are to Logan. Can you please just talk to him and figure out what's going on between the two of you?"

"For the love of—"

"Or don't. You keep saying we are running out of time together, and yet you are wasting your own." She kisses me on the lips and then twirls off into Max's arms, almost knocking him over with her force.

I sigh and plop down on the floor, leaning into the padded wall.

Someone blocks the light in front of me. A hand reaches down, and I blink against the glare around the silhouette.

Logan smiles, the straps of my shoes laced through the fingers of his other hand. "May I have this dance?"

I blink.

He clears his throat. "Well, it's how that Darcy guy would've done it, right?

"Unless he was zombie Darcy. Then it would've been more like 'graawwwrraaarrbrains.'" I claw at the air with my hands.

Logan snorts. "You're deranged."

I take his hand, and he lifts me to my feet, awkwardly pulling me into his arms. His hand slides to my back. We both seem to feel the eyes on us as we look up to face a narrow-eyed Mr. Weaver. Logan raises his hand slightly higher on my back, and Mr. Weaver nods, then moves on with a smile.

"You really are beautiful tonight, you know," Logan whispers, red creeping up through his cheeks in time with his words. "Uh . . . not that you aren't every other day!" He rushes to add.

A corner of my mouth lifts. "You're looking pretty handsome yourself."

He smiles down on me. We sway along with the violin solo of the song that flows around us like wisps of smoke, hazing the rest of the crowd out.

"You know, I don't think I've ever seen you in a suit," I muse.

He laughs, the lights glinting against his teeth. "Well, it's a good thing that pictures were taken, because it's never happening again."

"Oh, yeah?" I tease. "What about when you get married?"

The words tighten my throat, and I instantly dread going there.

He stops dancing for a minute and swallows. "Well, maybe once more—I guess that all depends."

My cheeks flame.

"Rena, I have some things I have to say."

"Logan . . ." I plead.

"No, please. Let me do this before what I am pretty sure the punch was spiked with wears off."

Logan continues to twirl me around in the light—I'm a feather in the eye of a storm.

"I have spent so many years infatuated with you. Your quiet strength, the way you've looked out for your sisters, and cared for your mother. I am sorry for all the things I've said that made you or Nikki feel weird about planning to get out of this town. That was all me and my own issues. You shouldn't feel guilty for having dreams. That's another trait of yours that I have always admired."

I suck in a breath as he dips me.

"Where did you learn how to dance?" is all I can utter, when the better question is, *Where is this coming from?*

He grins, lifting me back up. "YouTube. It's not just good for shirt weaving tutorials, you know," he says with a wink.

I blink fast, because tears form on my eyelashes as he continues.

"Deep down, you're this wild girl that a quiet little town like ours has never been able to contain. I know the last thing you want is a guy whose future runs along a small scale, and I know it's selfish, but as proud as I am of you, I just want to freeze this year. Every moment. That's probably why I have been hard on Nikki with Max. It's all changing too fast. It used to just be the three of us."

"Logan." I exhale, his face moving nearer. My hand goes to his cheek, his nose touching mine.

He whispers, "Infatuation is by its nature a selfish thing, so I know that what I feel for you is love. Despite how I feel, I want you to get out there and see all the sights you want to explore, and have all the experiences you crave. I want you to set the world on fire with your beauty and art . . . What's selfish is that I'll never give up hope that one day, you'll come back, ready to be with me."

"I—"

Logan places his finger softly against my lips. "I know. Like I said, selfish. I also know that you're going to point out the fact that we are only eighteen and I'm being ridiculous. As well as I know you, you know me. I am a creature of habit. I can tell you exactly where I want to be in ten years. I want to have expanded my dad's business and built a cabin that puts even your family's to shame, complete with a studio —all for you. Just a simple life. Here. With you. Babies if you want them, and freedom for you to travel for your art, wherever and whenever."

My steps falter, and he catches me. His arms are steady as always, but his voice breaks. "I've been one of your anchors ever since I can remember. Why can't I remain that for you?"

Tears stream down my cheeks freely, spilling onto his jacket. I glance away, unable to meet his gaze because I see it all. I know he's right. I know that I love him, probably always have. But I don't know what level of love it is that I have for him—or if it matches his for me. That aside, how do I make him see that we are just too different?

"I can't even tell you where I will be in three years, Logan. I haven't seen enough of the world. My wants and opinions are forever changing. How is that fair to you?"

His eyes glisten. "Do you love me?"

"Logan . . ."

He stops carrying us and locks me in place with his open, honest glare. "Do. You. Love. Me? It's a simple question."

I nod, blinking faster.

He smiles and wipes the tears from my cheeks. We slowly sway to the music. "Well, why don't we just focus on the time we have this year? I know what you're scared of, but I will never clip your wings, Serena. Why would I destroy what I love most about you?"

I can't breathe, or think, as his heady scent of home and the trees cocoons me with his sweet words. Everything feels out of place lately, leaving me uneasy. So when he moves in, nose brushing mine, I freeze.

Right before our lips meet, the burning sensation on my chest grows so intense that I shriek. I grip the chain and rip as hard as I can to stop the pain, but, again, the necklace won't budge.

"Serena? What is going on with you?" Logan gasps, his eyes huge.

The music cuts to dead silence, of course. Kids stare at me as Mr. Friske bellows into the microphone. "Time to announce this year's homecoming king and queen!"

The kids closest to us continue to stare, most of them laughing. Everyone claps, and pulled from my dream, I gasp in fear of whatever the hell is happening to me. That, combined with the realization that I was about to lead Logan on in the most epic way so far during our friendship, breaks me away from him. I take my shoes from his hand.

"I'm sorry," I mouth as I flee. I look over my shoulder only once. Logan's crestfallen face and red-rimmed eyes sucker-punch me. As I have just done to him.

CHAPTER 8

$\mathscr{L}$uckily, the bathroom is empty. I examine my chest in the mirror. A tiny blister slowly forms in the shape of the crystal.

I knew it wasn't in my head. Fear coils through my stomach, because this is the first burn that hasn't disappeared.

What does it mean? I lean into the path of the overhead light and twirl the chain of the necklace around, trying to remove the damn thing. Nothing. The clasp won't budge.

Cheering and music swell outside the door as I lean on the sink, feeling even worse for missing what was probably Nikki's crowning glory, if she and Max won.

The door crashes open, and Nikki comes "whooping" into the bathroom, shaking her rear, holding her crown in the air in victory.

"Not that there was ever any doubt, but . . ." She throws a tiara-laden fist pump into the air. "Please tell me you weren't in here the whole time and that you saw it!"

I don't answer, so she swishes over to me, a cloud of taffeta. When she takes in my expression, she drops the tiara on the counter. "What's wrong?"

"It won't come off. It b-burned me!" I stutter, fear and panic taking over. She rushes to my side, placing both of her cool hands on my feverish cheeks.

"Girl, you're on fire," she whispers.

"I know! Look at my chest! Family heirloom or not, help me get this thing off!" I beg.

We both yank on the chain, as hard as we can, without strangling me.

It doesn't budge.

I claw at it, but Nikki grabs my hands. "Whoa, Serena. Stop. You're going to draw blood."

She leans in closer. "Where did you say it burned you?"

I roll my eyes, beyond frustrated with the entire situation. "Right. Here. Under the crystal," I say, pointing at it.

"Uh, I don't see anything," she says quietly.

"No! It happened. I had a blister!" I glance in the mirror, down at the spot that was all but oozing pus moments ago—and seeing only creamy skin. It's not even red.

"What?" I exclaim. "That's impossible."

"Serena, I think we should get you home," Nikki says, giving me the same exact worried tone I have sent her way for months. Aggravated as I am with her in this moment, part of me wants to apologize, because holy hell is that annoying.

"No."

"No, what?" she asks, her eyes wide. She backs away from me a little.

I glance into the mirror, and I can see why she is reacting the way she is. I look like a crazy woman.

"No, you worked really hard on this stupid prank, and I am not leaving," I say.

"Really, it's fine."

"We are doing this," I insist. "I've let enough people down tonight."

"What's that supposed to mean?" she asks, still blinking at me like I am insane.

I wipe my cheeks. "Stuff went down with Logan—I ruined it."

"*What?*"

Someone pounds on the door. "Nik, it's 9:25," Max yells.

"Yeah, just announce that to the entire senior class, smooth guy!" Nikki shouts back, turning to me. "What happened with Logan?"

I grab the sparkling tiara from the counter and place it gently on my best friend's head, then slip my shoes on. "Don't worry about it. Tonight is about fun, right? Last dance and all?"

"We will do whatever you want," Nikki says cautiously, helping me wipe my cheeks. "But I think we should leave. You look like hell."

"Maybe it's just a sign that we should spread some," I say.

"Are you sure? Don't tease me, Alverson," she jokes.

I fist bump her and then lead the way to the door. Max and Logan stand on the other side. Logan refuses to meet my eyes as we all sneak into the girls' locker room and file into stalls to change into our prank costumes.

Nikki helps me convert my strapless white vintage Balenciaga gown that we scored from Callie's, eye-hooking it into a halter-neck. This reveals a hidden layer that we spent months hand-sewing red sequins to, so that it would be Carrie White's bloody prom dress without destroying it.

Nikki fixes her creepy-ass Mrs. Voorhees wig.

"Don't forget this, Carrie!" Nikki says, tossing me her tiara. Max hands Logan his own homecoming crown for Logan's Tommy Ross costume.

"See you on the flip side! Keee, keee, keee, ma, ma, ma." Nikki croaks the *Friday the 13th* line, impersonating Mrs. Voorhees's voice. Then she Frankensteins her arms out, walking backward into the hall. A jumpsuit-clad, hockey-masked Max twirls a fake machete, following her.

Logan comes up to me and offers his arm, still not looking directly at me.

"I just need to use the bathroom. I'll be out in a minute," I whisper.

Logan starts to say something, but stops himself and heads out.

I disappear into a stall, and when I come out, I laugh like a fool. I *would* get my period the day that I am dressed as Carrie White, because why would life provide me with anything less strange. Luckily,

I always have stuff in my purse because I have been waiting for this for-freaking-ever.

With a sigh of relief, because now I can at least let go of my health concerns, I head out into the hall and meet Logan.

"You ready for a bloody good time?" He asks, finally looking at me.

"What?" I snap, cheeks burning.

Logan holds the bucket full of red confetti up (because fake blood has no place on Balenciaga—for once, I think Callie would be proud) and adjusts his own crazy blond curly wig with a crown.

I smile. "Oh, I guess. This is insane."

"Let's just humor Nik one last time," he says. "I've been a dick to her and Max, feel like I owe her this."

It's freaking hard to remain unnoticed, but we somehow manage to sneak under the table next to the makeshift stage undetected.

Artemis, the tech expert from the drama club, meets us to take the bucket of red confetti, quickly rigging it to an impromptu pulley directly above the basketball hoop overhead.

When we hear the *Friday the 13th* theme music and the screams and laughter, we crawl out from under the table and take our places on the stage with our crowns in place.

On cue, red confetti rains down on Logan and me. I glance up, watching it sparkle and tumble down. A hush falls over the crowd. They stare at us, mouths gaping, some laughing. Max, in his Jason mask and with a fake machete, has hacked away at tons of random people, in addition to the ones who signed on to take part, spraying them all with fake blood.

My gaze falls on a familiar pair of eyes in the crowd—sea-glass green, peeking out from under a black hood. The guy who has been chasing me! My heart stutters.

Energy seems to shift, and then release, exploding in a sonic boom through the room, shaking the floor. I look out at the mass chaos ensuing. Kids scream and fall over.

I search for the guy from the cemetery, but he's gone, lost in the crowd.

"Logan?" I scream.

He wraps his arm around me, pulling me from the stage into the corner, covering me with his body.

What the hell? A bomb? That guy? My mind starts going through bad movie plots and flashes of news stories on terrorist attacks and school shootings.

"We have to find Laurel!" I yell over the din.

"I saw her sneak out with Turner over an hour ago. She's gone," Logan yells back to be heard over the crowd. Though I want to choke her for leaving with that loser, I'm relieved she isn't here.

My chest feels lighter, so I glance down. The necklace slowly lifts, the crystal floating before it's somehow jerked off my neck and disappears. *But how?* A strange metallic clink echoes throughout the gym. Looking around me, I note other pieces of jewelry scattered on the gym floor.

A bunch of football players and cheerleaders flee out the open door, into the night. *What the hell? Did they do this?*

I look at Logan and see my own fear and confusion reflected as the floor shakes again.

"We have to get out of here!" Logan yells.

Someone I don't really know stands at the edge of a group of kids. His body contorts at strange angles, like his bones are breaking and reforming in a new shape.

When he looks up, his eyes glow and his teeth grow into jagged points. I scream, pulling Logan toward the exit.

Mr. Friske yells something in a weird language. Everything falls silent. I turn to Logan to figure out why the hell he isn't moving with me and find him frozen in place.

"Logan?" I ask.

No response.

"Logan!" I scream.

Other kids are paralyzed, like he is, but not everyone. Zaltana stares over at me wide-eyed and then I see Nikki, blinking in shock.

I run over to her. "Logan—something is wrong with him."

"Max, too," Nikki whispers.

Within what feels like seconds, adults filter into the gym in silence. "What's going on?" I demand. "Shouldn't the sheriff be here?"

A well-dressed, dark-haired man steps forward—Roman Bishop. My legs turn to jelly, and not in a good way. I don't know him personally, only the stories I have heard. He is one of the most powerful men in our town. *What the heck is he doing here?*

Addie Beaumont whisks in behind Roman wearing knee-high boots, torn jeans, and a leather jacket. A sense of comfort and familiarity rush over me. On occasion, we chat in line at Coffee Haven, and she's even bought some of my jewelry.

"Addie? What's happening?" My voice breaks.

She shakes her head at me and Nikki, her dark glasses framing the annoyance flashing in her eyes.

Addie's assistant, Athena Lawrence, hisses. "Why did I know that this reeked of Nikkola? And you, Serena, what kind of friend are you to allow something so idiotic?"

"I—I don't understand," I say.

Nikki weaves her fingers through mine. "Addie, I'm sorry. This was my fault. Not Serena's."

Addie grabs Nikki's free hand, wrenching her free from me as she sets her down in a chair. Addie unwraps what looks like a tattoo kit.

Nikki's eyes widen. "What are you doing?"

My throat tightens. "Hey, what's going on? Are you giving her a tattoo? But . . . *why?*"

"We understand your concern, Serena, but you need to stay out of this. Why don't you go wait outside?" Athena murmurs. "Nikkola, please sit still. We don't want to hurt you."

Addie lines up different inks on a table, and Nikki struggles to break free from the arms that hold her down.

"There was clearly just some sort of a terrorist attack, and now you are giving a kid a *tattoo*? It makes no sense!" I yell.

"Please, Mr. Friske! I'm sorry!" Nikki howls in the principal's direction, but he turns away.

"Wait! Shouldn't her parents be here?" I demand.

"They're on the way, child." A raspy voice, evil as sin, fills the room. Ada Daryn, a blue-eyed brunette with an old-Hollywood vibe, who looks decades too young to be Stella's mom and Ellisyn's grandmother, struts toward us.

"Since they are not here to claim Nikkola, I act as guardian. Emergency contact and all," she says, flashing me a strange smile.

"No, my aunt is Nikki's emergency contact," I argue.

"Please do what you need to teach this young witch to mind her place," Ada snaps at Addie and Athena.

"What?" I gasp. Then I let out a nervous laugh. "Oh! Nikki, you got us all good. You were right! This is the most epic senior prank ever." I laugh until Ada clears her throat.

"Are you quite finished with your hysterics, or must I slap you?" She turns from me and returns to Nikki. "I am disgusted by this utter waste of your talent. You are officially warned."

Ada waves to Addie to continue whatever it is that Addie is doing, and then makes her way over to me, leaning in.

"My dear, you are absolutely on the cusp." Ada pats my cheek. Her eyes alight, she pivots, narrowing them at Roman Bishop as she bumps him roughly with her shoulder before she exits.

"What does she mean you're a witch?" I ask Nikki, who won't look at me.

Anger shoots into my veins—real and primal. A live wire entrapped. My entire body burns. I cry out and start to go down to the floor. Mr. Weaver suddenly appears at my side, holding me up.

"Alverson, you okay? You don't look so hot," he says, concern lining his forehead.

"I—I don't know. Can you please explain any of this?" I wrench myself free of him when Nikki screams.

"My powers!" she sobs. "Addie, why!"

What powers?

Athena sighs. "I'm sorry, Nikkola. It was decided by the Court. You have a temporary restraint on all magic until you appear before them."

"What is going *on*?" I yell. No one answers, but Mr. Weaver quietly shushes me.

Nikki's tears fall onto the birdcage tattoo that Addie formed on Nikki's chest, near her heart.

I rush to her side. "Nikki, I am so confused," I whisper.

She cries into my arms, and the painful current rips through me again. I lose my footing once more, but she catches me.

"Serena?" Nikki gasps.

Roman Bishop steps to the center of the room and thunders, "What was seen here tonight will only be remembered by the few who hear me speaking. You have a responsibility to keep it to yourselves. Any who abuse their power, or break this gag order, will be dealt with. As Nikkola Morris will be. We are better than this, kids. Remember that."

A young woman I don't recognize appears at Roman's side and whispers something.

"The wards are back up and stronger this time, to prevent another ill-conceived prank," Roman says to Principal Friske, who nods. Whatever that means . . .

One by one, the adults filter out as quickly as they came.

My body buzzes with restless energy. My mind is on a nonstop loop, trying to make sense of everything.

"What did Roman mean, we have a 'responsibility'? And what was Ellisyn's grandmother talking about? I mean, I know we joked about it when we were little, but there's no such thing as witches," I say to Nikki. "Right?"

Before she can answer, Aunt Brynna and Uncle Christian arrive, their ashen faces set in stone as they cart her away from me without even saying hello.

"No! Serena needs me!" Nikki screams.

"Nikki, why? Tell me what you know!" I cry after her.

Once Nikki leaves, the music starts back up, and the frozen kids all break free, moving around, laughing and poking fun at Max in his costume. Like nothing ever happened.

From the rambling, it appears they only remember him running through in costume, and nothing of the strange happenings that took place after. A few kids who weren't frozen look at me with solemn, knowing looks. I start to make my way over to them, but then Logan is at my side, laughing.

"That was hilarious." He pats Max on the shoulder as Max pulls his mask off, all sweaty and grinning.

"Where's Nik?" Max asks.

I swallow hard, trying to work through the buzzing energy swarming my body, doing my best to hide what really happened. Ridiculous as this all is, Roman Bishop scares the crap out of me, and something tells me not to cross him.

"Uh, her parents heard about the prank and came to pick her up. They were pissed. Think she's grounded." Pain shoots through my body, and I wince.

"Serena, do you have any one who can pick you up? I think you need to go home and rest," Mr. Weaver says, looking at me in a strange way. Only now do I realize that he has never left my side.

"Rena, you okay?" Logan asks.

The painful buzzing in my body is so bad I can't even answer for a minute.

"I can take her home, Mr. Weaver. I drove her here." Logan volunteers.

Mr. Weaver nods, and I lean into Logan as he leads me out. When my legs buckle once more, he picks me up and carries me to the Jeep.

CHAPTER 9

*A*fter an uncomfortably silent ride home, the conversation we had at the dance a silent passenger, we pull into my driveway.

"Thanks for driving, and for this." I hold my wrist up, playing with the red petals of the roses on my corsage. My body throbs as I slowly make my way out of the Jeep.

"Hey, easy!" Logan says, rushing from the driver's side to the passenger side to help me. Once the pain lessens, I test standing on my own, and he cautiously sets me free in front of my darkened house.

Laurel must still be out with Turner. Simon and Lena will still be in Grand Junction for a few hours at least, and who knows where Aunt Odette is.

Another volt of pain shoots through my body, and I cry out and fall.

"Serena! Seriously, do you need a doctor or something?"

"Logan, please go home. I think I just need to go to bed."

"No." Concern thickens his voice. "Look, I know I overstepped tonight, and I'm sorry if it made you uncomfortable. But I'm not sorry I told you the truth. And I want to make sure you are okay."

I push myself to my feet and nod. "I'm sorry for my reaction—I just have a lot on my plate right now and feel like I got hit by a truck. Maybe I'm getting some weird zombie flu."

He doesn't appear convinced. My cheeks flush with fever, and every cell of my body trembles. Am I allergic to these changes in my body? That must be it.

Or maybe the adults did something to me in the gym. If they said Nikki is a witch, what the hell are *they*?

A wave of nausea hits me as phantom currents and flames lick at my limbs.

I look over my shoulder toward the waterfall, glittering in the half-moon like a light tower directing me home. Tears sting my eyes, and a breath catches in my throat. I've grown up looking at it my whole life, without really seeing each facet—the most beautiful thing . . .

"Hey, why are you crying?" Logan's voice loses all mirth.

Ignoring him, I follow my body's pull to the water.

"Uh, are we going swimming? In our clothes, on a freezing night, Crazy?" Logan asks, pulling me out of my head. The gentle current of water teases my toes, kissing them, as I stand in the rocky sand and twigs.

"No, of course not. It's just . . . soooobeautifuulllll." Sobs cut me off, and his arms are around me.

"Uh . . . hey, we've done crazier," he says, using his thumb to wipe a tear from my cheek. Electricity zaps me, and I flinch away. Logan pulls back, wide-eyed.

"Did you feel that?" I gasp.

He blinks and flashes a weak excuse of a cover-up grin. "Happens to me all the time with the ladies. I say let's go for a dip if it will make you feel better."

The woodsy musk that has always been Logan's, and usually calms me, takes on a rancid twist for a split second. The thrumming in my body picks up, and I wince. Then he smells amazing again.

"Rena?" Logan asks, eyeing me. His lips are right there, like they were before everything went so horribly wrong. This time I want them in a way I never really allowed myself to in the past. All the questions and complications I created for us in my head seem like a faraway dream.

"I know what will make me feel better." I lean into him, grabbing his face.

Logan sucks in a breath and then pulls me into his arms.

I don't know who initiates it, but our lips whisper across each other. Not gently like the books describe, but with a burning that rivals the forging current that continues to ravage my body.

He trails his lips down my neck, whispering in my ear. "I've waited for this since like sixth grade."

I shake my head as he returns to me, smiling into his lips. Then we are in the water, my gown billowing around me. Logan's suit jacket is long gone. He breaks the kiss, to my frustration, and then his shirt slips over his head.

His scent even stronger, I'm drawn to his neck, trailing kisses down it as we move deeper into a cool spot.

The waterfall roars in the background. I can hear every single drop cascade down to her sisters, pooling around us. Everything feels lighter, and the buzzing bolts of pain leave my body. I raise my head to let out a sigh of relief.

When I move back to his neck, nothing is enough. My jaw hurts. I screech as tiny knives cut though my gums. *The pressure.* I just need to bite down.

His carotid pulses, and it's delicious.

Mine.

He's putty in my hands, and before I know what I'm doing, my teeth sink into his neck.

Logan cries out as sweet blood rushes into my mouth like the juice of a peach.

But it's not a peach. It's Logan's flesh. Logan's blood. My best friend, who is no longer pulling me toward him, or reacting in any way. He stills in my arms. Save for the buoyancy afforded by the water, I would never be able to support him like this.

Tiny bolts of electricity fire from my body, shooting into his under the water like little veins of a monster, and I scream.

"Logan?"

His eyes stay focused on mine, frozen in accusatory terror, as he floats in my arms.

I retch into the water next to me, coughing up his blood.

Blood. That I consumed.

Red droplets spider-web around rose petals knocked loose from my corsage, in a macabre two-step.

A wail tears from my lungs, but then it turns into a foreign laugh as the water rocks through me, a cooling salve to my searing worries. My tongue examines the tiny layer of daggers shielding my teeth.

The water trickles around, whispering in the same voice as the whisper in my dream on my birthday:

You're helping Logan, Serena. Water is birth. Water is life. Water is death.

Memories from over the years, of Aunt Odette and Mama, surrounded by countless floating dead men and lightning bolts striking under the surface, assail me, as though unlocked in my mind. I glance down and see my reflection—the smirking girl in the water.

His warm blood calls to me, so I dive back in to cut the remaining strands of life force clinging to Logan's feeble body.

CHAPTER 10

"**S**ERENA, STOP!" someone screams from the shore.

Suddenly, Aunt Odette is by my side. I'm shaking and dry heaving, and the buzz that left my body returns to my head and ears. My hand flies to my mouth when my gums are cut through once more, as the sharp teeth retract. I can see my aunt's lips moving, but can't make out the words as she pulls us to shore. Once on land, the buzz dulls enough that I can hear her.

"Get me a blanket." Aunt Odette's voice is calm and measured as it breaks through my hysteria.

"I don't know what happened . . . I—"

Her blue eyes flash. "Blanket. NOW."

I scramble to my feet. The weight of waterlogged gravity pulling on my dress causes me to stumble. I right myself and then run into the house, sliding on the hardwood floor and banging my thigh into the wall, but I barely register it.

I killed him.

I kissed my best friend, then bit his neck and killed him. *Who. Does. That!*

I grab the quilt from my bed and race back to her side.

"Should I call 911?" I gasp, my voice tiny as I picture a jail cell with no windows. Not that it matters, if he's dead. Nothing does. They can stick me anywhere.

"No." She drips a handful of water over Logan's neck, and the puncture wounds close, fading to nothing in front of my eyes. I let out a loud sob, and she yanks me to her side, covering my mouth.

"I know this is overwhelming, but pull it together, girlfriend."

I obey, and she slides over to make room for me, while putting an ear to his mouth and gently grasping his wrist to feel his vein.

"Sweetie, he's breathing. He just has a weak pulse. That can easily be remedied, once you return what belongs to him."

"What?"

She puts her hands on my shoulders. "Do you trust me?"

I nod without having to think about it. She nods back and positions my head over his. "Breathe into him."

I do what she says, and my throat closes. I'm choking, but nothing is in my mouth for me to choke on.

Aunt Odette holds me down, even when I try to pull away. "Fight through it, sweet pea. It will pass."

And she's right. Whatever it was moves from me into him. But nothing happens.

The numbness I had taken for granted in my body while in the water switches back to the thrumming, pent-up energy, but it's not as bad as it was. Really, when your friend is lying in front of you, possibly dying, your own pain means nothing.

"Come on, damn it!" Aunt Odette growls, pounding on his chest once. Logan's body seizes and stills. And then he coughs.

"Logan?" I choke through my tears and pull back, partially to give him some air, but mostly because I no longer trust myself anywhere near him.

He opens his eyes, dazed at first, and then terror returns to them. Logan has never looked at me like this before, and it kills me. His hand rushes to this throat and he tries to skitter away.

But Aunt Odette pins him down. Her eyes glow, locking on his as she whispers in a foreign language. A flashback of countless versions of

Aunt Odette, whispering to me in that same language over the years, eyes glowing, bombards me.

It doesn't make sense to my ears, but my brain understands what she's saying to him, and he settles down.

Aunt Odette continues in English. "Shhhh, it's okay! You fell into the lake and hit your head, Logan. Serena and I pulled you out."

He blinks, glancing back and forth between the two of us. *He will never buy it.*

"You." His voice is accusatory as he focuses on me. Then I realize that must've just been in my head, because his voice is soft. He whispers, "You saved me."

Tears stream down my cheeks. I shake my head, and Aunt Odette firmly grabs my shoulders.

Nails digging into them, she says, "She's being humble. Serena dragged you out of that water like it was nothing, Logan. You will be just fine, aside from whatever you swallowed."

He laughs, along with her hollow laugh. I can't stop crying.

"Hey," he says, pushing up on an elbow. "It's okay, I'm here. We can go back in."

"No!" This time it's me scrambling to get away from him. I run into the house as I hear Aunt Odette's soothing tone out in the yard with Logan.

I lock myself in the bathroom, the humming of my body so intense that I just need quiet. Remembering how the water helped, I fill the tub and sit on the side of it, leaning over the toilet just in time for the rest of my dinner to make its exit when the metallic aftertaste of Logan's blood lurches my stomach into action.

"Serena? Serena, let me in," Aunt Odette demands.

"Sick." I gag on the word.

She sighs. "Are you going to be okay if I drive Logan home?"

I murmur a lie.

"Don't you dare leave. I think we both know how badly you and I need to talk." She lingers a moment, and then her footsteps fade away.

I flush the toilet and then strip down and get into the full tub.

The water doesn't have the same effect that the lake did, but a bath is a bath. My tears drip into the water as I set my head back and try to relax. *He's okay.*

But I'm not. Every time I close my eyes, I relive it. The horror in Logan's eyes, his limp body, the blood. How some strange part of me reveled in it.

Me. The girl who can't even handle the thought of eating a cheeseburger.

I lower my head in shame, and a flash bleats through my closed eyes. I glance down to see tiny currents of lightning shoot upward from my submerged body to the surface of the water.

Just like with Logan.

I suck in a breath, blink, and it's gone.

I scramble to free myself of the tub, grabbing my robe from behind the door. I wrap it around myself, tears streaming down my cheeks as I rip the door open.

"Aunt Odette?" I yell.

Nothing.

She must not be back from taking Logan home yet.

Logan. The tears come harder when I remember him, lifeless, floating in the water.

Fear of this body I'm trapped in propels my feet up two flights of stairs, to my first home.

"Mama?" I choke on the word, clearing the room until I am at her side.

"Mama, I don't know what's happening to me."

She stares out the window, eyes vacant.

Anger over how my sisters and I have been robbed by losing both Mama and Daddy pulsates through my body, my fists balling at my sides.

"I need you, Mama."

No response. And that is my undoing.

I have tried to be strong over the years. Aunt Odette was there for us, making sure we were loved and cared for. But that has never erased the pain and grief of the absence of my parents. And now this—whatever this is—not having my Mama to help me through . . .

I crumble, anger deflating itself back into a bone-crushing grief. My body folds into the tiny space between Mama and the side of her chair as I curl up against her, like I used to when I was a little girl. My damp hair and tears dot the front of her nightgown. I feel like a jerk for soaking her clothes, but I just need her.

"Mama, I'm a monster," I whisper.

"No, Serena. You are magnificent." Aunt Odette's voice fills the room.

I turn around, wiping my tears to find my aunt in the doorway, light from the hallway haloing her.

"What?"

"Sweetie, you and I need to talk," Aunt Odette says, coming forward to help me off Mama.

I hesitate, glaring at my aunt, fear icing my spine when I see the look on my aunt's face—reverent. *But I almost killed someone.*

"What is wrong with you?" I shout, lowering my voice when Mama tenses against my side.

She sighs. "Serena, let me change your mother into dry clothes, and then I think we should take this somewhere else."

She nods toward Mama's rigid body. I rise to my feet, not wanting to upset Mama further, and realizing how selfish I was to get that close to her without knowing what is going on with me.

What if I hurt her, too?

My hands fly over Mama, checking for any damage. Then I remember that my hands are part of me, of this body—which is apparently a lethal weapon.

Biting my lip, I turn and flee to my room. I shut the door and curl up in the window seat facing the falls. As much as I don't want to look, I cannot deny the pull. It's not so much that my body wants to be in the water, but it feels like the water has claimed me. When I focus hard enough, I can still hear whispers woven into the ever-present clamorous rush of the falls.

"Baby girl, we should have talked a long time ago," my aunt says, stepping into my room. "Simon told me, but I didn't listen . . ." she adds, an afterthought.

This admission fans the flames of my anger anew.

I whirl to my feet, facing her. "You knew this would happen? And you told *Simon* instead of me, first? What am I? Why does the necklace you gave me keep burning me? Did you do this to me? Why did I almost kill Logan?" My voice breaks, but I continue. "Why does my body feel like this? God, I just want to crawl out of my skin."

Now that my mind is focusing on it, the buzzing grates on me, not quite painful any more. It's more like the pent-up energy of a limb that has lost circulation. Annoying, demanding attention. Only, unlike a foot that has fallen asleep, there is no explanation for this.

She drops onto my bed, eyes glazing. "The necklace, of course! Serena, where is it?" Her voice raises in alarm.

"I don't know. There was an explosion or something at the dance, and right after it happened, the necklace fell off. Which makes no sense, because I couldn't remove it, no matter how hard I tried. It kept burning me, ever since the night you gave it to me."

"Why didn't you tell me?" she demands.

I snort. "Oh, yeah, because that's totally an easy and rational conversation for me to have with you. 'Thanks for the necklace, not so crazy about the burns, though.'"

"Serena, you know you can talk to me about anything."

I narrow my eyes. "Do I? Because last I checked, you still haven't told me what's wrong with me, or why you're being so calm about the fact that I almost killed my best friend, and that you were able to stop it."

My heart stutters as I remember her eyes glowing, the weird language she spoke when calming Logan, and seemingly making him forget the whole ordeal. The weird déjà vu slams into me—Aunt Odette and Mama, surrounded by dead men in the water.

"Aunt Odette—what are *you?*"

She sits up straighter, appearing almost regal, even though her eyes remain sad.

"Serena, you need to know something first. They don't choose just anyone for an honor like this—we Alverson women are special."

"You and Mama, you're murderers. I was almost a murderer," I rasp.

"No," she says firmly. "We are not murderers, any more than God is. And tonight . . . well, that never should have happened. We need to find your necklace as soon as possible."

"What the hell does that matter right now?" I cry out, pacing in frustration at Aunt Odette's strange half-answers.

Her face pales. "That necklace is everything."

"Wait—can you just tell me what the hell we are, first?"

"Honey, I know this is scary and overwhelming, but there are a lot of moving parts in this explanation. I need you to sit down."

"No! You don't get to call the shots this time, Aunt Odette. I'm sorry, I love you, but—"

"Serena. Give her a chance." Simon's figure darkens my doorway.

He turns to my aunt. "I came as quickly as I could."

"Where's Lena?" Aunt Odette asks, panicked.

"She's reading, in the tavern. Don't worry," Simon reassures her.

Lena. Laurel.

"Is this going to affect them, too?" I ask, worry for my baby sisters trumping my own concerns.

Aunt Odette nods. "Now you see why we need that necklace."

"Actually, I don't. Because all I know is that it hurt me."

"The necklace is special. It has been in the family since we were first honored by this calling. Josie Alverson, the first siren, wore it into Havenwood Falls."

"So, we're sirens?" I ask, trying to rack my mind for anything I have ever read or watched on the topic, but nothing comes to me.

That superior look returns to her face. "Yes. When Havenwood Falls first formed, it was meant to be a haven for certain types—supernatural beings."

If this conversation happened a week ago, I would have laughed. But after what I witnessed tonight . . .

"Wait, Nikki really is a witch, then?" I ask.

"Yes."

"You knew? All these years, you knew that about Nikki, and me. You didn't tell me any of this?"

"Honey, I thought I was protecting you. The necklace is important because it is a form of training wheels for a new siren, so to speak. It reins your power in and controls the discomfort you feel when away from the water, until your body can learn to regulate its new normal. Your body prepares to siren as you prepare for your first period. I take it that happened tonight?" she asks.

My cheeks flame, and I don't meet Simon's eyes. Something tells me he is probably as interested in the floor right now as I am.

"Why is Simon here? No offense, Simon. Why does he know about us?"

Aunt Odette smiles up at Simon, whom I finally bring myself to glance at for a split second. He smiles down at her so lovingly that it's nauseating.

"Because he saw me for what I was and gave me a chance. Which is what I am begging of you right now."

"Would it help if I told you that I had a secret, too?" Simon asks.

I shrug, secretly curious, not sure if I even want to know.

"I'm a dragon shifter."

I snort, and then laughter erupts until I can't breathe.

"Right," I say between laughs. "That's enough *Final Fantasy* for you."

He feigns hurt. "Uh—my alter ego is way better than yours, so . . ."

This only makes me laugh harder, until his words pull me back to my own reality.

"Oh, God. This is real?" My head spins so I fold over, putting it between my knees, like my aunt used to tell me to do when I would get car sick.

"She's actually taking this a lot better than I thought she would," Simon murmurs under his breath.

"Honey?" Aunt Odette asks, bracelets jangling as she comes to my side.

I take a few deep breaths and then look toward the waterfall. The sight of it takes the edge off the nausea. When I watch the water froth and dance, something subconsciously comforts me. *This is right. Of course, it is.* Water has always been my haven.

"Is anyone in this town actually human?" I ask, keeping my eyes on the falls.

"Well, yeah, of course," Simon answers.

"Logan . . ." I say. "He's human, right?"

"And until we find your necklace, and get you fully trained, you must stay away from him, and other human men." Aunt Odette says.

"Why only men?" I ask, almost wanting to kick myself for my own stupidity, because it was only dead men that I saw in the flashes of Mama and Aunt Odette in the water.

"Mama was in the water at the Carnival the other day!" I say.

"Yes," Aunt Odette answers, carefully.

"How? She can't move."

"You're going to have to trust the limits of what I tell you for now. All I can say is that the siren in her is stronger than the prison she has built in her mind. I mostly handle the requirements the town has for the sirens on my own. There are usually three at a time, and always three Alverson sisters in each generation. Now that you are going to join me, it will help. We hold a massive harvest on October eleventh, every year. Your mother's pull to siren and the magic from the town allow her to step out of her own head to fulfill her responsibility on that night."

"What about her responsibility to us?" I whisper.

"Believe me, when she has a moment of clarity on that day each year, she begs me to fill her in on what is happening with all three of you. The hard part is that she forgets as soon as she remembers your father's death, and then goes back into herself. We have to start over again the next year."

My chin trembles. "She never wanted to see us on that day? I know I have gotten close a few times. You did something to me. I remember it."

"I had to wipe your memories of it, Serena. Those wipes are losing hold because you are transforming, so the repressed memories are returning."

"Why?"

"I told you I wanted to protect you. All those years that your period didn't come. The doctors told me you might be sterile."

"They never told me that."

"I asked them not to, while you were a minor. It was so hard. Part of me was excited that you might be the first of our kind to be able to get away and escape this. While it is an honor to protect our home, it comes at a dear price."

It suddenly hits me. "This is why you didn't want me to plan on college overseas."

Tears glimmer in her eyes. "Oh, baby, I wanted it for you," she cries. "I want the world for you, and deep down, I hoped. I came in here, so many nights after you fell asleep, laying the crystal of that necklace on your chest, to see if it reacted, but it never did. That lulled me into a false sense of security. I knew that you were going to Europe, at least for a few weeks this summer, so it was time to give you the necklace, as a precaution. I swear I was going to talk to you before you left. The first time it activates, sensing that you are close to sirening, it lights up the night."

I snort. "Yeah, I know. That happened after you went to bed, on my birthday . . ."

"When you went swimming," she finishes. "I should have known. God, I have failed you. I am sorry for that. I just wanted to keep hope alive that you could break free, but I didn't want to overly encourage a shining future that I wasn't sure you would be able to have."

"Why can't I just leave? I don't want this. I can't even stand to eat a chicken nugget, and you expect me to fry men and then drink their blood?"

"The blood part isn't totally necessary," Simon answers.

"You will get that under control." Aunt Odette tries to reassure me.

"No, I don't want to get it under control. I don't want this. What if I just leave?"

Aunt Odette sets her jaw. "You die. Or you end up like your mother."

My lungs refuse to expand as that punch lands in my gut. *She tried to leave us?* I don't remember that.

"If you remove yourself from your water source," Aunt Odette says, pointing to the falls, "the imbalanced electrons in your body will fry you."

"The buzzing?"

"Yes, that is a store of electricity that your body maintains to paralyze your victim in the water. It's like venom, in a sense. I know it sounds horribly inhumane, but it is painless. The current in the water paralyzes them, while we get to play out their deathbed fantasy. Clearly, you have always been Logan's. So that is what he saw."

My cheeks burn, and I hurry to change the subject. "So, I should stay away from Simon, too?"

"Nope. And that's why I told you the truth about what I am, Serena. You're not alone in this. And you can't hurt me. Well, I mean, you can *try*," he teases.

"We only Harvest human men that the Court and the covens overseeing town ask us to harvest," Aunt Odette says, rolling her eyes at Simon with a tiny smile.

"Why would they ask us to do something so terrible?" My mind goes back and forth from instinctively accepting this as right, because an ancient level of my subconscious already knew that this was my path, to the other part of me that bucks against it all in horror.

"Serena, this town is full of unique types who have been hunted since the beginning of time. Every so often hunters, or other humans with evil intentions, come to town and need to be dealt with. The town has magical wards, put in place by the Luna Coven, overseen by the Court of the Sun and the Moon. These wards help protect us, but occasionally someone bad gets through, and that is where we come in."

"We have covens?"

Aunt Odette smiles. "Surely, you didn't think Nikki was the only one of her kind? I know you saw some interesting things at the dance tonight. Brynna called before you came home."

"Are Addie and Roman a part of either of those groups?"

"Both are major players, actually. Why?"

"They were at the school tonight after everything happened."

"Honey, they were there to keep you guys safe. Before any of the supe kids accidentally hurt each other, or a human."

"Is Nikki okay? Everyone seemed really mad at her." Guilt tears through me for not having asked about her sooner and being so wrapped up in my own drama.

Aunt Odette winces. "Yeah, you won't be seeing much of Miss Nikki for a while."

"Is she grounded?" I ask.

Simon clears his throat.

"Honey, Nikki used her magic to breach the wards that the Luna Coven placed on your school. She is in very, very big trouble, and stands to lose all of her powers permanently."

"But, that doesn't sound like Nikki!" I argue.

"Serena, please don't take this the wrong way, but it might be time for you to entertain the fact that you don't know the real Nikki as much as you thought you did," Simon quietly advises.

"No! I know her better than anyone . . ." But the argument sounds weak even to my own ears. How well do I really know this girl I have shared so much of my life with? An image from the dance flashes in my mind and doesn't help.

"I saw a kid start to change into something else, Aunt Odette." I shudder. "It was horrible. Was it because Nikki dropped the . . . wards? Is that what you called them?"

Aunt Odette moves over to my side and wraps her arms around me.

"Yes, sweetie. It was a very foolish and dangerous thing for her to do. I know this is a lot to digest, and I know it isn't fair. I'm sorry. Please just know that even with the supernatural, there is a natural order to things. We coexist pretty well, most of us more peaceful than most of the human world outside our borders. When beings have been oppressed for centuries, they tend to be more sensitive to attaining peace, and then preserving it."

"But, I don't want to hurt anyone . . ." A memory of a man floating in the water at the most recent Carnival this week stops me.

"What is it?" Aunt Odette asks.

"Dr. Nance! I saw Mama take him down. Why? He was good. He helped me when I was little."

Simon works his jaw and crosses his arms over his broad chest.

"He was a sick man. He experimented on supes in his free time," Aunt Odette explains.

"There have been a few murders that were traced back to him. The police found evidence of tortured supernatural beings." Simon growls.

I cannot seem to pull enough air in, and scrub my face with my hands, to get rid of the tingling before I completely hyperventilate.

"So, a doctor is bad, but we are good for killing him?"

"No, not killing. Harvesting. We harvested his life force, merging it with the magical properties of the water in our falls, then we siphoned what is needed to help sustain the town's wards. Serena, we are the only ones in this town with the ability to turn pure evil into good. We are the silent guardians of our home, protecting everyone we love and care for. When we take the lives the Court asks us to, it's only after all the major figures in this town have exhausted all other choices for the individual—they are that dangerous. When we harvest them, they aren't even in pain. Compare that with the human form of the death sentence . . ."

"Logan was terrified!" I argue.

"Because you don't know what you are doing yet. I will teach you, and then, together, we will teach Laurel and Lena, so that the three of you can take over when my time, and your mother's, has passed."

My throat tightens, and my heart pounds. "No, not them."

Aunt Odette squeezes me. "I felt the same way for Karina, and your mother felt the same about the two of us, at first. It is completely natural as a big sister. But it's this or death. There's no way around it."

Aunt Odette glances up to Simon. "We need to find her necklace. She can't leave the house without it until we get her under control."

"I was at the school already and haven't seen it. Friske is on high alert for it, though. He will call as soon as he finds it. Multiple pieces were lost tonight," Simon says.

I have received so many answers that one of the more important things nagging at me has been neglected, and now comes bobbing to the surface of my mind. Sea-glass eyes. A hood. *He* was at the dance.

"Oh!"

"What?"

"There's something else. Simon, that guy, he is still following me. I think I saw him at the dance, right before the explosion."

Aunt Odette and Simon exchange the same look of pure panic.

"You don't think . . . How could they already track her? She's so new," Aunt Odette says.

"I never put anything past their kind." Simon spits the words out. "I'm on it." He disappears before I can say anything.

"What's wrong now?" I ask.

Aunt Odette doesn't meet my eyes. "It's nothing."

"No! Stop lying to me. Please."

"Simon told me about the guy in the cemetery."

"Narc," I mutter.

"No. He did the right thing. I told you how we take out hunters, right?"

My lungs freeze.

"Well, sometimes they have vengeful friends."

"I saw him by the water at the carnival! I am almost positive. I think he was holding a knife, and he was looking at you and Mama."

She purses her lips into a white line, the color draining from her cheeks.

"He was that close to you that many times?" she whispers.

I shrug.

"I'm going to go grab your sisters and call for backup. For now, do not leave this room. Stay away from the window and get dressed in case we have to move quickly." She tilts her head. "Do you think you could draw a picture of him for me?"

I nod, trying to swallow past the lump in my throat. *How do I go from being the unlikely hunter to the hunted within one night?*

She touches my cheek, her face lined with worry. "I know I threw a lot at you. I promise, I will be right here, helping you through it all. I will tell you as much as I can. There is going to be some stuff I must keep from you for a bit still, and I know that pisses you off. I get it. But please trust me. Other than this, have I ever let you down?"

I glance into her eyes, remembering the illnesses she lost sleep over, taking care of me, the baked cookies, the blanket forts, the stories, the endless supply of love and selflessness.

"I trust you, but please, no more secrets."

She kisses my forehead, then hurries out of my room, digging her cell phone from her pocket. Her voice carries down the stairs.

I slip into sweatpants and a hoodie, and then sit down at my desk, opening my colored pencils.

My fingers shake as the pale green eyes, peeking out from underneath a black hood, come to life in front of me.

Eyes belonging to a man who wants to kill me and my family.

WE HOPE you enjoyed this story in the Havenwood Falls High series of novellas featuring a variety of supernatural creatures. Read on for an excerpt of *Somewhere Within* (A Havenwood Falls High Novella) by Amy Hale. The series is a collaborative effort by multiple authors.

Stay up to date at www.HavenwoodFalls.com

ABOUT THE AUTHOR

Kristen has always had an intense fear of water—maybe it can be attributed to the dark world of sirens lurking under the surface of her subconscious. Or it's just because she cannot swim. When she isn't reading and writing, she's exploring creepy historical things with her daughter or attempting to cook (it's debatable which is scarier). You can find her on Facebook, Instagram, and Twitter. Oh, and if you're a dude going swimming in the wild, don't forget to bring a rubber inner-tube—it could buy you a couple of minutes.

ACKNOWLEDGMENTS

God, thank you for leading me here and allowing this to even happen.

Thank you to my parents, my Gramps, my Grams and Great-Grams (who fervently believed in my stories since I was too little for them to make sense), Aunt Jackie, Aunt Colleen, Nate, Shaina, Jen, Steven, Sean, and Damien for forever love.

Ryan, the last time that we were together before you died, I swore that I would follow through on this dream. A promise is a promise, little bro. Thank you for the years of mischief managed. I will miss you for the rest of my days.

Thank you to my own "Mr. Weaver" for seeing in me what I couldn't see when I was in high school.

Andrew Smith, your taste in indie music is impeccable. Nikki wouldn't be Nikki without your musical guidance, thank you! Jay Asher—you started out as one of my favorite authors, turned mentor, turned friend. You were there for me during some of the worst times of my life, encouraging me to keep writing, and to be kind to myself. Thank you for all you have done for me, and for so many others in this world.

Tina Sandoval and Tiffany Neal, "No, read *this* one." I would be lost without you both on the written page and off. Sam Sandoval—thanks for being my forever-teen-reader. Gina Kupfer, Amy Viscuso, and Chrystal Mook, thank you for cheering me on!

Regina Wamba, thank you for making Serena and me feel like princesses with this gorgeous cover!

Liz Ferry, thank you for polishing up my words!

A special thank you goes out to all the Havenwood Falls authors.

Thank you, E.J. Fechenda, Randi Cooley Wilson, Kristie Cook, Michele G. Miller, and Kallie Ross for sharing your characters with me!

Kristie Cook, when you offered for me to take part in this, it was too good to be true. Guess what? I finished. Thank you for believing I could!

Alexa, my baby girl, thank you for being the Rory to my Lorelai. P.S.: It's a belt bag.

Last but certainly not least, thank *you* for spending your precious minutes and hard-earned money on me and my imaginary friends. You are the reason that I do what I do!

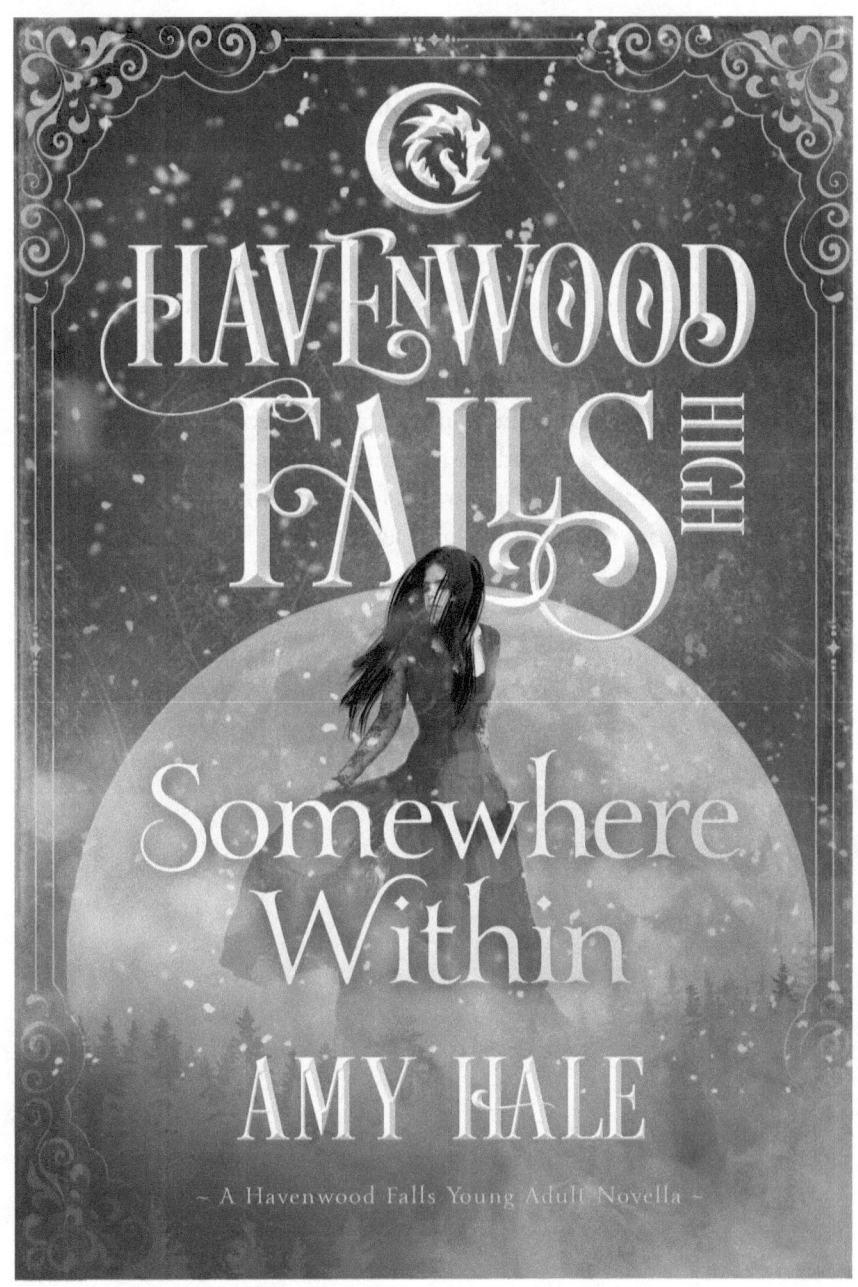

HAVENWOOD FALLS HIGH

Somewhere Within

AMY HALE

~ A Havenwood Falls Young Adult Novella ~

Somewhere Within (A Havenwood Falls High Novella) by Amy Hale

With her raven-black hair, porcelain-white skin, and shy demeanor, Zoey Mills has been the target of bullies since childhood, no matter how many times her family moved. She expects nothing to change when they relocate to Havenwood Falls, her parents' hometown. What she doesn't expect is to discover that she inherited her eccentricities— as the next generation of a long line of frost dragons.

As she learns to accept she's on the cusp of becoming a shifter, she finds out her new best friend isn't human, either. But the boy Zoey's fallen for is, earning the disapproval of her grandfather and patriarch and fueling the fire of a decades-long feud among her extended family. Elitism and prejudice take on whole new meanings.

While she wants to trust her instincts and follow her heart, Zoey discovers that hiding who she really is and playing by the rules would make life a lot simpler. But simple doesn't mean easy. She must find her strength somewhere within and embrace her destiny—or risk losing everyone she cares about. And all of this on the eve of her Sweet Sixteen.

SOMEWHERE WITHIN

AN EXCERPT

I glanced at the boxes still waiting to be unpacked as I attempted to relax in my new bedroom. The excitement that generally accompanied a new house was missing. I felt like we moved more than we stayed still. My dad had assured me this would be the last time, and while I thought he believed that to be true, I had my reservations.

My first memories of moving took place at age seven. I don't remember all the details, but I do recall a loud commotion, after which Mom had run out to the backyard to get me. She rushed me into the car, and we left. Just like that. No goodbyes to the neighbors. No "grab a few things for overnight." We just left. Two days later, my dad arrived at our hotel room, two states away, driving a moving truck containing all our belongings. At the time, I was afraid to ask what happened, but it had certainly crossed my mind with every successive move. I'd had an unpleasant sensation down in my gut each time I attempted to mention the subject, so I'd always chickened out.

So there I was, on move . . . what was it? Move eight? Yeah, I thought this was move number eight. One would think I'd be used to starting over, and over, and over. But the truth was that with every packed box, I felt like I'd left a part of me behind. Even if that part wasn't important, it was a segment of my scattered life that no longer felt valid. Those memories now lived in the past.

This latest move had been prompted by a family member. It turned out I had a grandfather here in Havenwood Falls, Colorado. My parents had never talked about him before, so I'd assumed my dad didn't know who his father was. It was the only logical explanation for never hearing about Grandpa Mills. You couldn't talk about someone you didn't know, right?

My parents had received a letter that my grandfather, Lawrence Mills, had become very ill, and was possibly dying. Mom and Dad seemed frustrated by the phone conversations they'd had with him afterward. Ultimately, I held the impression they'd decided it was time to mend fences. Granted, they'd never told me what busted the fences to begin with, but maybe someday I'd learn all the deep, dirty family secrets. All families had a skeleton or two in their closets, so I'd heard. I suspected my family to be no different.

I stood and opened the box closest to my bed. It contained some of my clothes and the most beautiful jewelry box I'd ever seen. It'd been a gift from my parents for my sixteenth birthday. I hadn't actually had that birthday yet, but it was only about a month away. Dad had said that he wanted to give it to me before the move. "Something special for your new room," he'd said. I thought he'd been attempting to bribe me so I wouldn't complain about changing houses and schools yet again. It kinda worked.

I ran my fingers over the smooth metal casing, and I could almost feel it vibrate beneath my fingers. I didn't know how to explain it, but it felt as if the box itself was alive. Every time I touched it, I felt a zing of positive energy pulse through me. No doubt these sensations all took place in my mind, but I allowed myself to indulge the fantasy just the same. As long as I didn't say it out loud, I should be safe. Admitting it to others would have been like saying I'd grown a third leg, but no one could see it.

I placed the gold box on my nightstand and studied the intricate design on the lid, which looked much like a maze, with lines darting out from the center in odd geometric patterns. From the moment I laid eyes on it, I'd tried to figure out if there were some kind of labyrinth hidden in all the chaos, but if so, I had yet to solve it.

Regardless, it was another great addition to what my mother lovingly called my "jewelry hoard." I did have a slight obsession with jewelry, but really, what teenage girl didn't? I wouldn't call it a hoard.

"Zoey, here's another box with your name on it." Dad pushed through my bedroom door and set the box on the bed beside me. "Sheesh, that's heavy. What do you have in there? Anvils?"

I rolled my eyes at him. "Yes, Father. I have an anvil addiction. You've found me out."

He smirked. "So much sass in such a little person."

I reached over and pulled the tape from the top of the box, then glanced inside. "Oh," I said.

Dad simply raised his eyebrows in curiosity.

"It's my jewelry boxes," I said quietly.

His soft laughter followed him to the door, and he sent me a wink. "Enjoy." He walked out of the room and gently closed the door behind him.

I looked into the box again. I had several jewelry boxes, most of them very full. *Okay, maybe I do have a jewelry-hoarding issue. Is there a therapy for that?*

Purchase *Somewhere Within* at your favorite book retailer.